THAT'S ALL I EVER WANTED TO BE

TO BE

SCOTT GENDAL

Printed in the United States of America

Published in Hellertown, PA

Cover design by Anna Magruder

Library of Congress Control Number 2023903493

ISBN 978-1-958711-35-4

For more information or to place bulk orders, contact the author or the publisher at Jennifer@BrightCommunications.net.

For my mother, Donna Gendal
You are all my reasons. You are all my rhymes…

PROLOGUE

They've all come to honor me, and all I want to do is hide. Every face is vaguely familiar—but unrecognizable. Everyone's lips are too chapped to smile. Every tan is fake. Every woman's hair is unnatural and colored. Every man's handshake is firm, like they have something to prove. The woman are caked in makeup; the men are doused in cologne. They look like imposters, and they smell unnatural. They reek of bullshit, and these are my closest colleagues and friends. I don't like these people, yet every one of them loves me.

My name is Evan Bloom. I am thirty-five years old. I am white, Jewish, and rich. I am handsome, smart, and kind. I am a fraud, a slave, and a liar. I would appear to be a loving husband and at least a decent father, and I'm being honored here in my own home. Apparently, I have done something significant. I am still trying to figure out what I have significantly done. I have made a lot of people a lot of money, and that makes me a hero to those gathered here. But would they be here if I'd never made them a penny? Would they laugh at my stupid jokes? Would they invite me for drinks? Would they kiss my ass and give a shit what I thought about the Knicks game last night? I doubt it. They pretend to love me because my friendship is a long-term investment in their children's future, and I pretend to love them because pretending is what I have done my whole life.

This should be the most important night of my life. Almost ten years of hard work went into getting to this moment. It is hard damn work taking the train and reading the *Wall Street Journal* every morning, analyzing stocks and trying to assess where I should put my greedy clients' money. It is hard because I find no pleasure in it. Having to wake up every day hating what you do and despising everyone you work with is hard. The fact that doing it has made me millions of dollars only makes it worse. It's monotonous, it's a bloodbath, it's a rat race, and it's my birthright. I was born and bred for this. I never wanted any part of it, yet this is where I ended up, a rockstar stockbroker, making the rich richer and myself miserable. I hate who I am, I hate what I have become, I hate the lifestyle I have become accustomed to, and I hate that my beautiful daughter will grow up in this environment. I am better than this. I am more than this. I am kind and compassionate. I have a heart. I have a soul.

I want to make a positive contribution to society. I have so much to say, but there is no one to listen. There is no love in my life except for my heaven-sent six-year-old daughter, Josie. She is the reason I continue. She is my meaning, my purpose. She is the only person who knows who I really am. My exquisite daughter is my only true friend, and with 300 of my fraudulent friends here tonight, my home has never felt emptier.

It's the first Friday in August 2013, and usually all these people would be out in the Hamptons. But they know that showing up here tonight could get them the dough to send their sons and daughters to college. My firm is the most reliable on Wall Street; we handpick the best. If you did not graduate from a top ten business school with a 3.8 GPA or higher, you'll be trading somewhere else. We have the brightest brokers, we get first-rate information, and we have connections everywhere in the corporate world.

Tonight, I become the sixth senior partner. But to me this only means I will have less responsibility and more vacation time. I like responsibility. And I hate vacation time, because then I have to constantly be around my wife. I watch her shop and spend my money, and I don't even get a thank you. I hate our counterfeit marriage and the angry, judgmental husband I have become. She refused to let me take Josie to Disney World. She insisted we go to France.

Our guests have come tonight to see my ostentatious home. I live in Kings Point, the small section of Great Neck, Long Island, made famous by F. Scott Fitzgerald who supposedly wrote *The Great Gatsby* here. Gatsby would've loved my home. It's over the top—like something you would see on *The Housewives of New Jersey,* but bigger and more detestable. With its two thick white columns out front, it looks like the White House, except it has no taste nor integrity. The front is dark brown brick with white awnings and shutters on the big windows that I have occasionally considered jumping out of. There is a living room, a dining room, a theater room, an entertainment room with a stocked bar and kegerator, a playroom, and a double-sided spiral staircase with a diamond chandelier above it. My kitchen could comfortably fit twenty. It has two Sub-Zero fridges, two ovens that have never been used, two sinks, an island with eight barstools, and a kitchen table that can seat twelve. The house has six bedrooms and seven bathrooms, and the master bedroom is bigger than a small home.

My backyard is eight acres. I have a white stained wood deck, two oversized Weber barbecues, an Olympic-sized swimming pool with a diving board and a waterfall, a putting green, a basketball court, and a tetherball court. I own four luxury automobiles and a cruiser, which is sort of like a mini yacht. I have never used it. It just sits at the dock.

To attribute all these possessions to my sweat and hard work would be comical. I pretend to work hard, but it all comes naturally. I have more respect for the average working American than I do for myself. They appreciate what they have and break their backs to earn it. And they make a difference. Teachers, plumbers, and sanitation workers change lives, just like doctors. They improve people's quality of life, and yet many are paid just enough to get by. I pretend to work hard, and I get paid millions for making the rich richer. What I do is easy for me, though having to talk to assholes is exhausting. It's hard to be surrounded by dirtbags all day and then come home to my wife. To avoid her, I instantly change and go straight into my daughter's room to play. It is the only place I can find some peace of mind.

My biggest problem is I never say no. I never learned how. I am good to everyone. Subconsciously, I must be seeking someone's approval. I'm the type of guy who is so nice that you think he's full of shit. When someone bumps into me, I say, "I'm sorry." I'm that guy.

It's really tiring always doing the right thing and always giving 100 percent. If you and I were having a conversation, you would have my undivided attention. My greatest gift is the ability to focus, and I really pay attention to detail. I do my homework, and I'm always prepared. I like to succeed, but it's never been about money. It's about doing things right. If you focus and prepare, you will succeed. You'll succeed at work, in life, or at whatever you hold sacred. The guests here tonight hold only one thing sacred: money.

I greeted each person as they arrived, and now it's time to play the game "how charming, funny, and cool can Evan Bloom pretend to be." I am a legend at this game, and the key is compliments. I throw them perfectly, like a quarterback, while I tell myself what I truly think.

"Lindsay, thank you for coming! You look stunning!"

("Lindsay, you fake breasted, botoxed whore. You've banged half my office, and Jonathan doesn't know about it. How do you live with yourself?")

To her husband, Jonathan.

"Jonathan, you're looking good, man. How about that tip on Tesla I gave you. How did that pay off for ya?"

"Bloom, you're the man. I don't know how you do it. I admire you. I really do. Congratulations. You truly deserve it!"

("You fucked my wife, and you think I don't know about it. You bang three hookers a week on company money. You do more blow than Pablo Escobar. Admire me? Blow me, you Manolo Blahnik-penny loafer-wearing piece of shit!")

Everyone is coming up to me, congratulating me. I smile, pat them on the back, and thank them for coming and sharing this night with me. They eat it up.

My wife, Lauren, is gingerly sipping a martini, pretending to listen to someone while taking inventory on what every female in the room is wearing—every pair of shoes, handbag, dress, necklace, earrings, and even hairstyle. Not only is she looking at what they are wearing, but *who* they're wearing. Chanel, Fendi, Vera Wang, Yves Saint Laurent. That is the only thing Lauren cares about at this party. She couldn't care less about me being honored. The only thing that excites her about my promotion is that I will be making more money.

I know she has fucked half the guys in this room, and lately she's been banging Andrew Feldman in his white Bentley. He is a Rolex-wearing, robber baron, hedge fund tool. It should bother me that she's cheating, but it doesn't. I am used to it.

My whole office is here, and so are a lot of my clients. Entrepreneurs, venture capitalists, surgeons, lawyers, and tech guys. I have a lot of clients in oil, but they could not make the trip. All of them treat me like a god. They bring me presents, Cuban cigars, Johnnie Walker Blue. They do whatever they can do to stay in my good graces. Funny thing, I look around my house, and everyone is dressed the same way: brown or white linen pants from Tommy Bahama, brown designer loafers from Bloomingdale's, soft cotton short-sleeved button-down shirts from Polo, and linen blazers from Banana Republic. It's the Hamptons look gone Great Neck for the night.

The women are all wearing pastel cocktail dresses, and they look like peacocks. It's a flock of asshole sheep, and I am dressed just like them, which makes me an asshole too—the asshole who is being honored here tonight. I must be the biggest asshole of them all! The king asshole!

The only things that separate me from the rest of the assholes in this room are that I have morals and I am ethical. Almost everyone else in this room cheats. They fuck each other's spouses; it's a kind of inbreeding. And most of the guys here do a lot of drugs—at work, at home, anywhere. They think it gives them a leg up. Both my legs are planted on the ground, and I do much better than all of them with no effort required, stone cold sober. It pisses them off that I am so squeaky clean. They have all tried to corrupt me.

I make it a point not to hang out with my bozo coworkers outside the office for two reasons. One, I hate them. Two, I am happier at home hanging in my office or playing with Josie in her room. Those are my safe havens, the only places where I can crack a smile. Going anywhere else is a chore.

What is fun about a night like this is playing with people. I'm such a nice guy that no one takes what I say at face value. When I say something rude or crass, they just think I am joking around because it is so out of character. But there's truth behind every joke. Frank Grafton comes over to me.

"Hey, Bloom, how does it feel to be the man of the hour? Maybe a shot of Jameson will get the stick out of your ass."

"Frank, maybe when I take the stick out of my ass, I'll take my dick out of your wife."

Frank smiles, laughs, puts his right arm over my shoulder, and says, "You're lucky I love you, Bloom. Anyone else says that to me, and I would be offended."

"Frank, I love you too. Thanks for coming. Glad you can share in this night with me. It means a lot. Let's get that shot."

"You got it, Bloom. I'm glad I can be here to honor you. Couldn't happen to a better guy."

Grafton is completely full of shit and a borderline criminal. He's a kiss-ass and has been bad-mouthing me forever around the firm, trying to get ahead of me on the corporate ladder. He's a real piece of garbage, and he envies me. I am a better broker and a more successful person than he'll ever be, and he knows it. He hates my guts, and he's my best friend here.

My firm is structured like a hedge fund but with no collaboration. We don't liquidate companies and restructure them. We don't work together or run ideas by each other. We're all free agents. You're on your own; kill or be killed. I'm the Godfather, and I provide a service, then make them an offer they can't refuse. There's never blood on my hands, and all my coworkers want to do is whack me.

I stand at the bar and listen to my colleagues' plans to buy and sell the world, and a familiar, overwhelming sense of panic comes over me. The world spins faster. My knees lock. Bad timing! This is not supposed to be happening now. But it happens almost every day. I feel the earth rotate, and my eyes become tight and narrow, my blood pressure rises, and my heart ends up in my throat. Now I take a big sip of scotch, praying the panic will subside. It increases. I know it will pass, but it will take about ten minutes. I sneak outside.

I stand in my backyard alone, looking back and watching people wander through my home, and it hits me: This really shouldn't be happening. Recently there's been a voice in my head. It speaks loudly. Sometimes it is deafening, and no matter what I do it won't go away. There's a constant heat down my spine, a discomfort that tells me I'm in the wrong place, and that I'm doing the wrong thing. The voice tells me things—that my life can change. What it says is what I want: freedom, autonomy, self-expression, liberation, the choice to do what I want when I want on my own terms. To just be and find out who I am. To find out what I enjoy. There's so much more to life than what I've experienced thus far. What does it all mean, this so-called success and these possessions? Multi-million-dollar homes, expensive clothes, gaudy jewelry. When you have everything, does anything have real value?

The voice tells me something I don't want to hear, although it is true. I don't know what it is to be loved—not by an adult. To have someone truly care about me. My parents bought me expensive clothes, luxury cars, but outside of that, I was nonexistent. My wife loves my bankroll, not me. My daughter loves me unconditionally. But besides Josie, I'm empty. Something has to change. A man having a panic attack in his own backyard at his own party in his moment of pathetic glory. Unbearable.

I need to find something real, something genuine, something pure. Someone who sees me for who I am, not for what I have. There must be someone out there who could understand me. Who could appreciate what I have to say. Every night I hope and pray for a different life. But my prayers go unanswered because I have no idea where to go or what to do. All I know is that who I am is not who I was meant to be. This life is not the life I should be living. This life, this wife, this job, this home. It's all wrong—except for Josie.

I head back inside and feel lost. I don't even know who to talk to or where to go.

Mort Faber, the firm's senior partner and principal owner, comes up from behind and throws his arm around me. "Evan, my boy, we're very honored to call you a senior partner. You should be proud of your accomplishments. Things will only get better, and your future only looks brighter. Cheers."

I hate to say it, but Mort always liked me and treated me fairly. I was his protégé. He taught me a great deal, and he always did right by me.

"It's time for me to make a speech in your honor, Evan. Stay right here," Mort says, then he walks over to the entertainment center in my theater room and picks up the microphone.

"Everyone, can I please have your attention? Please make your way into the room with the big screen and theater seats. I'd like to say a few words in honor of my good friend and new senior partner, Evan Bloom."

All the guests move into the theater room. I walk over and stand next to Mort, and he puts a hand on my shoulder and begins, "I remember when I first interviewed Evan. He was forthright, honest, sincere, sharp, and personable. I remember thinking, 'This kid is going into the wrong business. He should be a car salesman!' He could really charm the pants off you. I liked him instantly and knew within the first two minutes he was going to be a success. He was analytical, had a clear vision of the market and where money was flowing, and his resume was impeccable. University of Pennsylvania, Wharton School of Business, top of his class. MBA from NYU, top of his class. This kid was the full package, and we felt lucky to have him. From day one, Evan was a superstar. Not only an excellent broker, but great to have around the office—always making us laugh, talking Yankees and Knicks, providing us with solid analysis on the previous night's game, and most importantly, always prepared. He climbed the ladder fast. And tonight, Evan becomes a senior partner, after just ten years, a company record. The secret to his success is hard work and dedication. Evan, we thank you for all your efforts, and we're proud to call you a partner. Congratulations. Everyone raise your glass in honor of Mr. Evan Bloom. Salud!"

Mort gives me a nice hug, but it feels inauthentic, like when basketball players of the winning team hug the losers after a game. The bullshit, good game hug. Now it is time for me to give my speech and make everyone a believer. I grab the microphone. This will be interesting. I am going to throw caution to the wind. Gonna let it rip.

"Good evening, everyone. Let me first take this opportunity to thank all of you for coming tonight to share in this special occasion. I care for and love each and every one of you. Mort, that was an incredible honor you just bestowed upon me. I felt like you were talking about someone else. You sure you got the right guy?"

Everyone laughs.

"All jokes aside, I remember when I started at Zenith Capital. I was overwhelmed. Honestly, I wasn't sure if I was going to cut it. Mort, if I looked confident, it was an act of deception. The one thing I knew is that I was going to work hard, and if I went down, I would go down swinging. Twelve-hour days were common.

"It was work that I grew to love and take pride in. I relished in the fact that I started getting good at it. It gave me a great sense of accomplishment, and I felt like I was a part of something bigger than myself, something important, something that was making a difference in people's lives. This is what drives me. It's nice to make money, but it's also nice to provide comfort and stability for my clients. At the end of every day, I hold my head up high knowing someone will sleep better tonight because of me. I am hooked on that feeling, and I intend to keep working hard to earn it.

"I want to thank Mort and the rest of the partners for making me a senior partner. I'd like to thank all my colleagues for making my job fun and for creating an environment that promotes success. I want to thank all my incredible clients who made the trip to share in this moment with me tonight. And I want to thank my beautiful wife, Lauren, for all the happiness she has brought to me and for giving me Josie. Once again, I want to thank you all for coming. I raise my glass to you. Salud!"

Everyone raises their glass and repeats, "Salud!"

What cracks me up is that I beat out more than half my colleagues for this position, and even they're happy for me. I'm that good. I'm not much of a public speaker. I don't enjoy being the center of attention. I prefer to hide. But I feel like my speech was solid: short and to the point. I almost convinced myself that I am happy, healthy, and successful.

Everyone comes over to me, shakes my hand, congratulates me. Lauren even gives me a big kiss and beams at me. I am the man of the hour. But my feelings haven't changed. There is not a man in this room I admire or respect, not even Mort. He has an illegitimate son with a woman from Connecticut and has never given her a dime. That piece of shit! Mort really knows the business—the monkey business.

The rest of the night feels like an eternity. Finally, it comes to an end, a highly successful event. All the guests seemed to have a really good time. A lot of alcohol was poured, a lot of coke was snorted in my bathrooms, and I'm pretty sure Steve Dunham was fucking Brittany Rubenstein in my guest room. It was definitely Brittany; I recognized her moan. She gets laid at every party.

I am now alone. My wife has already gone upstairs. She didn't bother to say goodnight. There is so much home, so much space, so many rooms and places to go. Besides Josie's room, there is only one other place I love, my office, but I don't feel like going in there right now. I am not much of a drinker, but I grab a bottle of whiskey, sit on the white wrap-around leather couch that seats fourteen, and drink alone. The caterers are busy cleaning up, washing and putting away the silverware and throwing out the garbage. I put down the whiskey and get up to pitch in. They look at me like I'm nuts. Sure, I am paying them for their services, but I want to do something useful. I want to see someone leave this party with a genuine smile. With me helping, they will get home to their families sooner, and that will make me feel good.

Two Black women and a Hispanic man are washing the dishes and bagging up the trash; they look exhausted. I help them finish up. I offer all three of them a beer, and they accept. I ask them about their families and where they are from. The one woman is from the Bronx, the other woman is from Harlem, and the Hispanic gentleman is from Queens. I ask them what they thought of the party, and I ask them to please be honest with me.

All three say, "It was wonderful."

I grin and say, "Be honest."

The Hispanic man says, "Mr. Bloom, you're a very nice guy, and please don't take this the wrong way, but except for you, everyone else here was rude. They treated me like a slave."

I smile, then I ask the ladies, "Did you feel that way too?"

They look unsure if they should agree.

"There's nothing to fear. Just be honest with me."

The woman from the Bronx says, "One man offered me $50 for a blow job, Mr. Bloom."

"Jesus. I'm sorry for that. What's your name?"

"Serena."

"Serena, I apologize for that."

She thanks me. I reach into my pocket and give each of them an extra $100, and I thank them for their help. They thank me. They are very appreciative. This is the only moment I enjoyed all evening. Helping people always feels good. It never gets old.

I hate my house when Josie is not in it, and tonight she is at my in-laws. My in-laws are despicable, which is probably the reason Lauren is the way she is, a total bitch. I realize it is 1 am, and I have to be up to get Josie at 7:30. I head upstairs, get undressed, and watch my wife sleeping comfortably in our bed. It is hard to sleep next to someone you despise. It gets harder every night. I watch her rest so peacefully, wrapped in her goose down comforter, head deep in her goose down pillow, lightly drooling, with not a care in the world. Only the carefree sleep like this.

I lie in bed, and my palms turn damp. I become extremely anxious. I begin to sweat, my heart starts to palpitate, and my eyes begin to twitch. I go into the bathroom and throw some cold water on my face. I can feel my blood rushing, but I begin to calm down. My blue eyes look grey and heavy, and my face looks drawn and stressed. I look like I haven't smiled a real smile in a year, the kind where you can't not smile. I gaze in the mirror, and I don't recognize the person staring back at me. I am not the young man with promise anymore. I am not the young man on the rise. I am a worn out, run down, burnt out thirty-five-year-old man who looks like he is fifty. There is no hiding from your face, and mine tells a long, tragic story. There is no life behind my eyes, and I am not sure if there ever will be again.

Now calm, I head back to bed. The clock reads 1:33. I close my eyes and quietly fall asleep.

PART ONE
MY PAST

CHAPTER
ONE

Being a Gen X kid in the '80s was a really good time—especially being filthy rich, because I had everything, which sounds great, but it allowed me to appreciate very little. Don't get me wrong: I loved a new Nintendo game, I loved having a basketball court in my backyard, I loved my go-cart and my go-cart track, but it sucked not having parents. Yes, my parents were alive, but barely. My father was a stockbroker, a very successful one. And a successful stockbroker in the '80s made multi-millions. He was never home, and when he was, he was working. Sometimes I was surprised he remembered my name.

My mother had absolutely no maternal instincts. She took no interest in me—never drove me to baseball practice, never made me lunch, never even hugged me. What mother doesn't hug her son?

My parents were only parents in public. Once in a blue moon, they'd take me out to dinner with them and parade me around town like I was the chosen one. They made everyone think I was brilliant. They would tell everyone I was articulate and well spoken, but they hardly ever spoke to me. It made me want to puke. They paid no attention to me at home. As soon as my dad's Mercedes was parked in the garage, he'd head right into his office. My mother would get out of her car and head straight to the phone to gossip to one of her yenta friends. My family life was one big show, *Keeping Up with the Blooms*. I grew up alone. I received no love from my parents. It was just me, a TV, and Regina.

Regina was my nanny, the Jamaican woman who raised me. She was my real mother. I loved her, and I miss her. She looked after me and tried to teach me what's important in life. Regina was about sixty when I was born, and when I was eleven, she suddenly had a stroke and died. I was heartbroken. She was my best friend. I ate with her, did the laundry with her, cooked with her, and cleaned with her. I didn't have to do these things, but she told me chores build character and will make a man out of you. She showed me the correct way to do things, and she called me "Evvy." No one else has ever called me that.

Regina told me, "Family is everything."

I would think, *Tell that to my parents. You had to remind them it was my birthday.*

It was clear she had a disdain for them, especially my father. It was her job to look after me, but she treated me like a son. She'd buy me presents, and I felt bad because I knew she didn't have much money. She'd buy me a 3 Musketeers bar or a box of Cracker Jacks. My parents didn't know I liked those things. Three times a year, Regina would go home to Jamaica to see her family. One year, I asked my father if I could go with her, and he chuckled, "Her family would hold you hostage."

My father idolized Gordon Gekko from the movie *Wall Street*, which I've seen many, many times. To me, Gekko represents all that's wrong with this country. "Greed Is Good" was his motto, and it was my father's too; he was in a constant pissing contest with his peers. My father was a great financier, but a terrible father. He cared about one thing: my grades. He never asked how I was doing socially, if I was having trouble with a subject, or how I felt. He just wanted to see my report card. If I didn't have all As, he'd be pissed, and my father had a bad temper. For him everything was a competition. He had the biggest house, the nicest cars, and my mother looked perfect at all times. God forbid he didn't have the smartest, handsomest kid.

I had no choice but to conform. There was no room for rebellion because I was terrified of him and his temper. I was dying to rebel, but my old man would beat the shit out of me. So, I stayed in line, shut my mouth, and did what was expected. I got all As. I got a 1580 on my SATs, and my dad was pissed I didn't get a 1600. But I got into the University of Pennsylvania's Wharton Business School—the best business school in the country. It's where he'd gone. The only time my father told me that he was proud of me is when I got my acceptance letter to Wharton. I had no desire to go there. I didn't want to go into finance, but I had no choice.

The one thing my father really got into was teaching me about the stock market. I wasn't interested, but I had to listen, and from a young age he taught me a great deal about corporations, commodities, trends, pretty much everything. He would quiz me, and I had to know the answers. If I got something wrong, he would scream at me.

You might think a father teaching his son the family business was time well spent, but it wasn't. But it was the only way my father attempted to relate to me. He knew nothing and cared nothing about anything I was passionate about—music, movies, video games. He had no interest. The only interest we shared was sports, and for that I was his newspaper. The morning after a Knicks-Bulls game, I'd have to give him a detailed verbal report on what happened so he could talk to his colleagues about it.

Like me, my father had no friends, only business associates. He and my mother went out almost every night with clients at fancy restaurants in the city. After Regina died, I was home alone, an eleven-year-old in a mansion. I found solace in the arts: music, movies, and books. My best friends were Kurt Cobain, Forrest Gump, and Holden Caulfield.

My mother was an interesting woman. She had potential. She could've been a great mother. She was smart, cultured, beautiful—and a narcissist. All she cared about was luxury. Everything had to be first class, from her argyle socks to her diamond rocks. What's sad is that somewhere down deep inside her was an artist. She saw every Broadway show, went to the opera often and the ballet constantly, and she always had the best seats, first class all the way. She wouldn't even tell me she was going to see a Broadway show. The only way I knew is that I'd see the playbill on the kitchen table the next day. One time it was The Who's *Tommy*. I was obsessed with The Who, and that was my favorite album. I would've loved to have gone with my mother. She had no idea I was interested in either Broadway or that band. I don't think she even knew I listened to music.

My father scared me, and I didn't like him, but I wanted to get to know my mother and have a relationship with her. She seemed crazy, but interesting. All the jealous, backstabbing women around town looked up to my mother. She looked and dressed like a movie star. She was highly intelligent, and she knew it. But she could not see that her own kid needed some attention, some quality time.

We had more in common than she ever knew. I love art, and whenever my mother wasn't shopping or doing lunch, she painted. She had a studio connected to the back of our house with tons of easels and canvasses. Her paintings were beautiful, mostly landscapes, and I really admired them. Sometimes when she wasn't home, I'd go into her studio and look at her paintings. *Where did this come from?* I'd ask myself. Even though we had no relationship, I was impressed—and proud.

As a young kid, I was well liked. I was a good athlete, funny, smart, and polite. Kids liked me and teachers too, but I never really liked myself, and I didn't know why. Kids would invite me over to play basketball or football, and I'd make up some bullshit excuse not to go and just hang out with Regina. Looking back, that's where I felt safe. I had every reason to be an angry kid, to be disruptive, but I was the opposite. Outwardly, I seemed to be having a good time, and I projected happiness. Inside, I felt isolated and out of place pretty much all the time—not too different from the way I feel today.

There was only one place outside of my house that I really enjoyed being, and that was at sleepaway camp. Sleepaway camp is where Jewish parents ship off their kids in the summer for two months so they can take vacations in Europe. I know that sounds horrible, and the price to go to sleepaway camp is $10,000, which is ridiculous, but surprisingly, it's worth it.

Camp is where I would come into my own. The vibe was the opposite of the one I grew up with in Great Neck. At camp, you're not being judged. No one's keeping score on every sentence that comes out of your mouth. You're free to be yourself, express yourself, and be who you are. The more yourself you are, the more you're loved. I went every year from the age of nine to fourteen. Not only did I play a lot of sports, I hung out with my counselors, who were college students. They taught me about music, girls, and drugs. They taught me what was cool, and I worshipped them.

There was no one like this in Great Neck; everyone there was busy having their shoes shined. I doubt any other kid in Great Neck was listening to Pink Floyd at age twelve besides me. In camp, I made a lot of friends, but unfortunately, they didn't live in my town. This was in the pre-internet world, and there were no cell phones and no texting. So, to talk with one of them outside of camp, I had to call their houses. I was too shy to do that, so I only saw my best friends for two months a year. But those months would last me. Sleepaway camp was one of the few things in my life that I deeply enjoyed.

The biggest event of my childhood was my bar mitzvah, a ceremonial party every Jewish boy has at age thirteen. In front of everyone, you read a portion from the Torah, the sacred Jewish scrolls that were written by God more than 5,000 years ago. It's a rite of passage, and it marks the day a Jewish boy becomes a man.

It really sounds beautiful, and if you look at it as a sacred religious tradition that's been passed on through countless generations, it is. But in Great Neck, Long Island, it's all about the huge party afterward. Nobody pays attention in temple when the bar mitzvah boy reads his haftorah portion; they just try to keep their eyes open. But, as soon as the service is over, it's basically Caligula time, a free-for-all of unnecessary excess.

Every bar mitzvah is different, but they are all ludicrous. It's basically a pissing contest for the parents to see who spends the most money. My father spent more than $150,000, and that was small potatoes. Every guest is calculating the cost of the party in their heads. I've seen indoor bumper cars, the Harlem Globetrotters, and famous rappers perform. I've seen bat mitzvah girls wear three different dresses in one night. There's always a DJ with a hype man and ten dancers to keep the party going. I went to one that took place at Yankees Stadium. The service took place on the pitcher's mound! The bar mitzvah boy's face was on the jumbotron as he recited his haftorah.

When he finished, he ran around the bases and slid into home plate. Then a couple of Yankees came out and gave him personalized memorabilia. Mickey Mantle had to have been rolling around in his grave.

My bar mitzvah was quite the scam. I had all the goodies. It had a carnival theme. Why? I don't know. I was never asked. My dad thought it would be cool. We had games, kettle corn, cotton candy, goldfish, and an indoor petting zoo. Looking back, it was a stupid idea. It felt extremely bizarre. I had to pose for five pictures with a miniature horse! Having to pretend we were a happy family was even more awkward. That was the only time both of my parents hugged me. My mom even kissed my cheek. I smiled as if I loved them, and we tried to act like a happy family. But it must have looked forced. I felt like a figure in a wax museum.

I don't think either of my parents knew that I had seen straight through them at a very young age. I doubt they ever gave me enough credit. I never acted out nor misbehaved; I just observed. But I knew how neglected and mistreated I had always been.

I'm not happy they're dead. As much as I disliked my father, I know he would be very proud to see me as a successful stockbroker and miserable millionaire. I think the only thing that really mattered to him in terms of me was that I be a success. That way he could brag to his colleagues about me, like he always did, not giving a shit about anything else.

CHAPTER
TWO

By the start of high school, I had reached puberty, and everything changed. It became harder to hide. I was on the basketball and soccer teams, and girls started to notice me, which made me very uncomfortable. I wanted to be different. I wanted to express myself. I didn't want to wear Tommy Hilfiger and Polo shirts with pants from J. Crew. I wanted to wear Grateful Dead and Nirvana T-shirts, but I was terrified of what other kids would think of me.

That's a major problem that I have never dealt with. Right up to this very moment, I am conforming, scared to step out of line. Why? I don't know. Maybe by this point, I feel it's too late. Designer clothing to me is bondage, like the stripes on a felon doing hard time. I have had thirty-five years to free myself, but I never found the courage to do so. It looks like I will remain this way forever.

I had a lot of friends in high school, but I never felt close to any of them. I had no real connection to any of the guys I hung around with. They'd talk about bullshit: this girl's tits, that girl's ass, that guy's a dick, this guy's car's a piece of shit. Like me, they were all privileged, and on our sixteenth birthdays, we all got brand new cars—BMW and Mercedes coupes, $60,000 automobiles, yet we could hardly see over the steering wheels.

My parents bought me a black Jeep Grand Cherokee limited, which was surprising because it was less expensive than every other kid's car. But 1998 was the start of the SUV revolution, so my Jeep was cutting edge, and it was maxed out with black exterior, black leather interior, Bose speakers, and fully computerized. It was pretty insane. My parents never asked me what I wanted. I just came home one day, and there was a Jeep. The keys were sitting on the kitchen table with a note that said, "Drive safe."

My so-called friends loved hanging out with me, and I never understood why. We played basketball and soccer together—that was our common ground. I'm inherently shy, and I divulged very little about myself. My body language was pathetic. I walked the halls with my head down. I hid behind my locker. I generally didn't want to be bothered with people. The problem was I was smart and good looking, and girls were dying to get to know me. But I was scared of my own shadow, and girls made me feel threatened. I was always extremely nice and cordial, and looking back, girls were basically throwing themselves at me, but I was too blind to notice and too consumed with my own thoughts to care.

In the middle of my junior year, a beautiful girl approached me after lunch. Her name was Ashley. She came right up to me and said, "You're the smartest, best-looking guy in this school. We're going out tonight. What's your number?"

I was stunned. The balls on this girl!

She took out a pen and paper and commanded, "Give me your number, Evan."

I gave her my number. I thought about giving her a fake one, but I'd have to see her in school the next day so I couldn't do that.

"I'm calling you at 6 o'clock," Ashley said. "Think about where you want to go. I'll be at your house at 7 pm sharp. Look good."

"Okay," I managed too stammer.

Ashley picked me up. I got in the car. She drove a few blocks, pulled into a parking lot, stopped, then asked me, "Have you ever had a blow job?"

"Not recently."

"Not ever. Don't lie. It's okay."

Silence.

"Can I take out your dick?"

I was shocked and said, "Sure."

She took out my dick and said, "I want to be the first girl to suck Evan Bloom's dick. This is like the holy grail."

"Holy grail?!"

"Evan, every girl has wanted to be with you for three years, but no one had the balls to ask. I win the prize. Lie back and enjoy yourself," Ashley said, and she gave me a blow job.

I dated Ashley for the rest of high school. She was a snot, highly obnoxious, but she didn't ask too many questions. I didn't have to talk to her on the phone for hours. I just had to drop by her house every now and then, have sex, and leave. It stopped people from wondering about what I did in my free time. My parents approved because her father was a surgeon, and she was beautiful. I had the perfect setup to focus on what really mattered to me.

The academic side of school came naturally to me. It was effortless. Teachers liked that I was a good student and an active participant in class discussions. I was not shy in class. My studies took me out of myself, far beyond the insecure, negative thoughts that were swirling in my head. One of the nicer things my mother ever said to me in high school was, "You have everything going for you. Everyone can see it but you."

Was that a compliment or a wakeup call? It stuck with me and couldn't have been truer. No matter what I accomplished, I still saw myself as being beneath everyone else. But at least I had one outlet, one thing that made me feel alive. Special. Connected to the world and everything within it. And it's served me well almost every day. I have always had a very special relationship with music, a deep under-standing of it. I can feel it. Some people are born with the talent to create it, and I am extremely jealous of that ability. Music was always my passion, but because I couldn't play an instrument, I felt I would never be part of music beyond a certain point.

The first concert I went to was with a friend from camp. We went to Madison Square Garden to see Phish, which was already, and remains to this day, my favorite band. It might have been the most important night of my life. Live music, my first concert, Madison Square Garden, tenth row seats, and I got high for the first time. The lights went down, the music started, and it was electrifying. I have never felt such energy, from both the band and the crowd, and I had a moment, an epiphany, a spiritual experience. I saw my future. As I watched the band play their instruments perfectly, I thought, *I can't do that*. But as I listened to the lyrics, it came to me, *I can write that!* I felt like I had figured out the riddle of my life: I am a writer!

But how to start? As it happened, that Monday in ninth grade English class, we began to study poetry, and I thought to myself, *Song lyrics are a form of poetry!* I sat in the back and wrote my first lyric. My first poem. What an unbelievable feeling. The pen couldn't move fast enough. Words gushed out as if from a fountain.

The other kids struggled to write one poem in thirty minutes, but I wrote three. I had never felt so complete. The clouds had parted. I had found my calling. I had the ability to tap into my emotions and put them into words. As a budding poet, I came to realize that my heroes weren't Whitman, Emerson, Byron, and Frost. Mine were songwriters, beginning with Jim Morrison and Bob Dylan. Later I came to appreciate Bruce Springsteen, Neil Young, Nick Drake, Dave Matthews, Paul Simon, Kurt Cobain, and many more. I longed to be part of a songwriting team. In the Grateful Dead, Jerry Garcia wrote the music, but his best friend Robert Hunter wrote the lyrics. In Phish, Trey Anastasio writes the music, and his best friends Tom Marshall and Steve "The Dude of Life" Pollak write the lyrics. Elton John writes the music, and Bernie Taupin writes the lyrics. I desperately wanted a friend who was a composer or to find an egoless band that needed a writer. How would I find such a thing in Great Neck?

And so, until the age of twenty-four, I wrote with a fictitious band in my head: searing, psychedelic rock songs and introspective, alienated alternative songs. I wrote songs about hope, desperation, and love. I thought of myself as a poet because I had no music. My writing was all about expressing what I felt. When I am writing, I feel powerful, fearless, unbound. My writing time is the only time I'm not afraid to be myself.

I've been writing for more than twenty years, but I have never showed any of it to anyone. I have written thousands of pages of poetry, all on yellow legal paper, all locked in a file cabinet in my home office. A few nights a week, I end up in my office alone with the door closed, writing. Sometimes I write so fast that I don't know what the poem's about until I read it back to myself.

For all these years, writing has carried me through and made me feel special. When I see a blank piece of paper, I see an opportunity to find out what I think. With a pen in my hand, I'm Evan Bloom, poet, and that's all I ever wanted to be.

CHAPTER
THREE

In high school, I spent a lot of time smoking pot alone, listening to music. Getting high allowed me to hear things differently and made me analytical. I'd notice different elements of instrumentation, and I'd deeply analyze lyrics.

In college, I did only four things: study, fuck, drink, and get stoned. I always went to class and always did my work—that part still came easy to me. In college, I became less inhibited, and I'm sure drugs and alcohol had a lot to do with that. For an analytical, philosophical, private poet like me, acid and mushrooms were liberating. I loved to trip, think, listen to music, see live music—and have spiritual sex with beautiful, earthy girls majoring in sociology and psychology.

But I was still somehow caught in the Great Neck Bubble. I was the preppiest acid head in the history of psychedelia. I had to hide my headiness because I knew a lot of people from home up there, and I was at an Ivy League school, not the University of Oswego.

So, on a deeper level, I was still unfulfilled. And even worse, now I was more self-aware, so I knew I was despondent. My despondence led to more drugs and sex, and more drugs and sex led to more despondence. On the surface all was good, and I was having a great fucking time. I had straight As, so my parents weren't on my case. I was having great sex and getting high. But I still couldn't find a true connection with anyone. I had a ton of friends who hardly knew me. If you were to ask my friends about me, they would have said, "Bloom, what a great fucking guy! He's the best! Say, where's he at?" Somehow "the life of the party" knew how to disappear.

I wrote poetry alone and began to read poetry alone. Reading poetry by real poets was humbling. Byron, Blake, Whitman, Emerson, and Ginsburg were true geniuses. They were extraordinary and a thousand times better than me. I would hide out with my words and their words, and those were my favorite moments.

It was the night before I was about to leave for my junior year of college. My parents had gone on a European cruise for six weeks, so I'd hardly seen them, which had made it an enjoyable summer. I was set to leave the next morning for school.

It was around 8 pm, and I walked into the kitchen to grab some water. My father was sitting at the kitchen table reading a financial newspaper.

"Evan, sit down for a minute."

"Okay, Dad."

"Listen, I know we don't have a very close relationship, but your performance in school has made me proud. You are doing very well. You are going to make a lot of money someday, and you can have everything we have and more. Now, I know you have two more years, but I want you to start thinking about business school and getting your MBA. Think about that this semester—about where you might want to go. With an MBA, you could get a job at a top-notch firm, maybe even *my* firm. How about the Blooms working together? Wouldn't that be something? We'll take over Wall Street. 'Bloom' will be a household name like 'Trump.'" He chuckled, patted me on the shoulder, and said, "Keep making your father proud. Drive safely tomorrow."

He picked his paper back up and went back to reading. That was the last "conversation" I ever had with my father, and I hadn't said a word.

CHAPTER
FOUR

It was early October, mid-afternoon, and I was walking back from my economics class in good spirits. I had a date to take ecstasy with a beautiful girl named Stephanie that evening. I was really looking forward to it. I made my way through campus with a grin. When I entered my dorm room, my grandfather was sitting on my bed. I was stunned. I'd had two conversations with my grandfather my entire life. He and my father were estranged, and he was my only living grandparent. Of course, I instantly knew something was wrong.

"Evan, pack a bag. Your parents were killed in a car accident," he said.

I stood there with my backpack still hanging over my shoulder. I was not sure how to react. I stood in my doorway like a statue for thirty seconds. My grandfather didn't say a word. He didn't get up to console me. He didn't say he was sorry. Nothing. He just sat there and watched me try to process what he had told me.

"Pack a bag, Evan."

"How did this happen? Where were they?"

"Your parents were coming home from a client dinner in the city. A drunk driver hit them on the Long Island Expressway. I'll answer all your questions in the car. Pack a bag. The funeral's tomorrow. I have to get you home. We have a lot to sort out, and you have to write and give a eulogy, so let's go."

I packed a few things, grabbed a suit, and we drove in silence. I didn't have the energy to speak. I was confused. Not upset, confused. Although my parents were not major players in my life, they were still my parents. Everybody loves their parents, even if they're shitty parents. Although I had basically no relationship with either of my parents, I always dreamed I would someday. Now that possibility was gone. I was an orphan.

I looked at my grandfather at the wheel, and he was a stranger. Both my parents had been only children, just like me, so I had no aunts, no uncles, no cousins. I had no one. I had always felt alone, and now I really was.

That night, in our gigantic home, I sat in my mother's painting studio and devised a eulogy. Surprisingly, it wasn't hard to write. I talked about my father and his business savvy, my mother and her love of the arts. I lied and told everyone how they were such supportive parents.

The next morning at the funeral, I spoke these words in front of 250 people. I hate public speaking, but I was not the least bit nervous because nobody at that funeral meant anything to me. I felt like I was addressing aliens. A lot of the people at the service were probably happy my parents were dead, especially the ones who were there because they knew my father. I eulogized my parents and sat shiva in my home for three days. At the funeral, I was approached by random people telling me they'd call and check in to see how I was. I never heard from any of them.

I received a call from my father's lawyer asking me to come in and have a meeting. Apparently, my parents had left a will. I drove to his office and sat with him. He asked me how I was holding up. Surprisingly he was kind.

"Evan, your parents left a very hefty trust, and you are the sole beneficiary of that trust," the lawyer said.

"Okay," I said very calmly.

"Are you curious to know how much your trust is worth?"

"Sure."

"$30 million."

My heart stopped. My blood stopped flowing. My eyes turned to glass. My bones stiffened. I felt nothing, neither excited nor happy. I felt indifferent.

"Evan, did you hear me? You just inherited $30 million!"

I couldn't give a shit. I casually said, "That's very exciting," just to appease the lawyer.

$30 million? Most people would feel something. I felt paralyzed. Burdened even. Now I was a trust fund baby. Now I had no reason to work ever. I had enough money to last five lifetimes, and I didn't care. Life was never about money to me.

Now, looking back, I realize this was my opportunity, the chance to live on my own terms, to do whatever I wanted with my life. I was 21 years old and worth $30 million, and I was upset about it because I had always been labeled a rich kid, and I was a rich kid who wasn't like the other rich kids. I used to hear people say, "He's from Great Neck, but he's different." I liked hearing that. Money scared me, and it still does. It's never done anything positive for me. Money was always my worst enemy, and it's followed me my whole life and just made me think less of myself. I know that sounds crazy, but money is the bane of my existence.

Inheriting a fortune should've given me freedom. My parents had held me back from pursuing what I wanted, but now they were dead, and I didn't have to be my father's son anymore. And yet I followed a ghost's shadow. I was still too afraid to be different, to spread my wings and fly. I still cared what others thought.

Instead of changing majors from business to English to work on my writing and then pursue it professionally, I stayed a business major and honored a father who had never taken an interest in me. Worse, I went to business school at NYU and got my MBA. I did what I had been told to do. I had no one to turn to, to talk to. I could have done anything. I could have done nothing. I chose to do the opposite of what my instincts and intuition told me to do. Instead of creating the life I wanted, I lost myself pursuing the life I grew up resenting. I chose a world of "I," a world of greed. I was meant to live in a world of "us," a world of compassion. The choice now feels irreversible. I will die on Wall Street, wondering what could've been.

CHAPTER
FIVE

I graduated from UPenn with a 3.9 and could've applied to any business school in the country. I decided to move back toward home and get my MBA at NYU. Having my own money hadn't gone to my head; my life pretty much stayed the same—with the exception of one extreme purchase: a luxurious one-bedroom apartment in a doorman building in the Murray Hill section of Manhattan, where all the buildings look like upscale hotels. It made no sense to move to Murray Hill, which is between 31st and 39th, and commute to school clear down at NYU, which is in the Village. But how could I resist?

Murray Hill is full of beautiful girls whose daddies are paying their very expensive rents. These girls don't believe in subways or the bus; they take cabs or town cars. Buying this apartment was obviously the wrong choice for me. The little voice in my head told me to get away from rich people, get a place in the West Village, and find some wonderful bohemian woman. But, like always, I continued to ignore that voice—and ended up regretting it.

Business school was much like college, only easier. Pursuing my MBA was a joke. Accounting, business analysis, market analysis, and global finance were a walk in the park, which gave me a lot of time to party and to sit in the actual Washington Square Park and write. This is by far the greatest park in the world, where many great writers wrote.

I'd sit on a bench and picture Bob Dylan, Allen Ginsburg, William S. Burroughs, and Jack Kerouac writing on the benches around me. In the '60s, Timothy Leary had love-ins in that park. Writing there, I felt like I was part of something. I had daydreams of grandeur. I would be the Gen-X connection, continuing the work of that secret society, that lineage of writers, carrying it forward. Through all the madness of my parents' deaths, the writing continued and grew stronger. With every poem, I got a little better and a little more confident. I still got high, but writing got me higher.

The party scene in the beginning of the millennium in New York City was nuts, and I'm ashamed I took part in it. It was different from college. Fewer bong hits were taken, and mushrooms and LSD were a distant memory. Now it was all about cocaine, and I did a ton of it. Cocaine was expensive, but everyone in my circle could afford it. Everyone went to the same clubs: Capitalé, Café Deville, Ohm, Sweet Sixteen. It was a dark scene, literally and figuratively.

Here's how it worked. At each club there'd be some jerkoff promoter at the front of the line letting people in. You had to be on his list. These promoters were always the most insecure guys, dying for everyone to like them, though everyone's just using them to cut the long line and get into the club. I usually got a VIP table for free because I was "friends" with the promoter. My bottle service was usually free as well. There was a club uniform; every guy wore an expensive, dark, button-down shirt and black Cole Haan or Ferragamo shoes. I preferred Cole Haan, which were much more comfortable.

As in college, guys looked at sex as conquest. "Yo, I fucked Jill Smollen last night, bro!" Young male machismo. Who you managed to sleep with said something about you and your status.

The girls—women, actually, but we called them girls—all dressed like high-class hookers, with extremely short dresses that went just past their asses. They wore high heels and did a ton of blow, and by the end of the night, there'd be at least one fight between friends. They'd go to war for a week, then be best friends again. There was always one queen bee in the group, who all the other girls revolved around. And there was also always one who had a serious drug and alcohol problem, which helped everyone else believe that they didn't.

Clubs would get wild with the music blasting and the lights flashing. Back then it was mostly old school hip hop, early electronic music. You're coked out, you're drunk, you took some Xanax, and everyone else has done the same.

It was impossible not to get laid. I banged a boatload of chicks in my twenties in New York City. I took down numerous girls in every building in Murray Hill, and all the doormen knew me. And with every girl I slept with I felt worse about myself. It was a coping mechanism for my unhappiness. I felt empty inside, and getting laid filled the void. For ten minutes, the sex took my mind off everything else in the world. But after I got dressed and left the girl's apartment or she left mine, I felt even emptier.

Every guy's apartment looked the same. Conversations were mostly about what their fathers did for a living and what their fathers drove. Everyone was flexing their muscles, trying to figure out who was cooler and worth more. Saying you had seen someone famous somewhere obscure said something about you. The same for going to certain clubs on certain nights. If you were there that night, you were cool. The whole ordeal was completely superficial and obnoxious.

At least I can say that I always played it a little bit differently in one respect: Although I was in that scene, I actually listened to women when they spoke. I didn't just look at their bodies. I looked into their eyes. And I didn't just listen to get laid; I listened because I can't not listen. I always listen. I gave everyone my full undivided attention, even when I was drunk and coked up. If you were talking to me, I was listening. That said, I knew that I was not supposed to be there. I knew that I was still running from myself.

CHAPTER
SIX

It was late May and my parents' home had been sold when I graduated from New York University Stern Business School with honors, first in my class. When summer comes and you're in your early twenties, from Long Island's Great Neck, Roslyn, Syosset, and Jericho, Hewlett, or Woodmere, you get a room in a mansion in the Hamptons for the season. If you're from Merrick, Lynbrook, Melville, Dix Hills, Plainview, or Manhasset, you get a room in a run-down house in the Hamptons. Everyone else usually ends up getting rooms in a dump on Fire Island.

Everyone I knew that summer was at their beach house every weekend. I was invited to stay in numerous places, but I stayed in the city alone in my apartment for some self-reflection and analysis. I did very little besides write poetry in the park and jerkoff watching YouPorn. I thought long and hard about my next step. I could do absolutely anything. I could sit in the park writing for the rest of my life. Instead, I chose to continue down the narrow path of conformity. The next thing I knew, I was at my third interview at Zenith Capital, and Mort Faber, the founder and senior partner, was trying to intimidate me. He praised my father like he was some sort of god.

"Your father had a killer instinct," Mort said. "He could work the phones and clients like a rabid dog. Do you have that instinct, Evan? Are you a rabid dog?"

I thought to myself, *Boy, this guy is an asshole. What kind of a question is that?* But with no hesitation, I said, "Mr. Faber, my father was a rabid dog. I'm not my father. I'm like a basset hound. I'm a hunting dog, and I always find what I'm looking for."

Mort ate that bullshit up. I was hired on the spot, and my life as a stockbroker began. Zenith Capital was the most prestigious brokerage firm in the city, and it had a mystique like it was a secret society. My starting base salary was $250,000 with uncapped commission. Zenith Capital is the only firm that has that kind of base salary. If they offer you a job, you take it, and you're going to be a millionaire.

The sky was the limit. I had beat out numerous people for this position, and I should've been excited. I should have celebrated, gone out, gotten fucked up, done an eight ball of coke, and had sex with two girls at once. Instead, I went home, went to bed, and stayed in my bed all weekend. I felt like I'd been hit by a train. My body was telling me I'd made a huge mistake, but my head was giving me a big thumbs up. I had taken a huge step toward turning into my father. I was doing what he had dreamed of, and I knew I could be even more successful then him. The thought of turning back did not occur to me. Getting dressed the next morning, I felt like I was going to a funeral.

CHAPTER
SEVEN

The firm was composed of really bright, analytical dirt bags looking to make a ton of money. On my very first day, I was given a seat at a trading desk directly next to six other guys—all under thirty. They seemed instantly threatened by me. Instead of coming over and introducing themselves, they stayed glued to their phones. Hey, you can take ten seconds to say hi and introduce yourself.

As a young broker, you can't make a trade until you pass your Series 7 exam. My exam was not for six weeks, so I devoted myself to researching, reading, lining up contacts, and learning everything about every corporation that was public and on the exchange. I researched their CEOs and their CFOs; I wanted to get into their minds and envision their plans.

After six weeks of twelve-hour days, I felt like I had a pretty good grasp on the market. I felt confident and secure. And during all that time, I did not take part in one conversation with a coworker. I listened to their conversations. There was a lot of ego. The desk had about forty guys. There was a large central board, TVs all over the place showing CNBC, and huge computerized tickers on both sides of the office, with six large clocks.

We weren't trading penny stocks; serious money was at play. My coworkers, albeit deranged, were highly intelligent and ruthless businessman. It was kill or be killed. Yes, as glorified in most films that center around trading floors, my coworkers were doing blow in the bathroom, but they weren't banging hookers in the boardroom. The partners weren't giving pep talks. Excellence was expected, and if you didn't deliver, you lost your job.

Once I got certified, my first order of business was to cold call some clients and get their attention. Once I got their attention, I'd keep it because I was different from every other broker. I was honest. I would talk to them like a person. I wouldn't give the hard sell and promise them the world. Instead, I would provide information on the corporation, how it's been performing the past three months, and a solid reason why I thought its stock would rise.

I was prepared for every rebuttal. I never got flustered. I never got hostile. I never got excited. I was calm, relaxed, and informative. I know I seemed trustworthy because I was trustworthy, and my intention was to make my clients money and keep them as clients for a long time. I aimed to develop relationships. I didn't go after the quick buck like my shortsighted coworkers.

I stayed away from all my father's former clients. I wanted nothing to do with him. I wanted to do everything on my own. And unlike most brokers in their first year, I was highly successful, one of the top earners on the entire floor. I built a solid client base, which led to referrals.

It all moved forward, and regularly I had people calling me. Whether they wanted to buy 1 share or 50,000 shares, I treated them exactly the same. If you were my client, I was available to you at any time, day or night, Monday through Friday. If there was an emergency, they could even feel free to call me over the weekend.

My clients were greedy, pushy, backstabbing, jealous, and obsessive, but they loved me because I was both their broker and their psychologist. I listened to them. I was honest, and they told me how they really felt. I had numerous clients drop me illegal tips, which could have made me a ton of money *and* lost me my license. I would listen and thank them, but I would never use the information. My clients live in a world of lies and manipulation, and I'm the only honest guy they know. The client with the tip I didn't use would now trust and like me even more and turn into a client for life. And he'll send five guys my way.

I gave work my complete attention. I worked my ass off. And my first year, I made $2.5 million. That was a record in the firm. I was balling with the big boys.

But inside I was miserable, burying myself in work to mask my pain. Fourteen- and fifteen-hour days. In at 6 am, out by 10 pm at the earliest. My coworkers would congratulate me on my success and ask me for tips, and I was always helpful. They hated my guts! They hated my work ethic, they hated how I sold, and they hated that I was making more money than them by doing things the right way. I looked at it as helping people. That's the only way I could get through the day.

I was making a lot of people a lot of money, and I'd go home exhausted and get out the yellow legal pad and my Pilot G2 pen and write about how I felt. Writing was the highlight of my day, every day. I'd sit in my leather chair and look out my floor-to-ceiling windows, staring into the night sky and wondering where I should be and how I could find what was missing in my hollow, cavernously empty existence.

Everything I pursued, I accomplished, but nothing felt right. A constant voice in my head said "write" every night. So, I wrote. I stopped doing drugs and hardly drank.

I was turning twenty-seven, and everyone I knew had serious girl-friends, were getting engaged, or getting married. That seemed right. I'd been following the flock since I was a boy, so why stop now? It was time to find a wife.

CHAPTER
EIGHT

The only guy at my firm who I could somewhat call a friend was a guy named Jeff Gleason. We didn't hang out much, but I thought he was a decent person, a couple of years older than me and also from Long Island. One night, he invited me over to his apartment where he was hosting a pre-drink before going out to a swanky lounge.

I'm usually hesitant to hang out with anyone from work, but I thought, *What the fuck? Jeff's a decent dude,* and I headed over to his place in Chelsea not knowing what to expect. I walked into his large apartment, and there were maybe six guys and four girls. The guys were pretty douchey, but the girls were very attractive, in a classy, well-put-together way. They had fashion sense and didn't look like the women I saw at the clubs. I made myself a drink and went over to the group of girls, but no one sparked my interest. Then, as I walked over to talk to the guys, two more girls walked in. The one on the left would become my wife.

When I first laid eyes on Lauren Shapiro, I almost fell over. She was gorgeous in a natural, organic way. She didn't have to try to be beautiful. I took a good look at her, and even from a distance I could tell she had moxie. She was self-assured, confident, and beautiful, and she knew it. Lauren gave all the other girls fake hugs and told one girl, "I love your shoes," and another, "I love your hair." This is Jewish female protocol. I watched Lauren interacting, and it was clear she was the alpha female. The other girls envied her and deferred to her. I was intrigued. I decided to lie back, play it cool, and have her come to me.

About fifteen minutes later, she walked up and asked, "What's your name?"

"Evan Bloom. What about yourself?"

"I'm Lauren Shapiro. I've heard a lot about you, Evan Bloom."

"Oh yeah? Good things I hope."

She smirked. "Very good things."

"Like what?"

"I heard you're a nice guy, smart, and fun to be around. Is that true?"

"It depends on the company."

"You're in good company now. I expect you to show me a good time tonight."

"I'll have to think about that."

"The market's closed on Friday nights, get a drink, and loosen up. Live a little." And she walked away.

There were red flags right away, but I was so smitten with her beauty, I didn't care. For the rest of the night, the dialogue was different. We played Jewish Geography, the game where every Jew is able to connect themselves to another Jew they know from somewhere, usually camp, college, or grad school. Lauren was from Plainview, Long Island, a town composed of upper middle-class Jews pretending to be rich and trying to keep up with the rich.

We had a lot of friends in common. Lauren went to Syracuse, which should've been another red flag. Syracuse is a private university where rich Jewish girls go because they are average students. Spoiled Jewish guys go there to bang good-looking Jewish girls who all have limitless American Express cards and brand-new BMWs. I should have seen then that Lauren was on a money hunt. Her father owned a popular sporting goods store in Syosset, which I thought was cool and different, having been surrounded by finance people my entire life. Her mother was a homemaker, and her older sister was a speech pathologist, which was the hot new field for young Jewish females to go into.

Lauren was a buyer for a department store. She had a degree in fashion design and worked for Bloomingdales corporate. In my experience 90 percent of Jewish girls do one of three things: They're buyers for clothing department stores, speech pathologists, or teachers. The rare ones are lawyers, doctors, or psychologists; those are the driven women. Most of the Jewish girls I grew up with just wanted to stay at home, spend boatloads of money, and do lunch every day while their husbands busted their asses at work. Most Jewish girls from Long Island quit their jobs when they have their first child. Lauren had no interest in pursuing a career, and she saw me as a long-term investment, a big dollar sign with legs. And I didn't care. I was too blind and too lazy to care. I was going to see where this went.

As I got to know Lauren, she seemed to be genuine, pure. She had a sense of humor, and she listened to my stories and theories on life. We went to the movies and the theater, and we met up with her friends for drinks. They seemed decent—a little snotty but no worse than I was used to. Lauren's friends' boyfriends were normal and seemed alright. They had various professions, and we talked about sports and music.

Lauren was my ticket out of the house. She was my form of entertainment. We never fought. We never even argued. I bought her anything she wanted; she never paid a dime. I gave her the royal treatment. Bottom line, I was extremely attracted to her and could tell she felt the same. The chemistry was good, and I convinced myself that she was fascinating. I made myself believe that there was something special in this girl.

Lauren only knew what I told her about myself. She'd ask me about my parents. She always asked me about work, and for someone to take any interest in me was refreshing. I have had no one my whole life who truly cared about me besides Regina. I was under the impression that Lauren truly gave a shit. Now looking back, I realize that she was a drop-dead gorgeous con artist, and I was just a mark.

Things moved fast. After six months of dating, Lauren moved in with me. I'd be lying if I didn't tell you that it was nice to have someone to talk to, to watch TV with. Everything seemed fine, and I thought I was happy. I thought this was what I wanted.

Everyone I knew was getting engaged or getting married. Lauren's friends were all engaged. About three months after moving in, she already started applying the pressure. She'd drop hints. She'd constantly show me engagement rings on the internet. She'd talk about her friends' wedding plans in detail.

It was exhausting. I couldn't care less. I really didn't want to get engaged. To me, that would be the beginning of the end. I knew it would change the whole dynamic of our relationship. I had told her I loved her many times, and she had reciprocated, but when I said the words, it never felt sincere. It never felt real. It felt like I was saying it just to say it. There was no life behind it, and no life behind me.

I convinced myself this was all right, that I was in love, but in fact, I was only in love with the idea of being in love. I didn't know what love was. How could I? I had never felt love. I had never opened up to anyone. The problem was that I wanted some kind of normality, and I thought Lauren would give me that. I never dreamed that *having* "normality" would be an even bigger problem, one I could neither understand nor solve.

Lauren kept pushing me to get engaged, and I kept telling her that now was not a good time, that I was too busy at work. She was turning twenty-seven, so I decided to rent out the party room in a swanky lounge and throw her a huge birthday party. I invited all her friends—and even the degenerates from my company. Her parents and her sister came too. I hired a good band, and it was open bar, with plenty of great hors d'oeuvres. I really went all out. I even had a decorator decorate the place.

And the whole thing was a surprise. I had Lauren's friend Shayna meet her for dinner, and then Shayna told her they should stop by this lounge with her for two minutes, that she just needed to show her face. They showed up at 9 pm on the dot. To get into the room, they had to walk through a set of heavy, red velvet curtains. When Lauren emerged, the band kicked in, and everyone whooped and hollered. She made her way to the front of the room and kissed me.

I grabbed the microphone and said, "Give it up for the guest of honor, the birthday girl, Lauren Shapiro!" I started dancing with her. We had some drinks, and the night slid by. About an hour in, I hopped up on the stage, shushed the band, and took the mic. The room quieted down to listen.

"Tonight's a very special night," I said. "As you know, it is Lauren's birthday. And I'm hoping she's about to become my fiancé!"

"Fiancé!" her father yelled.

"Yes, Mr. Shapiro. I want to marry your daughter. That cool?"

Nonchalantly but beaming he said, "Sure, go ahead."

Lauren started to cry, and I reached out and pulled her up on stage and just kept going. "Lauren, you're the best thing that's ever happened in my life. I want to spend the rest of my life with you. I want the rest of my life to start tonight." I took out a three-and-a-half-carat Tiffany engagement ring, dropped to one knee, and proposed, "Will you marry me?"

She was hysterical. She looked at the ring and almost passed out. "Yes!" she said. "Oh my God. Yes!"

Everyone was cheering. It was amazing, and in that moment, I thought I had done something great. It felt right. It felt perfect. Everyone looked truly happy for us. Even my coked-out colleagues looked happy.

But when we got home and walked into our apartment, I suddenly felt extremely anxious. I was dizzy. Lauren went into the bedroom and waited for me to make love to her—engagement ring on. I could hardly breathe. I knew I had made a huge mistake. But it was too late. Lauren Shapiro was going to be Lauren Bloom.

After that night, my future wife became unrecognizable. Everything changed. Now it was all about the wedding, the guests, the dress, the invitations, the flowers, the décor, the music, the seating, and the gifts. And the money. I had made all her dreams come true. That ring certified that she was actually going to be who she had long aspired to be: a rich princess from Long Island who stays home, pretends to be a mother, gets a maid to take care of her kids, and does nothing but buy things and do lunch with her superficial, jealous, backstabbing friends, expecting only the best of everything. Lauren felt entitled to be entitled. She had dreamed of having everything and anything possible, and now having everything and anything possible was possible. She had won the lottery, and I was the winning ticket. Now she was free to release her inner bitch.

CHAPTER
NINE

As our wedding approached, I became more and more uneasy. Lauren made all the plans. I had nothing to do with the process. She picked the place, the date, the cake, the band. I just gave her my credit card.

"Whatever makes you happy, I want you to have," I told her. "I want you to feel special on your big day."

She'd kiss me on the cheek, tell me she loved me, and head out the door to drop thousands of dollars.

The only thing I had to deal with was the problem of choosing groomsmen. I had no real friends. I had no family. It was kind of embarrassing. Lauren had twelve bridesmaids, each of whom she considered her best friend. And they all were engaged or married, so I told Lauren their guys would just be my groomsmen, and we'd have each couple walk down the aisle together.

That's what we did, though it was pretty sad for me to look to my left and see a row of dudes I hardly knew representing me. My best man was Jeff Gleason. I'd asked him because I met Lauren in his apartment. By this time, he had left my firm, and we were hardly friends anymore, but he agreed to do it anyway.

The wedding was over the top, extreme in every possible way. Three hundred people. Weirdly, it was in the Great Neck Jewish Center, where I'd had my bar mitzvah. All during my wedding, I kept remembering how I'd felt that day back when I was thirteen. Even then I thought formal affairs, like my bar mitzvah, were bullshit. And my wedding was bullshit. It was all for show. It was as if I was in a time warp. Both events felt the same: I put on a smile, I danced, and I pretended to be happy.

My wife loved being the center of attention and the life of the party. I despised every second of it. The only thing about my wedding I really enjoyed was the music. We had a great twelve-piece band and danced for hours. I felt like I was at a Kool and the Gang concert.

All night long, people came up to us saying, "You are the most gorgeous couple," and, "This was the best wedding I've ever been to," and, "You are going to have such beautiful kids," and, "I've never seen a couple so in love. Mazel tov!"

But the marriage never felt right to me. And over the first months, as Lauren began to reveal her superficial nature and fundamental dishonesty, I withdrew more and more. Soon there was little between us except the physical chemistry. I didn't want to admit this and wondered if it was me or if it was Lauren. Now I can see it was both.

CHAPTER
TEN

One evening three months after the wedding, I came home late. It had been an extremely long, tiring day. The market had been a roller-coaster, and my clients were driving me crazy. I was beat. I walked into our apartment, and Lauren was sitting at the kitchen table. It was absolutely quiet. No TV. No stereo. She wasn't reading. There was no stimulation, and she looked like she had seen a ghost.

"What's the matter?" I asked. "Are you okay?"

"I wanted you to walk in and see me looking like somebody died."

"Well, you accomplished your goal. What's up?"

She looked up at me, cracked a little smile, stood up, threw her arms out, and exclaimed, "I'm pregnant!"

I felt like all the life was being sucked out of me. A million thoughts ran through my mind in an instant. I wanted to cry.

I put on a happy face, hugged Lauren, and said, "Oh my God! I'm going to be a father. You're going to be a mother! We're going to be parents! What a blessing. I love you!"

She kissed me, said, "I love you too," and hugged me tight for a long time.

I wanted to scream. This was the icing on the nightmare cake. Now there was no turning back. The divorce I'd been planning in my mind would never happen. There was no escape. I could not propose an abortion. She'd been praying for a baby. Her friends were having kids, and she knew I would not leave her if we had a baby in our life. I thought she was using birth control. Letting herself get pregnant was a strategic move. I was stuck, and all I could think of was myself. My life was over. Or so I thought.

As the months rolled by, Lauren started to really show, and she seemed less and less familiar to me. It was surreal. I had spent the past year and a half with her, but she felt like a stranger. And she didn't have a clue who I was. To her I was just "a rich stockbroker."

Nonetheless, as her due date slowly approached, I was all in— hands on. Doctor's appointments, crib shopping, preparing a room, all of it. I sold our one-bedroom apartment and rented a huge four-bedroom apartment on the Upper East Side, the neighborhood of choice for rich young Jewish families. I hated the Upper East Side! But it's where Lauren wanted to live, and I went along.

Lauren quit her job and spent her days buying baby clothes and lunching with young moms and other moms-to-be in upscale cafés. I went in to work extra early, and I stayed extra late. It scared me to be around her. I knew I was not cut out to be a father. I was incredibly depressed, and I put all my energy into work so I wouldn't hear the angry voice in my head that kept yelling at me, telling me my life was over. I had never felt so low, and I had only myself to blame. I realized I had married just to get married, and my wife was more in love with my money than with me. I had fooled myself into thinking that marriage would make me happy, and this baby was my punishment.

I was completely unprepared for fatherhood. The idea was too much to bear. Worse yet was the idea that Lauren was going to be a mother. Jesus! She was the most selfish person I'd ever met. I couldn't imagine her waking up in the middle of the night to feed the baby or change a diaper. She hadn't gotten up before 9:30 am in more than a year.

I was having constant panic attacks. I felt dizzy and nauseous. I wanted to talk to someone, but I had no one. I found solace in my writing after Lauren went to sleep at night. I would write about my fear and desperation. Soon I would be stripped of my independence. I would provide for my family because that's what men do. You don't run from problems; you solve them. And I was determined to find a way to turn a negative into a positive.

As Lauren's due date approached, I was a wreck. One day around lunchtime when I was extremely busy in the office, my phone rang. I saw the call was from Lauren and ignored it—so wrapped up in work that I completely forgot she was pregnant. When she immediately called again, I remembered, *Oh shit! This could be it.* I picked it up.

"Evan, my water broke," Lauren said. "There's no time for you to come home. Meet me at Columbia Hospital maternity right away!"

"I'm leaving."

I grabbed a cab and headed uptown, and as if in a movie I urgently asked the driver to "step on it." My mind was racing. I had so many thoughts I couldn't focus on any of them. I was terrified. By the time I reached the hospital, Lauren had already been put in a room.

Holy shit! This is really going down! This is fucking crazy! I thought to myself.

I ran upstairs and saw my wife wearing a hospital gown with her feet up in stirrups.

Before I could say anything, the doctor came in, checked Lauren, and proclaimed, "You're fully dilated. Let's begin to push."

I stood there like a statue, immobilized.

The doctor turned to me and asked, "Are you the father?"

Hesitantly I said, "Yes."

"Well, it's time for you to meet your daughter."

I had asked Lauren to keep the sex of the baby a secret from me.

I was having a daughter! A daughter! Holy shit!

I went into the bathroom and threw up. That's how scared and overwhelmed I was. I did my best to play the role of loving husband. I held Lauren's hand as she pushed. I breathed with her. I was there the whole way through, and I would be lying if I didn't say that I found the whole birthing process amazing. It felt like I was helping a stranger give birth because I had no connection to Lauren, but she pushed and she pushed, and when the head popped into view, I almost passed out.

One minute later my daughter, Josie, came tumbling out. I felt a blast of adrenaline and a blood rush, and my vision was the clearest it had ever been. It was cosmic, otherworldly, the most incredible sensation I have ever felt. I was overwhelmed by joy and the inherent understanding that Josie and I were meant for each other. All the misery, disappointment, and isolation had disappeared.

I had thought having a child was going to be my biggest problem. Instantly, I knew that she was the *solution* to all my problems. In that moment, I found my meaning and purpose. Josie had been the last thing that I wanted, but she was the greatest gift I ever received. I was on top of the world.

When I held Josie for the first time, I cried. I had so much love to give and now I had someone to give it to. My love for Josie was real, authentic, unwavering. I looked deep into her eyes, and I saw purpose. I was going to be the best fucking father of all time!

Over the weeks that followed, I no longer dwelt upon my distaste for Lauren. It was all about Josie all the time. I got up in the middle of the night and rocked her to sleep. I fed her. I changed her. And I loved every minute of it. I'd wake up early before work to feed her. I'd come home from work as early as possible to be with her. I'd watch her sleep.

Lauren watched us as if from afar. She seemed to have no maternal instincts. We hired a nanny, and my wife went back to spending her days shopping and meeting her friends. I didn't care. The less time she spent around my daughter, the better. I didn't want Josie growing up to be anything like Lauren.

Six years later, I would have happily told you that Josie was the only thing in my world that I have ever loved with every fiber of my being. When she smiles, it makes me want to be a better person. I want to make the future better for her. When things couldn't get worse, she appeared and changed everything.

Josie and I developed an unbreakable bond. We have an understanding, a world of our own making. We share inside jokes. We have our own language. She's honest, sincere, compassionate, funny, and kind. Watching her grow year by year has been my greatest pleasure. Seeing her is the first thing I do in the morning and the first thing I do when I get home from work. We hang out upstairs every evening, and we have a blast. We read books. We watch TV. We play. We watch movies—good movies! She loves comic book movies—live action more than animation. That's where the waddle comes from.

One evening I was clicking through the channels and found the Batman movie where Danny DeVito plays the Penguin. Josie went crazy! She loved the Penguin so much that she started walking like him, waddling. Now Josie and I waddle around the house all the time. We put our hands on our hips, point our heads out to the side, invert our feet, and off we waddle, calling "Aarrgh! Aarrgh!" out of the side of our mouths. When Lauren sees us waddling, it really pisses her off.

I have the feeling that I'm doing okay as a dad. Maybe being a father is what I do best—besides writing poetry.

PART TWO
THE JOURNEY OF POET

CHAPTER
ELEVEN

Awake! That's the best way I can describe how I feel. I'm awake for the first time ever! I jump out of bed. I feel taller, stronger. My limbs are loose, elastic, like rubber bands. I feel my heart pumping and the blood rushing through my veins. I feel light, buoyant. My mind is silent. The complaining voice is gone. My vision is crystal clear, eyes wide open, eyelids fluttering.

I look out the window, and the leaves on the trees are neon green in the flood lights. The grass is not green. It is bright yellow, strong, and electric. The light grey sky is streaking and textured like the coat of a wolf. The full moon wears a smile. Even from indoors, I can hear the water in the swimming pool as the ripples gently slap against the edge. Everything is exactly the same, but everything has changed.

I stumble into the bathroom and turn on the lights. It is so bright. In the mirror, I am unrecognizable. No longer tight, my face is now putty. My eyes are teal blue, like the water of the Caribbean. My face is cherubic, angelic. My skin is soft like fine silk. I have never looked like this before. It is me, but I am someone else. I realize I am looking at the person I was supposed to be. This is how I am supposed to look. I want to dance. I want to shout. I feel like celebrating. What happened?

I don't know what to do with the energy surging through me. It is the middle of the night, and I am standing in my T-shirt and underwear, exploding with the urge to do something, to move. I begin to walk, and it's as if I am a passenger and someone else is behind the wheel. I go out into the main hallway and take a long look around. A diamond chandelier hangs from the ceiling, and I want to swing from it. The paintings on the walls are in 3D. I examine each one in the dark. I feel the canvas. I smell the paint. The brushstrokes are big and vivid. I can't look away. I feel the artist's energy. I understand his emotions and feel them inside. Pure bliss.

I walk into the guest rooms. They are bare, but I feel like there's an invisible party going on, and I am the only guest. I peek into Josie's room, forgetting she's not home! She's at my in-laws because of my big party! I walk into her room, and I imagine I can see her there, sitting on her bed beside me, so beautiful. The images on her Harry Potter and Taylor Swift posters sway back and forth, as if I am on mushrooms. I can hear Taylor Swift singing. Harry gestures with his wand and casts a spell.

I take Shel Silverstein's *Where the Sidewalk Ends* off Josie's night table, sit on her bed, read a poem, and begin to cry. I have no idea why I am so emotional. I'm so grateful—grateful to be alive, grateful to feel this way. This is a new state of consciousness, some kind of spontaneous enlightenment. I don't know what is happening, but it is not a figment of my imagination. I know it is real. I have changed.

All my frustration is gone. I feel a sense of promise, of hope. I feel limitless, at peace in the moment. Now I'm standing in my massive kitchen. The marble countertops are gleaming, and I examine them closely. It's as if I am seeing things for the first time. A black veil has been lifted from my eyes. There is beauty in everything I see.

I take a red apple out of the fruit bowl on my kitchen table. I can feel its skin, its texture. I savor its smell and the weight of it in my hand. It's as if I've never held an apple before.

I walk over to my subzero fridge and open it, and I am overwhelmed. There are so many options. I'm not hungry, I'm not thirsty, but I want to taste something. I pick up the chocolate milk and drink it straight from the carton. As it goes down my throat, I feel prickly tingles. Nothing has ever tasted so sweet. The thick milk dribbles down my chin, and I finish the carton. I hold it up to my eyes and smile. God bless cows!

Where to next? I roam down the hallway and into my entertainment room with its bar and cocktail tables. Five hours ago, this room was filled with my clients and coworkers, but that feels like five years ago.

I take a seat at the bar and try to think, but there is no thought. My mind is empty. Did someone slice off the top of my head? Suddenly, I want to go to my office. I speed walk there as fast as I can, like a kid on Christmas morning. I turn on the desk light, grab my yellow legal pad and my Pilot G2 pen, sit at my desk, and write.

My pen flies down the page. It can't move fast enough to keep up with the swirling thoughts in my brain. I have no idea what I am writing; the words are coming from somewhere else. I am not in control. I look and feel like a madman. My face is down in close, just above my pen, almost on the paper. It is as if I am watching myself write, just an observer. The pen has a will of its own.

I write and write and write, but suddenly the pen stops. I sit motionless with my pen in my hand, examining the yellow paper. I am terrified to read what I just wrote. I place my pen down and lean back in my expensive ergonomic computer chair, breathless. I close my eyes and see spirals of green and red rotating. The more tightly I close my eyes, the more colors appear. I feel tension leaving my body. My eyelids twitch. The pain I've held deep inside is drifting away—fast. When I open my eyes, my vision is normal and clear. I look down at the poem. It is legible! I begin to read.

> *The uncomfort of silence sways below my feet.*
> *A shadow rises above my eyes.*
> *I peek through my clouded eyelids in the mirror*
> *Take off this plastic disguise.*
>
> *As it comes off, I grow cold…*
>
> *Is this truly the way others view me?*
> *The same way I see myself?*

Would you still want to pursue me
If I threw away my belongings and my wealth?

Today I start over with nothing,
Live off what others throw away.
It might sound strange to admit this,
But today is my very best day.

I have no hidden agenda,
No meetings, no quota to fill.
I walk the city streets paved in copper
With a tin can of change and a lonely dollar bill.

I feel so liberated.
I can now seek out my true joy,
One truth from the past I hold sacred.
My love for my daughter, nothing can destroy.

I begin to perform in the subway.
I write at night and read my poetry to crowds all day.
I'm inspired by the sights and sounds that surround me.
The response makes the demons in my mind go away.

The word spreads around the city far and wide.
People come from all over to see what I'm about.
I stand up on my milk crate preaching the gospel.
The love I feel leaves me no doubt.

One day at noon I look off in the distance,
As I read aloud my passage of the day.
Who do I see staring back at me?
The image I saw in the mirror that day.

Only now that image wears a smile,
An inner confidence and a glint to his eye.
I stop speaking and bow my head in silence.

I'm so proud I turned into that guy.

A man who gave up his possessions,
His family, his friends, and his wealth.
With hardship only comes the obsession
To become a better version of yourself.

I read it again, and again, and again. My body is shaking. I feel frozen. What does this mean? It came from me, but I didn't write it. It is a message of some sort. I try to make sense out of it. Streets of copper, lonely dollar bill? Write at night and read my poetry all day? The city far and wide? With hardship comes the obsession to become a better version of yourself? What am I supposed to do?

I close my eyes tight and lean back in my chair, but the colors have disappeared. There is nothing. No sound, just vast darkness. I sit silently for two minutes, and suddenly there is a jolt of adrenaline, and I almost fall out of my chair. My body trembles and shakes. It comes to me, all of it! This is who I am, this is what I'm meant to become, this is where I am meant to be. In the city. New York City!

I have to give it up! Everything: my job, my money, my identity. I have to free myself from my plastic disguise. No more hidden agendas. The time has come to become a writer, a poet! The time has come for Evan Bloom to live the life he was born to live. I title the poem "Poet."

It is a prophecy I must fulfill, and it must begin immediately. I will abandon my old life, head to Washington Square Park, and write.

I will have to leave Josie behind for now, but I will come back for her when the prophecy is fulfilled. How long will it take? Can she go without me for that long? I lean back in my chair, and the colors reappear. I search for an answer. I begin to sob. I know the answer. It's yes.

Tears stream down my face. I think of my life without Josie, and of the life she'll have without me. I will keep in contact with her, and our dear nanny, Petra, who loves her and whom she loves, will take care of her. But leaving her will be such a selfish act! Yet it is what I must do, for both of us. In the long run, Josie will need me to be my true self, the fulfilled, best version of myself so that I can give her a happy life, a real life, an authentic life.

Petra will be Josie's guardian spirit and make sure she is okay. Neither of them can know where I am or what I'm doing, but I need to know that Josie is safe, happy, and secure. Thank God Josie loves Petra so much. We can do this. We will find a way. My muse is my writing, and she is calling me.

I head out into the backyard. It is like an oasis whose beauty I have never noticed before. The turquoise waterfall tumbling, the white water splashing, the neon green grass sparkling in the moonlight. I am always so caught up in thought, but right now my mind is calm. I'm in awe of the reality around me. I lie down on a lounge chair and try to wrap my head around what has just transpired. I need to plan the next step.

Tomorrow night I will make my escape and leave behind my meaningless life of extravagance. If anyone knew what I was doing, they would think I have gone mad. But actually I have become sane.

The orange sun begins to rise above the trees, and the hummingbirds start to sing. Their song builds and builds and crescendos like a symphony. I haven't stayed up all night and watched the sun rise since college. It is like seeing an old friend. I have been too blind to appreciate what is right in front of me.

I head back inside my house and take a long look around. Everything seems unnecessary. It is a hollow dwelling composed of broken dreams. How did I allow this? When I leave, I will bring only what I need, the bare necessities.

I walk back into my bedroom. Lauren is still sleeping. I realize that I no longer feel hatred nor disdain for her. I accept her for who she is. From now on, I will accept everyone. I won't judge. Now I'm focused on Josie. I have to be at my in-laws' house in an hour to pick her up. I can't wait to see her face.

We are going to waddle and eat a mountain of pancakes, and I will savor every moment with her before I leave. Will she ever forgive me? Will she ever understand? My soul says yes.

CHAPTER
TWELVE

When we come back into the house, Josie scampers upstairs to her room for half an hour and blasts music, then comes downstairs to watch TV with me. I have so much on my mind I don't know what to do. I open a bottle of water and lean back on the marble kitchen counter. In less than 24 hours, my life will be turned upside down.

I settle into my office, take out a yellow legal pad, and plan my exit strategy in detail, listing everything I have to pack and everything I have to do. My list is ridiculously specific, almost minute by minute, but for me, writing things down brings clarity.

Lauren sleeps late, then heads off to do errands and later dinner with friends. Josie and I have a normal Saturday—PB&J for lunch, play for a while, watch a movie. Because I slept only for a few hours, I take a nap. It is spectacular, though I wake startled when I remember the plans I've made.

Josie and I are drawing pictures together and watching *101 Dalmatians* when Lauren comes home. She says she had a good dinner and she is tired and is going to bed. She gives Josie a peck on the cheek and heads upstairs. Josie and I stop drawing, then just watch the last part of the movie with full attention. We have Kraft mac and cheese for dinner and sliced apples with Peter Pan peanut butter.

As Josie's bedtime approaches, she heads upstairs, and I clean up our dishes. We usually spend the last hour of her day in her room play-ing, and then she gets into bed and I read to her. We both love reading time. I do voices for all the characters and sound effects. We usually read three or four books, and we also talk.

I have a theory that people become more vulnerable as they become more tired. Tiredness lets the truth come out. This theory runs true for my daughter. Every night as Josie winds down, she tells me how she feels, what's bothering her, if she had a good day. On this night, I really have to keep my emotions under control and make it seem like every other night, when in fact it will be our last night together for quite some time.

As I head upstairs, I close my eyes tight and pray. I feel like the worst father in the world. Yet what I am about to do is for her sake as well as mine.

When I walk into Josie's bedroom, she is wearing a black cloak and holding a wand in her hand. She's watching *Harry Potter and the Sorcer-er's Stone*.

She looks up as I come in, smiles, points her wand at me, and says, "Hecto patronum!"

"Am I dead now?" I ask.

"No, you disappeared."

"So, you can't see me right now?"

"I hear your voice, Daddy, but I don't see you."

"It is fun being invisible. If it wasn't summer, I would go with you to school, sit in the corner quietly, and watch you do addition. How's that sound?"

"That sounds fun. I like math."

"Well, how about spelling? Would you want me to watch you spell?"

Josie smiles wide and says, "No! I'm not a great speller, Daddy."

"That's not true. You just need to sound the words out. Spell nursery."

"Do I have to?"

"Please, sweetheart, just spell one word for your dear old dad."

"Okay. Fine. N-U-R-S…this is the hard part."

"Sound it out, Joze. N-U-R-S-ERY. Say "Errr""

"Err."

Now say "R."

"R."

"Joze, to turn that "R" into an "Errr" what vowel do you need?"

Josie thinks for a second. I can see her sounding out vowels in her head. She shouts out, "E!"

"That's my girl! See, you're a good speller."

"I'm getting better."

"It's all practice, Joze. Practice makes perfect. Hey, am I still invisible?"

"Nope, the spell wears off after a correct spelling word."

I grin and say, "I expect I'll never be invisible again. Bedtime's in a half hour. Let's read some books and then I'll tell you a special story."

"Is it a true story?"

"No. But, you'll like it."

Josie throws on her SpongeBob pajamas, jumps into bed, and gets under the covers. Of all the books I have read to her, her favorites are the ones by Shel Silverstein. Tonight, I read five poems from *Where The Sidewalk Ends* (my favorite Silverstein book), *The Salamander Room*, and *Guess How Much I Love You*, which is a little tough for me to get through without crying. "Okay!" I say then, shutting the book. "Now it's story time! And I have a new one that's pretty special."

"What's it called?"

"The Fish Who Swam Alone."

"Alone?"

"Yup. You ready?"

Josie smiles and giggles and says, "Yes."

Once upon a time there was a fish named Sal who always swam every-where as part of the same big school of fish. Everyone in the school of fish looked just like Sal, and all they ever did was swim together, going around and around the same reef.

Sal had a feeling that the ocean was bigger than he could see from that reef, and he wanted to see more of it, but none of the other fish were interested. One day, Sal decided he was going to go explore the ocean on his own.

It was scary to think of leaving everyone he knew and swimming off into the deep blue, not knowing what he would find or what would happen to him.

And he knew he would miss his friends. A lot. But he knew in his heart that he had to do it, even though it scared him. He knew he couldn't spend his entire life swimming with the same group of fish on the same reef, wondering what else was in the ocean.

So, Sal decided he would go exploring alone and learn what he could learn, and then come back and tell the other fish in his school what he had seen.

And that's what he did. One day he swam away. And his adventure began.

I stop talking and give Josie a squeeze. She looks at me, and we both smile.

"That's part one of the story," I tell her. "Next time, we'll find out what Sal discovered on his big adventure, and what happened when he came back."

She laughs and says, "Oh, Daddy, I can't wait! I hope he doesn't get eaten by a shark!"

I tuck her in, we say our goodnights, and from the doorway I take it all in. "I love you, Josie!" A tear runs down my cheek. She can't see it in the darkness.

"I love you too, Daddy. Sleep tight!"

CHAPTER
THIRTEEN

In my office, I distract myself by watching the end of the Yankees game. I get all my writing out, and I flip through and read old poems. Twenty years of my life is captured here. It's one of the few things I've done that gives me pride. I wrote it for myself as catharsis, as a way to feel. As I read, I stack the pages into three, tidy piles.

I go back upstairs, quietly slip into my tremendous walk-in closet, and shut the door. I take my oversized black duffel bag down from the top shelf, which is so high up I have to use a step stool. Quietly, I select some clothing and place it in the bag. Fortunately, Lauren sleeps like the dead—or at least the well tranquilized.

I take the duffel bag back to my office. I grab a plastic shopping bag and carefully place the piles of paper inside, then gather it tight with a rubber band. Everything else in the duffel bag is replaceable; my writing is not.

The few remaining items on my to-do list go into the bag. The last item is a picture of Josie. I look at it, and suddenly my body goes cold.

In my heart and soul, I know this is just as much for her as it is for me. Josie deserves to grow up in a different world. A better world filled with honest people who will truly love her, like Petra. A world where she is appreciated for who she is, not what she has. I want my daughter to grow up the opposite from the way I did. She deserves a better father and a better life, and I'm going to find a way to give it to her.

As I continue to look at her smiling face, I begin to feel better. I stare at it. It's like she's talking to me, saying, "Daddy, you're doing the right thing. This is your chance. Don't worry. I will always love you." That thought inspires and reassures me, so much so, I take an over-sized calendar out of my desk drawer and grab twelve pictures of Josie and me at various places: the carnival, a Broadway show, her school play. I place a picture on every Sunday of the month for three months. On a piece of yellow legal paper I write:

> Joze,
> Every day that you cross off this calendar brings us
> a day closer to being together again.
> Love,
> Daddy

I cross off day number one with a black sharpie and place the note inside the calendar.

I call a town car, but not the usual company car, which would bill my company and leave a trail behind me. I tell the driver to meet me on the north side of a small park that's four blocks from my house. I tell him my name is Dylan Gorman.

After the Yankees game ends, I watch the 11 o'clock news. It's supposed to be nice tomorrow: 75 degrees, not a cloud in the sky. I realize that I'd better add one more item to my list. It will be cold come winter, and I'll need a heavy jacket. What I am about to do seems crazy, but if I'm going to do it, I have to take it seriously and be practical about it.

I quietly slip into bed and lie next to Lauren with my eyes wide open watching the clock tick on my Breitling Aviation watch. It feels like an eternity. Finally, as 4 am arrives, I gently and quietly get up and head downstairs to my office.

I sit at my desk to write notes to Lauren and Josie.

Lauren,

I know you and I are both unhappy in our marriage. I'm going away, and you won't hear from me for a long time. Eventually, I'll get in touch. I'm sure you won't miss me. I want you to know how disappointed I am in our life together—disappointed in you and in me. We could have been kind and generous, but we were not. And you have been unfaithful to me—to put it mildly. But Josie is a miracle, and if we hadn't been together, she would not exist. So, I thank you for that. Please take good care of her in my absence. Here are all my credit and debit cards. The passwords on all of my accounts are "Josie13." Try not to spend everything; Josie will need to go to college.

Farewell,

Evan

P.S: Go ahead and keep fucking Andrew Feldman. You have my blessing.

Joze,

You are my #1. Like Sal the fish, I have to go away for a while, which breaks my heart because I will miss you very, very much. There is something important that I need to take care of, and I have to do it alone. Nobody will know where I am, but I promise you I will be fine. While I am away, I do not want you to be sad. I want you to be your happy, *wonderful self. I will see you as soon as I can, but I will think of you all the time. Remember to cross off each day on the calendar on my desk. Everyday is a day closer to us being together. When you waddle, imagine me waddling too. I will always love you with all my heart.*

Love,

Daddy

P.S: I promise I won't get eaten by a shark. I will swim back to you as soon as I can!

On my phone, I look up Petra's cell number, and I write it down twice. I put one copy in my pocket and the other in my duffel bag.

I place my phone in the back of a desk drawer. I take out my wallet and remove my driver's license and $500. Then I put my wallet in the drawer atop the phone. I put my license and $300 in an envelope that I then zip into a secret pocket at the bottom of the bag. Two $100 bills go into my pocket.

I leave all my credit and debit cards on the kitchen table, along with the note for Lauren, then quietly go up the stairs and head toward Josie's room. I gingerly open the door and look at her sleeping peacefully, a smile on her face, her blanket falling off, her little feet showing. I was going to place Josie's note in her room, but now I realize it would be the very first thing she would see in the morning, and I don't want that. But I want it to be somewhere that she'll read it before Lauren gets up. Josie watches movies on the widescreen TV in the guest room, so I go there, down the hall, and tape the note up in the middle of the screen. Then I poke my head back into Josie's room, silently tell her I love her, and shut the door. I wipe the tears out of my eyes and quietly head back downstairs. I grab my duffel bag, slip out of the house, and head for the park.

CHAPTER
FOURTEEN

For far longer than anybody alive remembers, Washington Square Park in Greenwich Village has been a gathering place for artists, writers, and activists, decade after decade of creative types, performers, sunbathers, students. In the 1950s, the beats hung out here, and the park was also surrounded by a cutting edge music scene. The Village Gate, the Village Vanguard, and the Blue Note regularly hosted the biggest names in jazz. The park is probably most famous for the development of the folk scene in the 1960s, when musicians from all over flocked there. Music clubs surrounded the park—Gerde's Folk City, the Bitter End, Cafe Au Go Go, and Cafe Wha? This is where Bob Dylan got his start and honed his craft. He lived right across the street, and folk legend Dave Von Ronk called Washington Square Park home as well.

Other artists who got their start in Village clubs are Jimi Hendrix, Bette Midler, Simon and Garfunkel, and James Taylor. The park is basically the Central Park of downtown. People protested the Vietnam War in this park. It's where LGBTQIA first gathered and fought for social justice. You can still feel the energy.

When I was getting my MBA at NYU, I practically lived here. It always felt like home to me to be there among the hippies, yuppies, burn outs, and college students. Comedians perform in the main circle by the fountain, when it's not running. Jazz musicians play Miles Davis and Thelonius Monk. The southwest corner of the park is loaded with tabletop chess boards, where cocky young players get hustled, mostly by wily, uncouth elderly Black men, and sometimes they hustle right back. Bobby Fischer, the greatest chess player of all time, came out of this park.

I've been all over the world, and the park is still my favorite place. Where else can a would-be poet like me stand next to a millionaire, a homeless man, and a trumpet player—all at the same time? There are no outcasts here. Nobody's weird. Everybody gets respect. In Washington Square Park, you are who you are. And that's all I ever wanted to be. Which is why I am here in the park on this life-changing morning.

The bright yellow sun is rising with rays of white lightning, and the bluebirds sound like a choir. I carry my black duffel bag over to a rustic, green park bench and sit down. I feel weightless and jubilant, jovial and childlike, and I don't move an inch for hours. I bask in all of nature's glory and watch the park come alive. Early risers walk their dogs. College kids head for morning classes. Homeless men and women rise one by one and stretch. The world is waking up. The yellow sun is everyone's alarm clock. And I suddenly realize time is on my side. All I have is time, and I am enjoying every second.

I'm ready to get to work, so I open my bag, take out a fresh new yellow legal pad and my Pilot G2 pen with blue ink, and the words come to me:

> When I look in your direction
> You will always feel the connection, and the love I have for you.
> Know this to be true.
> No matter where you are, I will be with you.
>
> When the sun hits your back
> And the clouds form within
> When your mind feels thick
> And your blood runs thin
> No matter where you are, I will be with you.

You will come to a crossroad in life
Where all you will feel is pain and strife.
You will feel confused, unsure of what to do,
But when you look in the mirror, it will be us two.
No matter where you are, I will be with you.

When the sun begins to rise
And the clouds part between your eyes,
When your mind has cleared
And your blood rushes true,
No matter where you are, I will be with you.

And on the day we meet again
And I get to hug my daughter and my best friend,
When all your dreams finally come true,
No matter where you are, I will be with you...

I title it "No Matter Where You Are." I don't know if it is good, but it feels good. I haven't read much poetry. I've never been around other poets or writers. I don't preconceive. For me it's not something I plan. It just comes out, and I really can't control it. A little voice in my head will tell me to grab a pen and a piece of paper, and the words spill out on their own. For five minutes the world does not exist. I am thinking about absolutely nothing and everything at the same time. It is another consciousness. I am addicted to that feeling, and it's really the reason why I ended up sitting here. I need to know what this is, and I need to know who I truly am. I know the two are interwoven.

I put my pen and pad away and sit in silence. I watch people going about their business following their daily routines. In the morning light, I am struck by the beauty of everything—plants, trees, dogs, squirrels, and not least of all people. It's a beauty I have taken for granted. Or, more precisely, ignored. For a long time, the world has been dull. My vision blurred. I saw no details.

Sitting here for hours I think about how cynical I had become, expecting everyone to be selfish, arrogant, and egomaniacal like me and everyone I know. I've met some good people, but no one I've let myself get close to. I trust no one. I have been alone most of my life, but now I want to be a part of something, connected. I want to meet people I can share myself with, people who will listen. It would also be nice to meet people who make me smile and laugh. I have always been afraid to say what's on my mind. Now I want to express myself.

Yesterday I was thirty-five going on seventy-five. Now my mind is lit up like a pinball machine. I keep figuring things out. Insight after insight. I want to live in the moment. My new routine will be not to have a routine. The fact that I have no idea what is going to happen next thrills me and makes me laugh out loud. Quickly I look around, self-conscious, and realize nobody has heard me. No one is paying attention to me. Nobody knows who I am. Nobody knows I am here. I am free, and my laughter is music to my ears.

CHAPTER
FIFTEEN

For a long time, I have been sitting on this bench in sheer bliss. All that was once black and white is now in hyper color. I am fascinated by everything. I observe the sky's shades of blue, the cloud formations, the hunter green leaves dancing in the summer breeze, and the ants and insects busy at work. I focus on the little things. I observe.

Over the past two days, I got up a few times to go to the bathroom at Starbucks. I treated myself to a tall coffee and ate two slices of stale pizza from Ray's Famous Pizzeria. I'm officially on a budget now. I have no idea where I'm going to sleep or how I'm going to eat, and truth be told, I don't care. I have absolutely no fear.

I was never a big believer in God. I think of him as a con man, the greatest salesman in the history of civilization. Religion is the ultimate scam. As a Jew, I respect my lineage and heritage: Two people from the same tribe made love 5,000 years ago, and here I am. But the whole Torah, temple, yarmulke tradition seems preposterous. When I walk into a temple, I feel like it is Halloween, like everything is just made up, for fun, fake.

When I used to get high, it seemed clear to me that all of us are part of something bigger. Sitting here now, in a mind-altered state, I feel I am awakening. I think everyone knows the life they really want, but taking action to pursue it is hard. In just two days, I've come to think that I can trust my instincts. Someone is on my side. God? A spirit? I don't know, but someone is looking out for me and wants me to be happy. And now that I don't have anything, it's clear that the main thing I want to do is write so I can give my writing to the world.

The park officially closes at midnight, but no one bothers me. I just sit and listen. In the quiet of the night, the dark is held at bay by lamps that look like they have been here for a century. I hear the sounds of the city. I listen in on people's conversations. This is New York City, so "yelling" is "speaking" here. When one woman calls her husband a "fat, lazy fuck," instead of getting angry, he calmly says, "That's your opinion." It makes me smile.

I can listen to strangers talk all day, but the best entertainment is watching drunk college kids try to find their way home. They're stumbling, stammering, sideways, and talking gibberish, and those are just the guys. Drunk girls are a mess. They walk in groups of four, looking like they woke up in the middle of the night. Their hair's a mess, they're carrying their shoes, walking barefoot, and they can hardly speak. Guys are loud and obnoxious, but girls look like the walking wounded limping home from war. They just want to get in their beds and forget.

I watch the homeless men and women settling into places to sleep. It breaks my heart. I can instantly tell who's just down on their luck and who's a drug addict or an alcoholic. It's an epidemic. I remember going to a Knicks game when I was eleven with a kid I knew from camp. I was surprised he had invited me because I'd never considered us friends. My parents were oblivious, and Regina allowed me to take the train to Penn Station. It was 1991, and New York City was not in great shape. The crime and homeless rates were high. I remember getting off the train, and Penn Station was filled with homeless men, women, and families. It was horrible. I felt helpless. I wanted to help those people, but there was nothing I could do. Some of them looked broken, some looked sick, and some looked like they just needed a bath and a place to sleep.

I will be homeless soon. Actually, I'm homeless right now. I live in this park. I might look like I've got a nice place somewhere, and if I wasn't devoted to changing my life I would go there. But right now, I feel more at home than I ever have before.

CHAPTER
SIXTEEN

The park is surrounded by New York University, the school I got my master's from. There are separate buildings for the various schools, some right at the edge of the park and others in the surrounding neighborhoods. These buildings are state of the art, like something out of Star Wars. Especially the Kimmel Center for University Life. Mr. Kimmel must be living pretty good in there. But these ultramodern additions notwithstanding, you can still feel the old Village energy. You can still feel the history.

I have been sitting in the park's northeast corner, near a sign that reads "Washington Square Park East." I walk over to the north side where I was initially dropped off, at the center of which is the most iconic of the four entrances. It features a tremendous arch dedicated to George Washington. It must be 150 feet tall. Right below it is a statue of him, decked out in full "father of our country" regalia. The arch itself is covered with images of war and peace and other fascinating details. Along the top of the arch is a quote from Washington himself: "Let us raise a standard to which the wise and the honest can repair. The event is in the hand of God." In the hand of God: I take that as a personal message of encouragement.

It's 11 am and a picture-perfect August day. This place will really be hopping in an hour. The tremendous circular fountain in the middle of the park is not spouting water today, so it will be filled with skate-boarders and young kids hanging out. Sitting on the outer rim are students studying and a young woman reading a novel.

During the spring, summer, and early fall there's always entertainment around the fountain. Over the years, I've seen comedy troupes, dancers, jugglers, and magicians. And it's not second-rate talent. The men and woman who perform here are fantastic, and on a nice day they will draw such a big crowd that you have to work hard to get close enough to see well.

It's too early for a show yet, so I wander over to one of the areas lined with tabletop chessboards. Some of the best chess players in the world play here regularly. As you walk by, they will challenge you to a game, and they'll probably let you win the first one. But you can bet your ass they're winning the next two and taking your money. I immediately get approached by a middle-aged Black man wearing a dashiki, with an old grey cardigan sweater on top of it.

"Hey, man, you wanna play?" the man asks.

I play dumb. "Chess? I don't know how to play."

"Man, you don't know how to play? I'll teach you."

"I appreciate the offer. I really don't have the patience to learn, but thank you."

"Hey, didn't I see you sitting on the east side yesterday? Was that you, man?"

"Yeah, that was me."

"You looked real serious. What were you writing?"

"I was writing some poetry."

"So, you're a poet?"

I own it. "Yes, I'm a poet."

"Well, poet, what's your name?"

It just comes out, "My name is Poet."

"Okay, Poet, I'm Bill."

I shake Bill's hand. "Nice to meet you, Bill. How long you been playing chess out here?"

"Twenty-five years."

"Twenty-five years! That's a long time. You must love it. Are you getting a pension and benefits out here?"

"Ya know, every year for the past twenty-five years, I say to myself 'this is the last year,' and every year in April, I sit right here in the same damn seat. It's got a hold on me. I love the game, and I love the camaraderie."

Bill raises his arms and gestures to the row of tables and the dozen or so players. "Hey, guys," he says loudly. "This is Poet."

That felt good. Really good. Probably the way Bruce Springsteen felt the first time someone called him "The Boss."

There's a broad smile on my face. "It's nice to meet you, guys," I say. "Don't take my money. I don't know a rook from a pawn."

"You'll still kick the shit out of Bill," says a short stocky guy with a long beard and a big grin. He's been here twenty-five years, and he's still looking for his first win."

Bill turns around. "I whipped your ass yesterday, Willie. You best shadow me all day. Maybe you'll learn something."

Willie waves his right hand at Bill dismissively. "Checkmate!"

"So, Poet, where do you live?" Bill asks.

Nonchalantly I say, "I live here, in the park."

"In the park? Clean cut white guy, schlepping around a big duffel bag is living in the park? There must be a story."

"No story. I'm just a guy learning to write. That's all. What you see is what you get. Where do you live, Bill?"

"I live up in Harlem on 147th Street. Been there all my life. I'm fifty-four years old, and there ain't nowhere I'd rather be. I love it up there. My family's up there, my kids are up there, and chess is down here. This is how I support myself: whooping people's asses at chess."

"You're that good?"

"Ya know, in chess, people like to use the terms 'master' and 'grandmaster.' I'm the master of the grandmaster. You sit at my table, it's slavery all over again. Only this time, the white man's getting whooped."

I laugh. Bill is full of life. He's fifty-four, but he looks thirty-four. He has a great way about him.

"Hey, Poet, I gotta get back to work and teach these kids a lesson. I'll see you later."

"Bill, go easy on them. They need their tuition money."

Bill smiles. "So do I."

And I walk away. I head over to the dog park, where there seems to be a lot going on. It has two separate fenced-in areas, one for small dogs and the other for big dogs. In both, the ground is covered with white gravel, and there are some doggy bowls set out, filled with water. A heavy musky smell hangs in the air, and I realize it's because little chunks of dog turd are scattered all over. I watch the drama as the dogs sniff one another out. A German Shepherd, a boxer, and a Labradoodle get into a tussle, and the boxer is getting the best of the Labradoodle. Suddenly the boxer's owner, a tall scrawny hipster, jumps into the gated area. He grabs his dog's snout and yanks on it. Hard. And the boxer trots away with his head down, looking distraught and whimpering. He is scared shitless of his owner. It's fun to watch the dogs mix it up and the owners scramble to break up the fights. Some of the owners really get worked up. I think about how the park is a place where both dogs and people get to meet strangers and become friends.

CHAPTER
SEVENTEEN

The park is starting to fill up. I head back over to the fountain, where two wildly outfitted Black performers are setting up. Each is wearing baggy red pants, a white winter hat with a red fuzzy ball on top, and a long baggy black T-shirt. Their red-and-white-striped tube socks are jacked up to their calves. They're funny-looking, but they are quite serious as they set up their props, including two big white buckets on the edges of the circle for donations. I honestly have no idea what's about to take place, but I have a front row seat.

The smaller performer stands up tall and begins to speak, projecting his voice like a master of ceremonies. "Ladies and gentle-men!" he announces, pausing to let people hear and pay attention. "Please make your way to the square if you feel like having a good time. If you prefer a bad time, you can have that instead. We don't discriminate. We aim to please. Ready, set…"

Both men start clapping their hands over their heads in a rapid-fire rhythm, chanting, "Let's go! Let's go! Come on, come on, let's go!" summoning the crowd from all directions. They keep it up, clapping and circling and climbing up onto the fountain's rim, and soon a good-sized crowd has gathered around them.

They keep clapping, and now they get the whole crowd clapping as well, and I'm clapping too. It is getting really loud, then suddenly they stop, and the audience's clapping pattern collapses into applause.

"All right!" yells the taller of the two performers. "Who likes to laugh?"

The smaller performer points to a teenager and asks, "Do *you* like to laugh?"

The taller one points to an older woman and asks, "Do *you* like to laugh?"

The smaller one runs over to a little girl, gets down on one knee, and asks, "Do you like to laugh?"

Then both performers scream, "Everybody, laugh!"

Everyone kinds of looks around like they are scared to be the first one to laugh.

The taller performer acts distraught and asks, "Why is no one laughing?"

The smaller performer says, "I didn't hear anyone laughing. I thought you came here to have a good time."

The taller one runs over to a hefty man and asks, "Didn't you come here to have a good time?"

The man nods, smiling.

The smaller one runs over to a mother with a baby carriage, looks into the carriage, gives a big smile, looks back at the mom, and asks, "Did you come here to have a good time?"

The mother grins back at him.

Then both men leap into the fountain and shout, "Everyone's here to have a good time, right?"

They then hold their hands to their ears again, and the crowd feebly responds with a scattering of, "Yeah!" and, "Yes!"

They both shout again, even louder, "Everyone's here to have a good time, right?"

They hold their hands to their ears again, and now the crowd responds more enthusiastically, "Yeah!"

Then they both scream, "Then let's all laugh together! Is that cool?"

And now the crowd shouts, "Yeah!"

The performers ask again, even louder, "Is that cool?"

And the crowd screams, "Yeah!"

"Okay, on the count of three. Here we go. One! Two! THREE!" and they both start laughing so loudly and manically that almost everybody else starts laughing at them.

"Louder!"

The crowd laughs louder.

"Louder!"

And now the crowd is howling in laughter.

"One more time! I can't hear you! Louder!"

The crowd erupts in cascades of laughter, laughing at the performers, laughing with the performers, and laughing at themselves for being manipulated into laughing.

"Now give yourself a big hand!"

The crowd starts to clap.

The performers scream, "Louder!"

Now the crowd is clapping like they're at a rock concert, trying to provoke an encore.

"Louder!"

Then one performer runs over and punches a button on a boom box, unleashing a driving rhythm with a pounding bass line, and for the next ten minutes, the crowd is mesmerized, mouths agape, by an astonishing performance of dance and gymnastics, the two men's bodies doing things that seem impossible. Just as the music and their movements come to a peak, the music stops dead and the dancers freeze while the final chord hangs in the air, then dies away.

The crowd bursts into applause as the performers grab the white buckets and quickly glide out into the crowd, keeping up a constant cheerful patter.

"Thank you for coming to our show, ladies and gentlemen, and don't forget to laugh. It's nature's medicine. Donations are accepted and are very much appreciated. A dime or a dollar, a ducat or a doobie, we thank you, and we appreciate your sharing some time with us. Good day and God bless."

It was amazing to me to see these two men take control of a crowd of 150 strangers and get them to let go of themselves and experience such joy together. It must feel good to be so fearless, so confident. Most poets and writers are not performers. I've given a few speeches for work-related events, but I despised it. These men clearly love to perform and entertain, and people were happily tossing dollar bills into their buckets. They had made at least two hundred bucks. And they earned every penny. They brightened everyone's day, including mine.

By afternoon, it's crazy in the park, so crowded that it's hard to get a bench. I walk around with my duffel bag, taking in the sights. I see lovers making out, quietly talking, hugging each other, smiling, and laughing. Young lovers, gay lovers, old lovers. I like watching older couples hold hands as they stroll.

Every conceivable subculture seems to have claimed the park as their own. You've got your skateboarders with shirts off, in beat-up jeans and black Vans sneakers. You have your hipsters, with long, perfectly trimmed beards, slicked back hair, tight plaid shirts, skinny jeans, and oversized, trendy sunglasses. There are the neo-hippies wearing yellow sundresses and tie-dyed Phish and Grateful Dead T-shirts, chilling on the lawn taking big hits from their vape pens. Frat boys turned preppies sport their white polo shirts, with brown loafers, flexing their beer-bellied muscles. Then you have your cool cats with grey and black striped fedoras, strayed vintage jeans, soul patches, and Ray-Ban Wayfarers. A group of fifty Asian-American students sits on the lawn in the sun, their faces filled with smiles while socializing. Some people who were cool sixty years ago are out walking their golden retrievers or reading the *New York Times*, maybe with a cheap beer in a paper bag, juicing it old school. And there are confused tourists, kids on their way home from school, and an artist daydreaming here and there, drawing away: a caricaturist doing quick chalk cartoon portraits, a guy selling prints of his photos of classic NYC landmarks, and a woman with a cardboard display board selling homemade papier-mâché earrings. It's an alternative cornucopia. This is Washington Square Park on a Saturday, and there's nowhere else I'd rather be.

As night falls, the park begins to clear out. I haven't slept in almost three days. Where to go? Where can I lie down and feel safe? I sit on a bench and brainstorm. The last two nights I have just stayed awake sitting on a park bench. I can't do that again. I'm starting to see double.

I'm in that zone where the world looks like a carbon copy of itself, and everything looks fake.

But there's one more thing I need to do, the most important thing: I need to speak with Petra. I'm worried sick about my daughter, and until I know she's okay, I won't be able to sleep.

CHAPTER
EIGHTEEN

I walk up 6th Avenue searching for a pay phone, hoping there still are a few left, and suddenly I see one—an ancient relic in a modern age. I put in some coins and dial Petra's number. Almost immediately, she picks up.

I believe everyone comes into your life for a reason. Petra Lubavitch was nineteen years old when she came to work for us as Josie's nanny. Spending so much of my time in the office, I only saw my daughter at night. Most of the time, Josie is with Petra, her surrogate mother.

While Lauren is out doing lunch, Petra takes care of Josie just like Regina took care of me. Petra and Josie are magic together—constant companions. Petra has Josie do chores with her. They play games. Watch TV. Bowl. Petra takes Josie everywhere. She treats her like a young adult and instills values in her. And every night Josie loved to tell me about all the details of her and Petra's day together. Josie would go on and on, and I just smiled.

Petra is from Poland and grew up playing soccer. When she was younger, Petra played competitive soccer. I enthused that she should teach Josie how to play. When Josie turned five, Petra would take Josie to the local high school and kick the soccer ball around with her. Josie grew to love soccer. Petra taught Josie the rules: how to kick the ball, pass the ball properly, even do head balls. Josie loved playing goalie. So, Petra taught her how to punt the ball and catch the ball properly.

I went online and bought Josie little goalie gloves and a goalie jersey. I also bought a miniature goal that I put on the right side of the backyard up against the fence. Josie goes in the goal, and Petra takes shots at her daily. I loved to watch them play soccer from the backdoor. I never went outside and disturbed them. It's their thing.

Petra has a small apartment in Queens that she lives in on the weekends, and she used to ride the bus to our house. I buy her whatever she needs for Josie, but when I try to give her extra money, she always refuses. She needed a car to get her around town to do errands and take Josie places, plus I didn't like that she had to take such a long bus ride. So, I bought her a new Nissan Altima, which belongs to her.

What's strange is that Petra is intimidated by me, no doubt because she sees me as her boss, though I have come to view her more as a friend, or even family. She calls me "Mr. Evan" even though I often told her to call me "Evan." She sees how close my daughter and I are, and whenever I enter the room they're playing in, she immediately leaves, even though I sometimes beg her to stay and hang out with us. All that matters is that my daughter loves her like a mother or a big sister, which makes Petra the second most important person in my life. Knowing that she and Josie love one another is crucial to me now.

"Hello, Petra."

"Hello, who is this?"

"Petra, it's Evan."

"Evan?"

"Yes, Evan Bloom."

"Evan! Mr. Evan!"

"Petra, are you alone?"

"No, I'm with Josie in her room."

"Can she hear you?"

"No."

"Perfect. Is Josie in bed?"

"Yes, she's lying down in bed."

"Is she awake?"

"Yes. Mr. Evan, where are you? Everybody's looking for you. Everybody is worried. Are you okay?"

"Yes, I'm fine."

"Are you in trouble?"

"No. I'm not in trouble. But I need your help. I need you to do something for me. I'm fine, I promise. Never been better. Listen, Petra. I'm going to have to stay away for a while, and I need you to watch Josie closely and reassure her that I'm okay and that I love her. I need to know my daughter is safe and happy, and it's so important to me that she is with you. I know how much you love her."

"You know I love Josie, Mr. Evan."

"I know you do, and she loves you, Petra. How is she handling me having disappeared?"

"She's been very quiet. I think she's a little confused. You know how attached to you she is and how much she loves you."

I tear up.

"I know. Listen, Petra, try not to talk about me. I don't want to upset her. Just reassure her that I'm going to be coming back, that this isn't permanent."

"Mr. Evan, are you in danger?"

"No, Petra. For the first time in my life, I'm safe. Watch my daughter, love my daughter. And it's important that you don't tell anyone you spoke to me. Keep it a secret that I called and talked to you."

"I swear, Mr. Evan. We never spoke."

"Petra, can I speak to my daughter?"

"Sure, Mr. Evan. Hold on."

I hear Josie in the background get excited and say, "It's Daddy! It's Daddy!" She picks up the phone.

"Daddy!"

I begin to cry hysterically, and I can't hold back the emotion in my voice. Josie can hear I am upset.

"Daddy, are you okay?"

"I'm okay. I just love you so much. Listen, Josie, Daddy will be away for a while."

"Where are you? When are you coming back, Daddy?"

"I'm away on business. Remember when Mommy and I took you to

Paris, and we walked all over and went to museums and parks? Well, I'm in a place that's kind of like that. And I have to be here for a while and take care of some important work things. I really miss you, and I'm glad Petra is taking care of you."

"Okay. But I miss you, Daddy."

"I know, honey. Don't worry though. I am okay. And Petra will take care of you and watch movies with you and take you to the mall and read you stories. And if you miss me tickling your feet, she can do that too."

Josie laughs.

"Listen, sweetheart, I love you more than anything. You are my #1. Don't ever forget that. I will call to talk to you as often as I can. And I want you always to remember one thing."

"What's that, Daddy?"

"I love you infinity."

"I love you too, Daddy. To infinity and beyond."

"Okay, baby. Put Petra back on. Bye-bye!"

Petra gets back on the phone.

"I'll call you as often as I can to check on Josie. But remember to pretend you haven't heard from me. That you are worried about me too. Nobody but you two can know that I called you and we talked. I am very sorry that I have to ask that of you."

"Of course, Mr. Evan. Yes."

"Thank you, Petra. Keep Josie busy. Play soccer with Josie more now then over. Take her over to the high school and put her in the big goal. She's ready."

"Okay, Mr. Evan. I will."

"I wish you could waddle with Josie because I know that's her favorite thing. But I won't ask you to do that."

Petra chuckles, which somehow makes me feel very good.

"I'll be in touch soon, Petra."

We say goodbye, and I put the heavy payphone receiver back on its hook. Josie suddenly seems very far away.

After I hang up, I am confused, and I wander around in a daze for a while. Eventually, I find myself on the west side of the park, between a bodega and a small boutique clothing store at the entrance to a tiny alley. It's very narrow, no wider than a king-size bed, very quiet and hidden, the thick branches of old trees hanging down over it. It's like a secret place. I go to the end of it, plop my duffel bag down on the black pavement, lie down on my back on the ground, and rest my head on top of my bag. Surprisingly, it makes a comfy pillow. The pavement's hard, but nothing I can't get used to.

As I relax, I feel my blood rush and listen to my heartbeat. As I focus on its steady rhythm, I know that I have made the right choice. Right here is exactly where I'm supposed to be.

CHAPTER
NINETEEN

The next morning, I am back on my bench, writing, and I find myself staring at someone. I'm not really sure how to exactly describe her. She has a presence, an aura, and I can't take my eyes off her. She's a little shabby, as if she just got out of a Nirvana concert and it's 1993, but honestly, she is the most incredibly beautiful woman I've ever seen. She is tall with long, light brown hair, and her skin is the color of cream. Her face is soft, with a sharp jawline and thin eyebrows. Her eyes are big, brown, and wide, with long eyebrows and extraordinarily long eyelashes. Her pink lips are wide, and her smile is wide too; it takes up most of her face. She is extremely thin and seems busty because her frame is so petite. She is wearing a cut-off Clash T-shirt, tight denim cut-off shorts, and beat-up low, black boots. She has on black nail polish. Her hair is pulled up and tied tight. She looks like an alternative porcelain doll and seems at home here. She has a magnetism. I can't look away.

But there is a sense of lightness and humor about her, as she warmly greets a group of dogs who all come up to her at once, each with a human tagging along at the other end of a leash. I watch her as she affectionately greets each of the eight dogs, and she has as much fun with the eighth as she did with the first. The dogs seem to love her more than they do their owners. I am mesmerized.

I try to casually observe, thirty feet away, as she pats the dogs and chats with them. I am trying hard not to stare. Somehow, I feel that I absolutely have to talk to her. But how? And what to say? I have no clue.

A ninth dog joins the group, leaping up and putting its paws on her lap. It's a little white toy poodle, and she bends down and buries her face in its curls.

She looks up at the owner and asks, "What's this little sweetie's name?"

The owner giggles and smiles. "Her name is Lexus."

She buries her face in the dog's snout and says, "Hi, Lexus, you're a luxury automobile, yes you are, yes you are. Only leather interior for you."

The owner is cracking up. I try not to laugh. I try to be cool. She is only fifteen feet away from me now and is radiating joy.

As she gets up, she looks at me with a shit-eating grin and sarcastically asks, "What's wrong? You don't find me funny?"

I am taken back and unsure what to say.

"Who, me?"

"No. The bench. You like watching me on your little bench over there, handsome?"

I'm Mr. Cool, an idiot who can't speak.

"I am watching the dogs, not you. You were blocking my view. I especially liked that toy poodle, and you ruined it for me."

She smiles extra wide and walks over.

"You got a name?"

"My name's Poet."

"Your name's Poet. What's your last name, Tree?"

I laugh.

She sits down next to me and says, "You have very blue eyes. You're scary. Stay away from me."

"Are you serious?"

"Hardly ever."

"So, what's your name, dog whisperer?"

She looks me dead in the eyes. My heart is pounding.

She reaches for my hand and shakes it as chills run down my spine.

"My name is Sarah Jones. My friends call me Sarah. Nobody's ever called me Ms. Jones; you can be the first. That way I'll never forget you."

I am transfixed. I've never been so instantly attracted to anyone in my entire life.

"So, Poet. What's your story?"

I play dumb. "What do you mean?"

"How did you end up in Washington Square Park with a big black duffel bag, unshaven and smelly?"

"I smell?"

"Well, you smell worse than me, so you reek, and, surprisingly, not like booze. Are you a junky?"

"No."

"So, you're not a junky, not an alcoholic, and you look really fucking normal. Like a cool guy from the suburbs. I'm right, right?"

"Kinda. I'm from Central Jersey. My apartment caught fire, and I lost pretty much everything. Except my daughter, who is living with my ex-wife's cousin. I have no friends to call, both my parents are dead, so for now it's just me, this bag, and this park. This bag and my daughter are all I have, and somehow, someway, this bag is going to bring my daughter back to me."

"What's in the bag?"

"Just some clothes and some personal items."

"Okay, so why the name Poet?"

"Because I write poetry."

"Damn, you don't look like a poet. You look like a guy at a sports bar."

"Looks can be deceiving." I laugh

She looks right back into my eyes and says, "I bet you're a wonderful poet and a wonderful father."

This touches me, and I say, "I'm an okay father who isn't with his beloved daughter and a guy who just happens to write poetry that may or may not be any good."

She places her right hand on top of mine and says, "Not everyone gets a great father. Anyone can get taught how to write a poem, but they don't teach fatherhood."

"They should."

"They really should."

I'm surprised to be shaken up.

I smile and say, "We just had a moment."

"A moment?"

"Yeah, that was a moment. A couple of years from now, I'll be sitting in this park thinking about this moment, asking myself whatever happened to that gorgeous, funny, brown-eyed, tall girl named Sarah Jones. She was really something else."

She smirks. "Something else, huh."

"Yeah."

"You know what you are? You're a cheeseball. Cheeseballs don't write good poetry. Cheeseballs write texts and emails using spellcheck. Poets are romantic; they're flirtatious; they take your breath away. You come up with 'gorgeous and funny'?! Those are the bullshit lines you want me to remember you by? Bring it real, Poet. Be a poet."

My mouth is wide open. I am embarrassed, and I am unsure if I am about to laugh or cry. This girl is something else. What a quick and honest wit.

After a long pause I ask, "What would you like me to do to prove to you that I'm a poet and not a cheeseball?"

"Two things. First, take off your baseball hat. Poets usually have unkempt hair. For the second thing, you have two choices. You can look deep into my eyes and poetically recite what you see, or you can let me read one of your poems. The choice is yours."

What? There is no fucking way I am going to look into this girl's eyes and "recite what I see." And no one has ever read my poetry before. Ever. This is a lose-lose situation. The third option is for me to grab my duffel bag and leave. But this girl is so beautiful and so interesting. I have never felt like this before. It feels fun. I feel inspired and happy. So, it has to be choice one or choice two. "Okay, well, after five seconds of thought, I've come to a decision."

"Oh, you have, have you. Have you decided to grab your bag, get up, and walk away? Tell me that thought didn't enter your mind."

I man up: "You're good. That thought crossed my mind. But I'm going to let you read one of my poems. And when you're done reading a poem of mine, you're going to propose."

"You're gonna give me a romantic poem to read?!"

"I don't write with intention. I write with emotion. Inside this bag are hundreds of poems. I'll open it up, you reach in, grab a folder, take it out, and read the poem on top. I don't know if it will be good or bad, but it's going to be something no one's read before. How's that sound?"

"That sounds kinda hot! And you just got a lot cooler, Poet. I knew there was something different about you. I always know."

I bend down and gingerly open my bag. My knees are knocking. My hands are shaking. I am a nervous wreck. Sarah looks down into the bag. "You have some nice clothes for a homeless poet. Are all these folders full of your poetry?"

"Yes."

"Do you ever sleep? There are millions of poems in here."

"I like to write."

"I can see that. These aren't old love letters to your ex-girlfriends and ex-wives, are they?"

"No, they kept those."

"So, I can reach in and grab any folder I want?"

"Sure."

"You look like you're about to shit your pants. It's okay. I won't laugh at you, and I won't judge you." She pauses, then winks. "But if your poem is a big piece of shit, I'm getting up and leaving. Just a warning."

She reaches into my bag slowly and pulls out a flat blue folder. The fear inside me is rising. I want to die! Sarah sees my discomfort.

She reaches over, rubs my back, and says, "We don't have to do this. If you don't want me to read your work, I won't. But I think you need this. It'll be good for you. I'm a great audience, and you seem like an incredible person. I won't laugh, and I think you'll feel relieved afterward. Okay?"

I try to be casual, but I stammer, "Sure. Read away."

She opens the blue folder, and my heart sinks to my toes. The poem on top of the pile is one I wrote in college, called "Time Is Never

Standing Still." There are probably 800 poems in that bag, and she has picked an extremely introspective one, a poem I wrote after tripping all night on acid.

Sarah looks up with a smile. "'Time Is Never Standing Still' sounds mysterious."

"I'm going to sit over there and go into cardiac arrest," I say, pointing to a bench about twenty feet behind her. "I don't want to watch you read it."

She looks at me, puzzled. "Poet, are you serious about nobody having read any of your poems? Hasn't *anyone* read your poetry before? Honestly?"

Hunched down, I look over and say, "Sarah Jones, you will be the first person to ever read any of my work."

"Okay. Well, it's about time. Go watch me from that bench, Poet. And when you see my head pop up, that means I'm done. And I like to read a poem twice. Once usually doesn't do it justice."

I limp over to the other bench and get comfortable. For some strange reason, the moment feels right. I am no longer scared. There is something cosmic in the air. I feel safe and secure. I don't mind that I'm about to be embarrassed.

Time Is Never Standing Still
Time is travelling by so fast.
I hope this feeling will always last.
I would remain in this moment now,
If this moment would last forever.

I don't know where I will be.
Or what is to become of me.
The message that the future holds,
I will receive in time.

Time is never standing still,
But it gives you free will.
What you do with the time you are given
Will be the legacy you have left behind.

I look back on the past.
My friends and family make up the cast.
Of the movie that is being filmed
Deep within my mind.

Time is much greater than me.
For production costs, you are charged a fee,
For your movie to make it on to the screen,
You are asked to donate your time.

Time is never standing still.
But it gives you free will.
What you do with the time you are given
Will be the legacy you have left behind.

When our time on Earth comes to an end,
We won't have to hide from ourselves and pretend
That the lives each of us has led
Have meant nothing in time.

We can look the Maker in the eye,
Wish our friends and loved ones goodbye,
Bow our heads, and think to ourselves,
Damn, did the time fly.

Time is never standing still,
But it gives you free will.
What you do with the time you are given
Will be the legacy you have left behind...

CHAPTER
TWENTY

As Sarah reads, her head moves closer and closer to the page. I'm not sure if this is a good sign or a bad sign, or if she just needs glasses. Finally, she quickly raises her right arm and signals me over. I walk slowly, like a cow ambling toward the slaughterhouse. I sit, and Sarah takes my right hand, looks up, and kisses me on the cheek. There is a tear in her eye.

"That was powerful, Poet. Powerful is the only word that comes to mind. I read it three times. That was not what I expected. Not at all!"

"What did you expect?"

"I don't know, but not that. You don't look like you wrote that poem, Poet. That poem doesn't look like you."

"You can't judge a book by its cover."

"Believe me, I don't. Right now, you know nothing about me. I'm just some pretty girl in the park who gets along with dogs. But you, my friend, are an enigma. You're a beautiful human being. You were handsome before the poem. Now you're in a different class."

I laugh and ask, "What class is that? The homeless-poet-in-a-park class?"

"No, you're in the class where the great artists live. Where looks don't matter. When you think of Bob Dylan, you think of his lyrics and music. When you hear "Like a Rolling Stone," you don't think about his face. When "Smells Like Teen Spirit" comes on the radio, it makes you feel something! You don't picture Kurt Cobain. You feel rebellion. You're a good-looking guy, but that doesn't matter. To me, those words are lyrics, not poetry. They are the lyrics to a trippy, psychedelic rock song. To me, that's even better than poetry."

I try hard to digest this, but it doesn't make sense. Of course, I like hearing "Kurt Cobain" and "Bob Dylan." It can't get better than that, so I should probably retire right now. I don't feel good. I don't feel bad. I feel numb.

I look at Sarah and ask, "So, you liked it?"

She looks at me and smiles. "No, I was just being nice. I think it's a giant piece of shit. Then she smiles. "It's all over, Poet. You popped your poetic cherry. Was the first time okay for you?"

"Yes."

"I want to tell you one more thing, and we can drop it."

"What's that?"

"I want you to know that you are a special person. I knew it the moment I saw you. There's something about you, a comfort. You see what's around you. You see things for what they are, and I think I do as well. And that's why we're gonna be a great team, like the fucking Yankees."

"A great team?"

"Yes."

"Everyone needs a partner: cops, married couples, gay men, lost dogs, dancers. We all need partners, Poet. Will you be my partner?"

Without thought or hesitation, I say, "Yes. What kind of partnership are we going to have?"

"Let's be tennis partners. You play doubles?"

I laugh. This is crazy, but it feels so right. "You already know I look like a sports bar guy, and I'll tell you about the rest of my life as honestly as I can. Anything about you that I should know right away?"

For the first time, Sarah is not smiling. "Yes, there's one thing. But first, are you gonna tell me your real name?"

"As it happens, that's the only thing I can't do, but everything else is on the table. So, what do you want to tell me? I won't judge you or think less of you."

"Okay. I'm a heroin addict. Four times a day, I get high. I've been an addict for a year and a half. I lost my career, my apartment, basically everything because of it. I have a deal with a guy who gives me heroin for free. I don't share needles. I shoot up alone; it's like taking medicine. That's my one and only secret, and around here it's not much of a secret. I'm not proud of it. I wish I could change it, but I'm not ready to take that step. So, Poet, four times a day for forty-five minutes, I won't be with you. But every other minute of the day, we'll be together, supporting one another, having fun. We might be homeless, but we're gonna have a ton of fun. That's my job description: fun. So, do you still want to have fun with me?"

I am stunned that this beautiful, smart, fun-loving girl is a drug addict. She has everything else going for her. Maybe she can't see that. Maybe I can show her. I have no interest in resisting or questioning the powerful force that has brought us together.

"I appreciate your honesty. Of course, I want to have fun with you. As long as you're safe and feel secure, I won't intrude. But if you feel threatened or in danger, tell me, and I'll help you take care of it."

She kisses me on the cheek. "Damn, you really do smell. I know a guy at the Washington Hotel, he'll let you shower in a room tomorrow. Lord knows, I could use one too."

She motions for me to come closer.

"What are you doing?"

"I'm giving you a hug for being my partner and the best Poet on the planet."

We hug each other really tightly for about a minute, swaying back and forth, and I realize that at this moment I feel loved.

CHAPTER
TWENTY-ONE

Sarah Jones and I are inseparable. We do everything together. The only time I am not with her is when she goes to get high. I never ask her about it, and she never asks me my real name. That's the deal. Other than that, we share everything.

Sarah was born near Des Moines, Iowa, an only child. Her father was a drunk who worked at the local grain elevator, and her mother was quiet and reserved and worked at the local library. Her father ruled the house, and Sarah was terrified of him. He'd take his anger and frustration out on her and her mother, and they'd basically just hide. But their shared nightmare did not make Sarah and her mother closer because they both pretended it wasn't happening, that everything was fine.

Around the age of fourteen, it became obvious to everyone that Sarah was extraordinarily beautiful, and according to her, it was a major distraction. Guys flirted with her; girls were jealous of her. Like me, she felt isolated and alone throughout her childhood.

Sarah had one friend in high school, Jeanine, who was a lesbian. They were together constantly. One day, Jeanine stole her father's car, and she and Sarah drove thirty-five miles to the nearest mall. While walking around the mall, Sarah was stopped by a stylishly dressed woman who said, "Have you ever thought about modeling because you, honey, you're a model."

Sarah laughed, but the woman was serious, gave Sarah her card, and begged her to call. "We'll take some photos. We'll see how they look, and we'll go from there. It won't cost you a dime."

Sarah told her she wasn't interested, but on the drive home Jeanine pleaded with Sarah to call. Two days later, curiosity made her pick up the phone. A month later, she had a meeting with an agent in New York City. Two weeks later, she moved here—without her parent's consent. Her father actually used the words "you're dead to me." Her mother just cried.

Sarah was not only anxious to leave the hell of her home life, but she was also excited to get out of corn country and experience the world. In New York, she became the model of the hour and got work all over—commercials, magazine shoots, and runway. In six months, she was making a lot of money and had a beautiful apartment in Soho. She was eighteen. She started partying, running with a fast crowd, sleeping with rich men, and doing drugs.

Before leaving Iowa, Sarah had only smoked pot. Now she was using cocaine. She was working every day, going out every night, and sleeping with celebrities, athletes, and other players. She was young, beautiful, charismatic, and impressionable, and by the time she was twenty, it all caught up with her. Sarah went from coke and pills to snorting heroin. When she started shooting heroin, it was the beginning of the end. She wasn't showing up for shoots, and when she did show up, she looked like shit, and her behavior became erratic. The work dried up, and she lost everything—her apartment and everything in it. She ended up with no job and a $100-a-day drug habit. And that's how she came to be curled up next to me in an alley with her head on a duffel bag, quietly trying to fall asleep.

Sarah has been completely honest in telling me about messing up her life. I on the other hand, have been lying to her since the day we met, and it tears me up inside. But I stick with my story—my apartment catching fire, my ex-wife hating me, my daughter forbidden to see me right now because I have no place to live—because I have to keep my secret. I know she doesn't buy it. One thing about Sarah: She is one of the most intuitive, perceptive people I've ever met. She didn't even graduate from high school let alone college, but she's extraordinarily bright, extremely witty and funny, and very fast with a smart reply. She can be a real wise-ass, but she is also by far the most compassionate, sensitive person I've ever met. She has a heart of gold. She is beautiful to look at, but she's even more beautiful inside, even after sleeping on asphalt in her clothes.

Everyone around the park is Sarah's friend, and our survival day by day is basically due to her beauty, brains, and personality. We live on the kindness of former strangers. For instance, Mustafa who is from Pakistan and wears a turban, is the owner of the bodega next to the alley. We've become very good friends with him. He likes me, he loves Sarah, and every night he gives us a magazine, some candy, water, a soda—always something. On the corner is the hot dog guy, Hector, who was born in Puerto Rico. He gives me and Sarah hot dogs for dinner every night. He usually gives Sarah two, both with onions. It's incredible. They say models don't eat, but Sarah never stops. She eats all day, and she's still only 110 pounds. We had a conversation about this the other day.

"How do you eat so much and not get fat?"

"I eat a lot?"

"You eat like a Roman at a bacchanal."

"And I'd look good in a toga."

"I'm sure."

"If you ate like I do, would you be fat?"

"Sarah, I'm Jewish. If I ate like you, I'd look like Jonah Hill."

"Jonah's cute."

"All chubby Jews are cute. But no one wants to sleep with a chubby Jew. I'm not vain. I just can't eat like that. Anyway, right now I can't afford to be a chubby Jew. I can't imagine how much you'd eat if you were pregnant."

"Let's find out!"

"You're someone I deeply care about. The first time we have sex won't be in an alley."

"So, keep jerking off in the Starbucks bathroom then, Poet."

"Crème de leche!"

Sarah smacks me lightly across the face. But we're both laughing.

CHAPTER
TWENTY-TWO

I constantly talk to Sarah about Josie. I talk about the waddling, Taylor Swift, and going to IHOP. We look at Josie's picture often. I'm pretty much in love with Sarah, but my daughter remains my primary focal point. I haven't lost sight of what I came here to do: write, figure out a way to get my poems read and heard, and get a book deal or something that pays me so I can support my daughter and myself. It might be insane, but that's the goal. And something tells me that loving Sarah will show me the way.

Sarah has boundless energy. She is always running around talking to random people, playing with dogs, or commiserating with and encouraging the park regulars who've become our friends. The homeless people who live inside and around the park are a little community. We look out for each other, try to help one another, and share the extras we receive. Well, at least Sarah and I do.

Some of my homeless friends are down on their luck, broke, broken, and desperate. Men wear ripped or frayed cotton cargo pants with brown dirt streaks running down the inseams. Their T-shirts are black and dirty and usually have three shades of brown dirt on the shoulders, stomach, and back. Their sneakers have no laces, and most of their teeth are yellow or missing altogether. Even the non-drug addicts' and alcoholics' eyes are yellow, and their pupils are dilated with fear.

The homeless women lug carts filled with clothes, bags, and cans. They wear patchwork frocks with legs unshaven and exposed. The younger homeless woman wear beat-up blue jeans that are too big at the waist with white strings as belts. Their hair is filthy, tied up in a knot with a rubber band. I talk to them, share food with them, and try to keep their spirits up. I reassure them everything will turn around. God has a plan, and God's plan is for everyone to find some peace, within and without. I like it when I make someone smile.

A jazz quartet called the Lange Trio plays a few times a week in the southeast corner of the park. They play some stuff I've never heard of, original tunes, plus classics by Miles Davis, Coltrane, and Herbie Hancock. They do a killer version of "Maiden Voyage." It's a great concert a few times a week. I've become very close with the sax player Reggie Lange, and I hang out with the rest of the band: Willie on organ, Tom on drums, and Scott on standup bass. All four of them are studying at Juilliard, and their concerts in the park are a great way for them to make some extra bucks and work on material. I enjoy their company.

I know a fair amount about jazz. I got into it when I took a history of jazz course in college, and I grew to love it. I ask them about composition, improvising, and their thoughts on the greats. They are young, ambitious guys. They play every Wednesday, Friday, Saturday, and Sunday afternoons, and those are the high points in our weekly lifecycle in the park.

Every Thursday at noon, a group of five middle-aged, normal-looking men play acoustic guitar, doing covers of classic songs from the '60s and '70s—a lot of Dylan, Neil Young, Crosby, Stills and Nash, and the Eagles. Sarah keeps nudging me to go in close and watch them play, but I'm shy. For three weeks, I watch and admire from afar. Then one day, they start playing the Grateful Dead's "A Box of Rain," one of my all-time favorite songs. I muster up the courage, get up, walk, move in close, and sit right in front of them. The guys smile, nod their heads, and keep singing.

As they launch into the chorus, one of them nods to me saying, "Join in!"

I smile and shake my head.

"Let's go, come on!" he says, and I figure what the hell. I'm homeless, why be shy too? I start singing, way out of tune, but it doesn't matter, and it is communal. A bunch of guys loving the same music, loving the same song. And from then on, every Thursday I sit with the guys at noon and sing. These guys are great guitar players. They all live in the city and work from home or are retired. They take a shine to me and want to know my story. One of them eventually offers me a job as a salesperson in his tech company. I decline.

"Poet, you're homeless, unemployed," he protests. "This is a way to get you off the streets instantly."

"Bob, I'm very appreciative, but I have other things in mind. I'm taking some time to reflect."

He doesn't judge me, nor does he understand. "The job is always there if you want it," he says.

There are a lot of homeless veterans in the park, and it really breaks my heart. Men who served and protected this country, but the country is not serving and protecting them. The stories they tell Sarah and me are horrific—both what happened to some of them in the war and what they've dealt with after coming home: month-long waiting lists at VA hospitals, even though they suffer from extreme anxiety and PTSD, terrible nightmares, sleepless nights, and trouble readjusting to the real world. Sarah and I listen to their stories, sympathize, and try to turn a negative into a positive.

Fred, a young, homeless Marine, talks about the guys his unit lost in Fallujah. "One of them was my best friend." The three of us are sitting with our backs against an ancient tree that was probably here during the Civil War. Sarah leans over and puts her hand on his arm, with a big smile, and asks, "Don't you think your friend would want you to go on and enjoy the rest of your life? You're so young. I'm so young. All three of us are so young. We have so much life to live. Poet will tell you: You cannot live in the past. It's over. You got to get up, pick yourself up, dust yourself off, and go home. Get to the VA hospital, get your checks, get some help, and start over. It's not too late. There's a next phase to your life."

Fred is motionless and silent for quite a while, but then he says, "Ya know, Sarah, you're right. It's over, and there ain't nothing I can do about it right. What's done is done."

"Damn right," I say.

Fred gets up, stretches, shoulders his bag, and says, "Now I'm going to take a walk. You all have a nice day."

Sarah and I never see Fred again. On average, two veterans commit suicide every day, and I know Fred could end up as one of those. I like to think Sarah helped him turn things around somehow with that moment of love and encouragement. And maybe she did. God knows in a matter of weeks she's changed my life.

Sarah and I are not the only homeless couple in the park. Plenty of us are all begging for the same change. Because Sarah's so fucking gorgeous and charming, we haven't had to resort to that, yet. People enjoy her company and conversation and slip her money, just enough for us to eat. Her kindness attracts kindness.

When I was rich, my heart always reached out to homeless men and women, and I would often slip some a few bucks. But now I see how transient and superficial my caring was. I never took the time to talk nor listen to a homeless person. Now that I'm living the homeless life, I see the situation clearly. Almost nobody really gives a shit about the homeless. Everyone is too afraid to get involved. And too busy. Once I create a new life and have Josie back, I will remember.

CHAPTER
TWENTY-THREE

Everyone around the park knows Sarah and me. We are the dynamic duo. Sometimes we'll get to know a new person for a few days, and then they disappear. But we have made some long-term friends, people we have grown to love. Jamie is beautiful in a geeky, quirky way, with dark hair, blushy cheeks, inquisitive eyes, and a big smile. She wears oversized round glasses, sundresses, and cowboy boots. She is adorable and funny and incredibly talented, and at twenty-one is an aspiring actress at the Tisch School at NYU. She's paying her way through college. She and Sarah took to one another like long lost sisters; they really love one another. Sarah and I keep telling Jamie to forget acting and pursue what she does every day in the park—play the acoustic guitar and sing. Jamie could make it and be successful. She has a unique sound, sweet and tender. You feel like you know her. She somehow taps into your emotions with hers.

Jamie plays right under the arch and always draws a huge crowd. Whether she's playing to three people, thirty people, or 300 people, it feels intimate. She does a version of Ryan Adams's "When the Stars Go Blue" that makes me cry. When she covers a song, she always puts her own spin on it. I keep telling her it's just a matter of time before the right person's going to walk by her in the park, hear her sing, give her his card, and make her a millionaire. Or at least put her on *The Voice*.

Today is Sunday, and for the past forty-five minutes, Jamie has been performing for a large crowd. When she takes a break and sits with Sarah and me, we watch people toss coins and bills into her open guitar case. She already made $100 today. I suggest to Jamie that she expand her repertoire by adding more songs that aren't so "folk." She has a couple, but I think she should do more, and she agrees.

Then Sarah chimes in, "Poet, you should write her a song."

I laugh, "Right."

Jamie says, "That's a great idea. Please write me a song."

I laugh again.

Sarah says, "Poet, grab your pen and write Jamie a fucking song."

"Now?"

"No, a week from Thursday. Yes now! Right now! Do it!"

"C'mon, Poet. Just whip something out with that weird brain of yours. I'm going back up there in like five minutes. I'll figure out the chords. Quick, go do it."

"You're serious."

"Yes! Do it!"

"You heard her, Poet. You've got five minutes!" Sarah says.

So, I scurry over to an empty bench, take out my notebook and Pilot G2 pen, and try to come up with words that would sound right coming out of Jamie's mouth. A whole series of images flashes through my mind as I try to ignore the busy chattering noise of birds and people and dogs and hear what Jamie is singing in my mind. I start writing, and once I start I don't stop. I'm writing as fast as I can.

"Time!" yells Sarah just as I finish.

I have no idea if it's any good, but I run my piece of paper over to Jamie, who takes it and reads it while she's walking over to her music stand. I see her lips moving, and she's playing around with some chords. Then she flashes a big grin and looks up and welcomes the audience, which gives her a nice round of applause. "Hi! I'm Jamie," she announces with a grin. This song was written by a man named Poet! And it's as fresh a tune as I've ever played. Here we go." She begins to sing.

Good Girl

It is so hard to be a good girl
In this crazy world today
I want to hide under the covers
Until this feeling goes away...

I can't help being good
When it is better to be bad.
I am looking for a man to be
The best friend I have ever had...

I look but nothing is found
I cannot find Mr. Right.
So, I turn off my phone
And quietly shut the light...

Chorus:
It is so hard to be a good girl.
It gets harder every day.
But one day, this good girl will finally find her way...

Bridge:
And on that day the clouds will part, and the sun will shine
*   its rays*
Onto my face, and it won't erase the light of brighter days.
I cannot wait for it to come.
I cannot wait till it is here.
I cannot wait till this girl's vision is completely clear...

Chorus:
It is so hard to be a good girl.
It gets harder every day.
But one day, this good girl will finally find her way...

I ask my girlfriends for a hand
An idea to solve my plight.
I lie in bed alone dreaming of a man

To tuck me in at night…

Outro:
It is so hard to be a good girl.
It gets harder every day.
But I know that this good girl will finally find her way
I'll find my way…

I keep smiling while Jamie sings my song. I don't remember what I wrote until I hear each line. Halfway through, Sarah flashes me a beautiful smile.

After the applause dies down, Jamie says, "Why don't we have the songwriter take a bow," and points to me.

I stand and give an embarrassed wave, but people clap, and I can't help but smile. It feels good to be acknowledged. I like it.

Another friend of ours is Henry the artist, who looks a little like Bobby McFerrin, with long dreadlocks and tan skin. He is a beautiful human being, a pure gifted soul. Henry can paint anything—portraits, landscapes, abstracts. He'll lay out five of his paintings for sale and set up a canvas and an easel and paint while park visitors shuffle past. A lot of people stop to watch.

Henry sells two or three paintings a day. If he's really caught up in what he's painting, I'll handle the transaction. One day, Henry decides that he wants to paint a portrait of Sarah and me. He tells us to sit on the bench across from his easel and not move. We sit for hours, then Henry calls us over. The painting is magnificent. Not only does it look like us, but he really captures our essence, especially Sarah. I'm wearing my stained, black Under Armour T-shirt, beat-up stained washed blue jeans, and worn-out white Nike Air Maxes. I have a scruffy beard, a smirk, and analytical eyes.

Sarah looks loose, limber, carefree, and comfortable. She looks like she's just said something amusing to me, and I'm trying hard not to laugh. Her head is on my shoulder, though we weren't posing that way. Henry has us sit back down in the same spot on the bench, pulls out his cell phone, and takes a picture of us holding the picture of us. I thank him and tell him he should sell it.

"Fuck off, Poet. Hang it in your alley."

I laugh and give him a big hug.

Henry packs up and heads home, and then Jamie packs up and heads home. It is 5 o'clock, and Sarah is going to go get high shortly. We usually eat first.

CHAPTER
TWENTY-FOUR

"I've been thinking," Sarah says as soon as we're both awake. "We need a way to earn money and since there's no high fashion runway in Washington Square Park, I think it's on you. I have nothing people want."

"That's bullshit. You make people laugh and smile."

"Yeah, but that won't put money in our pockets. You, however, are a pretty good poet. Or a handsome good poet. You might have a gift."

"Right."

"Own it! You better believe it, or no one else will. So, I've been wondering how we can use your gift to attract a crowd and make us some money. I think you have to be a poet in public."

"And what, sit there writing?"

Sarah gets excited. "Yes! That's exactly right. That's what you're supposed to do for people."

"And how am I supposed to do that?" I ask, shrugging her off.

"I'm working on it."

We sit silently, and I can see that her creative juices are flowing, maybe even racing.

"I have it! I have it!" she shouts. "Here's the deal." She gets up right in my face, her eyes locked into mine. "You always tell me you write your poems in five minutes, right?"

"Usually."

"Well, our business is going to be Personalized Poetry in Five Minutes."

"Personalized poetry?"

"In five minutes. We'll sit at a table with a sign that says, 'Give me your name, where you're from, and three things, ideas, or words that are meaningful to you, and Poet will write you a poem.'"

I give her my best "what are you talking about" look, but she keeps going.

"It's perfect. They tell you who they are, where they live, and three other things—three words—and you will write a poem that includes all those things—just like you wrote that song for Jamie. Right in front of them."

"Jesus! How long does the poem have to be?"

"It doesn't matter. However long it turns out to be. Ten lines? Twenty?"

"Twenty lines in five minutes with random stuff. Damn, that's going to be fucking hard."

"Yeah, but you can do it. This is nothing for you, no sweat."

"But I can't even type twenty lines in five minutes."

"Bullshit. Stop being a bitch! Just open your bag, get out your yellow legal pad and the fucking Pilot G2 pen, and try it!"

"I'm only going to try it because it's for you."

"Because you love me. I know. Everyone does."

"Well, I'm not everyone."

"Well, I love you too, so let's get going. Poem time."

I've got the pad and pen out already, and I stop and stare at her.

"You love me?"

"Shut up! Are you ready?"

"Yes."

"Write this down: Sarah, Iowa, soybeans, tiger, pajamas."

"Okay, weird. I got it."

"I'm gonna time you. Are you ready?"

"Wait, wait, wait." I settle in against the wall with the pad in my lap. "Okay."

"Poet, start your pen. Your five minutes begin…now."

I dive right in. I haven't even had my morning coffee, but I'm firing on all cylinders, trying to tell a story. This is not easy, but I enjoy the challenge. I'm planning ahead as I come up with each line I'm writing. I'm thinking about all of it at once. I'm going back. I'm rewriting. I realize that I'm really enjoying it. It feels like it's been a lot longer than five minutes, but just as I suddenly feel like it's done Sarah yells, "Time!"

(Sarah, Iowa, soybeans, tiger, pajamas)
When I drove to Iowa, I was forlorn.
I only saw soybeans and hay bales and corn.
I needed a place I could sit down and think.
So, I stopped in an old bar and ordered a drink.

I made a friend, Bob, and he showed me around.
He said, "I live large in this little old town.
Out here you can roam; out here you can rage,
And let your soul's tiger live outside the cage."

He asked, "Where you from?" I said, "Kalamazoo."
Bob said, "Michigan—that is a place I love too!"
"I came here," I told him, "to start life anew.
In that state way up north, there was nothing to do.

"I came here in search of a girl from my school.
I met her in psych class and thought she was cool.
She dressed in pajamas, but one day she left.
So, here I am, looking alone and bereft.

"She came around here. I'm hoping you know her.
She's near six feet tall and is strong, like a rower.
I'm worn out from searching, but really don't care—uh.
I just have to find her. Her first name is Sarah."

I look up at Sarah.

She smiles and points her finger at me right between the eyes. "Done, damn it! Nailed it. Stone cold." She gives me a hug.

She jumps on my lap.

"This is gonna be fucking awesome, Poet! This is going to work!"

"You think people will go for it?"

"Yeah, I think they'll find it fascinating. I do. To write something like that, with the random things, coming up with it all off the cuff like that but so fast. It's nuts and unexpected. Poet, people will love it! I'm telling you."

"From your lips to God's coin purse."

"Here's how I figure it. Let's find a table and chair. In this city, that part's easy. And we need to get some money for art supplies, because after you write the poem, I think I should letter it beautifully with markers and my handy dandy handwriting on a nice heavy piece of paper, so people have something to take home. A souvenir."

"Something tangible. I love it."

She offers me her hand. "We're business partners now! Our first project. Let's do it."

"Okay, but we need a celebratory kiss."

We both burst out laughing.

But I lean toward Sarah slowly and touch my lips to hers. Sometimes you don't truly know how much you care about someone until the first time you kiss. We both pull away quickly, jolted to realize at the same moment that we are already far more connected than we knew. Sarah is looking at me with a huge sunburst of a grin, her pupils dilated. I've never felt so good. I'm glowing inside and out. We smile at each other for a while.

Then Sarah pulls her legs up and stretches them on the bench, lies her head down in my lap, looks up at me, and asks, "Now that wasn't so bad, was it?"

I brush her hair back and say, "*I* was great. *You're* going to need a lot of practice."

"Is that right?"

I laugh.

"Poet, I want you never to forget what I'm about to tell you." She looks at me in a serious way. "You're the best person I've ever met. I mean that. You're special, and I don't think you know that."

"Sarah, the only thing that's special about me is that it took me an embarrassing number of years to find you." I laugh.

"You're still a cheeseball," she says and leans up and kisses me again.

CHAPTER
TWENTY-FIVE

Sarah and I go to work, rounding up what we need. One beautiful thing about New York City: There are always sofas, chairs, tables, paintings, and all manner of household items left out on the sidewalk for the garbage collectors and passersby. You can furnish an apartment in half an hour. We quickly find two chairs and a fold-up table that are light enough to lug around. Art supplies are trickier. We need markers, cardboard or heavy paper, and maybe some glitter pens.

I know Sarah has no money. I have been pretending that I have no money, when in reality, I have $350. I need to come up with a cover story, and I tell Sarah I am going to donate blood at a place I heard of a few blocks east of the park. I'm worried Sarah will want to donate too and come with me. But she knows as a heroin addict she can't. I head out of the park, and a while later I come back with $40 in my hand, just enough. We head to Pearl Art Supply. We are officially ready to find out if this fantasy can become reality.

That night, we are lying in the alley, and Sarah says, "Tomorrow's our big debut. You nervous?"

"No, we'll have fun like we always do, whatever happens."

She reaches over and caresses my face. "Just do you. That's all. Just do you. Do your thing." She makes a gang sign and says, "Word!"

We wake up, get a free bagel at the deli, and hang out for a while.

There is no reason to set up until 11 o'clock. Sarah feels it is necessary to make a big poster that explains what our poetry project is all about.

Here sits Poet. Give him five minutes of your time. Give him your name, where you're from, and three random words, and he will use them in rhyme. When the five minutes are up, his assistant will give you a framable version of your poem to take home.

It takes two trips to carry everything out and set up shop by the fountain. A few people walk by, read our sign, and look a little confused. So, Sarah starts selling—like a carnival barker, but charming, tactful, and beautiful. "You see this guy right here? He can make anything rhyme. He's a walking thesaurus. He's word crazy, as if Walt Whitman and Dr. Seuss gave birth to a son."

People laugh, but no takers.

Then Sarah shouts, "Five-minute poetry, five-minute poetry! Step right up. Read all about yourself."

Finally, a woman comes over and asks, "How much does it cost?"

"It's up to you," I explain. "It costs whatever you want it to cost. Give me your name, where you're from, and three random things, and I'll write you a poem containing those items. It'll be a nice little story."

Then Sarah says, "I'll letter the poem for you on card stock, and Poet will sign it. If you don't like it, don't give us anything. If you don't like the rhyme, don't pay a dime. If you like it, give us whatever it's worth to you."

The woman laughs, "Okay, I'm in. Donna from Fairfield, Connecticut. Salami, motorcycle, and butterfly."

I write those things at the top of my yellow legal pad. A few people have stopped to watch.

"Sarah, count me down."

"One, two, three …WRITE!"

I am off, and I write like the wind. I feel free and unselfconscious, and I am finished before Sarah tells me to stop.

"How long did it take?"

"Three minutes and fifty-eight seconds."

I smile and say, "That was fun. I think you'll like it, Donna. How about Sarah reads it to you?"

"Okay."

Sarah stands and orates it loudly and enthusiastically, with extravagant hand gestures.

> **(Donna, Fairfield, Connecticut, salami, motorcycle,
>   butterfly)**
> *Donna loves her deli salami and orders it every time.*
> *Because it is so salty, she washes it down with wine.*
> *She loves to lie in grassy parks and stare into the sky,*
> *In hopes to see a butterfly flutter while passing by.*
>
> *Her home is in Fairfield. I won't say what state.*
> *The green luster of its trees makes it lushly great.*
> *It's not far from Boston; some consider it New England.*
> *Red Sox and Yankees fans fight over this every season.*
>
> *Its roads are known to be kind to motorcycles.*
> *You'll bounce on a chopper, a Harley, or a scooter.*
> *If you want a smooth ride in the nutmeg state,*
> *Buy a yacht, and name it Shooter.*
>
> *The state is very beautiful, just like this deli fan.*
> *As she roams the rural roads, I hope she makes an eating plan.*
> *To cut back on the red meat and eat a lot more nuts*
> *And ride her bike with caution while avoiding all the ruts.*

People chuckle throughout and give me a nice smattering of applause at the end. Sarah immediately starts lettering it, titling it "Donna's Delight," and listing the three things. When she's done, Donna is grinning with delight and drops a $10 bill in our big, empty spring water bottle. All it takes is one to get the ball rolling. Other people step up, and I am soon writing like a madman. We draw a lot of attention. As the hours pass, it's tiring, but it's a lot of fun, and I love listening to Sarah bullshit with everyone at the table. She draws people in with her charm and humor. I keep the words coming.

Things go well day after day, and before you know it, we're actually making a nice living, considering we're homeless. On a good day, we make over $100 dollars, weekends $150. Slow days between $40 and $80, but it really doesn't matter. I am enjoying myself, and we are doing it together. I feel like we're Sonny and Cher. Sarah has the quick, witty one-liners, and I am the brunt of every joke. But whenever she makes fun of me, she grabs my hand to assure me that she is kidding.

We are about a week into it when I get a real ego boost. There's an older guy I've seen around the park occasionally—grey-haired, with a handlebar mustache, always smoking a pipe and usually wearing a fedora. He walks slowly with a cane and always has a book under his arm. I've seen him sitting on various benches, reading. Now he comes up to us at our poetry table.

"I really like your stuff," he smiles. "This is a great scene you've got going. You've managed to put writing poetry, having fun, and making a little money together, and that's hard to pull off. I'm impressed. My name is Jeremy." He sticks out his hand, and I shake it, and I introduce him to Sarah, who stands and curtsies playfully. The guy has a friendly sparkle to him.

It turns out Jeremy is a real local—he's been living near the park for years—and he's a writer.

"Not a particularly successful one," he adds, chuckling. "But I managed to add a few very modest volumes of lightweight levity to the canon of American literary eccentricity back in the day."

We talk about the park and its history for a while and all the writers who've lived in the area over the years, and then he leans in, puts his hand on my arm, and looks at me kind of seriously.

"Listen, Poet. I have the feeling you are really onto something here with your spontaneous writing. Maybe you'll keep doing the five-minute thing, or maybe it will lead you to something else entirely, but you have good mojo, and I think you should keep at it."

I kind of laugh, but he squeezes my arm more tightly and says, "Writing is a special thing, and you should take it seriously. Be brave. And if you keep going and you ever get to the point where you are ready to publish something, you should call my agent. I mean it. His name is Dean King. He's not as old as me, but he's been an agent for a long time, and he's represented all kinds of writers, even a poet or two. I think he would like you. So, keep him in mind. Dean King. But if you ever do call him, for God's sake don't tell him I sent you. I never made much money for the guy, though he was good to me and got all three of my books published. That was way back when I still thought I had a gift. Fortunately, about twenty years ago I realized that I'm only a so-so writer, but I'm one hell of a reader. So *that*," he lifts the hardcover book he's been carrying high up over his head and shakes it at the sky, "is what I've been doing ever since."

I thank him profusely, shake his hand, and assure him I am a million miles away from writing anything worth publishing, but I tell him that his saying that has really made my day and boosted my spirits. And it's the truth. I'm blown away that he took the trouble to come over and encourage me like that.

"See you crazy kids around," he says with a wave as he heads off. "Keep it coming. The park appreciates you!"

I look over at Sarah, and she's smiling as brightly as I am.

As the days pass, we get better at the poetry table and settle into a regular working routine. We wake up, grab some breakfast, walk around a little, read the paper, and then set up the poetry table. From 11 to 4:30, she advertises, and I write. Sarah goes off to get high around 12:30, and when we are done for the day, she goes again. As time goes on, this becomes more and more upsetting because I really love her, and to see someone you love doing something that's so dangerous is heartbreaking. Every time she leaves, I worry it will be the last time I see her, but I never say anything. I don't feel like it's my place. Her drug use doesn't make me love her any less. I just want to understand.

Late at night when we're all alone in the alley, Sarah tells me stories about her past. We truly are kindred spirits. Neither of us ever found a place to call home, and clearly the first place we ever felt comfortable was with each other. Sarah might be incredibly beautiful, but deep down she doesn't like herself. After her parental abuse, drug abuse, and losing all her money, she feels like a loser, which is hard to believe because she projects such positivity, and even as a homeless person, she is pretty much the life of the party.

CHAPTER
TWENTY-SIX

One day I finish strong with a poem I'm particularly proud of. It involves Charlene, cantaloupe, monotheism, a quince, and Coeur d'Alene, Idaho. As Sarah and I lug our gear toward the alley, she starts telling me about her parents, how her dad drank nothing but Schlitz beer and watched old Westerns, and her mom constantly cleaned their house. After she finished and everything was perfect, she'd immediately start over again. Aside from cleaning, all she did was cook and loaded everything up with oil and butter.

"It is a goddamn miracle I am 5'11" and 110 pounds."

After she tells me all that, she starts angling for some more details about my life, but as always, I focus on Josie. By now Sarah knows everything about her, but still loves hearing about her. She interrupts me and says, "I wish I had a father just like you."

It's like a stab wound. "What kind of father leaves his daughter?" I ask. "I'm a horrible father. She probably thinks I don't love her anymore."

Sarah quickly turns and says fiercely, "That's not true! Kids never forget. My father paid no attention to me as a kid and no attention to me as an adult, and I haven't forgotten that. I remember everything about my father from when I was Josie's age. I remember my father being drunk and angry. Once I was playing with a doll on the other side of the living room, and he got out of his chair, looked at me, and said, 'You were a mistake. Your mother was not supposed to be able to have children, but here I am stuck with you. Get out of my sight and go to your room. Go play up there. You're not allowed in this room anymore.' From that day forward, I rarely spoke to my father, and I haven't spoken to him in six years, my mother either for that matter. I honestly wouldn't care if my father was dead, not that I would even know if he was. I do wish I had a father like you. I mean it, and believe me Josie loves you. She might be hurt and confused right now, but she will always love you, and when this all comes to an end, she'll be proud of what her father accomplished. She will understand."

I am frozen in place, my mind reeling. "Sarah I'm so sorry you grew up that way."

"It was a long time ago, but I fight those demons every day. You make the pain go away."

I smile.

She says, "I have an idea."

"What?"

Cautiously, she says, "Why don't you write Josie a letter."

I have never thought of this. Mustafa, the owner of the bodega at the end of the alley, has been letting me use his cell phone to call Petra. She tells me Josie is okay, making friends, doing her work. If I write a letter, I can send it to Petra at her apartment in Queens, and she can give it to Josie. Sarah sees me considering the idea.

"If you wrote Josie a letter, and she knew you were okay and that you were thinking about her, it would make me feel better. If I was a little girl who loved her daddy and hadn't seen him in months, getting a letter from him would be like winning the lottery. You have to do it."

"I can't mail it from here. It would be postmarked with this zip code. I don't want anyone to have a clue where I am."

"So, we'll get on the subway, go uptown, and mail it from there. Listen, tonight, take your pad and pen, sit under a lamp in the park, and write to her. Believe me, both of you will feel so much better."

"Okay. You're right. I'll do it tonight. Thank you."

Sarah nods her head. We pick up our chairs and table and continue on to the alley.

Later, after it's dark, I grab my duffel bag and head back into the park. I am nervous, not sure if this is the right thing to do. I sit on a bench on the west side by the chess tables. I take out my pad and pen, cross my legs, and place the pad on my left thigh. I sit for five minutes with my eyes closed and picture my daughter laughing. I feel like she's sitting next to me. I begin to write.

> Josie,
>
> Not a day goes by when I don't think of you. You are my first thought in the morning, my last thought at night. I love you and miss you. You are everything to me. I'm sorry I had to go away for a while. When I finish what I am working on, I will be making you pancakes again, watching SpongeBob with you, and hugging you. I want you to know that I am okay. Don't worry about me. Don't ever forget how much I love you. I love you infinity. I miss you like crazy! Don't tell anyone except Petra that you heard from me. It is our secret.
>
> Love,
> Daddy

Back in the alley, I find Sarah leaning against the brick wall reading a magazine.

"Hey, did you write it?" She sees my face. "Oh. You did." She drops the magazine, gets up, hugs me really tightly, and rubs the back of my head.

We lie down together, and she nuzzles her head against my shoulder. We lie like this for awhile in silence, then quietly fall asleep.

CHAPTER
TWENTY-SEVEN

When I wake up, I head to the bodega and buy a stamp. Mustafa gives me an envelope. Sarah and I enter the West 4th Street subway station, and I buy a $10 metro card for us to share. What train to take? I haven't headed uptown on the subway in years, not since I took Josie to Central Park. I ask an older woman what train will take us uptown, near Morningside, and she says, "Honey, you need to jump on either the B or C."

Nobody is waiting for the C train, which means it just came. Sarah and I walk downstairs and hop on the B. It's around 11 am, and the train isn't too crowded, so both Sarah and I get seats. I'm seeing the subway in a completely new light. In a way, it's beautiful. All races, nationalities, and religions are peacefully contained in a small space. Everyone's accounted for. Black teenagers wear purple and orange sweatshirts, long black jeans, and brightly colored sneakers. An elderly woman is sitting quietly wearing a light sweater and a long heavy skirt. Businessmen, young and old, are wearing slim-cut suits, skinny ties, with perfectly combed hair. They look down, reading artfully folded newspapers. There's an old Hasidic Jewish man wearing a big black hat, beat-up black shoes, with tefillin streaming down, reading a prayer book. A young mother rocks a stroller gently while her baby sleeps. A young Asian couple is holding hands, both wearing navy New York City sweatshirts.

A dapper-looking French man walks over to Sarah and me with his wife and is trying to ask me something. I can't understand him. He points on a map and I say, "Oh, the Museum of Natural History."

I point out the stop on the map, and he shakes my hand, smiling with appreciation. As they step off the train Sarah says, "Have fun."

At Columbus Circle, a homeless man in a ratty purple sweatshirt enters the train with all his gear in black garbage bags. It saddens me. I am living the homeless life, but I'm sure not him. Sarah and I have a little money from the poetry stand, and we've had a lot of good fortune. Although we are filthy, the guy who runs Starbucks on the east side of the park lets us use the bathroom and wash up whenever we need to. And the manager of the Washington Hotel lets us shower in a vacant room a couple of times a week. I now have a lengthy beard that's itchy, and my hair is all over the place and thick, but I control it by always wearing my Yankees baseball hat. Clearly, this man is worse off than I am. His grey sweatpants are so filthy they are almost black. His purple hoodie is smeared in black tar. He's wearing beat-up high-top sneakers that have no laces. His hair is knotty and dotted with tiny pieces of paper. He has a long scruffy salt-and-pepper beard, his pupils are jet black, and the whites of his puffy eyes are yellow. He holds a sign that says, "Homeless for nine months, no food, no shelter, please help me." It is clear he is alone and afraid.

Sarah and I made $80 the day before, so I do what feels right. I reach into my pocket and palm the bills in my hand. The train pulls into our stop, and as we move toward the open doors, I gently place the money in the hat that he's holding out. He doesn't see me do it; he is looking in the other direction. Sarah and I get off.

Sarah takes my hand, turns to me, and says, "I don't know if I should hug you or slap you."

"He needs it more than us."

She takes my right hand, kisses the top of it, and says, "Thank you."

We climb the stairs out to 107th and walk down the street. We stop in front of a blue postal mailbox, and I pull out the letter, but I pause. I take Sarah's right hand and say, "Let's just stand here with our eyes closed tight and think of Josie. Picture everything I've told you about her and open your eyes when you feel you see her. We'll send her a love charge. Here we go."

We both close our eyes. I see my daughter right in front of me, smiling, dancing, singing into her microphone. She is right here with me. When I open my eyes, Sarah's are still closed. I watch her for a couple of seconds. It's touching.

She opens her eyes, smiles, and says, "Put the letter in that mailbox. Your daughter needs it!"

I kiss the envelope and gently drop it in.

CHAPTER
TWENTY-EIGHT

"Get the fuck up!"

I've been kicked hard in the center of my ass. My bones flare; my nerve cells fire. My eyes fly open at warp speed, and there is a steel, silver Colt .45 pointed at my temple. Somehow, I am as cool as a cucumber, calm, at peace. I am terrified, but in complete control.

"Get the fuck up and get the fuck out of here, you piece of shit! Get up, mothafucker! I'm here for the girl! I'll blow your fucking head off if you don't get the fuck out of here now! Now! Don't test me! Don't fuck with me!"

Sarah wakes up basically wheezing, turns over quickly, and sees the gun.

"Poet! Jesus Christ! He's gonna kill you! Get up and get the fuck out of here! Now! Get up, Poet!"

Then the man calmly says with a snide grin, "Tell your faggot boyfriend to be smart and leave before he ends up dead." Then he spits on me.

Somehow, I remain calm. I stand extra slow with my arms stretched up and wide, palms up like I'm searching for a higher spirit to save me.

Slightly above a whisper I ask, "Listen, man, what's your name?"

"What the hell does that matter, you motherfucker? You're gonna die."

"I'll call you John. Your name's John."

He shakes his pistol at me. I can tell he's scared. "We're not playing games here! You're a dead man! Get the fuck out of here! Leave! Leave now!"

I stay super cool. "John, chill, man, relax. You don't want to do this. You really don't. Trust me, man. This is a huge mistake. Attempted murder, rape. You're gonna get caught. It's inevitable. We know everybody in this park. Plus, rape? You know what they do to rapists, John? In Attica, they buttfuck rapists. Don't get buttfucked, John. You can kill me, but I'm not leaving here, not without Sarah. Not happening."

He is now trembling. Now he's scared of me. "Poet, I'm gonna fucking kill you and piss on your grave! I will!" Now he's serious. His right arm is extended. The barrel of the gun is five feet away from me. My knees are knocking, hands trembling. I feel like I'm gonna throw up in fear. But he doesn't notice.

Still calm, I say, "Come on, John. Relax. You kill me, that's murder. Twenty-five to life. Say goodbye to the world, John. Your bedroom is now a cell. Your life will be shit. You will die isolated and alone."

He screams, "Who the fuck are you, dickhead? Who the fuck do you think you are? A faggot who writes in a park. You're a fucking loser! You deserve to die! What the fuck do you think you're doing?"

Still chill, I say, "John, I'm just a regular guy. A guy who cares about that girl very much. I love her, John. I do. I love her, and if I abandon her, I couldn't go on with my life. So, that's why you're either going to kill me or leave, because you're not going near her with me around. We're a package deal, John. You rape her; you rape me. You kill me; you kill her. We're interconnected. Our souls are one. We love each other for better or worse. So, John, if you're going to rape Sarah, you have to kill me first, and if you do those things, you're going away for life. So, you'll be dead too. Getting buttfucked in Attica. No one to save your ass."

I can feel his fear. He stutters and screams, "I've been watching her all day. I need to have her! I need her! She's mine! She belongs to me!"

Somehow still cool, I say, "John, 'need' and 'want' are two different things. You need to eat; you need to have clothes on your back. You don't need Sarah. You want her. Which is understandable, she is hot, but she doesn't want you, John. She doesn't know you. And holding a gun to my head isn't making a great first impression. So, John, why don't you put the gun down and let's have a conversation. It can be about anything, whatever you feel like sharing. Just put down the gun slowly and softly."

Sarah has been listening quietly; she hasn't said a word. She's frozen. I am focused. I got this guy. He's gonna put the gun down. I'm in his head.

I look and feel like I do when I'm writing on the bench—100 percent present and in the moment. "Listen, this will be our little secret. No harm, no foul. Nothing ever happened. I'll even buy you a cup of coffee. You a coffee drinker, John?"

John has gone pale. His face is now jaundiced. His gun is still pointed at me, but he is confused and starting to pace.

"Put the gun down, and we'll walk to McDonald's and get a cup of coffee, John."

Slowly, he lowers the gun. I take a deep breath, and I can feel the air in my lungs dip in my diaphragm. I look at Sarah, and she is in tears with the blankets almost over her head.

"Thanks, John. You just saved three lives. You should feel good about that."

John looks like a deer in the headlights—his eyes dilated, his pupils bulging. He's extremely shaken up. So am I.

"You want that coffee, John?"

"I'm good on the coffee. I'm gonna go take a walk and think things over. I feel sick."

"Thanks, John. You have a nice night, and if you ever need someone to talk to, I'm here."

"What's your name?"

"I'm Poet. Everybody knows me around here; just ask. This is Sarah."

Still wrapped in blankets, Sarah waves her right hand and fakes a smile. "Hi."

"She's a good person. She's grateful."

"Thanks, John."

"My real name's Steve."

"Okay, Steve. It was nice meeting you. Have yourself a good night. Thank you for saving us."

"Have a good night, Steve," Sarah says.

Steve quietly walks away with his head down. He is walking sideways and looks disoriented. Sarah sits up and throws a pillow at my head.

"You're a fucking lunatic. A lunatic!"

"You think I was leaving you with him? No way I was gonna let that guy rape you. Are you crazy?"

"How do you know I couldn't take care of myself?

"He had a gun, Sarah."

"You saved my life. I'm forever in your debt. I love you, Poet. I fucking love you!"

"I just did what needed to be done, hun. No sweat. Walk in the park."

"You're fucking nuts! Nuts! How'd you know how to talk him and calm him down like that?"

"I once read that it's important to use names in moments of crisis. It helps rapists to see the victim as a person, not an object. We're people just like him. I also know it's important to not show fear."

"You weren't scared?"

"I was terrified, but I wasn't gonna let him know that."

"I was so scared I couldn't say anything. That's how you know I'm scared, Poet. When I'm speechless. I nearly shit my pants. I have to change my underwear."

As I laugh, I start to pace, basically walking in a circle. I'm a ball of nervous energy now.

"So, it happened!"

"What happened?"

"It had to happen!"

"What?"

"Something like this! We needed a bump in the road, and we worked our way past it. This was a test."

"A test?"

"Yup. We needed a reality check. Not everything will always go according to plan. I'm glad we got that out of the way and no one was hurt. Are you okay?"

"I'm fine."

"Jesus, Poet, you were straight out of *Law & Order*." Sarah makes the signature "dun-dun" sound effect. "That was impressive and attractive, Poet. I like you brave, Poet. Now I see who you really are: Super Poet!"

"Okay, Lois. Superman's tired. He's crashing now, big time. How about we go back to sleep."

We rearrange ourselves and the blankets, snuggled together with my arm wrapped around her. I have a tremendous smile on my face as I look up at the night sky.

I kiss her forehead. "Nobody will ever hurt you while I'm around."

"I know."

She kisses my cheek, and we both fall asleep instantly.

CHAPTER
TWENTY-NINE

I went to Hebrew School, I was bar mitzvhad, I respect my Jewish ancestry, but overall, I think religion is a giant scam that has done more bad than good. But I have faith in faith, and faith is a positive thing. It gives people hope. It gives people joy. It gives people belief, and I am all for believing. That's why I came to this park.

I always notice a man of the cloth, and I have been watching one in particular since my first day here. He is Black, tall, about 6'2", with puffy cheeks and a cherubic face. He wears an old school pair of Adidas sneakers, like the ones Run-DMC wore, a long burgundy cloak, and black wind pants. When he walks by the poetry stand, we often make eye contact, and he smiles, and his smile is so infectious, it makes me smile. This man is even smiling when he is not smiling. Everyone seems to know this man, and everyone stops to converse with him. He often sits to talk to strangers. He has a way about him. He does not so much walk, he strolls, and he looks at peace, rested, self-assured, and calm. It is endearing. His serenity permeates the park.

I ask around and find out that he is Reverend Frank Emerson. It seems like he was drawn to the cloth for all the right reasons. He's deeply concerned about preparing the next generation for the future. Jamie tells me he is selfless: "He puts everyone in the world in front of him and provides spiritual nurturing for anyone and everyone."

A very intelligent homeless man named Jack tells me, "I've spoken with him many times. He is extremely spiritual, and he provides counsel for many homeless men and women. The reverend's a noisy activist; he fights on the front lines for many social issues. He holds demonstrations for same-sex marriage, interfaith dating, right to choose, and the equal treatment for LGBTQIA. He's led anti-war protests and holds significant fundraisers for the poor and homeless, and he allows Jewish people and members of any faith to be a part of his church."

I'm also told the reverend drives a van for the homeless to get them proper healthcare and conducts same-sex marriages anywhere—in the park, church, downtown, uptown, cross town. If you're gay, and you want to get married, Reverend Frank Emerson is the man to call. He is part of the Church of Christ and the Baptist Church, and he is traditional in the sense that he follows the Jesus of the Bible who privileged the poor and outcasts, the sinner and not just the saint.

When Sarah and I close up the table and she leaves to get her fix, I often grab my duffel bag and head over to the church. At the top of the steps, I have a beautiful view of the sun setting over the park, and I love to write here. I tell myself the sunset is the reason, but I am also hoping to talk to Reverend Frank. The church has about fifteen white marble steps; it could be mistaken for the Colosseum in Rome. They lead up to massive double doors that look like the entrance to heaven. The church is old, an incredible piece of architecture—brown brick with a huge, white cross hanging from the top. It really is something else. Somebody told me it is the only building surrounding the park that New York University has not bought. That is probably why I am drawn to it.

Every day I quietly sit and write and watch all the different types of people who enter the church: gays, lesbians, Hasidic Jews, Blacks, Whites, Puerto Ricans, Hispanics. The place is like the DMV. I am curious about everybody in the passing parade, but I'm mainly engulfed in my writing. I usually write for about twenty-five minutes, and then I watch the sun set. I listen to my breath, hear my heartbeat, feel my blood flow, and relax in a quiet, meditative way. And every day, the reverend in the burgundy cloak walks by. He looks at me for a couple of seconds, nods his head hello, and quietly heads into the sanctuary.

CHAPTER
THIRTY

It's the day before Halloween, and I'm on the church steps, and I've just finished a poem I feel pretty good about. I slip it into a folder, zip up my duffel bag, sit back, and relax. I am so deep in thought I don't even notice that the man in the burgundy cloak is sitting next to me.

"This sunset never gets old, does it?" he asks.

"It seems to become more beautiful every day. It really is amazing."

"You know, I've been a reverend at this church for over forty years, and I've never seen anyone sit and admire this view for three weeks straight. You know how to appreciate beauty. Either that, or you have nowhere else to go."

"Rev, I've sat on every bench and all the steps in every direction around here, and for some reason I end up sitting here every day. Let me ask you something. What drew you to becoming a minister?"

"Son, only one source has the answer to all our actions and decisions, and some people refer to Him as God, I like to refer to Him as the Really Big Guy. So, great admirer of beauty, you got a name?"

I extend my hand. "My name is Poet. It's nice to meet you."

He shakes my hand softly and says, "The pleasure's mine, Poet. My name is Reverend Frank, but you can call me Reverend Run if you like."

I'm taken off guard. "You're a Run-DMC fan?"

"Oh yeah, big time. Got the Adidas sneakers and everything."

I grin. "I saw those. So, you dig hip-hop. And other music?"

"And *all* music." He smiles. "Music makes the world go 'round. Let me ask you something. I watch you everyday writing poetry for people with your friend."

"Sarah."

"You two look like you're having fun. Is it fun?"

"You know, Reverend, it is. Honestly, some days I don't really feel like writing ten poems, but I always enjoy spending time with Sarah, especially when we're around other people, making up stuff. When you spend so much time with someone, having a conversation is almost like playing a game. You say something funny, and you know that something funny's coming back."

"It sounds like you two have a special relationship."

"We support each another. Sleep next to each other. Eat with each other. What's mine is hers; what's hers is mine. I've never been so close to anyone before. Reverend, do you ever feel like that with anyone? So close to somebody that you feel lost without them? I mean, I know you're a reverend and all, but have you felt that way before about someone?"

"I feel that way with four people."

"Who?"

"My wife, Donna; my daughter, Holly; my best friend, Al; and God."

"You're married?"

 "Yep. I'm a Reverend, but I'm also a ladies man. This cloak really turns them on. Do you remember Madonna's 'Like a Prayer' video? It's based on me."

I don't know if he's messing with me or not. "But seriously, you're married?"

"Fortunately, I am," he says and smiles.

"I thought ministers couldn't marry. Aren't you supposed to be married to Jesus?"

The reverend arches an eyebrow. "He wasn't my type."

I laugh. "How long have you and Donna been married?"

"Fifty-one years."

"Jesus Christ! It's none of my business, but how…"

"I'm seventy-four."

I'm shocked. "Seventy-four? You look forty-seven."

"Well, that's what walking in the park will do for ya."

"How old's your daughter?"

"Forty-nine."

"Is she part of the church too?"

"She's a social worker. So, with us in spirit. And she's here all the time."

"What about your wife?"

With a smile, the reverend says, "She's home watching *Ellen*."

I laugh. "I got to go meet Sarah in the alley. Do you mind if I come back here tomorrow?"

"You are always welcome here, Poet. How about we sit here and chat at around the same time every day for a while."

"Okay. They'll be my confessions. But I won't have to do Hail Marys, will I?"

"Not unless you're trying to catch a cab driven by the Mother of God."

I laugh again, stand, and grab my duffel bag. "Rev, I'm looking forward to my next confession."

The reverend gets up and asks, "Is there anything you need—a blanket, some food, some water? Or anything I can get for Sarah?"

"I really appreciate that, but we're all set for tonight."

"The heavens declare the glory of God; the skies proclaim the work of His hands."

"I like that. What was that?"

"Psalm 19:1."

"Well, Reverend, I hope the skies declare the work of my pen."

"Poet, your words are your declaration. The skies are on your side."

I nod my head, smile, and extend my hand. "Goodnight."

The reverend shakes my hand. "Goodnight, Poet."

I head back to the alley, where Sarah is leaning against the wall immersed in a crossword puzzle. She looks up and says, "I fucking suck at these things. What's a six-letter word for getting something back in return?"

With no hesitation I say, "Refund."

"Go fuck yourself, Poet. I hate you. How did the writing go today? Did you write 'Leaves of Grass' yet?"

"It was a pretty good day. I'm happy with what I wrote."

"Good."

"Yeah, something else went down though."

"Did you meet a new girl? Should I be jealous? Are we gonna have our first fight? Are you kicking me out of the alley, you cheating piece of shit?"

"How did you know? You think you're the only smoking hot ex-model in this park? The place is loaded with them."

"So, what happened? Did you make yourself lucky in the Starbucks bathroom again?"

"No, but I had a long conversation with Reverend Frank Emerson."

"Shut up! The guy in the burgundy cloak you've been obsessing about?"

"Yeah."

"What happened?"

"When you leave at 5 every day, I go write on the church steps. It is really beautiful up there. Today I wrote a poem, and I was sitting there admiring the sunset, and he sat down and struck up a conversation. It was pretty incredible."

"What did you guys talk about?"

"Honestly, I hardly remember. It was deep in a light kind of way. But he seems to be a music freak, so that's good."

"Get the fuck out."

"Yeah, and he asked me about our poetry stand and if I enjoy doing it."

"What did you say?"

"I told him the truth."

"What's the truth?"

"Sometimes writing ten poems a day can be tiring, but I love being around people with you. You make it fun."

"I make it fun?"

"No, I was lying. It's a terrible experience because of you."

Sarah hops into my lap, puts her arms around me, and says, "I love doing it with you. I love every second of it. I love you."

She pulls her face close to mine and says it again. "I do love you. You know that, right?"

I do love Sarah, but it isn't easy for me to say it.

I look down. "I love you too."

"Look at me and say it like you mean it."

I look her directly in her eyes and say, "I love you, Sarah. I loved you from the minute I met you, and I always will."

She smiles wide and puts her nose to mine. "I love you too. I always will. I promise." And she kisses me.

CHAPTER
THIRTY-ONE

I go to the church every day, and the reverend and I make our confessions. Sometimes we just talk about pop culture. We both love classic rock. The rev was at Woodstock. I have a mild obsession with Woodstock, so I drill him about what it was like, and I flip out when he tells me he was twenty feet away when Hendrix played "The Star-Spangled Banner."

One time, he tells me how he was always a very spiritual person and that he wasn't raised overly religious, but he always enjoyed going to services as a kid. He always felt comfortable at church, but for most of his teenage years he fought that feeling. In his group of friends, the church was really uncool, but when no one was looking he'd get in his beat-up Chevy and go to church, but he didn't know why. He kept it a secret. He didn't tell his parents, certainly didn't tell his friends, but it's where he found solace.

He told me he had a mentor, a Black minister who was both religious and into cultural things. Reverend Tom was down with Dizzy Gillespie and Jesus Christ simultaneously, and Reverend Tom showed him that just because you work in a church doesn't mean you have to only like choral music and be uptight. You can be yourself, whoever you are, and use the Bible as your guide. So, during college the reverend had an epiphany: "Be who you are and do what you love."

He loved to help the poor and indigent, fight for civil rights, and try to instill in everyone the awareness that they deserve to love and to be happy. The reverend doesn't care who you are, what you do or did, or what you look like; he just cares about your character. And if you are unhappy with yourself and your life, he believes it's never too late to change. If you are willing to put in the work to better yourself and better your life, he will do anything he can to help you because helping others is his calling.

The reverend tells me all kinds of personal, real things about his life, and I basically tell him nothing. It is very hard for me to open up. All I do is talk about music, what took place earlier in the day or the night before, and that is about it. The only person I ever talk to him about is Sarah. I tell him how worried I am about her drug use. He always asks if he can help, but I tell him that I think she would feel like we were ganging up on her. It's not the right time.

But today when the reverend is talking about his daughter, I crack, and out of nowhere I blurt out, "I have a daughter!"

The reverend says, "I'm not surprised. A father is more prone to looking out instead of looking within. What's her name?"

"Josie."

"That's a beautiful name. How old is she."

"Six. With each passing day, I grow more and more distraught."

"How long has it been since you've seen her?"

"Three months."

"Would you like to see her? Because I will find a way to make that happen."

"The timing's not right. I haven't accomplished what I set out to do yet."

"What's your ultimate goal, Poet?"

"My goal is to live an authentic life on my own terms, making enough money to provide for my daughter doing what I was born to do—sharing my gift with the world."

"Poet, how long have you been homeless."

"Three months."

"What were you doing before this?"

I hesitate, wondering if it is safe to tell him my story. "Rev, you've really got to keep this confession secret."

He nods.

I take a deep breath, listen to the birds chirp, and plunge in. "My real name is Evan Bloom. I was a stockbroker. I was a multi-million-aire. I had a mansion, luxury cars, a huge swimming pool, a wife I hated, and friends and coworkers who were 100 percent full of shit. I was living someone else's life. I was the son my father always wanted, a man other men admired. I had it all, and I was the loneliest man alive. I hated my life. I hated myself, and I hated what I stood for. Besides my daughter, the only thing that gave me pleasure was writing poetry."

I tell him the whole tale, and then we sit in silence until the reverend says softly, "Poet, you will find what you're looking for. I think you've already found love, and love is the greatest power. Love can change the world. And you love to write, you love to share your gift with the world, and you love Sarah. One day, your daughter will understand your quest of self-fulfillment, she will understand your sacrifice, and she will love you even more for it. Love has brought you here, and love will take you further. Cherish the time you spend with Sarah because that kind of love only comes to a person once. When you get back to the alley, give Sarah a hug for me, Poet." Standing up, he says, "Your truth is safe with me. Keeping secrets is what I do."

The reverend puts his hand on my right shoulder and looks up at the sky. "Great admirer of beauty, look at that half-moon. Can you see it? The other half is yours."

CHAPTER
THIRTY-TWO

Our confessions continue. We talk about sports every day. The rev keeps me up on the Rangers and Knicks—who played well and what he thinks about the future for each team. We discuss movies, new and old, actors and celebrities. But most of all, we discuss music. The rev is a music historian—jazz, blues, folk, funk, modern and classic rock, hip-hop, and pop. He moves from Lady Gaga and Beyoncé to Muddy Waters and Chick Corea. He tells me moving stories about meeting Martin Luther King Jr., about the day JFK got shot, and about his brother who lost his life in Vietnam. He says Vietnam is this country's third greatest tragedy. The other two were our late entrance into World War II and slavery.

The reverend is married to a white Jewish woman, which I find fascinating.

The conversation goes both ways. He sees me as a mystery—my upbringing, my college experience, my previous career. The rev tries to wrap his head around the idea of me walking away from wealth. He wants to understand how my perspective changed and why I'm happier now than I was then. I love telling him tales of my old life, which only deepens my sense of how distorted my worldview had been: all the extravagance, all the luxury, the need to impress others. Buying 25,000 shares of Apple for a rich trust fund college kid from

Connecticut. My wife buying me a $75,000 Rolex on a Sunday after-noon. The reverend just takes it all in. He listens patiently, and at the end of every story he always has something insightful and clever to say, followed by a passage from the Bible.

The Judson Memorial Church—the reverend's church—is a special place. To me, it represents the spirit of Washington Square Park. The church is open to everyone; if you have a heartbeat, you are welcome. The reverend's church has been a catalyst for social change since he got there in the '60s. It holds fundraisers, NA and AA meetings, free coun-seling; if you need any kind of help you can find it there, or the church community will help you find your way to it.

My favorite thing about the rev is his belief in artistic expression. Every Wednesday night, he hosts an open forum for artists. Writers, actors, dancers, comedians, and painters are all invited to share their talents, and anyone can come and watch. On a good night, there are maybe 175 people there, and some of the performances are as good as anything you'd pay money to see in a club or an off-Broadway theater. A concert, a reading, dancing, doing stand-up in a church—it all sounds pretty fucking crazy to me. But I guess Reverend Frank sees the gathering of like-minded individuals as a way to honor God, and it's hard to disagree with that.

What the reverend finds fascinating is my relationship with reli-gion. I have allowed him to read some of my poetry, and he knows there is a great deal of spirituality in my soul. He's puzzled that I have no relationship with my religion and Jewish heritage.

"Why?"

"Reverend, when I walk into a synagogue, I don't feel that there's any spirit there. It's just a beautiful building with books, scrolls, and funny hats. Also, when I walk into a Christian church, I feel over-whelmed by all the images and ritual. It's hard to take it seriously. The only things I take seriously are my writing and the love I have for everyone I encounter."

"But when you introduce yourself, you introduce yourself as a Jew. Yet you don't practice Judaism nor do you believe in any religion. Explain that, Poet."

"It's funny you ask me that. I've been thinking about it recently, and I really don't have an answer. 'I'm a Jew' just sort of comes out, like it's a predisposition. Maybe I respect my lineage and heritage. It wouldn't be because of my parents, grandparents, or my bar mitzvah, but I do think the history of the Jews is miraculous. We've been under-dogs for 5,000 years, and we're still here to tell the story. It doesn't make sense."

"See, you said 'we.' 'We've been the underdogs.' You do feel a kinship. I think one day you'll rediscover your Jewish roots."

"Rev, I usually think you're right, but this time you're dead wrong. I will never be in a synagogue, and I won't make Josie go to Hebrew School, and any other kid I might have won't go either. Trust me, I'm done with religion."

The reverend puts his hand on my shoulder and says, "Well, I can always baptize you, Poet."

I shake my head. "I was never much for swimming."

"Think of it as a dunk tank; be the clown."

"Rev, I've had a red ball on my nose my whole life."

CHAPTER
THIRTY-THREE

The reverend really wants to meet Sarah, to speak with her one on one. He is fascinated by her—a young girl of such beauty, such a zest for life, so loving, yet plagued by heroin addiction. The reverend knows that Sarah and I are in love. He sees us together, he can see that she is special, and he knows how much her drug use is taking a toll on both of us. He sees her compassion and empathy. He knows about her harsh background and upbringing, and he appreciates her unique sense of humor: the way she can call me a "fucking pervert" and in the same sentence tell me how lucky Josie is to have me as a father. I tell the reverend that if Sarah called me an asshole, I would hear "I love you." The reverend knows she's a beauty with a foul mouth and a pure heart, and he is dying to help her. He has been trying to figure out the best way to get to know her, without setting off her defenses.

Sarah knows all about the rev and loves hearing about our confession sessions. She calls them the "meetings of the minds." She knows the rev is a catalyst for change, positivity, and prosperity, but she is reluctant to meet him. She won't go near a church and has no interest in sitting down with a man of the cloth.

"I don't do religion," she tells me.

"How about if he comes down here and spends time in the alley with us?"

"No." I think what Sarah really fears is the reverend trying to talk to her about her addiction. The needle is my competition and my enemy, and it scares me. I can't lose Sarah. I would not be able to go on.

It is a windy cool day, the Monday before Thanksgiving, and the rev and I are sitting at the top of the stairs.

"Poet, what are you doing for Thanksgiving?"

"Probably eating a turkey sandwich and potato chips with Sarah. How about you?"

"Donna, Holly, Holly's boyfriend, and I were just going to have a quiet dinner. But last night I ran an idea by my wife, and she liked it. She is going to cook a complete Thanksgiving dinner in the church for about thirty people. Of course, my family will be there, and I invited some other homeless men and women, and other people in need, but I saved a special spot for you two. I want you and Sarah to be our honored guests. I won't take no for an answer."

"Reverend, you know how Sarah feels about churches. It's not gonna fly."

"But, Poet, how does she feel about food?"

"She weighs 110 pounds, and she eats like an elephant. She feels pretty good about it."

"This is your chance to get her in here. This is our shot!"

"Rev, it's not gonna happen."

"I have an ace up my sleeve."

"What's that."

"I'm writing her a personal letter."

I laugh. "Okay, go for it, but don't put it on church letterhead."

The reverend grins. "Open your duffel bag. I'm writing it on your yellow legal pad."

"If you do that, you have to use one of my Pilot G2 pens."

He chuckles. "You writers and your pens. You're like priests with their Bibles: They all have their favorite model."

So, the reverend crosses his legs, takes a pad, and writes.

Dearest Sarah,

Your friend Poet tells me you're afraid of the church. The only things to fear in church are cheap suits and ladies wearing big hats, and we have neither. Basically, no one wears a suit, and the only hats I've seen around these parts are Yankees hats, usually the ratty one worn by Poet. So, if you don't mind the Yankees, please join me for Thanksgiving dinner. Sarah, I'll even give you a drumstick. Might I add there will be sweet potatoes, stuffing, and cranberry sauce, and my wife, Donna, is baking an apple pie. Imagine a scoop of vanilla ice cream melting down the sides of a slice of sizzling hot apple pie. More importantly, you'll have fun, and you'll meet good people who make great company. You and Poet deserve a good meal and a night out. I'm dying to meet you. I already feel like I know you. Please come share Thanksgiving with me and my family. I'll save two seats for you. I haven't really met you yet, but I'm pretty sure you and Poet and I are going to be good friends for a long time.

Sincerely,

Reverend Frank Emerson

I walk into the alley, letter in hand, and find Sarah reading a beat-up romance novel with a tiny flashlight.

She looks up, sees me, and asks, "What the hell is that?"

I play dumb. "What?"

She points her finger and says, "That. What is that? Is that a letter from your pen pal in Tokyo?"

I give her a baffled look.

"What address did your pen pal use? The Alley, 101 Washington

Square Park East, NYC 10025. Did she make it out to Poet-san or The Poet?"

"You're such a funny girl, so funny. Ha Ha Ha! This letter happens to be for you."

She perks up. "For me? Do I have a secret admirer?"

"You do." I hold it out.

She snatches it. "This better not be perverted."

She cracks it open and begins to read. I watch her face and as she makes her way down the page. I watch her grin grow wide, and when she finishes, she tries to hide her excitement.

She turns to me and asks, "You sure there won't be cheap suits and big hats?"

"No way."

"Okay, I'll go, but on one condition—and keep in mind, I'm doing this for you, not for me."

"What's that?"

"You shave, and you don't wear your Yankees hat."

"So, this is all about headgear? Are you sure it has nothing to do with the drumstick, cranberry sauce, stuffing, and apple pie with vanilla ice cream?"

"Absolutely not. I just want you to look proper at the dinner table. You're a reflection of me, and my mother taught me manners. I'm a very proper dinner guest. I'm a classy gal, and I can't be accompanied by a scruffy man who looks like he's been sitting in centerfield for three months."

I crack up. "Sarah, I'm gonna look good, no worries. I won't embarrass you."

"Poet, I know it means a lot to you. And I want some fucking stuffing! I'm sick of potato chips, and it's time I met the reverend."

"He's dying to meet you."

"Who's not? I'm the hottest homeless chick in New York."

I laugh. "You're the hottest *chick* in New York."

"From your lips to God's earlobe." She kisses me and goes back to her romance novel.

CHAPTER
THIRTY-FOUR

It is Thanksgiving morning, and the park is filled with families, walking, laughing, and posing for pictures, everyone with huge smiles on their faces. I think of Thanksgiving with Josie, of sneaking pieces of turkey off her plate and making her laugh. I called Petra late last night, and she said Josie is doing relatively well, but she found her in my office the other day sitting in my computer chair and marking days off the calendar.

"And Josie's not the only one who misses you," she added.

"I wish we were all celebrating Thanksgiving together today, Petra. Please keep her spirits up. You have to be strong for her. I'm being strong for her. We'll make it."

"Wherever you are, please take care of yourself, Mr. Evan. Be safe."

"Thanks, Petra, Happy Thanksgiving."

"You too, Mr. Evan."

I have been looking forward to Thanksgiving dinner at the church. I know the rev's wife is going to go overboard. The reverend has told me so much about her and about their daughter, Holly. He says one of his greatest pleasures in life is messing with Holly's boyfriend, James. Her boyfriend asks a ton of questions and goes off on long monologues, hoping to get a conversation going, and the rev just sits silently, with no expression, then gives one-word answers. But he really likes James, and Holly knows it.

Sarah and I have been together for more than three months, and today is the first time I've seen her nervous. Apparently, she doesn't like formal gatherings and forced conversation, especially in a church. Sarah might be homeless and no longer has a closet with designer clothes, but she cares how she looks. It's hard to be homeless and look good, but somehow, she finds a way.

Juan at the Washington Hotel lets us briefly use a room to get ready, right at checkout time, before it gets cleaned. It is a very nice gesture, considering it is probably one of the hotel's busiest days of the year. I get dressed first, and as promised, I shave off my beard. I even bought a $3 bottle of gel and slick back my hair. I throw on one of my grey sweatshirts, my cleanest pair of Levi's, and of course, my Nikes. I walk out of the bathroom, looking fresh, and Sarah smiles, comes over, and kisses me.

"There's the face I fell in love with. Where's he been hiding? You remember when we met, I called you handsome."

"Yes."

"This is when you're the most handsome, when I can see your face."

She rubs her right hand on my left cheek and says, "I love this face," then kisses my cheek and neck. "I wish we had time to get in that bed together."

"They'll be plenty of time for that. I promise."

"There better be. I gotta stop reading those romance novels. I'm like a furnace right now."

"Sarah, you're killing me. Go in the shower and get changed. We have to be out of here in ten minutes."

She kisses me, gives me a strategic squeeze, and says, "Okay."

Ten minutes later, she reemerges, and I almost pass out. She is stunning in a tight, red cotton dress that flares at the waist with black ruffles—and just enough cleavage to make me crazy, without overdoing it since she's about to socialize in a house of God. Her lipstick is bright, and she has on black stockings with her trademark black boots.

Her hair is combed out and hangs down to her shoulders. She looks, not surprisingly, like a model.

"Hot, right?"

"Like a goddess. I want to bow down to you. I'd kiss you, but I don't want to shmear your lipstick. It's too perfect. Forget the turkey; I want to eat you."

"I like when you talk dirty, Poet. We need more of that in the future." She hugs me. "You ready for apple pie?"

"Let's overeat!"

We kiss. I take her hand, open the door to the hotel room, and head for the park. Food and the reverend await.

When we get to the church steps, Sarah says, "Maybe we should've brought something."

I laugh due to our poverty. I grab Sarah's left hand; she is extremely nervous. We slowly make our way up the steps and walk in.

Sarah takes a big look around. "It's beautiful in here. Maybe I should convert."

"You're Catholic, right?"

She looks at me. "I'm not sure what I am, but *my* church didn't look like this."

When the reverend sees me, he gets right up from the table and walks to us with a humongous smile. "This is great! This is so great!" He gives me a giant bear hug and says, "This is Christmas come early. This is exciting!" He pats me on the back. "We're so honored to have you."

"Rev, the honor is mine."

He hugs Sarah and jubilantly exclaims, "She's here! She's here! This is already the best fifteen seconds of my Thanksgiving. Thank you so much for coming, Sarah. This means so much to me. So, what do you think of the place? It's not too bad, right?"

"Nice digs. I think I went to a rave in a place like this when I was sixteen. I'm happy to be here too. Thank you for inviting me, and thank you for your thoughtful letter. You might think I'm here for the food, but I'm here for you, and I'm here to thank you for all the time you spend with Poet. Don't tell him I said so, but he loves you, Reverend. You mean a lot to him, and he means everything to me, so the least I can do is honor you and your wishes to have me here tonight."

"So, Sarah, let me confide in you. I've never quite met anyone like him, and I think you've been an integral part of his self-discovery. You bring out the best in him, and he recognizes that. His eyes really light up when he talks about two things: you and Josie. He thinks the world of you, so take care of him, take care of each other. He has a good effect on people. And I've seen a lot in my day, but I've never seen a poetry table like you two have. And I'm sure that's just the first of what will be many grand collaborations. It's the start of something beautiful."

I overhear their whole conversation and watch the reverend hug Sarah again. Those two people are my whole life right now.

The Thanksgiving table is set up on the stage, and it looks magnificent. Mrs. Emerson has organized everything, and she is bustling about, greeting people while making final preparations. There are appetizers on tables in front of the stage—various crackers, cheeses, salsas, chips, and homemade breads. As all the guests shuffle in, Sarah introduces herself to each one, and everybody stands around talking.

We are not the only homeless people here. There are about ten of us, and two, Jerry and Roger, we know, both very nice guys. Roger is about my age and lost his wife and daughter in a car accident and has not been able to recover. Bipolar, he was too sick to work or even get out of bed and started drinking. He's now an alcoholic and homeless. Early in the day, before he's had a lot to drink, he's a sweetheart. But if you catch him at night, he can be temperamental—not mean or scary, just strange and disoriented. It's heartbreaking, and we sometimes give him food. Roger is a burnout from the Vietnam War. He's been in and out of shelters since the '70s and has wild stories about living on the streets in different parts of the country.

There are two homeless transgender women. I had never met someone transgender before, and it is fascinating. Gloria, who is about forty-five, tells me how all her life she felt like she was a man trapped in a woman's body. I ask her when she decided to make the change, and she told me five years ago. She'd been living a lie for over forty years and just couldn't do it anymore. When she decided to make the change, everyone disowned her—her family, her friends, everyone. She was fired from her job. I tell her to sue on the basis of discrimination, but she tells me it isn't so easy. But the reverend is helping her work on it.

There are some young gay men and woman here too, most under the age of twenty-one. Many are from small towns where they were bullied, and their parents didn't accept them. They fled to the big city, seeking equality and peace of mind, a place where they could feel accepted and not judged all the time. New York City is one of the few places on Earth like that. Yes, big strides have been made societally, and gay marriage has been legalized, but in small towns discrimination is still strong. These young kids came here with $5 in their pockets, looking to find some freedom. They are broke, and they have nowhere to go, so they live on the streets and try to find a way to support themselves. Some end up turning tricks, some beg, some commit crimes, and I understand why they resort to these things. I'd rather be homeless and be myself than live in a small town hating myself and being hated by everyone else, including my parents.

The reverend had also invited three women who openly describe themselves as prostitutes. Two were born in the city, and the other one is from the Midwest. All three have been arrested numerous times, and their lives are hard. They would rather do something else, but they barely make enough money to survive and keep going. None of them, surprisingly to me, are serious drug users, and they all have young kids to support. The two NYC natives say their mothers watch their kids at night and are fully aware of the work they do.

I ask what their mothers think about them being sex workers, and one says, "She's disgusted, but it's better than my son going to bed hungry."

All three say the reverend is trying to find them real jobs. The woman from the Midwest says he got her a couple of interviews. "One was janitorial; the other was doing filing at a drug rehabilitation facility. I was very upset that I didn't get hired for either of them. I thought it was gonna happen for me. I am way beyond ready."

Meeting Donna Emerson and their daughter, Holly, is a delight. Just like the reverend, Mrs. E. has a huge smile, and you can feel her compassion. She is attractive for an older woman—long dyed blonde her, hazel eyes, and a good figure. She's very warm and seems excited to meet me. I could tell she wanted to take time and talk with me, but she was so busy preparing for dinner we didn't get the chance to have an in-depth conversation.

She kisses me on the cheek. "Frank says you're special, that you're a gift from God. He doesn't say things like that, Poet. My husband loves you, and he talks about you all the time. When he found out you and Sarah were coming, he was beside himself. Oh, by the way, Sarah is sweet and absolutely beautiful. Look at her talking to Gloria, making her laugh. I've known Gloria for two years, and I've never seen her laugh. Stay next to that one; don't let her go."

"This is truly magical, Mrs. E. Thank you."

She pinches my right cheek and says, "It's our pleasure."

Holly is a trip. She is the cool girl the guys like to hang out with, not hung up on her looks and with a great sense of humor. Like the reverend, she knows everything about everything. We have a fifteen-minute conversation about the Rangers. Her boyfriend is cool too and gets in on the conversation. Sarah chimes in and says that fighting in hockey should be its own sport.

"It's better than boxing because there's no rounds. It's better than a bar fight because it's on skates. Brawling in hockey is fucking exciting. The only thing that would be better would be fighting in the Ice Capades or Disney on Ice. Can you imagine Pluto and Mickey taking their big heads off, throwing them down, then kicking the shit out of each other on skates in a rink? That would be the ultimate. Snow White beating up on the Seven Dwarfs? If I had any money, I'd pay to see that."

We switch gears, and Holly talks about the work she does with her father: counseling addicts, the homeless, and disabled veterans, and she tells me it is really rewarding. And her father helps get her clients work.

"It's way outside his job description, but my father sleeps better knowing the people I'm caring for are being taken care of."

All this talk about counseling and helping people gets me thinking that the girl I love and sleep with every night is just as in need as the people they're talking about. She is a functioning addict, but there's still a lot I don't know. How does she get her drugs? How does she pay for them? How do they not seem to affect her the same way they do other addicts I see on the street? It just doesn't add up. But this is a boundary I cannot cross. And how can I object to Sarah placing that limit because I haven't been totally honest with her. She doesn't even know my real name. I really want to get Sarah help, and she has the tools right in front of her. The counseling, the support system, the meetings, it's all there. I have to find a way to make it happen.

The Thanksgiving feast lives up to the hype. The reverend saves a seat next to him for me, and Sarah is on the other side. She gets her drumstick, eats two servings of stuffing, two servings of sweet potato pie, a serving of cranberry sauce, and a piece of banana bread. Faces are smiling, but no one's grin is as big as the rev's. This is his dream for the world: people from different walks of life sharing in food, conversation, and laughter.

There are many highlights of the evening, but for me the best is watching the reverend and Sarah connect. I think having him in her life will bring her one step closer to getting the help she needs. I now consider the reverend family, and I've come to realize that I can't imagine my life without Sarah anymore. I miss her when she's not around, and I'm with her twenty-one hours a day. I started this journey to find myself, but the best thing that's happened is that I found someone else.

We say our goodbyes. I hug the reverend and thank him for an amazing night. He takes Sarah aside and whispers something to her.

She comes back over to me, and as we leave I yell, "Goodnight, everyone, happy Thanksgiving!"

Everyone yells back, "Goodnight, Poet. Goodnight, Sarah!"

When we get outside, I ask, "What did the reverend whisper to you?"

"He said to remind you of the time you were sitting on the steps looking at the half-moon. He says I'm the other half: the lit-up part."

CHAPTER
THIRTY-FIVE

The days are frigid, the nights are frozen, but somehow, Sarah and I manage. We each wear four layers of clothes, cover ourselves with three thick blankets, wear thermal gloves and knit hats, and rest our heads on my duffel bag with two pillows without pillowcases. Most importantly, we have each other, and that definitely makes the cold more tolerable.

In early December, I begin to notice that Sarah is slipping away. I am very concerned. Naturally, I think her drug use is increasing, which frightens me. One day, she gets up to leave at noon, even though she'd already gone away at 10 am.

"Where are you going?"

"Taking a walk."

"Where?"

"I'd rather you not know."

"Sarah, in four months, I have never asked, but now I'm asking. I want to know where you're going."

"You think I'm going to get high again, don't you."

"Of course. That's exactly what I think. Every day, you leave here at 10 am to get high. You used to go four times a day. This week, it's been five times. I'm worried next week it will be six."

"You really want to know?"

"Yes, I do! If anything happens to you, I won't be able to go on. That would be it for me."

"Okay. I wanted to keep it confidential, but since you're so concerned, I'll tell you. Every day at noon, I have a tuna fish sandwich with the reverend."

"What? Really?"

"Yes."

"Why would you hide that from me?"

"Because I wanted it to be between him and me. I didn't want you asking questions about what we talk about or anything like that. It's like therapy. It's private. We're working on my issues and trying to sort them out."

"Are you making progress?"

"I'm not sure, but I always feel better after I eat my sandwich."

Sarah's beautiful face has always been loose, relaxed, and usually smiling, but if you look closely, there is a lot of hurt. There is a lot of pain. But lately, I'm beginning to feel like she's more present, more self-aware. She seems more comfortable, more complete. Her shooting up is obviously terrible, but it seems like she doesn't feel as guilty about it. For now, she seems to own it. I think she sees it as just a part of who she is. It doesn't define her. It doesn't make her a bad person.

Of course, I still go to confession. Today the rev says, "Poet, here at the church every Wednesday night at 7:30 is artists night. I have told you that, right?"

"Yes, rev, about a hundred times."

"I'd like you to come tonight and do a reading. It's time. And Sarah should come too."

"Rev, I can't even read my poetry to her. How am I gonna read it to strangers?"

"Poet, this is the most open-minded crowd you'll ever play to. If you intend to read your poetry and share your gift with the world, this is the place to start. It's junior varsity, maybe only sandlot. Good and fun. It's the perfect place to take your game up a notch."

"I'm not looking to play. I'd rather sit in the top row, or even under the bleachers, with my notepad. That's my comfort zone."

"All the great poets read their poetry out loud. You have to bring it to life. Deliver it to people. I heard Ginsburg read in the park lots of times. He was very good. Somehow the way he recited each poem made you understand it better. You've got to believe in yourself, Poet. If you really are a poet, then you need to do what poets do: Read your poems to people. Believe in yourself. Proclaim your words."

I sit motionless and silent. I take long, deep breaths. I feel a tingle, that enlightened sensation. Things are very clear.

I smile at the rev. "For you, I'll read tonight. It's time start the next chapter of my life."

Back in the alley, Sarah is lying down, reading a month-old copy of *People* magazine.

"Hey, Poet, Jennifer Lawrence's phone got hacked, and somebody released her private nude photos. How fucked up is that?"

"Where can I see them?"

"You're disgusting, Poet. What, are you, fifteen? You think Jennifer Lawrence is hotter than me?"

"No, but she's got nude photos."

"And when she wants you to see one, she'll send it to you."

"If I ever have a home. Fair enough. Hey, I made a promise to the rev. I told him I'm going to do something he really wants me to do. Guess what."

"Artists night!"

"How did you know?"

"He's been telling me for weeks he was going to try to get you to go."

"Why didn't you say anything?"

"I figured the rev could handle it on his own and would eventually wear you down. It is a pretty good idea, after all."

"I wrote a poem for the occasion."

"Just now?"

"Yeah. After I talked to him"

"What's it called?"

"'The Arch of Heaven.' I wrote it with a crowd in mind. It's long. We'll see."

"'The Arch of Heaven'—like the big arch at the entrance to the park on 5th Avenue?"

"Wow, that didn't even cross my mind, Sarah. I like that."

"Oh my God! I can't wait to see you up there on stage doing your poet thing. I'll probably cum in my pants."

"I'm a nervous wreck. I feel like I'm reciting my haftorah."

"Your what?"

"When a Jewish boy turns thirteen and has his big coming-of-age ceremony, he reads Hebrew in front of all his family and friends. That's the haftorah. You're a nervous wreck, and it's awful. I don't even do public speaking, let alone recite my poetry to strangers. I can barely read it to you, for crying out loud."

"But it's so beautiful. Just go for it. Don't be afraid. And if you get scared, just look at me, and I'll pick my nose and make you laugh. Hey, it's just going to be artists night in a church; you're not being judged. It's not Madison Square Garden. You could go up there and recite 'Mary Had a Little Lamb,' and you'd get applause. You'll be great."

"If you say so. I don't know if this is really my thing."

"Let's find out. If I had ten bucks, I'd bet on Poet being a pretty good performer."

A few hours later, we are making our way across the park, my duffel bag in my hand, and I am a wreck. I never took an acting class. I'm not a musician nor a performer. I'm a writer, a poet, and we're the invisible guys. That's what I like about it. But tonight will be different.

Sarah is bouncing along, as excited as if we *are* headed for a concert at Madison Square Garden. She's completely changed her tune, and now she's pumping me up, telling me that this is just the beginning of a big damn deal. I don't think it's helping.

"Poet, this is your major label debut. You're playing *Letterman* tonight."

Even though I'm only going to be reading a fucking poem. Who cares? Suddenly I realize that both Sarah and the reverend care. They care about me deeply. And they think that me doing this is a really big step. I appreciate their love and support, but I know it might suck big time. My body is stiff; my mind is racing. I'm already not having fun.

It's pretty crowded in the church. Up in front of the pulpit, there's a stage that some people are finishing setting up. As I scan the room, I realize that there are not only homeless people here—gays, transgenders, and junkies—but there are plenty of "normal" people, people who live in homes and pay mortgages, who have jobs, families, and regular lives. I kind of forgot these people existed. Seeing them only increases my anxiety. I consider sneaking out, but just then the reverend and his wife come over and give me and Sarah huge hugs.

The reverend pulls me to the side, puts his hand on my shoulder, and says, "You're nervous. Loosen up. You're gonna kill! There's some milk and cookies over there. Go have some."

"I'm too sick to eat. The only person on planet Earth who could have convinced me to do this is you. I hate you right now. Pray for me."

The reverend says, "Poet, you don't need to be prayed for. You've already been blessed." He slaps me on the shoulder, says, "Just be yourself," and walks away.

Sarah and I grab some milk and cookies, three each. Sarah eats hers in a few bites, then takes two of mine and gives me a cutesy grin. I look back at her with disdain.

The reverend takes the stage, adjusts the microphone, and says enthusiastically, "Welcome to artists night, everyone!"

The audience claps. There are a few whistles. "We have a lot of good stuff in store for you tonight. We have a pair of ballerinas, we have two singer/songwriters, a painter is here to show you some of his work, we've got a saxophone player whose gonna blow—in a good way, and tonight we also have a poet." He winks at me.

The rev says, "First up is Christina, to play an original song she wrote on her acoustic guitar."

It could be Tina Turner up there or Christina Aguilera. I'm not paying attention. I'm lost in space.

When Christina finishes, the rev gets up again and says, "Come on up, Frankie. It's time to blow."

Frankie gets up there and plays a mean sax. I normally would have enjoyed it, but right now it sounds like a funeral dirge to my self-hating ears.

And then it happens. The rev takes the stage and in what feels like slow motion says, "Next up is a young man who spends his free time on the steps of this church writing poetry. Please welcome Poet."

I slowly get up, and Sarah slaps my ass and says, "Go get 'em!"

I walk to the stage as if in a dream.

The rev shakes my hand and whispers, "It's time to let the tiger out of the cage."

I take a long look at the crowd, and suddenly all my anxiety dissipates. I was born to do this! The room disappears. There's only me and the paper, and the words are huge. They are almost illuminated, like scripture. I begin to read. There is no crowd, there is no noise, there is nothing. I am surrounded by white light. I am not in my body. My vision is blurred. All I can see is the words in front of me. I am not in control. I don't know what is happening, but I feel more alive than I ever have felt before. It's just me and my words. I feel liberated, free.

The Arch of Heaven

I entered this park homeless.
I entered this park alone.
I became a man in this place I now call home.

I look at those around me,
See the beauty that's inside.
And I'm grateful for this park that stretches two blocks wide.

Yes, I have nothing, but also I have it all.

I have freedom. I have pleasure.
I have time. I get to speak.
I converse, and I am not judged.
Express myself openly and never feel like a freak.

I am witness to the world.
I watch the sun rise and set.
And the beauty of the Earth
Makes time easy to forget.

I see a dog that is happy.
A woman wears a smile.

I watch someone in the playground,
Rediscovering their inner child.

Some are playing chess.
Others play guitar.
An actor walks around the park,
Dreaming of becoming a star.

There's a juggler and a painter, a comedy troupe and a jazz
    band.
A toddler runs, falls down.
And six people rise to lend a helping hand.

Why can't the world be this way?
Why can't we share in each other's lives?
Why can't we help whoever it is we are standing right beside?

Help your neighbor, your family, your coworker, and your
    friends.
Be proactive and contribute.
Don't stand apart and play pretend.

Pretend to worry, to care, to go on your merry way.
Stop living for tomorrow; the time for change is today!
Don't live your precious life in fear.

In fear of being accepted.
Afraid of being who you are.
Scared of being considered,
Never feeling like a star.

Some hide behind a shadow that feeds on wasted time,
Scared to explore the buried treasure that's deep within their
    mind.

We're all born happy.

We're all born pure.
But then you're told the way to be and are not yourself
    anymore.

And so many get lost, lose track, lose heart,
Find comfort in drugs and alcohol, in need of a brand new
    start.

We're innately good.
We all innately care—
About our fellow humans, but to share is way too rare.

More kind words to another,
Make a fresh new start.
And they'll try anything

To stop the voice inside their head
That keeps them up at night as they lie awake in bed.

Their instincts and intuitions can find the path.
But they hide behind a mask and pretend to be someone else,
Terrified of what might be inside.
The outcome would be beauty.
The outcome would be grace.
The outcome would be blessings for the entire human race.

We're all innately good.
We all innately care
About our fellow humans, but to share it is too rare.

And that's so sad.
It breaks my heart.
Mere kind words to another make a brand-new start.

That's why we're here.
To share in a dream.

And at the end of the day
What does it all mean?

The life we live,
This world we share,
What do you hold sacred?
What's your cross to bear?
Do you love your family?
Do you love your friends?
Do we love one another?
What's our legacy when it ends?
Can you look in the mirror and like who's looking back?
Can you hold your head up high?
Are you different from the pack?
Or just a sheep among the flock?
Obsessed with things, constantly checking your stock?

Don't be afraid to be great.
Don't be afraid to be good.
Don't be afraid to be completely misunderstood.

Because some will never see it.
Not everyone is built the same.
And that's what makes life beautiful.
And much more than a game.

It's not about possessions—
Money, things, fame, or cars.
I praise altruistic values,
Seeing people for who they are.

Love can change the world.
Love can change your life.
You were born to love.
So, express it day and night.

And when your life is over,
When it's all been said and done.
Be surrounded by your loved ones.
Be surrounded by your friends.
Be surrounded by your family.
Be at peace when your life ends.

Don't look back and feel regret.
It's just the beginning of your life.
Concentrate on what's ahead.
Another life you get to live.
Eternity and more.
No one knows what the future has in store.

So, die with a smile,
Holding someone's hand.
Leave this life fulfilled.
Leave with head held high.
And at the Arch of Heaven, wave to me and say goodbye...

I finish, and I am disoriented. Everyone is standing and clapping loudly. What the hell just happened? I am frozen, a deer in the head-lights, under anesthesia.

The reverend steps back on stage and says, "That was the debut of Poet. Remember this face; it will be familiar soon." The reverend hugs me really tight and says, "That was perfect. You are on your way." He beams me a big smile. "Well done, my friend."

As I stumble off the stage and back to my seat, people are still clapping. I don't look at Sarah; I just plop down next to her. I feel like I just gave birth.

Sarah grabs my face, puts her nose up to mine, and says, "That was the best fucking thing I've ever seen in my entire life. Goddamnit, I love you." She kisses me and says, "I want to have your babies. I want ten Poets."

I am confused. "It was good?"

"Multiple orgasm good. It was that good!"

"I don't remember it. I was outside myself. It was like someone else was talking."

"You were like a preacher. Hands flying. Manipulating your voice with emotion. Telling a story with your words. An intense performance, but real. Everybody was with you, hanging on every syllable."

"With whom? The person on the stage? It didn't seem like me."

I get up, go to the bathroom, and stare at myself deep in the mirror. Scruffy beard, long curly hair, clear blue eyes, I am unrecognizable, and I realize that I have become what I have been telling everybody I am. I am Poet.

CHAPTER
THIRTY-SIX

By the beginning of December, the park has settled into winter mode: fallen leaves, barren trees, quiet and serene. Lots of the regulars are gone. No Jamie, no Henry, no comedy troupe, no jazz bands, and not much chess. Now it's just me and Sarah in the alley.

It is starting to get really cold, on the verge of dangerous. There is often snow on the ground, and we shiver and shake at night, noses running, teeth chattering. We both lack energy, and funds are running thin. With fewer people spending time in the park, the poetry business is not viable, so we start begging, with a sign that reads "If there is a God, He blesses you." The main park visitors now are the dog walkers.

Despite our distress, we appreciate the quiet winter beauty. With the leaves gone, you can see the entire park at once, east to west, north to south. Sarah still wears a smile, but I can see the stress on her face. Both of us are still meeting with the rev every day, and he can see we are in trouble, slipping into dark times. Sarah refuses to go to a shelter, and I'm not crazy about the idea either. In my mind, I live in a beautiful home with simple architecture, a nice leather couch, surrounded by art, with Sarah lying beside me. I'm fulfilled.

Today after confession, the reverend says, "I spoke to the parishioners, the members of the church. I told them about you and Sarah and that you are very special to me, and I asked them if they would let you live in the church basement until spring. They were hesitant, but I won them over. There's a shower and a cot, and I'll leave some food out for you in the kitchen every night before I leave. Does that sound good?"

"Jesus. Are you serious?"

"Yes. It's pretty minimal, but the basement's yours if you want it."

"Reverend, I don't know what to say. This is crazy. I can't tell you how grateful I am." I hug him. "I've been worried about Sarah's health, and honestly, my own as well. Thank you!"

"I take care of the ones I love," says the rev. "I love everyone, but you and Sarah are family."

I drop my head. "I had a family, but it didn't feel like a family. You're the closest thing to a father I've ever had. I didn't know they made people like you. How can I ever repay you?"

"You can repay me by not being afraid of who you are, what you are, and what you stand for. You're living proof that money is just paper but that words are priceless and have the power to change the world. So, embrace yourself and give yourself an ounce of credit because you've made the impossible possible. Everyone can see it. Everyone can feel it, but you."

Flashes of my past ran through my head. Lauren, my old office, my house, my cars, and there is an image of Josie, so beautiful. Her hair is down, and she is giggling. "I've been Poet for almost five months, Rev. I was beginning to forget."

"Poet, your story is who you are. Now go back to Sarah and tell her the good news. I'll leave the side door unlocked for you at 9 pm. The basement's yours till 7 am every day."

When I get to the alley, Sarah is sitting with her back against the wall, wrapped in blankets. She is very thin.

"You and the rev were kicking it."

I grab a blanket, sit down next to her, and snuggle close to give her some body heat. "I've got something serious to tell you."

"Are you alright, Poet? Are we okay?"

I smile and say, "We're great."

"We're great?"

"Yeah, never better."

"Poet, don't fuck with me. I'm too cold."

"We're gonna be warm very soon. The reverend's made arrangements and said we can stay in the church basement! Sarah, there's a cot, a shower, and soap, and he's going to leave us food every night!"

"Don't you dare fuck with me like that! That's not cool."

"Sarah, I swear to God: We're out of this alley in four hours. We get to shower and sleep in a bed in a heated room! He says we can stay there every night until spring. We just have to be out by 7 am."

She hugs me. "This must be what it feels like to win the lottery. A bed! Oh my God, Poet, you might get laid." She grabs my face and kisses me.

That night, we enter the basement of the church and find a small room with a light on. There are two big wool blankets, a little shower in the corner, white sheets on the bed, a pillow, towels, and a brown bag with four sandwiches: two turkey and two tuna fish. There's a note that says, "Sarah, I made the tuna just for you. Not too much mayo, of course. Hope you like it. Sleep well kids—Rev."

The room is half the size of my old walk-in closet, but I feel like I'm at the Plaza and this is our honeymoon suite. I take my first warm shower in over a week, and it's magnificent. I shave my beard, brush my teeth, and put on my last set of clean clothes. I feel like a human.

Sarah hops in the shower, shaves, combs her hair, and puts on her dark red lipstick. She throws on her vintage Rolling Stones T-shirt and the old raggedy jeans she keeps in my duffel bag. Being with her every day, I sometimes forget how beautiful she truly is. Now I stare at her, transfixed. I can hardly believe this is the woman I love and the woman who loves me.

CHAPTER
THIRTY-SEVEN

We are lying silently with smiles on our faces. It is midnight. I kiss Sarah's forehead and tell her I love her. I'm caressing her stomach with my fingertips, and I'm wondering if now is the right time to talk to her about getting clean. My head is spinning. I am afraid because I know how sensitive she is about her addiction, and how ashamed.

"Sarah, I want to talk to you about something."

"Anything."

"I want to know where you get your drugs."

There's a pause. "No, you don't."

I prop myself up on an elbow so I can see her face. "I do. I love you, and I've been worried about you constantly for months. I feel like I need to know."

"Why?"

"I should know where you are in case there's an emergency. Or if you don't come home someday, God forbid. It would make me feel better to know where you are. I would sleep better."

"We're in a nice warm bed. You'll sleep fine."

"Please now," I say emphatically. "I want to know."

Her anger flares in response to my insistence. "Fuck you. I don't even know your real name!"

"You've never really asked."

"Well, I'm asking now. I want to know the name of the most impor-tant person in my life. I'm in love with Poet, so who the fuck are you? What are you hiding from? I'll tell you where I get my drugs if you tell me your real name, where you're from, everything! I know about Josie, but I want to know it all. I want to know about your parents, your ex-wife, your fucking dog, your goldfish—everything! I want the truth! You tell me your secret, and I'll tell you mine."

"If we do that that, will you think about going into rehab?"

"That, I cannot do," she says quickly.

"Why?"

"I'm not ready."

"Well, when do you think you might be ready?"

"I don't know, but not now."

There's a moment of silence, and she looks at me and says, "If I tell you what you think you want to know, you might not love me anymore. Are you willing to take that chance?"

"Sarah, no matter what you tell me, I will not love you any less. I know this is true. I promise."

"You've been warned."

"Okay."

"Two years ago, I was at a club in the meatpacking district. It was filled with models and celebrities. I had just started using. Toward the end of the night, a celebrity, a very famous actor, approached me. Let's just say everyone wanted to fuck this guy. He came up to me and said, 'Why don't you come back to my place. We'll hang out and get high!'

"I said to myself, 'Free dope, why not?' So, I go back this guy's townhouse in the West Village, and we shoot up, and then he starts to rub my leg and gets touchy feely.

"I get up and say, 'No, no, no. Hands off.' This deflates his huge ego.

"He says, 'What the fuck! Every woman in America wants to put their hands on me. Who the fuck are you! You're just a face. You're useless, talentless.'

"I say, 'Go jerk off to a picture of yourself, you fucking tool!' and head for the door.

"He says, 'Come back here when you're broke and need a fix, then you can suck my famous dick!'

"A year later, everything had fallen apart for me. My habit had taken over my life. I had lost everything, was absolutely broken, about to be evicted, and had no friends left, nobody to turn to. I called him. He knew exactly who I was. I went to his place, gave him a blowjob, shot dope, and every week for the past year, I have done that: traded a blowjob for a week's worth of dope and a clean needle. So that's my story, Poet. That's the fucking secret you were so anxious to know."

I am shocked. Sarah begins to cry. "And every day for the past year, I wake up and think, 'Today's the last day.' And it's been over a year. I'm tired! And I'm scared! And I'm sick of living like this!"

My heart is ripped apart. I hug her and tell her it's going to be all right. We're going to figure it out together. I stroke her head as she sobs.

"Do you still love me?"

"Of course, I love you. This doesn't change anything. It took so much courage for you to share that. I love you even more. I swear."

"You sure?"

"Yes, Sarah. I'm sure. Just let me help you. We can fix this. This problem can be solved. I'll do anything in my power to change this. Just give me a chance."

"I'm not ready."

"Okay, whenever you're ready, I'm ready."

She kisses my cheek and says, "Okay."

We lie silently for a while in the dark, and I hold her tight. Then she sits up, turns on the light, takes my hand, and softly asks, "What's your name?"

"Sarah, my name is Evan Bloom. I'm Evan Bloom."

She moves her face in close to mine and whispers, "Evan Bloom."

She says it again, "Evan Bloom."

And again, "Evan Bloom."

She laughs, "It's such a cool name. It's what God would say to a flower. Evan, bloom! It fits you. It's beautiful. So, who is Evan Bloom?"

I feel very uneasy.

"Sarah, what I'm about to tell you has to stay just between us, okay?"

"I swear."

So, I tell her everything, all of it. I open myself up to her in a way I've never done with anyone, ever. It all comes out: childhood, parents, money, isolation, drugs, success, secret love of writing, Josie joy, bad marriage, misery, self-hatred, inspiration, my vow to write and become a poet, the great escape, meeting her, renaming myself, confessions with the reverend and how I told him my name and identity—the whole improbable story, step by step, everything, talking on an on for an hour, right up to my recent huge realization that the destiny I am seeking isn't just to write, to be a writer, but also to be with her.

"I was put here for you. I've come here for you! And you have changed everything. You have given me the love and support I needed. You've made me a better man, you've given me confidence I didn't know I had, and you've taught me more about myself than anyone else ever has. I am still here because of you, and I never want to leave you. And I know in my soul that we are going to escape this life together soon. I don't know how, but I know that we will. So... that's who I was, and that's who I am."

I curl myself around her, and we snuggle together, wrapped in silence for a while.

"Can I be your muse?"

"You already are."

CHAPTER
THIRTY-EIGHT

Four days before Christmas, the city is lit up like a palace. Green and red lights are beaming from every building, department store window displays attracting tourists. Salvation Army Santas ring bells for donations. The smell of Christmas trees lingers in the air. Sarah and I take long walks, holding hands, pretending to be normal. I study the happy families out in the cold, enjoying themselves, wearing long winter jackets, scarves, earmuffs, smiles. I look at Sarah and imagine Josie between us, holding both of our hands, and us swinging her. Me and my girls, laughing, smiling, taking in a Broadway show, eating a great meal. What would be better? But it's just a dream, a Christmas wish.

Trading our stories has brought Sarah and me even closer together. We spend every moment together, except when she is off on her mission, and it kills me to know what she has to do to get her dope. I imagine myself following her to that guy's apartment and fucking him up. I even fantasize about killing him. But what would that get us? I'd be in prison, and Sarah would still be an addict, but with no way to deal with her habit. I keep my mouth shut, but on the inside, I am screaming.

The next day, we decide to take a holiday from panhandling and just enjoy the city. We have $18. We go down Bleecker Street for the best slice of pizza in the city, at Joe's Pizzeria, and we each get a cup of high-end coffee from a café, then spend the evening at the reverend's apartment. He'd invited us for dinner. He lives in Stuyvesant Town, now a kind of a hotspot, which is all the way on the other side of the island, by FDR Drive and the East River. He's been there for thirty-five years. Tishman Speyer Properties bought all the Stuyvesant Town apartment buildings for $4.2 billion, supposedly the largest real estate deal ever. They turned all those old, rent-controlled apartments into cool, modern yuppie pads, and a lot of professionals moved in. It's strange: You see older people and families mixed with young go-getters in their twenties.

There's a nice park there, and you sort of feel like you're outside the city because of all the trees and grass. The only problem is it's a bitch to get to the subway. The reverend has a rent-controlled apartment that's decorated in a very antique-ish sort of way. He has thousands of old books, cool knickknacks, and signed pictures of him with various dignitaries; it's like a museum of the past fifty years. The reverend loves board games, so we play Scrabble. I win, by a lot. Donna makes lasagna, and Sarah eats a serving big enough for four. It's the best meal we've had in six months. I forgot how good Italian food is. Donna also serves us a homemade chocolate mousse, and it's fucking amazing. Words can't express how incredible chocolate tastes when you haven't had it for months.

We get back from the rev's and turn on the lights in our room, and Sarah seems strange. Distant.

"Are you okay?"

She says she's fine, but I can tell something is on her mind.

"Do you wanna talk about it?"

With a strange stare, she says, "I'm fine, Evan. I'm really fine. Maybe it's something I ate."

"That was five-star lasagna."

Instead of going on some hilarious rant, she says, "Yeah, it was good. I'm gonna take a walk."

"Now?"

"Yeah, I need some alone time."

"Okay."

CHAPTER
THIRTY-NINE

No, Sarah! It is midnight! I don't know what to do! The thoughts rolling through my mind are scaring me. Rape, murder, suicide. This is New York City. Anything's possible.

Sarah got high for the fourth and final time earlier tonight, right before we went to the reverend's. She looked funny before she left. Staring off into space, I can see her wheels turning. Self-awareness is the first step toward change. Maybe she's ready to get clean. Maybe that's what it is. I pray.

No, Sarah! It is now 2 am! I have searched the park. I run to the payphone on West 4th Street, and I'm having trouble catching my breath. I call the reverend and wake him up.

"Hello."

"Rev, it's Poet!"

"What's wrong?"

"Sarah's missing!"

"When was the last time you saw her?"

"Four hours ago!"

"Come over. We'll call precincts and hospitals."

"I'll be right there. Start making calls, Rev."

"I'm on it."

I sprint through the park, run down 1st Avenue, and hang a right on 14th Street.

Sweating in the cold, I get to the reverend's building, and he buzzes me in, I hop in the elevator, he opens the door, and he looks up at me concerned.

"My wife's been calling hospitals. I've been calling precincts. No sign of her yet."

"I need a Bible passage."

"Psalm 46:1: God is our refuge and strength, a very present help in trouble."

"Rev, I knew something was gonna happen tonight. I felt it. Sarah was acting weird. She went for a walk without me. Before we came here for dinner, she used, and that was the fourth time today. You know, Sarah only gets high four times a day. After dinner, she looked like she had seen a ghost. Something was on her mind; it was heavier than usual."

The rev asks, "Donna, did you call Mount Sinai?"

"Frank, just got off the phone with them. No Sarah!"

"Alright, Ev. Let's call precincts."

I can tell the rev has a bad feeling. He keeps sitting down then standing up. When I'm nervous, my body shuts down. It is strange. I become numb, and I feel like I'm going to pass out. On the way to my parent's funeral, I fell asleep in the limo. I am struggling to keep my eyes open. I am holding on to the arm of the sofa to keep myself upright like I'm on a rollercoaster. I have lost the capacity to speak. Sarah better be okay.

The rev calls every precinct around the West Village. No Sarah! Now the rev is pacing around the apartment, which is making me very nervous. I am scared.

"Evan, get ahold of yourself. I need you to do something."

I stutter and ask, "What?"

"Go on the computer and look up the numbers of precincts in the East Village and write them down."

I struggle to get up and hop on the reverend's desktop Dell computer. He still has dial-up. I Google police precincts around the

East Village and write them down. I hand the sheet of loose-leaf paper back to the rev. Mrs. Emerson is still calling hospitals in the bedroom.

The reverend calls on his cell phone. "Hello, this is Reverend Frank Emerson. Was a young girl named Sarah Jones brought in tonight? No. Thank you."

Another call. "Hello, this is Reverend Frank Emerson. Was a young girl named Sarah Jones brought in tonight? No. Thank you."

He calls another. And another. And another. And another. My heart is in my throat. I can't swallow. I get up to grab a glass of water, and my hand trembles as I pick up it up. My knees are knocking.

"Hello. This is Reverend Frank Emerson. Was a young girl named Sarah Jones brought in tonight? She was? Really! Thank God! Oh. Thank God! Praise Jesus! Is she okay? Yes! Where is she? She's in a holding cell. She was arrested? What's the charge? Possession. We'll be right down."

CHAPTER
FORTY

The rev and I grab a cab. The drive from Stuyvesant Town to the 9th Precinct is five minutes. It's 3 am; there are no cars on the road. I still can't talk. I'm relieved she's in a precinct and not a hospital, but this is my worst nightmare. Now Sarah's addiction is very real. She is what she has been telling me she is: an addict. A beautiful, brilliant girl with an addiction.

But I realize this is a sign. This is God telling Sarah that it is time to stop. Now I hope she's ready to take the next step—to live the life she was meant to live. Everything gets worse before it gets better. This arrest will be her moment of clarity. It is a blessing. I can feel it.

The rev and I get out of the cab. The 9th Precinct is an old-looking building with modern amenities. I feel like Detective Andy Sipowicz from *NYPD Blue* is about to walk out the huge steel double doors. I am still a wreck, but now full of nervous energy. I can see the rev is thinking about how we are gonna play this. We have not spoken since we left his apartment. He stops me in front of the precinct and asks, "You okay, Poet?"

"I'm alright."

"You have to be strong in there. Who knows what Sarah has been through tonight. She must be terrified and ashamed. She will feel like she let us down. You have to be supportive. Smiles. Words of encouragement. Positivity. Keep telling her it's gonna be okay. Because it will be. It always is. We'll figure it out. Stay next to me. Let me do the talking."

We walk into the precinct, and it is a lot more modern than I expected. It sort of looks like a Verizon store, but not as trendy. The rev walks over to the officer at the front desk, and I follow behind. The reverend says to the female officer, "I am looking for a young girl named Sarah Jones. I was told she was brought in tonight."

The female officer looks at her computer. "Sarah Jones, yes."

"Can we see her?"

"She's in a holding cell. You'll have to wait till morning."

"Ms., what's your name?"

"I am Officer Hayley."

"Officer Hayley, my name is Reverend Frank Emerson. I have been the reverend at Judson Memorial Church for forty-seven years. The girl you picked up is homeless and has nowhere to go. I care for her. Do me a favor: Let me and this young man have five minutes with her. I just want to make sure she's okay. It can't wait till morning.

"Reverend Frank, I know who you are. My son's gay and attends artists night all the time. He met his boyfriend in your church. You're a saint. I'll see what I can do. Give me five minutes."

"Thank you."

"Jesus Christ. You might as well be Mayor Bloomberg," I say to the rev.

The officer comes back to the desk. "Okay. I got you five minutes, Reverend. She's through those glass doors, first room on the right."

We walk slowly. The reverend stops me in front of the door. "Remember: positivity. A lot of 'it's okays.' Big hug when you get in there. Be strong now. She needs you."

"Okay."

The reverend opens the door and walks in first. Sarah is not smiling. She's slumped down in her chair with her hands clasped behind her head. She gets up, gives the reverend a big hug, and digs her head into his right shoulder. He massages the back of her neck. She's crying. As I walk in, she becomes hysterical and screams, "I'm so sorry."

I hug her tightly as her tears splash on my cheeks.

"I'm so sorry! I'm so sorry! Don't hate me."

"I don't hate you. I love you. It's okay. It'll be fine."

I massage the top of her head.

The reverend says, "Sarah, it's fine. As long as you're okay. Are you okay?"

"I'm okay. I'm fine. As long as you two don't hate me."

"We love you."

All three of us sit down.

"Tell us what happened."

In an exhausted, stressed out, crackly voice, Sarah says, "I just didn't feel right after dinner. At the church, I was having flashbacks and hallucinations: my parents, modeling, getting evicted, being homeless and alone. All of it. I needed a hit. You both know I only shoot up four times a day. This is the first time ever I snuck away for a fifth. Poet, the other day while you were at the church with the rev, I sold a pair of sneakers and an old Led Zeppelin T-shirt to the vintage store on 6th Avenue for some extra cash. That gave me the 60 bucks for the heroin. I always get high at Tompkins Square Park. I walked around the park looking for a dealer, waiting for someone to call me over. Finally, a beefy guy singles me out. I walk over, roll up the 60 bucks in my hand, and place it in my palm. I shake his hand, we make the exchange, then he kicks me in my left shin. Hard! He pins me down on the pavement! Then he stands me up, throws me against the brick wall, and says, "Drop the bag! You're under arrest. He cuffs me tight and recites my Miranda rights. I was caught in between tears, shock, and rage. I was so confused. Everything ran through my mind in an instant: Evan, the poetry table, the alley, tuna with you, Rev. My whole life. Over! The undercover cop called an unidentified cop car that rolled up at lightning speed. Before I could breathe, I was in a cell in tears, body sore from the pavement. They told me heroin possession is a class D felony, Poet. Ten years in prison!"

Sarah is in hysterics.

"I'm looking at time, Poet. I'm going away! I'm gonna have to leave you. I'm going to prison. I'm a homeless junkie, a felon! An addict. Nothing more! Nothing more!"

I rise out of my chair fast. Sarah's head is down on the table. She is wailing. I somehow keep my cool. "It's gonna be fine. We're gonna figure it out. Everything happens for a reason. This is our reality check. Now, we start over. You start over. It all starts with you. You went looking for that fifth fix for a reason. You wanted to get caught. This is a blessing."

The reverend takes our hands and kisses them, then he puts his hand on top of mine. He simply says, "I'll be right back."

Five minutes later, the rev bursts through the door. A yellow light is hovering above him. I can see his aura. I know he has worked his magic.

"Listen, kids, I have news. Sarah, you are staying here for the night. Poet, back to my apartment for some sleep. I woke up Captain Flanagan and explained Sarah's situation. God's on our side. He runs this precinct. I have a meeting with him first thing in the morning. He is an old, dear friend of mine, and he attends services every Sunday. I asked him for a favor that he couldn't refuse. Sarah, I asked him to let you go if you agree to go to the methadone clinic on 14th Street for inpatient rehabilitation. I will monitor your attendance and will report back to him on your status. But I will only do this, Sarah, if you promise that you will stay there for ten days, go to meetings, take the methadone, and fully comply. Sarah, my reputation is on the line. You cannot let me down. Do it for me, do it for Poet, but most importantly, do it for yourself. Now is the time. The rest of your life starts tomorrow."

"Rev, you're a miracle worker. Sarah, what do you think?"

She tears up again. "I think I'm scared. What if I don't follow through? Maybe this is who I am. Maybe this is what I'm meant to be: a homeless junkie! Reverend, I don't want to do this to you. I don't want to hurt you. I don't want to let you down! Poet, you don't deserve this. You don't need this! You have enough to worry about. Maybe you are better off without me!"

I jump out of my chair and shout, "Not another word from you! I am nothing without you! Without you, I'm just Evan Bloom. A miserable millionaire! Gutless! Soulless! A walking corpse! You are me.

When you hurt, I hurt. When you're sick, I'm sick. You're not a junkie! You're sick! If you're sick, we're all sick! We're a family! We support each other. We love one another. Sarah, this is nothing. I have never been so sure of anything in my life because deep down inside you don't want to get high anymore. You don't need it! You have us. Love is all you need."

CHAPTER
FORTY-ONE

Sarah is already dressed and has a smile on her face. Her bags are packed by the door. She looks excited, like she is going on vacation, like the methadone clinic is a cruise ship. She looks relieved, stress free. It is bizarre. I stare. She already looks clean.

As I hop out of bed, she leaps on me, crosses her feet behind me, and hangs off me with her fingers interlocked behind my neck, kissing me.

"It's a brand-new day, Poet."

"You do realize that in about eight hours, you're going to kick heroin's fucking ass!"

"Bring it on! Pain's gonna be my new high. I'm making heroin my bitch!"

The whole walk down to the clinic, Sarah does not stop talking. It's pure nervous energy, and I just listen. I am even more nervous than she is. I know that she's up against a harsh reality. I've seen documentaries, and they're not pretty. I'm sure the clinic we are heading to on 14th Street is not a luxury resort.

We get there at 7:30, but the place doesn't open till 8. I put down my duffel bag, and we settle on the steps.

Sarah has finally gone silent. She has her red hoody pulled up over her head.

I rub her back. "You okay?"

"I'm really scared, Evan." She looks out at me from underneath the hood. "I can do this, right?"

Calmly I say, "Sarah, I truly believe there's nothing you can't do. You're afraid of yourself, not heroin. Heroin's just something to blame yourself on. You're better than heroin. I'll be here for you, but you need to want it, Sarah. You have to do it yourself. I know you can. I have complete faith in you."

Like she always does after I say something that she knows comes from the heart, she puts her right hand on top of my left hand and rests it there. We don't say any more. There's nothing left to say. I feel her hand tremble. It's the longest twenty minutes of my life.

One of the two big doors opens, and a heavy Black woman in a long black skirt and black Rockport sneakers peeks out. She looks mean. Sarah and I go in and follow her to the front desk, which is surrounded by bulletproof windows.

Sarah's tongue-tied and looks at me.

"Good morning," I say. "My girlfriend would like to be admitted for treatment."

"Well, honey, she has to admit herself."

I turn to Sarah.

Sarah is frozen.

"Sarah, speak to the lady."

She snaps out of her daze. "Okay."

The woman asks Sarah a zillion questions and then gives her a batch of forms to fill out. We sit in the waiting area. There is no one else there yet.

Sarah looks at me. "I hate filling this shit out."

"So do I, but it's necessary. The first step. I told you this would be hard!"

When Sarah hands the clipboard back, the formidable looking but actually nice woman smiles and passes it on to another woman behind the barricaded front desk. My right leg is shaking. This place really makes me nervous. The walls are bland pink, cream, blue, off-white, and it smells like formaldehyde. It's dreary. I hold Sarah's left hand and try to project calm, but I am freaking out. We wait twenty minutes with very few words spoken. I rub Sarah's thigh to comfort her, but she seems more comfortable than I am.

"Evan, stop fucking rubbing me. You're making me nervous. I'm checking in, not you."

I give her a fake smile. Finally, we are called in.

We follow a woman who's about my age into a room. She sits behind an old metal desk that looks like it could have once been a teacher's desk in the '80s, and she invites us to take a seat.

"Hello, Sarah. Welcome to the West Village Clinic. We're happy to have you here, and I applaud you for taking the first step toward recovery. It's a big step; you're very brave."

Sarah nods her head with a catatonic smile.

"And who are you?"

"My name's Evan Bloom. I'm Sarah's companion."

"Boyfriend?"

"Yeah, something like that."

"Sarah, do you consent to Evan being here?"

"I wouldn't be here if he wasn't here."

I grin at her.

"Sarah, I have some questions I need to ask you before we take you in to get your vitals."

"Okay."

The woman looks at her file.

"So, you're twenty-four."

"Yes."

"Originally from Iowa?"

"Yes."

"Are your parents deceased?"

"I don't know."

"Would you like me to contact them?"

"No."

"Do you have a permanent residence?"

"Not at the moment. Evan and I live in the basement of a church."

"Which one?"

"If I told you that I'd have to kill ya."

The woman smiles.

"How long have you been using?"

"About two years."

"How many times do you use a day?"

"Four. Same times every day."

"And what times are those?"

"Every three hours. 11, 2, 5, and 8."

"This is a positive. Sporadic use is harder to control. It should be easier for you to break a consistent habit, instead of a habit that's completely out of your control. Here we might be able to tinker with time, reset your watch. This is a good thing."

I give Sarah a promising look.

"Do you take heroin intravenously?"

"I do."

"Do you share needles?"

"No. I do it alone, by myself with a fresh needle every time."

"You take heroin by yourself?"

"Yes, I like to be alone. I don't enjoy the company of other people when I'm getting high."

"How much heroin would you say you do a day?"

"I do the same amount every day. About a gram."

I can't help myself and ask, "Is that a lot?"

"It's a significant amount. How long have you been homeless, Sarah?"

"Six months."

The woman asks at least twenty more questions and tells Sarah what's ahead: She will have a psychological evaluation and a physical, and then treatment will begin. Every day she will be given a dose of methadone, at a different time of the day. The dose of methadone will be about the equivalent to the amount of heroin she injects a day. Every day Sarah will take part in group therapy and art therapy. Her diet will be observed, vitals will be taken regularly, and there will be medical staff on hand twenty-four hours a day. This woman seems genuine, and I can feel that she truly cares.

When Sarah goes to use the bathroom, I say, "That girl right there, she's the world to me. She's a very special person. Please, please help her."

The woman looks me in the eye and smiles. "I can tell how you feel about each other. I promise you we will take special care of her."

I mouth, "Thank you" as Sarah returns. She looks to be in good spirits, a smile on her face, walking tall. She outwardly does not seem nervous anymore.

I ask, "How much does the treatment cost?"

"$200. Then social services will pick up the rest."

"Evan, we don't have $200."

I reach into my duffel bag and remove $200 from the $350 that remains in the envelope.

"Jesus Christ, Poet. Where did you get that?"

"Been saving it for an emergency. This is an emergency. This is what it's for."

"My God, all those nights we went to bed hungry. We could've been full."

"Yes, and we wouldn't be able to get you in here right now. This will be the best $200 we ever spent. Don't waste it."

Sarah nods her head. "I won't."

She gets up to use the bathroom again. Apparently, she *is* nervous.

While she's gone, the woman leaves her chair and raises a brow at me. "Homeless and hungry, and you held onto enough money to help your girlfriend? That's impressive."

"She saved my life. I'd give anything."

Sarah walks back in, takes a seat, and asks, "This is a ten-day program?"

"Ten days of residency initially, but the whole program is six months. We use a tapering system. Every thirty days, you receive less methadone than the previous thirty days. This makes the transition smoother and helps you stay opiate free."

"So, ten days from now we'll start coming here every day for Sarah to get methadone?"

"Yes, every day, Sarah, it will be your responsibility to come here and receive your dose. We will be keeping track of your maintenance. Evan, this might be your most important role, escorting her here every day so she can take her dose."

"It will be my pleasure."

"During the first ten days, can he visit me?"

"I'm afraid not."

Sarah is a little upset. "Can he at least come to the therapy sessions? I'd like him to be here with me."

"I know you would. But it's in your best interest to be isolated for ten days. It's what's best for you, sweetie. You have to trust me on this. This program works."

I try to be helpful. "Is it okay if I come by every day to at least get an update? You could give me an update, right?"

"I'll do everything I can do for you, Evan. Just come by, and I'll let you know how she's progressing. But you won't be able to see her. Okay, it's time to get you inside, Sarah, and get started."

I grab Sarah's hand, and I grip it tight.

"This is it. Time to be a champion. Be my warrior."

Sarah tries not to smile but does.

She leans her head forward and touches her nose to mine.

I whisper, "I love you," and she whispers, "I love you back," and turns and follows the administrator through the door that leads inside.

At the last second, she looks back, flashes the big Sarah smile, and says, "Behave yourself. Write some fucking poetry."

And she's gone.

CHAPTER
FORTY-TWO

I wake up smiling, shower, get dressed, and make my way outside. It's a beautiful January day, a little dreary, but warmer than usual. At the top of the church steps, I take a big stretch and throw my arms in the air like Rocky Balboa. I've been counting the days, and this is the one I've been looking forward to. Sarah is reemerging into the world. I am so excited. It's been a struggle. Some people like to be alone, and I have always been one of them, but I've missed Sarah. Life without her is depressing.

When the clinic opens, I'm the first person in a line that doesn't exist. I am very nervous, very excited, and very thankful. The doors swing open, and the nice lady we had first dealt with, who I now know is Bernice, welcomes me in.

We chat a bit about the unusually warm weather, and then I ask about Sarah, and she says, "Oh my, that one is an entertainer."

"An entertainer?"

"Baby, she had everybody rolling. Her humor lifts everyone's spirits. She never complained about anything. She's happy to be here. When I see her upstairs, she'll ask me about my day, talks about what's going on. She's totally engaged with everyone. It's almost like she works here, one of the staff, not a patient. Every day I bring her up your candy bars or one of your poems, and she'll light up. She'll read your poem to everyone and share the candy. What a sweet person."

This is music to my ears.

"What time do they usually let patients out?"

"Usually around 10 o'clock. Why don't you go and get yourself a cup of coffee and come back in an hour or so. Or you can just wait here and talk to me. It's your choice, sweetie."

"How about I grab us both a cup of coffee. How do you take yours?"

"That's very nice of you, sugar. You don't have to buy me coffee."

"I want to."

"In that case cream, two Sweet'N Lows."

"I'll be right back."

We chat over our coffees for a while, and then I sit and wait. I don't have the patience to read a magazine. I watch the clock on the wall until finally, it's 10 am. I look down the hallway to see Sarah coming toward me with her usual swagger. She hasn't seen me yet. She looks amazing. Well rested, her skin is less pale, a deeper shade. She's put on a little weight, and her hair is perfectly combed and banded up in a ponytail. She is in her trademark outfit, but she has a glow about her and looks relaxed. She's smiling, and not your average Sarah smile. It looks like she earned it, and she knows it.

They take her into the same office where she was initially evaluated.

Bernice says, "Let me see if you can go in."

I wait.

She comes back and says, "They'll be ready for you in two minutes. Sarah's just filling out some paperwork and going over post-treatment plans."

"Okay."

Five minutes later, the administrator comes and gets me.

We start walking toward the office, and I ask, "On a scale of one to ten, how did she do?"

"She was an eleven."

I walk into the room, and there she is. She jumps up, grabs my hands, pulls me in, and hugs me tight. She kisses my right cheek, and I feel her tears. I take my thumb and wipe them, and she gives me her wise-ass smirk.

"So, how many girls did you sleep with while I was gone? Two or twenty."

"More, Sarah. I live in the basement of a church. Women can't resist that. I cheat on you, then I confess. Never happened."

She smiles. "Sobriety's made me horny. We're having a ton of sex tonight. I hope you weren't jerking off in the house of God."

"No, that's what the Starbucks bathroom is for."

She smiles, and then we both realize that the administrator has been standing there the whole time. I am a bit embarrassed by our stupid banter.

But the administrator gets it. "Grande or venti?"

We all crack up.

Sarah says, "More like a tall."

The administrator laughs "Have a seat, you two. We have some quick things to discuss. Evan, I need you to listen here: Two heads are better than one."

"You have my full attention."

"Sarah has had no noticeable physical or mental complications. We gave her 300 milligrams of methadone at a different time every day to break the pattern of use. She would get a bit antsy at times, but that's completely normal. She slept well. She slept a lot—on average nine hours a night, which is great considering I know she's a light sleeper. So now, she's well rested. She was regulated by a physician: All her vitals are good. She had an HIV test, and it came back negative.

"Thank God," I say.

"She met with a therapist every day, and the feedback from the therapist was very positive. She's in a positive mental state. She has no severe trauma nor hallucinations. Sarah also participated in group therapy, and this is where she really shined. Sarah's warmth, humor, and compassion made group fun. Usually patients hate group, but Sarah would entertain them—tell a story, read your poetry, but most importantly, she took the time outside of group to listen and help everyone. Sarah helped a lot of people in here. I have never said that about a patient before. Sarah, in my professional opinion, you should be a therapist or social worker one day. The world needs more of you."

I take Sarah's right hand and squeeze it. I am so proud.

"So, here are the next steps. Every week, you will be given a schedule with the day of the week and time for you to come and take your methadone. We follow the schedule religiously. For the next twenty days, you will receive 300 milligrams. The next thirty days, you will receive 250 milligrams. Every month over the course of the next six months, you will receive 50 milligrams less than the previous month. This is the tapering system, the most effective way to clean up. I know six months is a long time, but if you follow the schedule exactly, your success rate increases by 500 percent. How's that sound?"

"Sounds good," Sarah says.

"Evan, you can be instrumental in this process. Remind her, watch the clock, do whatever it takes to help her come in every day and stay on the program."

"I'm on it. Walking here together will be our exercise. It will help us get in shape."

Sarah feigns outrage. "You think I need to be on a diet?"

"Sweetheart, I think you need a donut."

The administrator chuckles. "Good call. Now I know we'll be seeing a lot more of the both of you, which is great. Sarah, every Tuesday night there's a meeting I'd like you to attend. Evan, you're welcome too. Both of you can really help us out. You are proof that even under extreme circumstances, you can still be positive and do great things. Will you join us?"

I look at Sarah, who nods.

"Great," she says and hands Sarah her schedule.

"So, we'll see you tomorrow at 11 am."

"Tomorrow at 11."

Sarah hugs the administrator warmly. "I haven't gotten the chance to fully thank you and your staff for giving me a second chance on life. I'm so grateful for everything you have done for me and for Evan. Really, thank you."

"You've saved two lives here," I add. "I don't know where I'd be without Sarah. One day, when we're in a better position in life, we'll give back. Thank you."

"You two are sweet. Now go out and enjoy the day and each other. Sarah, you earned it. You're on your way."

Sarah and I exit the clinic's doors and fall into a huge, long hug in the clear clean air. I feel like she has won an Academy Award. I am bursting with pride and relief.

Holding her tight I say, "I was lost without you. I didn't know where to go, what to do. I was clueless. I was worried sick. And now I find out that not only did you ace the program yourself, but you helped everyone else too. Are you sure you're not Mother Theresa?"

"Well, she wasn't a junkie. But I felt for everybody in there. I am them, with one difference. I have someone who loves me, who cares about me. I have a place to go, someone to confide in. Some of them have no one, so I was able to shine some light and give them hope and tell them it can turn out alright and that miracles do come along. And it made me feel good to make them laugh. It's how I rehabilitated. Let's eat."

I kiss her with every emotion I could possibly feel all at once.

"So, Poet, what the fuck do you want to do today?"

"I have some ideas."

"Let's hear 'em."

"Well, we have $120 left. I thought we could get you a haircut and a massage."

"Fuck that!"

She pokes my chest with her finger, emphasizing every word, and says, "I don't feel like being primped like a poodle. Let's have some fucking fun!"

"Like?"

"I don't know. Let's do something we both can enjoy that will make us feel good. But sex is not an option. Not yet."

"Okay. A movie? With an extra-large popcorn and two large sodas."

"That's a first date. Too ordinary. Something cooler."

"Such as…"

"I'm not sure."

She pauses. "Oh wait, I got it!"

"Okay!"

"I got it! It just came to me. We have $120, right?"

"Yes."

"And we should spend it all, right?"

"Down to the last ducat."

"How much is a ticket at Irving Plaza?"

"Depends on who's playing. Maybe 40 bucks."

"Beautiful." She pauses, then says, "Let's get two tickets for tonight's show, and I don't care who's playing, we're going. So that's like 80 or 90 bucks. Then, we'll take the rest of the money down to Magnolia Bakery and spend it all on those kickass cupcakes. We'll buy like thirty, eat as many as we can, and whatever we can't finish, we hand out to our homeless brothers and sisters in the park. A concert and a cupcake for everyone. How's that sound?"

"Like the best fucking idea I've ever heard in my life."

CHAPTER
FORTY-THREE

We make our way to Irving Plaza. In my younger days, I saw a lot of music there, by people who were on their way to becoming huge, like Blues Traveler and the Dave Matthews Band. It's a great venue. It probably holds around 1,500 people. The first floor is rickety, warped wood and gets really packed; there's a small stage and a huge bar in the back. The balcony is very narrow and has a smaller bar. Back in the day, I used to smoke weed on the side of the balcony, and maybe I'd be tripping on acid or mushrooms. I heard some amazing music there.

Now Sarah is strutting down the street like a kid in a candy store—like she owns the world. She looks extraordinarily beautiful and, of course, is getting looks. I am pumped to see live music. After I got married, this part of my life disappeared. Lauren wouldn't be caught dead in a place like Irving Plaza. She might occasionally see a Broadway show or the ballet because those things are expensive. And when she did go, she'd barely pay attention.

Sarah turns to me and says, "I hope it's going to be some hardcore punk band. I want to throw you in a mosh pit."

When we arrive, it's around 11, and the box office has just opened.

Sarah sticks her head into the box office window and asks the guy, "What you got going on tonight?"

"Pretty Lights at 10."

I pop my head in beside hers, "Who's Pretty Lights?"

"It's EDM, electronic dance music. The place will be jumping."

"Jumping, like in dancing?"

"Like insane dancing. If you've never heard EDM, try it. You'll like it. We're talking wall-to-wall nonstop dancing, glow sticks, kids on ecstasy, chugging water. It's gonna be a sweat fest."

Sarah turns to me excited and says, "That's exactly what we're looking for, a sweat fest!"

I had been thinking more in terms of rock 'n roll, but what the hell. It's a new day, so why not a new kind of night.

"How much are the tickets?"

"$40."

Sarah turns to me. "Perfect."

I ask, "What time does Pretty Lights go on?"

"Around 10:30."

Sarah says, "So, we'll be sweating at 10:31?"

"Guaranteed, or your money back."

"I'll hold you to that. Two for the sweat fest, please."

"Eighty bucks."

I reach into my pocket, grab my wad, and roll off four twenties for him.

"Is it gonna sell out?"

"Within the hour."

Sarah pumps her fists and says, "Extra sweaty!"

I thank the guy, and Sarah and I head toward Magnolia Bakery.

Sarah turns to me and says, "You're dancing your fucking ass off tonight, and I don't mean any of that head-bobbing, awkward hip-shaking white boy dancing, I mean *dancing*. Please tell me you can dance, Poet."

"I can do the Watusi."

"Fuck no. Not tonight. We're going all the way. The tango or nothing."

CHAPTER
FORTY-FOUR

At the Magnolia Bakery, there's a line down the block. Ever since it was featured on *Sex in the City*, it's been a major food destination. It's like the whole world has lined up to buy a cupcake.

There's a French couple in front of me. An Irish family behind me. There are people from Japan, Korea, and some maybe from Serbia or Croatia. It's a scene. And we're in the middle part of the West Village, where the rich people live, mixed in with regular people who've lived here for eons. Beautiful six-story townhouses line the streets. Every passing dog is some odd purebred, and they're all beautiful and have had their fur coiffed. The West Village has always been my favorite part of the city. It has a neighborhood feel, almost communal, and old, and there's an unspoken camaraderie among those who live here. If I could live any place in the world, it would be here. It's a pretty good place even when you're homeless, but it would be awesome to live comfortably here with Sarah and Josie.

It's a little cold now, and I'm hugging Sarah with my arms from behind to keep her warm. We don't exactly have ski jackets. We're wearing layers with giant sweatshirts and on the outside beat-up jeans. She's wearing her favorite weird grey winter hat that has bunny ears, big eyes, and big eyelashes on it. It's unique and very her—fun and funny.

While we're waiting in line she says, "I haven't had a Magnolia cupcake in five years. I so wanted to be Carrie Bradshaw, and I came down here and waited in line for an hour for one of these overpriced, overrated things."

"So, if they're overpriced and overrated, why are we here?"

"Because they're still fucking delicious!"

"Overrated how?"

"The buildup. Remember how excited you were for each of the *Star Wars* prequels?"

"How did you know I like *Star Wars*?"

"Evan, you have a penis, and you write poetry. You like *Star Wars*."

"Hey, I'm offended."

"Relax. It's a beautiful story with lots of themes. It's right up a poet's alley. So, the *Star Wars* prequels sucked, right? Too much buildup, they couldn't live up to the hype. Same with the Magnolia cupcake. You see it on *Sex and the City*, and Carrie goes nuts, so you expect that when you take a bite of the red velvet one, you're going to have an orgasm. You finally take a bite, and no orgasm. But it's still fucking delicious."

We finally get inside. It's such a small bakery. Very quaint. To the right are trays and trays of cupcakes. In the center are four big cakes, and then on the left are even more cupcakes. The smell is rich, warm, and complex—a mix of chocolate frosting, fresh custard, a hint of lemon, and Febreze. If the cupcake is as good as the fragrance, an orgasm is not out of the question.

As we peer into the glass cases, Sarah is giddy. She is standing on her toes and clapping gently and quickly, like a kid, like she might explode. I slowly take it all in. I examine the baked masterpieces as if the shop is the Eighth Wonder of the World. What strange magic explains their power? There are too many choices. It's a cornucopia of delights.

Sarah turns to me, eyes wide. "I want them all. Ask them how much the store costs. Ask them."

I laugh. "If it's not more than $50, we're good."

"How many can we get? They're $3 each."

"We can get fifteen."

"Fifteen. Perfect! Which ones do you want?"

"Let's get the seven we want, and another seven can be a mixture for the people around the park. And I want to get the one called Heaven for the rev."

"The rev will love whatever we give him. But I see him loving peanut butter."

"Really? I see him loving chocolate peanut butter."

"What are you getting, Poet?"

"One red velvet. That's it for me. All the others, you can pick out."

Sarah got herself a Boston Crème, a key lime pie, a chocolate cheesecake, and a plain vanilla. We got the chocolate peanut butter for the rev, and the rest were for our friends. We were excited imagining their faces with the first bite.

Once we are outside, Sarah asks, "Now where are we gonna eat these things?"

"Great question. How about we buy some milk and grab a bench on McDougal Street."

"I have a better idea. Let's get some milk, head back to the park, and sit on the bench where we first met."

"Outside the dog park?"

"Yes, where you stared at me for fifteen minutes and didn't have the balls to approach me. And I had to come over to you and say, "Hey, handsome."

"I remember it like it was yesterday. Talk about being in the wrong place at the wrong time." I grin and kiss her. "Let's go."

We pick up a carton of milk on our way back to the park, which is empty, desolate. Not too many people are visible, but we know where our fellow homeless are hiding. We'll find them after we eat our cupcakes. We go to our bench, and we both take a long look at it. It looks like every other bench in the park, just some wood with a green steel support. But this is no ordinary bench. This bench is sacred. We sit and open the box of fifteen glorious cupcakes.

Sarah turns to me. "I feel like we should say a prayer or something."

"A prayer?"

"Poet, say something. Bless these cupcakes."

"Okay. Supreme Being, or God, Spirit of the Universe, there are many things I want to thank you for. I want to thank you for giving me the strength to start over and discover what it is I was born to do. I'd like to thank you for my daughter. Thank you for keeping her safe, secure, and happy. And thank you for bringing Sarah into my life. And for giving her the courage to get help. Thank you for all that God. I'm shutting up now because I want a cupcake."

Like always when I say something that touches her, Sarah rests her right hand on my left hand in silence.

Then she screams, "Cupcakes!" and opens the box.

I grab my red velvet, and Sarah grabs a Boston Crème. I inspect it, examine it, sniff it. I'm trying to understand this cupcake.

"Just fucking eat the thing. But let's take our first bite at the same instant. I want us to cum together."

I laugh.

"Alright, on three. One, two, three!" And we each take a bite.

Sarah doesn't even let me chew. She kisses me with both of our mouths full. I begin to chew, and I swallow, and I quickly realize that this cupcake is better than sex. Even an ordinary baked good is ecstasy to a homeless person. But this cupcake is like chateaubriand to a connoisseur of beef who's been eating at Arby's. Sarah is elated.

She turns to me and says, "I take it back. I'm wet."

I crack up. We're both chomping down cupcakes and guzzling milk. I end up eating three and feel like I'm gonna pass out. Sarah is holding her fourth in her right hand, the key lime pie, and her head is down low.

She looks up and says, "I don't know if I got it in me, Poet."

"Save it for later."

"No. It's now or never. I don't believe in leftovers."

"Well give it to Ron or Frank. It's one more we can hand out."

"This is key lime pie. I saved this for last. It's the sweetest. It's my orgasm. The rest were foreplay; this one takes me there."

"Do you want me to support you, cheer you on?"

"Yeah, get a Sarah chant going."

"Are you serious?"

"Yeah. I'm serious. This is key lime pie. This is no joke. Chant, goddamnit!"

I start laughing and begin, "Sar-ah! Sar-ah! Sar-ah! Sar-ah!"

She takes a huge bite and grabs my right shoulder like she's about to fall over. She's chewing with her eyes closed and a look of ecstasy on her face, and says, "Keep chanting, asshole."

"Sar-ah! Sar-ah! Sar-ah!"

She takes another bite, a huge one and chews for over a minute, pausing to guzzle milk. Chew, milk, chew, milk, chew. She takes a final gulp of milk and says, "Poet, you ever give me as much pleasure as that cupcake just did, I'll marry you."

With a smile I say, "I may not like key lime pie, but I can make an apple turnover."

She smiles. "That was smart and funny, but you're still a cheese-ball," she says, then laughs.

We sit for a while, satiated, then head off to hand out the last eight cupcakes, seven for other homeless folks in and around the park and the one for the rev, God bless him.

CHAPTER
FORTY-FIVE

Back in the church, we spiff up for our big night out. I wear my usual beat-up duds, grey sweatshirt, beat-up jeans, Nike Air Maxes, but with clean underwear. Sarah goes into her bag and comes up with silver, confetti-colored leggings, a ripped vintage black CBGB T-shirt cut off at the sleeves with a black tank top underneath. She puts on her ancient black high-top Nikes, puts her long dirty blonde hair up in a ponytail, and applies dark purple lipstick and heavy mascara.

The band is supposed to go on at 10:30. We get there at 9:30, and it's already crowded. The guy at the ticket booth's description was accurate: There are a lot of water bottles and dilated pupils. Oddly enough, to me all the guys look like they might be homeless. Apparently, my look is in right now. Most of the girls are wearing trucker hats tilted to the side, with leggings and high tops, just like Sarah. We fit right in.

Hugging Sarah from behind, I say to her, "You're the trendiest one in this room, and you haven't bought a piece of clothing in two years. What's up with that?"

"Evan, I'm a model. I set the trends. These girls are just catching up. They're two years behind."

By 10:30, the place is packed. Sarah and I are standing toward the back in the middle, about thirty feet from the bar. A couple of guys try to strike up conversations with her.

One comes over, eyelids fluttering, swaying from side to side, and says, "I feel like I've seen you before. Were you at the Philly show last night?"

I anticipate a classic Sarah response, and I am not disappointed.

"Yeah, I fucked Pretty Lights last night. And I gave him herpes. Might not be a great show tonight. He's probably itchy."

I crack up. The guy's fairly high and very confused. He's not sure if she's kidding. He walks away.

She turns to me, "Evan, I've gotten hit on every day since I was fourteen, and guys just don't get it."

"What don't they get?"

"That if you just walk over, introduce yourself, look a woman in the eye, and honestly take an interest in what she is saying, you will eventually get laid. It's as simple as that. Don't be a moron and try to impress us with bullshit. Be your fucking self, represent yourself. Girls respect honesty. Unless you look like a guy who works at Walmart, in which case you're so screwed you won't get screwed."

"Walmart?"

"The one by my old house in Iowa was scary. All the men looked like they were cousins, and they probably were."

I shake my head smiling. "Where do you come up with this shit?"

"Evan, sometimes I think nasty. I'm not proud of it, but if you spend a lot of time around models, you start to think like a model, and models think in a very disgusting, jealous, competitive manner. I was the anti-model model, but some of it still rubbed off on me. You know what? I need to go into former models rehab. I need to de-model."

I have no idea what to say so I just kiss her forehead and keep my mouth shut.

By 11, the show still hasn't started, and already Sarah and I are drenched with sweat. I'm hugging her from behind and swaying us back and forth. I honestly have no idea what to expect. Who are Pretty Lights? I know it's an electronic dance act. But onstage I can only see an elevated table. Is Pretty Lights just one guy? If so, wouldn't he just be Pretty Light?

Sarah turns around and passionately kisses me. We are wrapped in each other, making out like crazy in the middle of the room. In most places this would be considered extremely weird, but in here, it's not. With all these youngsters on ecstasy, hormones have saturated the air.

When the lights go down, the crowd roars, and Sarah starts jumping up and down. I just take it all in. I'm surprised we are here, embedded in a crowd. I'm not much of a dancer, but tonight I have to suck it up and move. I need to keep up with my girl.

It turns out Pretty Lights is just a dude in a jumpsuit working a console. He starts with a bass and synth beat, real slow, and Sarah starts fist-pumping. The bass and synth beat builds, and builds some more, and keeps on building till you think it's reached its zenith, but then it just keeps building, and the crowd gets wound up tighter, anticipating the beat to drop. He adds a gangster rap sample that blends in with the mix he's built.

Sarah has her hands up in the air, and her smile is as big as it could be. It's infectious and makes me grin too. It's a joy to watch her get wild. The tension builds and builds, and just when it feels there's nowhere to go, no more room, that my head is about to burst, the beat drops, the lights detonate, and a wave of energy explodes through the room, as if we are one huge body, one huge mind. Everyone goes nuts! Sarah leaps on me. I jump up and down as I hold her. Incredibly, her sheer joy gives me the strength. I'm thirty-five years old. I'm homeless. I'm raving in New York City. Life doesn't get any sweeter than this.

CHAPTER
FORTY-SIX

The streets are full of black slush, which splashes up as the cars plow through. I try to place my mind somewhere else. We are still managing. I am writing every day. We walk to the methadone clinic every day and attend a recovery meeting there every Tuesday night. I am still reading my poetry at artists night every Wednesday and have begun to really enjoy it. I still get anxious before I perform, but once I get going, I feel like I become myself.

Sarah and I find one another's quirks amusing. Although we get naked when we have sex, I won't change my clothes in front of her, which she finds hilarious and ridiculous. As I'm getting ready to shower, I throw a towel on over my boxers and then pull my boxers off under the towel. She tries to pull the towel off, but I just won't let it happen. In contrast Sarah is basically a nudist. She doesn't wear clothes unless she is going somewhere, which doesn't bother me because she's drop-dead gorgeous, and I love her body, but I find it amazing that anyone can be so free.

She finds it inexplicable that I am a neat freak, and I am obsessed with washing my hands. I'll admit: I'm OCD, but since when is being homeless a cure for that? Sarah doesn't give a fuck about needing to use public toilets or washing her hands. If she has to pee, she'll go anywhere she can. A park, on the side of a building, she doesn't care. It blows my mind. She keeps a wad of toilet paper in her pocket, and she just goes.

"Evan, a guy can whip his dick out anywhere and pee. But you run to McDonald's every hour so you can take a leak and then wash your hands. What kind of a man are you?"

"The kind who likes to have clean hands. What kind of woman pees on buildings?"

"I look at it like this, Evan. How often do those building façades get cleaned? Not often. I put my urine where it can do some good. If there were more brave women like me out there, real estate values would go up. Let's start Pee on a Building Day. It would help clean up this city."

Sarah's eccentricities make everything enjoyable. Her outlook on life is unique. I can't bullshit Sarah. She is always one step ahead of me. And she certainly knows more about people than I do. She can see a person's spirit and instantly know how to make anyone feel good, or at least feel better. White, Black, Hispanic, Asian, gay, straight, she can put a smile on anyone's face. If the person is having a bad day, she knows the perfect thing to say to make them feel good, and that's infectious. She knows I'm a thinker, dwelling on things that have absolutely nothing to do with what's going on at that current moment. She's the only person I've ever met who can always garner my full attention. She knows my weaknesses, she knows my flaws, she knows my dreams.

What I am trying to figure out right now is how my writing is going to get us out of this situation. I left my old life with an intuitive certainty that my writing will one day be read by many people. But how? And when? My instincts tell me the answers will come, and I've been patient. I've enjoyed every moment I've spent since I left my old life behind, and I do feel blessed. But I'd like to see my daughter and live under a roof that belongs to us, not to God. I dream of a simple life. A kitchen. A sofa. A bedroom. Even a TV so Josie can watch her cartoons. That's all I want.

One night after a long, frigid day, there is a knock on the church basement door. It is pretty late. It's the reverend, and he doesn't have his normal spirited glow or large smile on his face. As he comes down, he is clearly carrying some type of heavy load.

"Hi, Rev. Why the sour puss? What's the problem?"

"I'm afraid I have some bad news."

I tense up, and my heart starts to pound. Sarah and I exchange a look. No smiles.

"Listen, guys, as you know, this room is usually used for guests of the church. There's a priest coming in from St. Louis who needs to stay here for a while. I tried to find another solution, and I fought for you, but I lost. You won't be able to stay here after January 31st. I'm so sorry. Now don't panic, I have ideas."

"It's okay, Reverend," I quickly reassure him.

But I am horrified. It's freezing out. I imagine us lying down under a pile of blankets, me wrapped around Sarah, trying to keep her warm.

I look over at Sarah, and she looks stoic, which I've never seen before.

"If I had the room in my apartment to take you two in, I would," says the rev. "But you guys have been to my place. It's a small, one-bedroom. But listen, I've got something lined up for you already. There's a shelter on 29th and 7th right near Madison Square Garden, and I'm friends with the director. You two are all set. You can sleep there every night, get a free hot dinner, and you'll be taken care of and safe. I know it's a shelter and you want the same privacy, but you'll still have me. We'll still have dinner at my apartment, and both of you are always welcome at all our events. Sarah, I've already talked to the methadone clinic on 27th Street, and your medicine will be there. And Evan, I expect you to keep reading your poetry here every Wednesday. You know I love you two, I consider you family, but I'm hamstrung on this. I feel awful that you can't just keep staying here."

There was a pool of silence for a moment, and we looked at each other.

"Sarah, you look spooked," says the rev. "But I think it's going to be okay."

"I'm worried about our safety, Reverend. Shelters scare me. I feel safe with just the two of us at night. I'm worried about sleeping in a shelter, even with Evan to protect me. They're not friendly places. I think we might be safer on the streets. I really do."

"Evan, what do you think?"

"I think nothing is permanent, and we have to give it a shot. Sarah, it could turn out to be a good thing. If you're right, and we don't like the shelter, we'll leave. I trust the reverend, and if he tells me it will be okay, then, Sarah, I truly believe it will be. We should go in with an open mind and see how it is. You're not doing this alone. We're doing this together."

"Trust me," says the rev. "I would not put you in a dangerous situation. But if it doesn't work out, we'll put our heads together and find an alternative. I asked all around, and also priests, ministers, social workers, and my daughter asked around. I reached out to everyone, and this is the best I can do right now. I've spent a lot of time there, and it's a good place. The staff is great, the volunteers are amazing, and they have showers and toilets. You can come and go as you please, and there will be a bed for you every night. They open at 5 pm, and you have to leave the premises by 7 am. You both know you can come back down here and sit in the church all day to stay warm if you want. You won't be that far uptown."

"We have to make money to eat."

"Dinner is covered by the shelter, and whenever I come by, I'll bring you supplies—tuna fish sandwiches and all. Evan, you look confused."

There was another silence while we all pictured our imagined versions of what lay ahead. "It is what it is, Rev. I appreciate the time we were given to stay here. I'm very grateful for that. I know you've done everything you can, and of course, I appreciate it. We've just got to stay positive and roll with it."

I turn to Sarah and softly say, "We're survivors. This is just another bump in the road. We'll be fine."

Sarah puts her hand on top of mine.

"You have two more cozy nights here, guys," said the rev. "Make them count. It might be awhile before you get alone time again. Cherish the next two nights. I'll take the two of you over to the shelter personally on Wednesday and introduce you to everyone. You'll be receiving special treatment, I promise you."

As soon as the rev closes the door, Sarah crawls into bed and curls up into a ball.

"What's with you and homeless shelters?" I ask, cuddling in beside her.

"We don't belong there, Evan."

"What are we, the privileged homeless?"

"We're not homeless, Evan. Not really. We're better than this. We have a bright future ahead of us. You say it all the time, and I believe it. I'm fucking sure of it! People in homeless shelters are fragmented, pulverized, lost. I don't feel that way. Even when I was a junkie and alone on the street, I never felt that way. I always believed the next day would be a brighter one. I'm afraid that in a shelter it will be hard to see the light. I don't want to get pulled down into darkness."

"Sarah, I was broken for thirty-five years, as broken as anyone in that shelter. Accept our circumstances; accept this card we've been dealt. This is just the next step on our journey to all the beauty that the future holds in store for us. As long as we are together, it doesn't matter where we are: Paris, Fresno, China, some shelter on 29th Street. It's just another step. It just adds more to our story. In my mind, we're already there: Comfortable and successful, and Josie's in the kitchen eating pancakes. This all took place already in my mind, and we will catch up to it. Just have faith—in me, in yourself, and in us.

"It's weird timing because I've already been thinking it is time for us to do something to change, even before the rev brought us the news. So, maybe this is part of it. What we need to do is figure out the next step with writing, with what we do for money. We need a big new idea like the five-minute poetry table. Something that attracts attention. We need something unique, something special, and I need you to come up with it."

I pull Sarah in tight and whisper, "It's all gonna be alright. We'll make it work, together, like we always do. Maybe we can even help some other people feel better about themselves and their situation, and maybe the shelter will turn out to be a plus? Who knows?"

I shut off the light, get back in bed, and rub her stomach, and she falls asleep. I lie awake with my eyes wide open. I meant everything I said, but at the same time, the truth is I am freaked out about living in a homeless shelter.

CHAPTER
FORTY-SEVEN

The rev, Sarah, and I are on the uptown C train, headed for our new no-home, not talking. The reverend tries to break the tension by telling me how much the Knicks suck, but I am hardly listening. I am rubbing Sarah's hand to comfort her, or more truthfully, I am rubbing her hand to comfort me.

Although we are only moving twenty blocks, we might as well be moving to a different state. In the city, every neighborhood has its own identity, its own flavor. Sarah and I are comfortable in the West Village. It's our small town. We know the park residents; we know the store owners and employees; we have the rev close by. We feel safe.

Midtown is a whole different world. Up there, it's all about business, and it's nonstop commotion. The streets are filled with people. Cabs are constantly honking. Everyone's walking fast. Tourists are everywhere. If you are looking for the true, real deal New York City experience, the hustle and bustle, the grit and grime, then midtown is the place to be. And that's where we are, in front of a building I must've walked by a hundred times but never noticed. It is relatively small by New York standards, only eight stories. It's an old brick building with no name, no sign, nothing written above the door. Not even a number. Normally so charismatic and jovial, Sarah looks as if she is at a funeral. I have on my tough exterior, and I try to look confident, borderline cocky, to reassure her.

"This is it. It's on the third floor."

"What about security?"

"These doors are locked between the hours of 5 pm and 7 am every night," says the rev. No one can get in or out unless there's an emergency. So, you have fourteen hours of safety every night. Let's go up. I'll introduce you to Cindy, the director, a very good friend of mine. She's expecting you guys. I told her all about you, and she's excited to meet you."

We walk out of the elevator, and there are two tremendous wooden doors that are wide open. Sarah and I step inside, and I see that she is tearing up.

"Let's go back to the alley."

"Let's give this a shot."

The shelter completely occupies one enormous floor of the building. It is massive. The ceilings are relatively low, about ten feet. The floor is made of old warped hardwood, and it creaks when we walk on it. The walls are off-white. There are no paintings, no decorations, nothing—just hardwood and a room filled with empty cots. There must be 150, eight to a row, all neatly made up with clean white sheets, a pillow, and a grey wool blanket.

There's a kitchen next to a big area of plastic picnic tables, which have red plastic covers draped over them. Next to the kitchen is an administrative office. This is not the Waldorf Astoria. I feel like I've hit rock bottom, and I know Sarah feels this way too. But, if living here is what we have to do to keep from freezing and getting sick, so be it.

"Let's go meet Cindy."

As we follow the rev, Sarah rests her head on my shoulder. We enter a small office where a smiling woman sits behind an old, wooden desk.

"Hi," she says warmly. "I'm Cindy Shulman, the director here at 29th Street Shelter. Have a seat."

Cindy looks like she's been pumped full of helium: long red skirt, long-sleeved green shirt, short blonde hair, rosy cheeks. She looks like Mrs. Claus. She wears a huge smile, like Ronald McDonald.

"Morning, Reverend. You've brought two very good-looking people here this morning. They could be movie stars."

"They're like Bonnie and Clyde, only Sarah's Clyde. She's the tough one."

That was pretty funny, but I don't have laughter in me right now.

"So, Reverend Emerson has told me so much about the both of you, all good. He warned me you two might shake things up around here."

"How so?" I ask.

"It's Evan, right?" she asks.

"Yes, but I go by Poet."

"Okay, Poet. The Reverend says the two of you have a knack for lifting people's spirits. He says the both of you will be, and I quote, 'beacons of light.'"

"Cindy, we'll do whatever you want us to," says Sarah. "We'll be glad to chip in and help in any way we can. I just want to feel safe when we go to sleep at night."

"Sarah, under my watch, everyone here is safe and provided for. If there's a medical issue, it will be attended to. If there's an emotional problem, come to me. Rest assured you will be safe. I promise."

I look at Sarah, and I can see she liked that response. She seems to loosen up, and her tense stone face has a little bit of life again.

"So, the reverend and I have been talking about you and your talents with people and with words, and we would like you to help us develop some new projects here. You'll be adjuncts to the staff. Sarah, the idea we came up with would be for you to read the newspaper every day and then, after dinner, give an informal presentation to the residents who are staying with us that night: talk about the day's events, what's going on in the world. Not everyone will pay attention, but some will. My thinking is that you can both entertain and inform them at the same time.

"Poet, I know you are a writer, and I would love if you start a writing group for whoever is interested. Again, maybe only a few will show up. I don't know. But you set up a circle of chairs, or just use the dining tables if you prefer, and spend some time every evening. You could start by reading some of your own work, then get everyone to write and learn to tell their own stories. And people can share their writing and help each other. However, whatever you want to do is fine. I'll get whatever supplies you need.

"You can figure it out as you go along. But I think these projects will help people, if you'd be willing to take them on. What do you think?" Cindy looks at us and smiles.

I let Sarah answer. "It's a deal, Cindy. I'll be the newshound, and I'm sure Poet will make a good teacher. Thanks for this opportunity. We're very grateful."

"I think you two will be happy here. Better than sleeping in that alley at least, yes?"

Sarah smiles, which makes me smile, and says, "I love that alley. I'll always love that alley. But I'd rather be warm."

Cindy adds that because we'll be helping out at the shelter, we will be assured entry every night, and we won't have to wait in line to see if there's enough room. She says she has already had two cots set up for us, side by side, in the back corner.

We keep talking for quite a while, about the programs she has in mind and about our lives. Sarah tells Cindy about the methadone program. Cindy tells us about the shelter and the types of people who stay there—a mixture of individuals and families down on their luck, the mentally ill, alcoholics, drug addicts. She says the staff of volunteers is amazing. We end up feeling pretty good about the whole prospect, and when we get up, the rev, Sarah, and I follow Cindy all the way down the back wall to where are cots are set up side by side.

"Here's your spot. This is where you'll be sleeping." Cindy tells us to go ahead and settle in and leaves us with the rev.

We chat a bit, and then he says he has to go. He hugs us both and says, "Poet, I want two new poems from you by artists night on Wednesday. Sarah, don't let him slack off. He has a knack for procrastination." He grins and says, "If you need anything before then, let me know," then waves goodbye and leaves.

Sarah and I sit on the cots and look at each other in silence for a while. Nothing is said, but everything is said. We need each other now more than ever. This will be hard. Our privacy is gone. Ironically, now that we are going to be with so many others, we feel more homeless than we did when we were on our own.

Cindy comes back over and tells us we can leave our stuff under our cots if we want, so we don't have to lug it around all day. "We close the building. It'll be safe."

"Thanks, but I always keep my duffel bag with me."

"Sarah, what about you?"

"Yeah, I'm gonna put my stuff under the bed. Thanks!"

"It'll be fine, and you can come in at a quarter to five, before we open up."

"Okay."

"So, guys, it's 8 now, so the shelter is closed for the day, but we'll see you back here at 4:45 tonight, okay? It's baked macaroni and cheese night, and I promise you it's good."

"Sarah will eat anything. She's like a goat."

She play-slaps me across the face, points her right index finger at me, and says, "But I don't eat tin cans. Behave yourself, Poet."

I shoulder my duffel bag, and Sarah and I head toward the exit.

Out on 29th Street, it's crowded, and people dressed in stylish Manhattan work outfits are zooming by, looking haggard and hurried and generally anxious. I grew up twenty-five minutes away from here, and I've lived in the city, but this is the first time I've felt like a foreigner. Life in the West Village was relatively slow, mellow. I feel like we are standing amid a stampede.

Sarah turns to me and asks, "Where do we go now?"

I'm usually quick with an answer. "I don't know."

"How much money do we have?"

"$55."

"Okay. I have an idea. This is a special day. Why don't we go to that diner we like and get pancakes, then just walk around, scout the area, explore, and figure out where we'll spend our time."

"Sounds like a plan. Pancakes it is."

The chocolate chip pancakes are delicious. But this is Midtown, and two orders of pancakes, one order of scrambled eggs, and two coffees comes to $24, almost half of what we have. I hate to have less than $50 on me. It seems dangerous. And even $50 won't get you far in this city. Being so low on cash makes me anxious, and Sarah knows it. "Let's go sightseeing," she says. "Let's see the hand we've been dealt."

We wander around for hours. The storefronts are mostly tourist shops, discount jewelry places, cheap clothing stores, and bars. The east-west streets have pretzel and nut vendors and guys selling old books and incense on picnic tables. There are upscale bars around Penn Station and Madison Square Garden. Back when I lived in Great Neck, I spent a lot of time in Penn Station and at the Garden, which is on top of it. Madison Square Garden is the home of the New York Knicks and the New York Rangers, and the venue for every major concert, the circus, the rodeo, and the Westminster Dog Show. It bills itself as the World's Most Famous Arena, and it may be, if you don't count the Colosseum in Rome. It's my second favorite place in the city —after Washington Square Park.

Now Sarah and I find ourselves standing in front of the entrance to Penn Station.

"This place should be perfect for us," she says. "There are tons of people. It's warm. There are bathrooms. There's food."

I am a little hesitant for only one reason: There's a chance I might be recognized here. Most of my former coworkers take the train through here every day, and I don't want to get caught.

But then I realize how unlikely that is. Who the hell would recognize me now? Who in their right mind would think I'd be looking like this, a dirty homeless guy? Would any of the idiots I used to work with even look at me, let alone recognize me? Absolutely not.

I turn to Sarah. "You're right. Let's spend our days here."

I grab her hand, and as we ride the long escalator down, I gesture grandly and say, "Welcome to our new office."

CHAPTER
FORTY-EIGHT

I know Penn Station well. It has the feel of a giant basement department store—drab, but busy, like an old Woolworth's, but with commotion: people waiting for trains, people running for trains, people missing their trains and waiting for other trains. A couple of subways feed in down there underground. The New Jersey transit trains, the Long Island Railroad, and Amtrak all go in and out of it, and each has its own big room full of display boards, with track numbers and departure times and everybody staring at them as if they're watching the most interesting TV show ever.

Around the edges of the coming and going, there is always some entertainment by the A, C, and E subway lines. We go past a Black bass player who's very good and extremely friendly. An African woman in a floral dashiki sings soul and gospel accompanied by a little boombox. She's not so good. And there's a group of Peruvians who play wooden flutes in front of McDonald's. I've seen them many times, and it always seems like they're playing the same song—one big jam session that's lasted twenty years. Fortunately, it's a pretty good song, and it makes me feel like I'm up in the Andes.

There's a lot of food in Penn Station, all of it overpriced and none of it very good: Moe's Southwest Grill, the Cheesesteak Place, Starbucks, McDonald's, Au Bon Pain, Hot & Crusty, Jamba Juice, Planet Smoothie,

TGI Friday's, Nathan's, Pizza Hut. A pizza place called Rosa's is surprisingly good. I've eaten many, many slices there over the years. There's a Duane Reade and a Kmart; there's a shoe shine place and a couple of little bookstores that nobody seems to go into. Penn Station is kind of a worn, subterranean, minimal version of our country. God bless America! Comin' through.

By 9:30 am, rush hour is dying down, and Penn Station is half as crowded as it was when we arrived. We take it all in. We walk by every restaurant, every store, the subway entrances, and the transit waiting areas. We are hunting for the right place where we can sit down with our sign and engage with commuters. Sarah points to a spot about forty feet from the escalators, across from Kmart, right by the entrance to New Jersey Transit.

"That's it. People coming off the escalators, people going to the escalators. It's not too far from the bathrooms. We can get people's attention there. I think that's our spot. Poet, what do you think?"

"It might work. And if it doesn't, we'll move. I like that it's away from the big crowds and heavy traffic and that the musicians aren't around here. People will be able to hear us."

"Exactly."

"Let's try it out tomorrow. We got nothing to lose, everything to gain."

"And hey, either way we'll be warm."

"Exactly, that's what's most important. And you can pee in a bathroom, not in the bushes."

"Sweet. So civilized."

We have all day ahead of us, till the shelter opens at 5. And because we had a big breakfast, we decide not to eat until we get back there.

"I need to read the paper. I gotta do the news tonight."

"That's right."

"Let's work on that."

Sarah goes into a Hudson News store—they're all over Penn Station—and buys the *Daily News*. We sit in the spot we have picked out for ourselves, and we read the paper cover to cover. We pick out four stories: one on immigration reform, one on the death penalty for the Boston Marathon bomber, one about Mayor Bill DiBlasio putting an end to stop-and-frisk, and one about actor Channing Tatum and what his life was like when he was a stripper preparing for his role in *Magic Mike.*

Sarah asks, "Did you see that movie, Poet? Guys don't admit to it, but I know you saw it."

"I did, and it was a good fucking movie. It was much more than a strip show. There was a story in there, and the thing was well directed."

She grins and says, "Please admit that you're gay. Come out. It doesn't make you a bad person. Embrace it."

I look at her and say, "It's true. I'm gay. And when we have sex, I'm thinking about Channing Tatum."

"Well, that explains a lot. I knew you were too straight to be true, dammit! You think you know someone. But you're a poet. Aren't a lot of poets gay?"

"Poets are the best lovers," I chuckle. "We're such romantics."

She laughs, play-slaps my face, and says, "Don't toot your horn. You're average at best."

"Maybe average *is* best."

"Maybe you'd rather fuck Lauren?"

"I'd rather fuck Hitler."

"That's messed up. I will allow you to have the last word this time, but don't get used to it." She pulls my head in, kisses me, and cracks up. "I love it when you're nasty. It's hot!"

"You're a complete smart-ass, and I find it extremely attractive."

"I can't deny it. I am attractive."

"Oh, I know. Because every guy that walks by stares at you."

"Every guy I've ever met is an asshole, except you. I'm in love with the only non-asshole. Pretty lucky."

For the rest of the day, we hang out in Penn Station, wander around and explore, share a large cup of coffee. We people watch and make up silly games, and before we know it, it's time to head back to the shelter.

It is freezing outside. It can't be more than 20 degrees. I thank God that we will have a hot meal and warm beds tonight. As we turn onto 29th Street, we see a line of people stretching all the way down the block, all homeless men and women hoping to spend a warm night inside. I feel awful that Sarah and I are assured that we have cots. I'm not sure what to do: Get in at the back? Go up to the front? We just keep walking, and when we get up to the door of the shelter, Cindy is there, checking people in.

"Poet," she waves us toward her. "You and Sarah come on inside."

We slip in through the door and make our way upstairs. As we walk into the main hall, we are met by a bunch of smiling volunteers. Sarah and I introduce ourselves, I thank them, and we make our way back to our cots. We sit, glad to be warm, and watch people file in. It is happy and sad at the same time: Happy because everyone is clearly grateful to have a place to stay. Sad that so many are sleeping in a shelter. And every person who comes in has a story. I realize it's a living library of sad stories. Some people lost their jobs, some lost their houses, some lost loved ones. I see there's a single dad here with his daughter, and it brings me to tears. I can't imagine Josie going through this.

The room is now filled, the doors have been shut, and every cot is taken. People are lining up for dinner, and Sarah and I get on line. The line moves quickly. They serve us salad and baked macaroni and cheese. It doesn't look too appealing, but I'm so hungry I'd eat anything.

Sarah and I sit at one of the big tables, across from each other. Next to her is a tall Black man with frizzy hair who looks like he hasn't eaten in a while. He has on a dirty orange sweatshirt and doesn't seem to be in the mood to talk. Next to me is a heavyset woman with a smile on her face. She has long, frazzled brown hair wrapped in a red bandana. She's sort of wearing a frock and looks like a homeless pirate. I'd guess she's around forty.

"How you doing?"

"Fine, how are you doing?"

"I'm great. Happy to have a warm meal. This mac and cheese is excellent. It's usually a little watery, but tonight it's very cheesy."

"It is. Almost as good as Kraft."

"Oh, Kraft Mac & Cheese. I lived on it growing up."

"Where did you grow up?"

"I'm from a small town in New Hampshire."

"How long have you been in the city?"

"Oh, about fifteen years. I came to the Big Apple to be an actress. It didn't work out. I was waiting tables for a while, and I was living with a guy. He wasn't very nice to me. I didn't handle the break-up very well, and I had trouble keeping jobs. I ended up with no job and no place to live. Both my parents had passed away, and the only place to go was the streets. I've been homeless on and off for six years. I've spent a lot of nights in this place. And other places. They're amazing here. This is definitely one of the better shelters."

"I'm sorry about your parents."

"We all come and go; it's just a matter of when and how—and what happens in between."

I think about that while I eat my delicious mac and cheese.

After dinner, Cindy comes over to Sarah and leans in. "Did you get a chance to look at the newspaper today?"

"I did."

"Do you feel like presenting the news? Are you ready?"

"Sure."

Cindy claps her hands and raises her voice to get everyone's attention. "Good evening, everyone. Tonight, we have a special after-dinner treat. Allow me to introduce Sarah. Starting tonight, she's going to be giving us all an after-dinner presentation, an update on the day's news. She'll be letting us all know what's been going on. Take it away, Sarah."

Sarah stands on the table, brandishing a piece of my yellow notebook paper with some notes, and she dives right into the stories she picked out. She talks about what's happening with stop-and-frisk and then gives her take on the issue. She starts with the news itself, laying out the story, but then she puts her own humorous spin on everything, making jokes. And it ends up as a sort of a round table discussion, as she asks people what they think and gets a conversation going. Before you know it, it's been thirty minutes, and everybody has had a relaxing good time.

Cindy is beaming. "Thank you, Sarah. We'll look forward to your next report, tomorrow night!"

A fair number of people were listening, and I see a lot of smiles.

Sarah sits, and Cindy asks me to stand. She introduces me as a writer and says that I will be starting a creative writing group. She invites everyone who is interested to join me at a big table in the back, and about fifteen men and women head back there with me and sit. I pass out the yellow legal pads and pens Cindy got for me. I am not sure where to start. I can't just ask everyone to write a poem, cold. I want to keep it simple. So, I read them a poem I wrote about Harker, one of the dogs I know from the park. It gets a few laughs and kind of loosens everybody up. Then I suggest that all of us take ten minutes to write about our day.

This goes pretty well. Everyone sits there writing and seems to be into it. When the time is up, I read my paragraph out loud. It's my take on Penn Station. And then we go around the circle, and everybody reads their piece. After each one, we talk about if anybody has any thoughts to offer. Most are kind of straight-forward, and a couple make people chuckle.

One piece in particular really affects me. An older man describes how a bunch of kids verbally assaulted him and one of them kicked him. This really makes me angry. When he reads the part about how he didn't understand why this happened, I feel like crying. When he finishes, I am choked up, and I thank him for sharing the story. He says he doesn't understand why nobody who saw it happening did anything. I tell him I think the world is filled with good people, bad people, and the disturbed.

"You and I, we're good people. New York City drivers who run red lights are bad. Kids who kick people for no reason are just plain disturbed."

This makes him grin. I call on Sarah to read her paragraph last, because I know it's going to be funny, and it will leave everyone in good spirits.

Sarah reads, "Today I woke up in a church, kissed the man I love, and was escorted out of that church by a reverend who I revere. I spent much of the day riding on escalators. I shared a coffee with my guy, but he put too much sugar in it, so it wasn't as good as it should have been. I have not forgiven him yet, and maybe I never will. A coffee ruined is a loss forever. Nonetheless, I love him with all my heart and always will. I also had pancakes for breakfast, so who cares about the coffee? Thank you."

Everyone chuckles at this. I thank them all for joining in. I get a round of applause, which makes me feel really good. Sarah walks over to me, gently bites my ear, and whispers, "You really did fuck up that coffee. And I won't forget."

"I have a sweet tooth."

We settle into our cots next to one another, holding hands, and she says quietly, "You know, this place is not so bad, Poet. Much better than I expected. We can do this. I feel relieved."

I kiss her forehead. "Always trust in the rev; he'll never let us down. Where would we be without him?"

"Frozen solid."

"He's the best man I've ever met."

"He's only my second best."

She nestles her head on my shoulder, and they turn off the lights.

CHAPTER
FORTY-NINE

It's morning, and we head out with our trusty old "If There Is a God, He Blesses You" sign in hand. It has always been good to us, and for a few months it helped bring us enough money to eat. We are optimistic about Penn Station, with its massive foot traffic and high energy, confident that there will be plenty of opportunities to strike up conversations.

Wrong! Very wrong. All morning, nobody pays attention to us. Everyone is in a big rush, driven, focused on moving as fast as possible. We are distractions—obstacles—and people want nothing to do with us.

Every now and again someone goes by walking slowly, and Sarah has a chance to say something. "I like your sneakers. What are those, Nikes?"

"Yeah, I just got them around the block at Foot Locker. You like them?"

"Oh yeah."

Then she points to me and says, "He's got a pair just like them."

Keep in mind I have a long beard, my jeans are filthy, and my pair of Nikes are completely worn out.

"What did you pay for them?" she asks.

"$80."

"If you paid $80 for sneakers, can you please spare a dollar for the compliment from a fellow Nike enthusiast?"

The guy reaches into his pocket and gives us a dollar. He thanks us and tells us to have a nice day.

Now usually she can do that kind of thing all day, but we see only two guys going slow like that all morning. It doesn't take us long to figure out that the only hours you make some money in Penn Station are between 10 and 3 when it's quiet and less crowded. But it turns out that during that prime time there is a lot of competition.

We aren't the only homeless people. We probably look more normal than most, which might work to our advantage or our disadvantage, I'm not sure. But Penn Station's homeless are really down and out. Some are so out of it they can't sit upright against the wall like Sarah and I do, and they are curled up in a ball on a piece of cardboard. And everybody has a sign. Most say things like "Homeless and hungry, please help" or "No job, nowhere to go." And then there's "Why lie, it's for booze." I appreciate the honesty. My heart goes out to all of them.

We spend our first days in Penn Station getting familiar with the scene and trying to figure out what our approach should be. It's good to be warm in here, but we need to make money. The place is loaded with cops and soldiers on homeland security duty. Sarah and I get into conversations with some of them about politics, foreign policy, social issues, and healthcare. I talk sports with the guys. Like us, the cops and men and women soldiers are stuck in Penn Station all day and are more than happy to chat.

As the days pass, we of course make friends. By the end of the first week, soldiers are buying us coffee, and the cops give us the newspaper after they are done reading it. In Penn Station, you're not supposed to be allowed to use the bathrooms unless you have a ticket for one of the train lines. Those rules don't apply to us. They let us do what we want.

We also become friendly with the restaurant employees and the people who work behind the counters at the Hudson News stands. They like me because I am courteous and a nice person, but they are all in love with Sarah. And as always, she leads us to perks like free food, candy, and drinks. It's kind of odd and nice to be homeless, in a relationship, and in love with someone who can get whatever she wants for free. And nobody is ever disrespectful to her. Of course, if they were, she'd kick their asses.

So, we still face our dilemma: How do we make money in Penn Station? The musicians are doing okay. There is some decent talent, but even the shitty musicians get paid, and it is frustrating to watch.

One day, Sarah turns to me and says, "Evan, remember how well we did in the park with the five-minute poetry?"

"Of course."

"We need something like that."

"That would be awesome, but I don't think there's a market for poetry in here. I can't set up a table and write poems for people. They don't have five minutes."

"We need to think of a way where you can write, and people will stop and listen."

"Sarah, no one would care about some guys poetic ramblings in here. It's not artists night. There's no audience."

"We have to create one. We have to turn the people who are waiting for the trains, standing around, under the big board, into your audience somehow. You need to give a performance about something they care about."

"All people here care about is getting home."

"Of course, but there has to be something else on their minds."

"Yeah, their day."

"Right. You need to brighten their day somehow. Make them laugh, give them information. People are so caught up in their own lives!"

She pauses, gets even more excited, thinking, and says, "I got it! I got it!"

"Got what?"

"I don't know if it's possible, but if it works, it would be awesome!"

"What, Sarah!"

"Okay. Every day at 6 o'clock, you stand up on a milk crate right by the information booths, and you deliver the news."

"Deliver the news?"

"Yes, but you just don't read the news, or tell them the headlines.

You recite a poem that tells everybody the news for the day, with your take on it. It'll be headline poetry!"

"Wait, I'm confused."

"Every day while people are standing there in a crowd staring up at the schedules, you get up there and recite your take on the day's news as one long poem."

"Every day? Write a poem about the news?"

"Yes! Evan, you could do it. Make the news into a poem, like you do at artists night!"

"Perform it? How the hell am I going to get anyone to listen?"

"Stand up on top of a milk crate and speak loud and clear. You just do it."

"No one will pay any attention. I'm just some homeless scruffy dude. But maybe if you, in all your Sarahness and beauty, get up there and introduce me, that would grab people's attention."

"That's a great fucking idea! I'll wear a "uniform"—my black boots, black leggings, short black skirt, yellow flannel shirt with the black stripes unbuttoned, and my tank top."

"Perfect."

"I'll make a sign that says, "THE POET RECITES THE NEWS." Maybe I'll use a bullhorn! I'll announce the day's date then say, 'HERE YE, HERE YE, HERE IS YOUR POET!' And you stand up on the crate and do your poet thing. Preach like a possessed televangelist. Exorcise the demons!"

"That's absolutely, positively insane, and it might be the best idea I've ever heard. You're a fucking genius!"

This feels like how Sarah and I have done everything so far: by being different, by doing things that don't make sense. That's how we survive, and it's a large part of why we love one another. Crazy for most is sane for us. And whatever it is we're doing, we're having fun. That's how we know we're on track. Piece by piece, we figure it out.

So, how are we going to make this thing happen? We have it all figured out. It's February 12th, and we decide we want our grand debut to be in two days, on Friday, which is Valentine's Day. Right at 6 pm seems the perfect time—in among the peak train departures. There's a twenty-minute gap in there, and we'll fill it. We sketch in our minds how it will work, and we go study the area, and I start playing around with some writing. Then there's only one problem we need to solve: By the time we finish our show, the shelter doors will already have closed. Cindy has already done so much for us, but we have to ask her for another favor.

After dinner, we knock on her office door, and she opens it with a smile.

"Can we come in?"

"Sure, Poet, Sarah, have a seat. What brings you crazy kids in here tonight?"

"Cindy, I want to tell you how grateful Sarah and I are for everything—the housing, the cots, the food, the showers, the people, the special projects, everything. It's truly been a blessing."

"The pleasure's all mine. You two have been so great for the shelter. Doing the news and the writing—those things put smiles on people's faces and help them in a real way. You take the time to really talk to people, to connect. It means a lot. You guys are the blessing."

"We appreciate that, Cindy, and I'm glad to hear it because we have a kind of situation, and we need to ask you a favor. You know about the poetry business we had going down in the Village? Well, we have a new idea, and I think it's even better…"

I tell her the whole thing, and as I do, I realize that it sounds a little nuttier than I had even admitted to myself, and yet as I'm talking I get all charged up and realize how excited I am about it.

"The one catch, Cindy, is that the best time to do it is 6 pm, when there are as many people as possible passing through the station—the biggest potential audience for us. But if we hit that time, we won't get back here until maybe 6:30 every night. And I know the shelter doors are locked at 5."

Cindy thinks only for a couple of seconds, then leans forward and reaches for pen and paper. "Let's do this. On your way home from Penn Station, go by the pay phone on 28th Street and call me. I'll meet you at the front door and let you in." She stands and hands me the paper with a big smile. "Here's my cell phone number, use that. Now go forth and spread the word, you two! God bless you. Just make sure you have enough energy left when you get back here to do the news and your writing workshop after dinner. We need you."

I give Cindy a big hug, and Sarah does too. And as we walk back into the residence hall, we are elated. Tomorrow will be our debut—the Big Show.

CHAPTER
FIFTY

Sarah and I wake up invigorated and excited. I'd rather sit alone and write, but I've come to enjoy performing. It's a shot of adrenaline. Sharing my thoughts out loud with the world has become rewarding, beyond the money. Doing it in Penn Station will be terrifying, but it's *go big or go home* time. Sarah and I now look at it as performance art.

"Poet, why don't we make some flyers."

"Flyers?"

"Yeah. Some cool cheap advertising to get people to check out our performance."

"You think that will make a difference?"

"Absolutely. Even if it only gets a few more people to listen to us it'll be worth it."

"But we have only like 30 bucks left. You know I get extremely nervous when we are below fifty."

"This is an investment and will pay for itself. Let's go to Kinko's, and I'll make something right there, then we'll print 'em up and hand 'em out in and around Penn Station throughout the day. We'll get people interested, and I'm sure some of them will come check us out."

"What will the flyer say?"

"'Poetic News at 6 pm live in Penn Station—Under the Big Board by Track 20.' Let's keep it simple."

"That works."

We get to Kinko's and design and print some flyers. As we leave, Sarah's pumped, as if she'd printed a pile of $20 bills. Just walking to Penn Station, she hands out like fifteen of them.

"Sarah, go easy on the flyers. We only printed fifty."

"I'm feeling righteous, Poet. Like a Jehovah's Witness handing out the *Watchtower*."

I laugh.

We get to Penn Station and go right to work. Sarah walks over to the Hudson News guys and asks for a milk crate. She is wearing her mini skirt and tank top, which shows just a hint of cleavage, and is extra flirtatious. How can they refuse? They give her one, and she goes over to Starbucks, flirts with a curly-haired pimply faced kid, and gets some cardboard. Next, she hops over to Planet Smoothie and gets a free banana that we share.

We have $18 left. I take out $5 and buy the *New York Times*, the *Daily News*, and the *New York Post*, and I begin to read, taking some notes on what I might want to incorporate into my poem. I don't want it to be too long, just enough to grab and hold their attention for a few minutes.

I'm just into my reading when Sarah turns to me and asks, "Are you going to be a dick and not read your poem to me before you recite it to everyone who's here at 6 o'clock?

"There is no way you're pre-reading my poem, Sarah. That would be bad luck, like me coming backstage into the dressing room and checking out what you're wearing before you hit the runway."

"The other models backstage can see me."

"The other models are looking at themselves not you, sweetheart."

"That might be true, Poet, but the other models aren't sucking your cock, and this one is, so you're gonna show me."

"Sorry, no can do."

"I'm never blowing you again."

"Fine, then I'm never eating your pussy again."

She turns to me, grabs my cheeks hard, and says, "Fine, you win," and we both crack up.

"I'm going to sit in the New Jersey Transit waiting room and write," I tell her. "Do me a favor. Please go sit in the Long Island Railroad waiting room where the cops are. See if you can get them to come to our premiere tonight. I'll be back in a half-hour."

When I sit down to write, it's very difficult at first. I go through all my notes several times, waiting for something to happen, and then it does, and suddenly I'm in the zone, and the words are flowing, and the pen is trying to keep up. Everything else kind of falls away. I keep at it and am really getting comfortable with the feeling of doing it, of thinking to myself as a kind of transmitter, assigned to tell my fellow citizens what the world has been up to while they were rushing around the greatest city in the world getting things done. Suddenly, I realize I have what I need. It's finished.

When I sit next to Sarah, she asks, "How could you be done already? I can't write my name that fast. Is it good?"

"I have no idea. We'll find out."

"Poet, please let me read it. Let me make sure it's alright. This is important."

"Have I ever written something you didn't like?"

"No. But I like some of your poems better than others."

"It's the news, it rhymes, and there's some humor in it. And it's not too long. It will be fine. Trust me."

She points her right finger at me and says, "If you mess this up, you lose all sexual privileges for life. We become friends with absolutely no benefits. Not even a hug. I won't even let you hold my hand. Never again. Nothing!"

"But if it goes well," I respond, "and we get donations, and people seem to really enjoy it, and if we have fun, then we go up to that hidden bathroom above New Jersey Transit and make sweet, sweet love?"

"Poet, it will be the best sex of your life. So, there's some incentive. Get up on that crate and kill it, and our night is made. You better hope your poetry is up to it."

"Oh, the poetry's good. Possibly better than you are in bed. We shall see."

"We haven't had sex in two weeks. You'll last five seconds anyway."

I smile and say, "But it'll be a great five seconds! I'm going over to that quiet corner so I can memorize my poem."

CHAPTER
FIFTY-ONE

It's five minutes till show time, and I am a nervous wreck, pacing and chewing gum frantically. We have figured out the ideal place to set up: in the main waiting area of the Long Island Railroad, right underneath the gigantic electronic signboard that periodically lights up with track assignments.

This is one of the biggest rooms in the terminal, and it is full of hundreds of commuters, all standing there looking up at the board, waiting for their gate assignments to appear. When a new batch of numbers pops up, the crowd surges forward, splitting off toward various gates, everyone hurrying to get a seat. But until that moment comes, they are standing there, looking up, facing toward the sign— and the spot where I am about to step up onto our 17-cubic-inch plastic milk crate stage.

We have figured out that if we start in one minute, there will be just enough gap between departure times for me to do my whole show. The room is swollen with people waiting and staring up at the board. That is the attention we are about to redirect to ourselves.

Sarah puts the crate down on the floor and opens one more button on her shirt. She comes in close to me, takes my face in her hands, and gently shakes me a little. "Poet, calm down. Just do what you do in the church. Do your thing. Get into it. Focus on the crowd. Set yourself free." She looks at all the people standing in the hall, then back at me. "I love you. Break a leg. Here we go."

She turns and steps confidently up onto the stage and shouts, "Ladies and gentlemen! Lovers and lonely ones of the world!" Her voice really carries well, loud and clear, and people are looking up. "HEAR YE! HEAR HE! Today is Friday, February 14th, Valentine's Day 2014! Did you get your sweetheart something? A card? Some chocolate? A box of candy hearts? It's not too late! Kmart's up the stairs! But now, it is my honor and pleasure to introduce to you the love of my life. Happy Valentine's Day to all of you, and now let's give a hearty welcome to the one, the only, the Poet!" And Sarah steps down, gesturing to me.

There is a smattering of clapping, and even though I am scared shitless when I get up on the crate, I know I am radiating confidence. I stand tall and proud, my hands out like Jesus blessing the crowd. I envision a white light radiating from my body onto the crowd. I take a long look around the room, seeing one face after another after another. All eyes are on me, and I feel the energy pouring into me, though my knees are lightly shaking. I sing at the top of my lungs:

"Happy Valentine's Day to you! Happy Valentine's Day to you! Happy Valentine's Day, dear commuters. Happy Valentine's Day to you…" I feel a big smile explode on my face, and it's mirrored back to me from numerous grinning visages.

"I am the Poet!" I shout. "And now you know it!"

> *Am I stuck in the snow? No.*
> *I'm homeless, and I live in Penn Station.*
> *I have absolutely nowhere to go!*
>
> *What a winter it's been.*
> *"More snowfall tomorrow," they say. We shall see.*
> *You'll be sad if you're a shoveler.*
> *Happy if you ski.*
>
> *The mayor said, "Keep all your kids home from school."*
> *So rare in this city, so rare.*

Home is where the heart is, but cooped-up kids too?
You may end up pulling out your hair!

"Virginia's for lovers," the state slogan says.
More true today—with the yes same-sex ruling
Overturned! Something learned! No one spurned!
Conservatives heart-broken,
But love found a way today.
Screw the venom the Republicans are spewing!

Pope Francis to get into the Valentine's spirit
With thousands of couples engaged to be married
His advice to all future newlyweds:
Make sure love is never borrowed, but carried.

From the Facebook realm
More gender identifiers for users to use.
Options! Options!
Man. Woman. More.
The intersection, so many sexians.
Who are you? The call is yours.

Sochi Olympics
Are you sick of them yet? I am.

But without TV, I cannot see the Olympics. No, ma'am.
And did you know in Russia it's 59 degrees?
But wait, are the Olympics in Russia? Or in Belize?

And the money Russia spent on the games,
Soon they'll wonder where it went.
Hey, Putin, you wasted all your dough.
And now the whole world knows:
Mr. P's an ass—WHOA!
Watch your language, Poet.
No international incidents, if you please

My goal is to inform you.
I aim to please!

Big win! We picked up three medals in slopestyle skiing.
But I must ask:
What is that please?
Not skiing on the flat?
Down country skiing perhaps? Or up?
What is slope? I'm a clueless Olympic dope.

ACHTUNG!
Take note of Germany's big relay win.
In luge. It's huge.
Please raise your hand and give someone skin.

HEY!
Carmelo says he may go.
The Knicks have got to plan.
Five years, 120 mil to stay.
If you can spare a quarter, then I'm your man!

Hockey's on pause for Olympic break.
Every Ranger in the Olympics is still undefeated.
Lundvist saved 26 shots last night.
Lundvist is "The King" of shutting out Sweden.

So, safe trip home, Valentine lovers.
Be sure to open your heart.
If you've found yourself in a lovers' quarrel,
Your partner should give you a fresh start.

"My name is Poet, and it's been an honor to share my words with you. Please feel free to drop a donation in the Poetry Fund bucket. Thank you! Happy Valentine's Day! Sarah and I will be back here tomorrow. In advance, we appreciate all your ducats…"

I time it perfectly. Just as I finish, some new gate numbers appear on the board, and the crowd starts to shuffle forward, with a smattering of applause, a woo-hoo! or two, and a lot of smiles.

I'm filled with emotion. And strength. I feel tall and confident, like I conquered the world. As I step down off the crate, Sarah grabs my hand and squeezes it tight. She's talking to people as they throw money into the bucket, and a lot of people are congratulating me, chuckling. Someone shakes my hand. Sarah is answering questions. Yes, we're homeless. I've been writing poetry all my life. She's chatting away, and I can't stop staring at the people who are looking at me. They don't see a homeless man, someone down on his luck. They're trying to figure me out. I'm an anomaly, and I enjoy the confusion. The more perplexed they are, the more powerful I feel.

CHAPTER
FIFTY-TWO

Sarah and I have been performing in Penn Station for two months now. We have a fan base, a following. Commuters love us. They look forward to Sarah and me performing every day and supplying them, in our weird way, with the news. We're basically the stars of "The Penn Station Show."

The reverend comes and checks out our act and brings his whole family. I spot him as I stand up there reciting away, and I throw him a big smile and a slight, respectful nod. He is the straw who stirred my drink and forced me to share my poetry with strangers. At the time, I was not happy about it. Now I enjoy seeing the pride on his face.

It's been about nine months since I saw Josie, who turned seven last week. I was distraught. I mailed her a card wishing her a happy birthday. I promised her that we would be having pancakes together real soon. I placed a $20 bill inside the card and assured her I was fine and happy and that I think about her every day. That's all I wrote. I didn't have the heart to write anymore. It hurt too much.

I called Petra and asked her to take Josie shopping and let her spend the $20 on whatever she wanted and to keep it a secret between her and not tell Lauren. Of course, I also asked Petra to intercept the card, hide it from Lauren, and give it to Josie and tell her I love her.

It's the last week in April, and I have been feeling sick for a while. I have downplayed it with Sarah, who's lying next to me, still asleep. I have no energy, a slight wheeze, and I am sweating profusely. It's usually cool in the shelter, but I feel like I am in the Sahara. I get up to stretch out, and my knees are shaking. It's only 5 am. We still have two hours to sleep.

When I lie back down, I feel worse. The room starts to spin. I have little black spots in my vision, and my cough is stronger. I never get sick, and even if I did, I would never admit that I am sick. You can chop off my finger, and I'll point out that I have four more. But something feels different this time. It's scary not to be able to breathe properly. But maybe I'm just being a pussy. I cough, and Sarah peels her eyes open, and I cough again, and this one is really deep, and I have trouble catching my breath. She slowly gets up, sits cross-legged on her cot, and gives me a concerned stare. I cough again.

She puts her hand on my forehead, leaves it there for about fifteen seconds, and says, "You're burning up."

"Bullshit."

"Don't mess with me, Poet. I'm in no mood. When did you start coughing?"

"In the middle of the night."

"Has it gotten worse throughout the night? Seriously."

"Yes."

"Does your chest hurt when you cough?"

"Yes."

"Are you dizzy? Do you have trouble standing up?"

"What are you, a doctor?"

She points her right finger at my eyes and says, "Don't fuck with me. This is no joke. Get your clothes on; grab your bag. We're going to the emergency room."

"Fuck that."

She shouts, "I will get up, throw you on the bed, strip you butt naked, and drag you by your balls to the emergency room if you don't get dressed right now! Move!"

Walking to the hospital emergency room, every step hurts my chest. When we get there, Sarah does the talking.

"This is my boyfriend. He's very sick. High fever, deep cough, wheezing, profusely sweating. I'm guessing bronchitis."

The receptionist gives Sarah a bunch of paperwork to fill out. We sit. An emergency room in Manhattan is like a zoo of pain. Every illness is on display: broken bones, swollen body parts, people wrapped in blankets, babies crying, psychiatric patients pacing and screaming, people in pain, grimacing, and me, sweating and weak. It's an ugly scene.

Sarah is putting my information on a form.

"Poet, what should I put for an address?"

"Just write 'No residency.'"

"What happens if this is really serious? Wouldn't you want to be covered by insurance from your old life? You probably still have some."

"No. I'm going to be fine. Don't freak out. They'll give me some pills, and in a couple hours I'll be right as rain."

"Well, I hope you're right. I gotta stay positive. Think happy thoughts—not-coughing thoughts."

I let rip with a deep one, and her eyes go wide. "Jesus, it sounds like your lungs are being ripped out. I hate it."

I spit the phlegm into one of the paper towels I got in the men's room. Sarah finishes filling out the papers and takes them back up to the receptionist.

Three hours have gone by. This is absurd. As *Daily News* columnist Liz Smith would say, "Only in New York, kids. Only in New York." Sarah's having a nervous breakdown. She's sitting like a statue, as if she were comatose.

As my coughing gets worse, it starts to go in long jags when I can't stop. People nearby are looking at me like I've got the Ebola virus. I'm actually making a scene in the ER. Sarah reaches over and feels my forehead every few minutes. She is stone-faced and just sits there, occasionally rubbing my back. She's speechless.

Finally, my name is called, and a nurse leads us into an exam room. We sit in there alone for twenty-five minutes before a doctor comes in. I'm coughing and wheezing and can't keep my head up straight. Sarah's sitting in the corner, silent.

The doctor asks, "Are you comfortable with her being in here?"

"I'd be really uncomfortable if she *wasn't* here."

He smiles.

He then says, "You sound very bronchial. The deep cough, the wheezing, it looks like you've got a fever. Tell me how all this started."

"Well, I haven't felt right for weeks."

"Weeks! And you've kept it a secret?" Sarah has finally managed to say something, and she is pissed.

The doctor says, "Tell me about the past twenty-four hours."

I begin to talk, but coughing interrupts me. Sarah takes over and brings him up to date on how my symptoms have dramatically advanced.

"Okay. Let's start out by taking your vitals."

It turns out I have a temperature of 103.2. The doctor launches into a series of exploratory rituals—listens to this, pokes that, touches that, takes some blood.

"I'd like to take a look at your lungs," he says. "A nurse will bring you a gown. Put that on, and we'll wheel you down to the x-ray department."

When we're alone and I've put on the flimsy gown, Sarah comes over and cradles my head in her arms. "I wish I could trade places with you, Poet. I wish I could make you feel better. Is there anything I can do?"

"Make me laugh! That's your specialty."

"You want to laugh?" she asks. "Go look in the mirror. You look like my grandmother."

We crack up. She puts her forehead up against mine.

"I'm probably contagious, you know."

"Fine, if you die, we both die. I'm not going to be your widow-like former girlfriend. Fuck that!"

I smile. "I'm not going anywhere. I promise."

"You promise."

"I swear on Josie. I'm not leaving without you."

"Okay," she says. "If you evoke Josie, I believe your sincerity, though it seems to me you aren't really in charge of the outcome."

When I get back from the x-ray, Sarah is relieved to see me.

"How'd it go?"

"It went."

We wait quietly, holding hands. Finally, the doctor comes bustling back in, and he doesn't look happy.

"You have pneumonia," he says. "And also, a blood infection. I don't like what I see. I'm admitting you into the ICU for twenty-four-hour surveillance. This is serious, but we'll get it under control. Evan, try to lie back and relax. Breathe slow. They'll come for you in a bit, and I'll see you guys at the ICU. Keep calm. Stay positive."

With a rush of panic, I remember that Jim Henson died of pneumonia. He had no idea he was so sick until it was too late. I'm not ready to die and leave Sarah and Josie. It is simply not an option. Fuck that!

CHAPTER
FIFTY-THREE

I'm rolling down a hallway while the face of an angel hovers above me. They wheel me into the ICU, and then I'm in a bed and I'm delirious. Everything is a blur. There is constant beeping and strange machine noises. Nurses come and go all the time. When I look at Sarah, she appears to be stricken. It's all dreamlike and surreal, and I'm in and out of consciousness. Apparently, my vitals are worse. My fever is now 104, my blood pressure is sky high, and my respiration is shaky. Something is beating the shit out of me from the inside.

Sarah is so distraught that it is making me upset. It hurts to talk, but I tell her to sit down and hold my hand, and she does. She keeps reassuring me, whispering, "It's going to be alright" over and over. I fall asleep.

I wake up ten hours later. Sarah is still holding my hand, and she has her forehead down, resting on the post of the bed, as if she is praying. I move my hand, and she sits up.

She wipes my sweaty brow and says, "Don't talk. Just nod your head: once if you are better, twice if you are worse, three times if you feel the same."

I nod once to appease her, but I have no idea how I feel. My chest hurts when I breathe, and I am weak. It even hurts to nod my head. I am very stiff and extremely uncomfortable. I look up at the clock, and

Sarah asks me if I want to watch TV. I haven't watched TV in almost nine months, and I have no desire to start now. It strikes me as insane that she asked that, and then I wonder if I am even awake. Maybe I'm dreaming. My eyes are closed.

I hear the doctor come in, and he's talking to Sarah. "Evan has fallen into a septic coma, hence the high temperature, rapid heartbeat, and fast breathing. If things don't improve, he's going to need to be on a ventilator."

I watched enough *House* and *ER* to know that needing a ventilator is not a good thing. Sarah asks him what's ahead. When will I improve?

"I don't know, Sarah," says the doc.

I have no clear memory of the next five days, except for hearing the doctor brief Sarah about my condition. I hear their voices but can't understand what they are saying. And I remember hearing the rev's voice, sounding upbeat, and Mrs. Emerson reassuring Sarah. And I hear Sarah sniffling and blowing her nose. And sometimes I am aware that she is holding my hand. These are the only moments of light I can recall from the long darkness.

Now my eyes are open, and I see Sarah—her lush, creamy skin, strong jaw, full lavender lips, oval brown eyes with yellow rose petal streaks, bleached dirty blonde hair. A face so familiar and so astonishing now. Staring at it, I feel like I am home.

She sees my eyes are open and leans in over me. "Poet? Poet?"

I nod my head, and one of her tears splashes directly into my right eye. I feel like I've been baptized, and I smile. Gently, she places her cheek against mine. Her skin is like silk.

Crying, she smiles. "You promised you'd never leave me, and you stayed. Thank you."

My throat is dry, but I manage to cackle out, "A promise is a promise!"

She brushes my hair back off my face. "But don't ever fucking put me through this again!"

"I'm sorry. I'll speak to my antibodies. Heads will roll."

Later I am awake, and Sarah is in the cafeteria, so the doctor brings me up to date. "You had us worried, Poet. Sarah stayed at your side

THAT'S ALL I EVER WANTED TO BE 253

the whole time and hardly slept for five days and nights. She fought as hard as you did! We begged her to go home and get some rest, but she wouldn't leave. You're lucky to be alive, and you're lucky to have someone who loves you that much. We're going to keep you here a little longer, but you're going to be okay. Urge her to go get some rest, okay? We don't want her to get sick from exhaustion."

I told him I would. "Doc, thank you so much for your care. You and the whole staff here. We're so grateful. In fact, it's been a pleasure. I've had fun. Good times!" I smile to be sure he gets my humor.

"The pleasure's all mine, Poet." He gets it.

I convince Sarah to go home to the shelter and get a shower and a good night's sleep after her epic vigil. I lie awake late into the night, grateful to be alive.

In moments of crisis, you learn a lot about yourself, and about others. I know I love Sarah and want to spend my life with her, and I love Josie more than I can say, but in my mind the two women in my life were separate. Only on my near-death bed have I realized how much I want them to be together. For us to be a family.

CHAPTER
FIFTY-FOUR

It takes a few hours to check out of the hospital, and a lot of people seem to know my story and come by to say goodbye and wish us well —nurses who were taking care of me and who helped Sarah during her long nights, doctors, staff. Everybody likes that a homeless couple made it out of a tough spot. And people were moved by Sarah's caring for me. A lot of people give her hugs.

When we finally finish up our paperwork and Sarah wheels me down the hallway toward the door, nurses and doctors are slapping me five. It's a really good feeling. I get up out of the wheelchair and hug Sarah tight. She is the angel who watched over me. Without her spirit and love, I would've died completely misunderstood—a failure who threw away everything for a dream that never came to fruition. She changed my life months ago, and now she has saved it.

And she saved Josie. Although I haven't seen Josie in almost nine months, she knows I'm out here thinking of her. If I had died after disappearing for so long, without saying goodbye, Josie would have been crushed, and would surely resent me and suffer. Fortunately, it wasn't my time. I can make my life work and make those I love happy.

Back at the shelter, we get a warm welcome with plenty of hugs. Cindy gives me a bear hug, with a tear in her eye, and says, "Poet, I want you to leave here someday, but not like that."

"Cindy, hospital beds are pretty comfy, but my good old cot is where I want to be right now. It's good to be back."

She laughs, "Go make yourself comfortable. You look hungry. It's mac and cheese tonight, your favorite. Maybe Sarah will need three servings instead of her usual two. She's pretty worn out."

I smile and say, "Make it four. She can have one of mine."

"There's a visitor waiting for both of you by your beds. I've got a feeling you'll be happy to see him."

I walk out of Cindy's office, squint my eyes, and look all the way down to the end of the room. I see what looks like the reverend. Sarah is already sitting on her cot, next to him. I smile wide and walk fast with my duffel bag in hand.

I give him a huge hug, and he says, "You trying to check out early? Who the hell are you, Kurt Cobain?" He examines my face and gives my shoulder a tight squeeze. "I never had a doubt."

"A doubt?"

"That you'd get through that. No way my son was leaving without saying goodbye, and without finishing his story. Only you can write the end of it. This is your masterpiece. No fade to black on this one. You've got to finish it proper, by yourself."

"Rev, have you been smoking blunts?"

"Poet, I'm straight as an arrow. Don't you see what's happening here?"

I play stupid and say, "Yeah, I was stupid and ignored my body and almost kicked the bucket."

"But you're only in Act Two. The hero never dies in Act Two. You die in Act Three. That's how it's done, son."

I laugh.

"You didn't get to the happy ending yet, and you've got to keep going."

"Rev, you've got to get out more. You spend too much time watching AMC. Start doing something constructive like feeding the homeless, counseling gay youth, and conducting anti-abortion protests. Good shit like that. I'm worried about you."

He laughs, pulls me in close, and says, "Honestly, kid, I was worried sick. I had everyone I knew praying for you—at the church, the synagogue, the mosque. You were covered by three religions. Sarah was a basket case." He gives her a warm nod. "I was almost as worried about her as I was about you. I sat with her every night. And we talked a lot about you."

"Good things, I hope."

"We talked about how many lives you've touched in such a short period of time. Day by day, you quietly touched thousands of people, and you did it while hiding behind a false identity, not even being you. Since the day you showed up in the park, you've changed the whole scene just by being positive and by writing poetry. You've given hope to other homeless people, there and here in the shelter. You write poems that give people pleasure, you inspire people at artists night, you read poetry to hundreds every day in Penn Station. And you got Sarah to address her drug addiction. And you two fell in love. Not bad for a guy who lives out of a duffel bag. I feel like what's happened to you confirms the universal truths."

"Universal truths?"

"Yes, universal truths. Can I recite a verse of scripture?"

"Of course. You're the reverend."

"Mark 11:24: Therefore I tell you, whatever you ask for in prayer, believe that you have received it, and it will be yours. That's what I'm talking about. Poet, what are the things that you think about all day?"

"I think about getting paid to do what I love. I think about my poetry and writing inspiring people. I think about Sarah and Josie and having a nice two-bedroom apartment overlooking the park. Nothing crazy, just a comfortable place with a nice view and a kitchen table, with me, Sarah, and Josie eating pancakes on a Sunday morning."

"Well, then that's exactly what you're gonna get. Might not be today, might not be tomorrow, but it will happen, Poet. Focus on what you want, and imagine it's already happened, and you will receive."

"That sounds way too easy. If anyone else in the world told me that, I'd laugh in their face. But hey, you're the rev." I give him a hug. "Thanks for being there for Sarah. It means everything to me."

"Well, I kinda came to see you too, amigo. Thanks for staying alive."

Sarah comes over and hugs the rev tight and thanks him five times. After more hugs all around, the rev leaves.

With a tear in her eye, Sarah turns to me and says, "He's the real deal." Then she makes her right hand into a gang sign, grabs her crotch, strikes a pose, and says, "He's one cool mothafucking holy man!"

I laugh. We lie down, and I put my arm over her. We look at each other for a couple of minutes and don't say a word. There is nothing left to say.

At dinner, Sarah finishes off four servings of mac and cheese, and we go to bed. We plan to head back to Penn Station in the morning. I look forward to writing and performing again. Maybe I have been making a difference. If so, I want to make an even bigger one.

CHAPTER
FIFTY-FIVE

The next day, it is beautiful outside, absolutely perfect. It's an awesome feeling to break out your first T-shirt after a long winter, even if it's an old plain white one. Sarah has her summer wear going: Clash T-shirt, black stockings, short jean shorts, black mini boots. Haven't seen that in a while. This is the Sarah I first met nine months ago, dressed the exact same way.

Because it is so warm, we don't have to hang out in Penn Station all day. We go into Macy's in Herald Square, the famous one where the Thanksgiving Day Parade ends up. It's across the street from Penn Station and Madison Square Garden. I haven't been in a big store in almost a year. It's surreal and disorienting to walk around the men's department. I check the price tags and nearly shit my pants. A button-down shirt is $75. I used to pay that and more for shirts back in the day, but Sarah and I can live on that for a week.

What is pretty amazing is seeing Sarah in her element. She goes down to the perfume and makeup section and gets her makeup done for free. Then we go upstairs, and she starts trying on dresses. Suddenly I feel like I am at a fashion show and can see her professional self. She's obviously a model. She's striking: tall, thin, a bit busty for her frame. She shows me how she used to walk the runway. She throws on her "model face." I am mesmerized. It's like she's acting, playing an uninterested diva who looks like she's saying, "Yes, you know you want me." It is incredible to actually see her in this mode. I am dating a model! The thought has never occurred to me. I wish I had friends to brag to.

In late afternoon, we head back to Penn Station. I am pumped! I haven't been up on the crate in weeks, and I'm really looking forward to it. I buy my newspapers, study them, make notes, and then head up to the New Jersey Transit waiting room so I can sit alone and write. It feels good.

Back in my old life, I'd write maybe once or twice a week, at night, if I was lucky. Since I came to the park, I've written every day for hours at a time. My rhyming is freer, and I feel confident enough to be more playful.

Now it's 5:30, my new poem is done, and as usual I'm agitated, as nervous today as I was on day one. Sarah brings the crate from the Hudson News guys. She has our cardboard sign ready.

She turns to me and says, "Okay, Poet, I'm going to make a big deal about you being in a coma, and I'll explain where you've been. I'm really going to play it up. When the room is chanting your name, that's your cue."

"What?"

She laughs. "Here we go!" And beaming me with a big smile, she hops up onto our mini stage.

"Welcome! Welcome, people of the train world! Have you missed us? I have missed each and every one of you. All of you!" She has the crowd's attention. I see smiles. She points a finger at a guy with an old-fashioned briefcase and says, "I missed *you*!" Then she points at two more people. "I missed *you*. And I missed *you*!" She points at a woman with purple hair. "I missed *you*." At a dour-faced old guy, "I even missed *you*! I can't believe I did, but I did. I missed ya! And you all look beautiful tonight." She wags her finger at somebody, "Not you, I didn't miss you."

The crowd laughs.

"Just kidding. Just kidding."

The crowd laughs again.

"Ladies and gentlemen, tonight is very special. Tonight's the night!

Tonight is a miracle. We have been touched by the heavens! Tonight is comeback night! Yes, it's true. The Poet has been in the hospital. He was in a coma for five days! Five days! And tonight is his triumphant return. The man. The myth. The legend. I am about to introduce to you the one…the only…Poet!"

Sarah is proclaiming like a Biblical prophet. "He is back! He's back from the dead! From the dark hallows! He saw the raven take flight, and he's here to tell us today's news! He's back for you! He walks the Earth once more. So, let's get a chant! Let's chant him back up here! He needs your support! He's your Poet! He's our Poet! So, let's go!" And she starts chanting, "Po-et! Po-et! Po-et! Po-et!"

Suddenly, the crowd is chanting my name. "Po-et! Po-et! Po-et!' Penn Station is rocking. People are pumped. I can feel the energy. I feel it welling up in me. I am ready to explode. Sarah steps down, and with a devilish grin she bites my ear, smacks my ass, and says, "Get up there, Poet. Give them what they want! You're a God!"

I step up onto our miniature stage, raise my hands in the air palms up, and turn, blessing everyone. The crowd goes wild, and I pump my fist to the Poet chant. "Po-et! Po-et! Po-et!" This is my moment. This is it. It can't get any better than this. I try to feel it, be in the moment, immerse myself, and let go. Three hundred strangers are chanting my name, and I am towering over them like an orchestra conductor. Now I slowly use my arms to bring the chant down, and when they are quiet, I begin my oration.

"This is the greatest moment of my life. When I was in that coma, I was gone. I never thought today was possible. I never thought I'd be back up here. But here we are! Tonight, like so many nights over the past months, we share in something. We share in each other's company! We feed off each other's energy! Right now, we are one! All I do every day is recite the news poetically. That's all, nothing more! And all I really want is to make you happy. My amazing girlfriend, Sarah, and me, we want to loosen you up after a long day. We want you to know we care about you, and we want to make you feel good. And she, by the way, is an angel, and just saved my life…"

I pause, then continue, "Do we make you feel good?!"

The crowd yells, "Yeah!"

"Do we have fun together?"

"Yeah!"

I raise my voice and shout, "Does anyone want to know what's going on in this big old crazy world today?!"

"YEAH!"

"Okay, here's the freaking news..."

I launch into my poem, and the crowd hangs on every word and laughs at all my jokes and obscure references. I feel like they are inside my mind. And I am getting off on their attention. They are following every word, as if I am a musician and they are hearing every single note.

From the news, I spiral out into some more riffs about the moment, hanging onto it, not wanting the connection to end. I improvise some lines at the end about how moved I am and how grateful I am for my life. I leave them with a whoop and a wave and step off the crate, and the crowd goes wild.

I hug Sarah as if I haven't seen her in years. I feel like I've never seen her before. Like I was just born anew. Like this is the World Series, and I just hit a grand slam. I am overcome with emotion. People are patting me on the shoulder as they move past toward their trains.

Sarah grabs my face and says, "This is our time, Poet! This is our time!"

"From your beautiful lips to God's ear, Ms. Jones."

"God's been listening for months, and tonight he told you, 'Fuck yeah, your time is now!'"

CHAPTER
FIFTY-SIX

Sarah doesn't say much on the walk back to the shelter. She just rubs my back and watches me glow. I can't even blink. I stop in the middle of the sidewalk, pull her in, and kiss her passionately.

She smiles, I put my arm around her, and we slowly make our way home.

The next morning, after pancakes, we head back over to Penn Station. It is raining, so we figure we'll stay inside and hang out all day. I talk to Officer Mattola about the Yankees and how crazy it is that it's Derek Jeter's last season. I hang with Sergeant Malloy, and we discuss politics. We share our thoughts on the Middle East and on pulling our troops out of Afghanistan, and we talk about President Obama.

Sarah hangs out with the girls from the Bronx who work at Planet Smoothie. She is very close with Jen and Jackie. They always talk celebrities and gossip. They show her what's up on Twitter, who's dating whom, and what they were wearing at this event or that.

At 3, I go over to the Hudson News stand and buy my papers to prepare for tonight's performance. Sarah is sitting in the Long Island Railroad waiting room reading *People*. I tell her I'm going up to New Jersey Transit to write.

I'm sitting there taking notes, head down, in hyper-focus mode, when I look up to see a professional-looking woman, in heavy makeup with short brown hair, right in front of me, smiling. She's attractive.

"Can I ask you a question?" she asks.

I'm on guard. She has a strange vibe.

"It depends. Who am I talking to?"

"My name is Stephanie Cohen."

"Okay, Stephanie Cohen, it's nice to meet you. How can I help you?"

She reaches into her pocketbook and takes out a phone. "Can I show you something?"

"The highlights from last night's Yankees game? Most definitely. I'd appreciate that."

"No, I want to show you something else. Do you read poetry here every evening?"

"Yeah, sometimes."

"Then you'll want to see this. You'll like it, I promise."

"Okay."

She holds her phone in front of my face so I can see it clearly. It's a video of Sarah, last night, introducing me. I hear the chant: "Po-et! Po-et! Po-et! Po-et!" and see myself get up on the crate and address the crowd. She pauses it.

"I'm from Channel 7 Eyewitness News. And this video of you two was posted on YouTube. It has 10 million views. I'd like to interview you and your partner, tape your performance tonight, and report on your version of the news on our version of the news."

Penn Station has just turned upside down for me. "Let me see the rest," I say.

She hits play, and I watch. I'm buying time.

I am so confused. If I am on TV, I will be exposed. Lauren will see me. Wait. If that video has 10 million hits, then I'm already exposed. This is bad. But it's also amazing. I need to talk to Sarah. The video ends, and I stand and shake the reporter's hand.

"Come with me, Stephanie. I need to speak with Sarah about this. She's downstairs."

My heart is racing. My palms are sweating. I hurry ahead, down the steps, slide up to Sarah in a hurry, slightly out of breath, and look back at Stephanie Cohen, who's coming down the escalator.

"What the fuck is wrong with you? You look like you've seen a ghost."

"Sarah, you see that woman coming down. She's a reporter. She wants to interview us. Someone taped our performance last night and put it up on YouTube. It went viral. We got 10 million views."

"What the fuck! She wants to interview us?"

"Yeah."

Sarah's eyes are wide; she's in shock. "Do you know what this could do? Make you a fucking star! This is the break, Poet. This is it!"

The reporter comes over to Sarah. "Stephanie," I say, suddenly grinning. "It is my great pleasure to introduce you to Sarah, the love of my life, and the other star of our show. Would you please show Sarah the insane video you just showed me? It's all Sarah's fault."

Stephanie sits down between us and brings the video back up. It's called "The Homeless News Poet of Penn Station." I feel as nervous about watching it again as I do when I'm getting ready to perform. Stephanie hits play, and we hear the sounds of Penn Station. The track numbers being called. The chatter. The sound of commotion. Then out of nowhere in the middle of the screen, we see Sarah rise above the crowd and shout, "Welcome! Welcome! Have you missed us?" Sarah and I look at each other and smile. She's incredible up there. Messing with the crowd. Pointing people out. She has the whole room's attention. She looks beautiful, she's stunning, and the crowd is hanging on her every word. Now everybody is chanting, and the place is going wild. It's amazing to watch.

Then I get up on the crate, and I can't even recognize myself. How could that be me? The pride in my eyes. The joy I radiate. The positive energy I give off. It's like watching a stranger. I've never seen myself perform, of course. The best part is watching me recite my news poem and seeing the faces in the crowd listen, laugh, wince, and look at others for their reactions. The camera caught it all. And I suddenly realize that the mean, miserable stockbroker me is gone. I don't even resemble myself anymore. I've become someone else. Myself. Poet!

I have always been one of the most insecure, unconfident, self-deprecating, self-despising people in the world. Now I am someone else. I like this guy!

The video ends.

"So, who are you two?" asks Stephanie. "I want to hear your story. I found this video and then tweets and posts about your performance down here last night. I did a little research and asked around, and here I am. What you are doing is pretty unusual, and I like it. If you don't mind my asking a few questions, let me start with this: What are your names?"

"My name's Sarah, Sarah Jones, and this is Poet."

I give Sarah the look of death, but she couldn't care less. She squeezes my hand.

"How long have you been doing this?"

"About three months."

"Poet, do you write all the poetry?"

"Yes."

"And you both are homeless?"

"Yup."

"Do you do this to earn money?"

"Yup."

"Do you mind if we film you performing tonight, after we do a brief interview on camera before? You can tell us a little about your process, answer some general questions. It's local news. It'll be a one-minute story. Nothing too crazy. Just a human-interest piece. With all the buzz on YouTube, it should grab people's attention. I think people will love it. Would you be okay with that?"

Sarah looks at me steadily, and a thousand words pass unspoken between us. She smiles, and a wave of joy and peace washes through me.

"Okay!" I say.

"Perfect. My crew will be here in an hour. Hang tight for a couple of minutes, if you don't mind. I need to make a few calls."

CHAPTER
FIFTY-SEVEN

By 4 pm, Penn Station is starting to get busy. Sarah and I watch the camera crew while they set up. The reporter, Stephanie, is getting her makeup redone and looks elegant in that fake, wax museum sort of way. Sarah is enjoying the preshow and ends up doing a bit of dolling up as well. She borrows some makeup from the girls at Planet Smoothie, combs her hair, and pulls it back into a tight ponytail that accentuates her facial features. Even without makeup, her skin and complexion are always perfect. Her face is angelic and radiates beauty, which makes the foul language that comes out of her mouth that much more ridiculous. When she says, "I'm gonna give you a blowjob," it's like she's fulfilling the fantasy of a young guy looking at a beautiful model in a men's magazine. Playing around with my sexual wiring is what she's doing, just for the fun of seeing sparks fly.

I love her soul and her character, but her amazing looks are a bonus. I, of course, look like shit. I haven't had a haircut in months. My beard is shaggy. I look like a guy who would be selling nitrous at a Phish concert. Sarah looks super-hot in a funky down-and-out way. I just look like some homeless guy. Maybe the contrast will make our story more interesting for TV.

Once everything is set up in a corner of the hallway, with the station in the background and all the shop fronts and people hurrying by, they start the cameras rolling. Stephanie asks us some questions. It only takes a few minutes. How we met, who came up with the idea of performing here in the station, how I write my news poems, how it feels to be up there doing it.

Then she starts in about our being homeless and asks us where we're from. Sarah instantly says, "Iowa. Right outside Des Moines."

Stephanie turns to me, and this is where I stumble. I am suddenly terrified that if I tell her too much, it's going to begin the unraveling of my new life with Sarah—my anonymity, my independence. It will expose me and reconnect me to my old world, to everything I left behind.

"I guess I'm kind of a local," I tell her. "At least I've been rooting for the Rangers, the Yankees, and the Jets for quite a while."

The reporter turns to the camera, does a kind of wrapping-it-all-up comment, and then re-films that part a couple of times with variations. Then they turn off the cameras, and we are done.

"You are an interesting couple," Stephanie says to Sarah and me, and it seems like she means it. "I'd like to know more about you, hear your whole story."

"Let's see how tonight goes first," I say, trying to laugh it off. "Hey, I'd better go polish up my news poem and get ready!" I shoot Sarah a look that I hope says, "I'm sorry!" and I turn and hurry off to one of my writing spots.

CHAPTER
FIFTY-EIGHT

It might have been our best performance yet. I don't really know, because I never saw it, but at the time it felt like we were riding an immense wave. Sarah was truly amazing.

As she steps up onto the crate, she immediately shoots her arm out, pointing at somebody, or pretending to. "LADY!" she shouts. And points to someone else. "GENTLEMAN!" And then she amps it up to full volume "LADIEEEEES AND GENTLEEEEEMEN!!! We are back! Moms! Dads! Hard-working laborers blue and white, WE SALUTE YOU! And we salute YouTube, where last night's show, from right here, went ballistic with a viralistic viewership. We're talking 10 million views. Twenty million eyeballs, or maybe a few less if there were one-eyed pirates in the crowd. To whoever put that video up there, we thank you!"

She's blowing kisses from both hands, tossing them out over everyone like candy and beads at a Mardi Gras parade.

"And now!" she continues, "here we are again! Tonight! Me—your mistress of ceremony—ready to introduce the man with the golden Pilot G-2 pen, who is here, once again, as promised—and now hereby delivered—to give you the day's events, the newest of the news, in verse. So PLEASE WELCOME… (and here she blows my mind by beat boxing a rhythm—with no microphone): "Boomp, kaboompa boomp bah boomp) THE MAN (boomp, kaboompa boomp bah boom) WHO BROUGHT YOU (kaboompa boomp bah boomp) ON YOUTUBE (ba boomp)—TEN (Ka boomp boomp) MILLION (ka boomp boomp) VIEWS! TEN MILLION VIEWS (boomp boomp) and suddenly arms shoot up all over the room and pick up the chant, and it's loud and strong. "TEN MILLION VIEWS! TEN MILLION VIEWS! TEN MILLION VIEWS!"

"I GIVE YOU," shouts Sarah, turning and gesturing to me, as if there is a spotlight burning on my face, and yes I am beaming right back up at her, with more smile than I thought possible. "THE POET!!!"

Mostly I have no idea what I said that night, though I know I improvised a lot. Suddenly, I am watching the faces of the crowd carefully and watching myself watching them while some other part of myself is talking, performing—a part that knows what it's doing, that has total confidence. I feel no anxiety—just joy and overwhelming peace, as if I am radiating my essential self out into that improbable crowd in that claustrophobic hall. Like I am spreading magic dust all over the world.

And there is something else going on, another level of thought. Suddenly, I know that this is the last show. That I have taken it as far as I can. And even though people are sincerely enjoying what I am doing and are listening to my words, and I am feeding off that energy, I realize that the poems themselves are limited in some way. And I know that I am limited by how little I actually know about writing poetry, by how little poetry by other people I've ever even read.

I feel an explosive combination of sensations—pride at being able to reach out and connect, love of words themselves, and the joyful certainty that I have somehow set myself free to play within language. Yet I have a new awareness that I want to go deeper—that everything I have dared to do is just the beginning of something more.

And with clarity, I see that it is now time to reconnect with Josie and bring her into this new life. If I think about it any deeper at that moment, I know I will be overcome with horror at what I have done: leaving her for so long and going off on my own. But my rational mind shuts that horror down and reassures me that all of it is connected: the success and the failure, bound together. And that I need to keep going.

So, I realize I am at a turning point and that is all okay. And at that moment it's as if the sound is turned back on, and now, I am the guy performing. The smiles and the yelling of the crowd are pouring right into me. And this part I remember clearly: I shout to the crowd, "What are we doing here together? For five minutes a day, we share something, and it's more than the news. We share joy! We share passion! We have fun! We are in this life together! Right here. We might not have money. But we have time. Right now. Let's share it through rhyme!"

I launch into my news poem. At the end, the crowd roaring, I step down off the milk crate, ready for whatever is next.

CHAPTER
FIFTY-NINE

I am having a nightmare about my marriage to Lauren. I'm watching us yell and rage at one another, though I can't hear anything. I'm floating in the air, observing my own life, like Jimmy Stewart in that Christmas movie. Our faces are ugly with anger, and neither of us is listening, just spitting out words. It's horrible. I recoil in terror, and suddenly I am awake on my cot in the shelter, and it's quiet and dark. I look over at Sarah, who is sleeping deeply. I turn in to her, put my arm around her, and lie there thinking for a long time.

I'm staring at her when she finally opens her big brown eyes and greets me with a wonderful smile. She reaches over and pinches my nose, and I gently kiss her.

"Time to get up!" I say. "Remember, last night we told Stephanie Cohen we'd do an interview today. She wants to put us on their national broadcast. We don't have long to get over there."

"Okay, superstar," says Sarah, kissing me. "Let's get dressed and go get some pancakes. We need extra strength if we're going for the big time."

"Make sure you look good," I joke. "I don't want the world to think Evan Bloom the Homeless Poet is dating a seven."

"A seven? You're a two at best. Why don't you shave and cut your goddamn hair? You look like a guy from *The Deadliest Catch*.

I stare at her blankly.

"The reality show about going out in the Arctic Sea and catching crabs, for months on end, where all the fishermen look like shit! That's what you look like. Yet somehow, you caught me."

"I'm not shaving. This is hobo chic, and today I'm unleashing it on the world."

"Good luck with that."

We go into the bathrooms to wash up and change. I come out in my T-shirt and jeans, the same ones I always wear, and Sarah comes out in her standard outfit of black stockings, short denim shorts, black boots, and Clash T-shirt. We are going on TV as ourselves because this is who we are, and I'm proud of how we appear. Just because you're homeless and funky doesn't mean you can't accomplish big things. We're living proof.

On our way home that night, I think about telling Sarah what I'd realized about no longer performing, that I needed to move into a new phase with writing, and that I'd realized it is time to bring Josie into our lives. Now, over pancakes, I tell her about my nightmare, and what I figured out in the early morning hours.

"Sarah, you were right somehow about Josie and about me and Lauren. Our marriage couldn't have become so horrible if I were perfect. It wasn't all her fault. Part of why I hated my life is that I was being an asshole. And if I was an asshole, why am I surprised she was a bitch? What did I expect, if I was willing to be as mean to her as she was to me? I've got to find a way to change all that, to connect with her in a new way so we can be apart but still be Josie's parents. And be good at it. We weren't meant to be happily married, but we need to be happily divorced. Do you see what I mean?"

"Poet, that's one gigantic crab of wisdom you hauled in during the night. You still look like shit, but I think your soul is getting clean. I'm proud of you."

As we guzzle the last of our coffee and walk toward Penn Station, we talk about how I can keep going with poetry and get better at it. I want to read as much as I can get my hands on and start trying to get something published in a magazine. I'd like to connect with other poets—maybe go to some readings over at the Poetry Project at St.

Marks Church in the East Village. During our wanderings, we'd gone by there several times and read their big sign announcing various poetry readings and classes.

"The other thing I feel good about is the workshops I've been doing at the shelter," I tell Sarah. "I think helping other people write and helping them figure out how that can help them and open themselves up will help me go deeper myself. I love performing, but I don't want to be a big ego freak about it. Whatever this whole thing we've got going is, I want to keep at it and see if I can not only do some good work, but also do some good for other people. Does that make sense?"

"Not bad for a fisherman, Poet," she smiles. "Now you can be a fisher of men, like that great poet Jesus. Isn't he the one who wrote "Howl"? No wait, that was Allen Ginsberg. Jesus wrote "Blessed Are," my favorite poem." She gives me a huge warm smile and hugs me, just as we turn the corner and Penn Station comes into sight. "I wonder where Stephanie's truck is going to be?"

Then we realize that on 32nd Street, a whole line of media trucks is parked outside the main entrance to the station.

"Wow," she says. "It's gonna be a shit show in there. You feel okay?"

"I feel great."

We enter Penn Station and take the escalator down. There aren't any reporters on the first floor. We peek around the corner and down to the ground floor and see a whole line of cameras set up and reporters with notes clutched in their hands. I look at Sarah and smile, and she smiles back. I take her hand.

We are halfway down the stairs when I hear someone shout, "There they are!" and we are mobbed as reporters and people with cameras hurry up to us. Everyone is talking at the same time, trying to get a word in.

I raise my hands for calm, and when it quiets, I say, "Sarah and I will be glad to talk to all of you, just be patient!"

I spot Stephanie and the crew from her network, but there are logos from every news organization I've ever heard of: CBS, NBC, ABC, MSNBC, FOX News, and CNN.

"We promised Stephanie Cohen first crack at us," I say, waving her over. "So, why don't all of you just hang tight. We'll go with her first, up to the Long Island Railroad waiting room and talk there, and when she's done, we'll talk to each of you, okay? There's no rush. We'll answer whatever question you want to ask, unless the answer is really embarrassing."

"Will you be performing tonight?" one reporter yells.

"No, I'm officially retired. I'm leaving at the top of my game. I'm working on a book." I hold up my big duffle bag and pat it. "It's all right in here."

Several hours later, we are talked out. I feel empty, but at peace. As we leave the station holding hands, I shake my head and ask Sarah, "How do you think it went?"

"I don't think it could've gone any better."

"Did we say too much?"

"Sure, but people are going to want to know more. It was perfect."

"Well, I imagine a gazillion people will see us tonight. What the fuck is going to happen?"

"I have absolutely no clue. Don't be surprised if we wake up in the morning and find out that people are lined up outside the shelter waiting to talk to us."

"Like who?"

She gives me that wiseass smirk. "Like President Obama. He's going to want the name of your barber."

We decide our efforts and our exhaustion justify another splurge, so we go to McDonald's. As I eat my fries, with lots of salt, and wash them down with a soda, I find that I am extremely happy—and getting happier by the minute. "I think I like being retired," I tell Sarah. "And I'm also inspired. I'm going to write an epic poem about you. I'll call it 'The Lady in the Park.'"

"Well I've been writing a song about you. I'm going to call it, 'Why Don't We Do It in the Shelter?'"

We take our time walking home. It's a perfect night.

CHAPTER
SIXTY

Sarah and I are usually early risers. Sleeping in late, for us, is 6 am. So, when I wake up and see that it's already 10:45, I'm shocked and instantly fully wired. We were supposed to be out of the shelter over two hours ago! What is going on? I look around to see all the other cots are empty.

Sarah is still sleeping, and she looks so peaceful I hate to disturb her, so I give her fifteen seconds more, and then gently take her ear lobe between my thumb and forefinger and give a gentle pinch.

"What the fuck?!" she startles awake and reflexively slaps my face, actually a little bit hard. "Why'd you wake me up? I was in the middle of a hot dream!"

"I'm sorry. But we gotta get out of here. It's a quarter to 11."

"Holy shit! The last time I slept this late was after a night of doing cocaine in Bungalow 8. Hop to it, Poet. Go get dressed. We have to find out if all that face time we gave the TV reporters amounts to diddlysquat."

Aha! Sleep has completely erased my memory; it's hard to believe we spent yesterday afternoon in front of the cameras. We both leap up and head for the bathrooms to get dressed, and within minutes I have my duffel bag over my shoulder, and we are walking toward the exit.

Just then Cindy calls us, and we see her beckoning to us from the doorway. "Poet, Sarah! Could you please come down to my office?"

I look at Sarah blankly, and she raises her eyebrows at me. We head down the hall.

Cindy's office is a relatively small space. You could probably fit five people in there, max. As we walk in, we see a well-dressed woman sitting in one of the guest chairs, sharp, attractive, distinguished looking, and probably in her sixties. She looks extremely familiar.

"Have a seat," says Cindy, gesturing to the other two chairs.

As we sit, Sarah smiles at the woman and asks, "Are you from the FBI? Because if you are, we didn't do it. I swear. At least I didn't. Poet? Maybe."

The woman laughs and reaches out her hand. "I'm Betty Wall, and I'm a journalist with CBS, from *60 Minutes*."

Sarah says, "*60 Minutes*? The baking show!" and I crack up.

"It's a long-form journalism show, Sarah," says Betty Wall patiently. "We're on Sunday nights at 7."

"Sarah's pulling your leg," I laugh. "Everybody knows you're the number one news program on television. I'm a big fan, Ms. Wall. I've loved your work for years."

"Well, Poet, everyone loves the work you and Sarah have been doing. I know you two are kind of sheltered here in the shelter. Do you have a sense of what kind of reach your story has had overnight?"

"We honestly have no idea," I say. I feel a tingle at the base of my spine.

"Let me put it this way. Everybody picked up on the interviews you did yesterday; they were all over the news last night, to the point where, at a press briefing this morning, the President was asked to comment."

"Holy shit! That's insane," says Sarah.

"He had seen the stories, and what he said was..." and Ms. Wall looks down at the notebook she has in her lap, "'Evan and Sarah embody passion and creativity and determination and prove that even when the chips are down, if you have somebody to love and somebody to collaborate with, you can do the seemingly impossible and make a difference.'"

My mind is kind of blown, and I am just grinning.

"You are all over social media and cable news," continues Ms. Wall. "You have 100 million views on YouTube. People want to know more about you, and that's why I'm here. I want to find out if you would be willing to spend some time with me, tell me your whole story, how you found each other, how you've survived on the street, and how you started doing the shows and the poetry."

Sarah and I lock eyes, as if asking each other, "This isn't really happening, is it?"

"We'd like to air the piece on *60 Minutes* next Sunday, so you and I would start out by just having a long informal conversation off-camera. Like maybe you'll let me take you out to brunch, and we can just get acquainted, and I can get a sense of what all we are going to want to talk about and film. Then over the next couple of days, we'll have our crew, and we'll film the interviews, go around to some of the places you've been living, and talk to some of the people who know you."

She stops and smiles, as if to give us a chance to let what she's saying soak in. "What do you think?" she asks, looking from one of us to the other. "Would you be comfortable doing that?"

I look at Sarah, and we smile at the same time, then she looks at Betty and asks, "Where are we going for brunch?"

"Your choice!" Betty laughs.

Since it's Betty Wall's treat, we jump in a cab and head up to 52nd Street to our favorite over-the-top restaurant, Serendipity 3. The main thing about it is the amazing desserts, specifically, the frozen chocolate milkshake. I brought Josie here for her fifth birthday, and she freaked out. She loved it. Sarah had told me she used to have any guy she went out with bring her there, to find out if he had a fun side.

From the street, it's an unassuming little place. It looks like a dry-cleaning shop. It's nothing. But when you walk in, it is magic, a colorful idiosyncratic world, with big clocks all over the place, white chairs and tables, white-and-pink tiled flooring, Tiffany glass chandeliers everywhere, paintings, and all kinds of odd colorful decorations. It is kind of cheerfully surreal.

Sarah and I order burgers, which in the menu photos are beautifully arranged with huge chunky fries. Ms. Wall orders a salad, and Sarah is outraged. "That's like going to a steakhouse using ketchup! I hope you at least go crazy on dessert."

When the burgers arrive, I go after mine like a seagull grabbing snacks on a beach blanket. Sarah is her usual careful, meticulous self, taking bites out of the burger in just the right places while she methodically rotates it. Sarah always plans how to eat her food, coming up with a precise strategy of some kind. I notice that Betty Wall is taking it all in, our banter and humor with one another.

We tell her about the past ten months, how we met, and what it was like living in Washington Square Park. We tell her about our first poetry project, the reverend, performing, and about Sarah's career and drug addiction. I tell her about the pivotal night when I gave up on my old life, and I tell her about poetry as the secret core of me and how that one poem had changed everything and set me off on a quest to make poetry the center of my life. She's taking notes all along and asking us a few questions. But she says she mostly wants to wait for the formal on-camera interviews to get more deeply into things. We'll start in the morning, doing some interviews in the shelter. She's already received permission from Cindy.

By the time we get to dessert and all three of us are pigging out on our huge extravagant chocolate milkshakes, we seem to be pretty comfortable with one another. We ask her about how she became a big-time journalist, and she tells us a little bit about that. But she is more interested in us. I tell her about Josie, and we tell her how the main thing we want now is to get off the streets and live together as a family. As I hear us talking about what we want, it sounds pretty good. Being in such a surreal restaurant makes it doubly surreal that we are talking to Betty Wall in the next few days and how we're going to be doing a *60 Minutes* piece. I'm counting on it helping us keep moving forward, toward our dream, toward our real chocolate milkshake.

CHAPTER
SIXTY-ONE

Filming interviews in the shelter feels a little weird at first, but we warm up to it. Cindy has arranged for them to do it after everybody leaves in the morning, and Betty talks to us while we sit on our cots. At one point, I open up my duffle bag and show her all the poems, talk about that, and read a few. I even show her my secret weapons: my yellow legal pad and Pilot G2 pen.

Betty interviews Cindy a bit, and they shoot a bunch of footage of the place. And then we head outside, and our interview continues as we walk along together on the sidewalk. The crew films us as we talk all the way to Penn Station, and one of them holds a big sound mike on a pole right above us all the way. We show Betty around the station and tell her about our routines in there. She has me buy some newspapers at the Hudson News stand, like usual, and she films me while I sit in the spot where I always wrote my news poems, pretending to write one.

Then Betty interviews a few of our Penn Station friends—a couple of the cops, our favorite Starbucks barista (who used to slip us day-old cinnamon rolls), and Sarah's pals at Planet Smoothie. Betty says she has plenty of footage of our performances, but they do some shots of the waiting room with the crowd milling around and staring up at the schedule board.

And then we all make our way back to the shelter. They want to get some footage of dinnertime, everybody hanging out afterward, and the room full of cots. They ask first if anybody minds, but nobody does except one old guy named Jesse, who smiles and waves and goes off to wait it out in the bathroom. Betty does an interview sitting at the rec room table talking a bit with a guy named Freddy, who's in the writing group I've been leading.

From the start, Freddy has been one of the most enthusiastic and serious writers in it. One evening, a few weeks before, he'd read a piece out loud to all of us. It gave an hour-by-hour account of his entire day on the street, complete with his conversations with other homeless people, what he thought about all day, and the things passersby said to him. It was heartbreaking and beautiful and completely hilarious all at the same time. I'd told him he should send it to the *New Yorker*, and he did, but didn't include a return address.

"If they like it, they'll print it," he told me.

When Betty Wall asks Freddy about me and my poems, he gives her a grave look and shakes his head slowly from side to side. "Poet is a great guy, and he has helped me and inspired me a lot, but I'll be honest with you. I think he might be insane. I mean, the guy used to be rich, and now he lives here and writes poems that I don't understand and sleeps on a cot." He arches an eyebrow at Betty. "We're thinking of having him committed." He lets that hang there for a second and then bursts out laughing and reaches up and offers me a high five.

They shoot some film of Sarah talking to the group she leads, talking about addiction and recovery. She tells a pretty intense story about how addiction had affected her career when it was at its very peak. She is so open—and though it is serious stuff and some of it painful, she is great at using her sarcastic sense of humor to make fun of herself and keep things loose. I can see that Betty is impressed.

We spend the next day, which is beautiful and warm and breezy and energizing, filming outdoors in Washington Square Park. It's a sweet homecoming, and Sarah and I are excited to give Betty a tour of the world we'd lived in for nine months. We show her the spot where we first met, and as we are sitting there kind of choking up about it, an adorable Yorkie comes over and starts nuzzling Sarah, quivering with excitement.

"This is my previous boyfriend," she tells Betty. "His name is Bruno. About ten minutes after I met Poet, I dumped him, and the poor guy still hasn't gotten over it."

At one point, Betty and the crew go off with Sarah to film her by herself, and I sit in the sun and watch the park, which is blooming with people. I can hardly believe what is happening to us, and that our story is going to be on TV. And not just on TV, on *Sixty Minutes*.

Growing up, I rarely watched television with my parents, but every week after Sunday night dinner we'd watch that show. When I was a kid, some of the subject matter was over my head, but as I got older, I found it more and more interesting. A lot of the stories are about politics and war, but some are about other things: a scientific breakthrough, a new technology, somebody who'd done something extraordinary, or just something interesting. I figure that's the category Sarah and I are going to be in: how surprising that our lives, which to be honest are kind of rooted in failure, have become interesting. I think about all the people I used to know who will be shocked to see us on the show.

The one person who seems to take our being profiled on big-time TV for granted is our friend and biggest fan, the rev. The crew sets up in front of his church and films him sitting in his spot at the top of the stairs, where he likes to hold his meetings. He starts off talking about how he met us, and I don't watch it all. I think it might get embarrassing, so I wander away so they can have some privacy.

But the weirdest moment of the day is when Sarah and I take Betty to the alley where we used to sleep. When Sarah and I sit down there, right next to our spot, I am unexpectedly overcome with emotion. I have to excuse myself and go over to the dog run and find somebody who will let me scratch behind their ears.

CHAPTER
SIXTY-TWO

On Sunday night, Cindy rolls out four old TVs and spaces them along one side of the dining area. After dinner, everybody stays in their chairs in anticipation of the show. The rev and his wife have come to watch with us, and Sarah and I share a table with them.

Somebody yells, "Where's the popcorn?" and Cindy blows everybody's mind by coming out right then with a cart full of big bowls filled with freshly microwaved, hot, buttered popcorn and handing them around.

Sarah is pretty agitated. "I hope my parents are watching," she says to me quietly. "I hope my father is sitting in his Lazy Boy and shits his pants. And I hope the bastard calls me up, so I can say 'Fuck you!' and hang up."

"Sarah, we don't have a phone."

"Good point. But if we did, that's what I'd say."

"I don't know how my parents would react if they were still alive. I'm sure me being a homeless poet is the last thing my father would ever have expected. You know, if he were still alive, I don't think any of this would have happened. I'd still be stuck, living in his shadow, living the life he planned for me."

"So, you're glad he's dead?"

"Of course not. I can't say that. But I think it's true that his death set me free and brought me joy—not at the time, but it led me to the joy of being with you. And of being Poet."

"I think that's who you really are, and always have been, and one way or another you would have found your way to being yourself."

As *60 Minutes* begins, the host runs through the teasers about each of the night's segments, and in the last one there are Sarah and me, laughing together on a bench in the park: "A story of love, inspiration, and redemption, of two homeless people who found each other and found their way." And then there's a glimpse of me standing on the crate, pumping up the chanting crowd of commuters in Penn Station. "They found a way to help others through poetry." Then they cut to a commercial. Sarah grabs my hand, and I bring it up to my lips and kiss it.

When our segment begins, near the end of the show, everybody in the shelter starts clapping, and the rev shoots me a beaming smile. Watching the segment is surreal. They've found a photo of me in my stockbroker days, wearing an Armani suit with my hair slicked back. I am wearing a fake smile. I look unhappy and lost.

I hate watching myself, and the things I say seem stupid. But I love the parts about Sarah. She tells about her career as a supermodel and being on the cover of *Vogue*, and they show a clip of her standing next to Anna Wintour at some glitzy event. Sarah is so honest and clear when she talks about her heroin addiction and fighting through that, and she comes off as a tough survivor. And she's never looked more beautiful.

Most of what the rev says cracks me up, but I am moved when he says that I am, in my own way, a kind of preacher, and that I am like a son to him. After they tell about all the hoopla at Penn Station and show the footage and the crowds and the poetry news and YouTube, they end the segment with me reading to Sarah from one of my poems, the stack of yellow paper sitting on top of my duffel bag. In the last shot, Sarah and I walk off through the park holding hands.

After the last image of the ticking stopwatch, the show ends, everybody claps and cheers, and there are hugs all around. We finish up the popcorn, and nobody wants the evening to be over. But in the end, it is just me and Sarah back on our cots in the dark, and I start crying. We hold each other, and I whisper in her ear, "Thank you."

CHAPTER
SIXTY-THREE

On Monday morning, we pack up and are heading for the shelter door, with no particular plans for the day, when Cindy intercepts us and asks us to come into her office. We sit, and she tells us how much she enjoyed the *60 Minutes* broadcast and having everyone together. "That was definitely the biggest night the shelter has had since I've been here," she says.

She smiles kind of shyly and tells us the shelter staff got us a thank you and congratulations gift, and she hands me a package. I unwrap it, and it's a prepaid cell phone.

"I think you might be needing this," she says. "In fact, I know you will." She tells me that she has already received both an email and a text message from Betty Wall, asking her to have us call her as soon as we can. Betty has received some messages for us and wants us to check in. "I already put her number in there for you, Poet."

We all share a big hug, and I tell Cindy I'll call Betty in a bit. "We've got to have celebratory pancakes first. Last night was exhausting, and we are starving!"

Sarah and I thank Cindy, and head for the diner.

After breakfast, we walk clear down to Washington Square Park and settle in on one of our favorite benches. I call Betty Wall and thank her profusely for the show and tell her about watching it with our big gang at the shelter. She tells me she was happy with the piece too and that a bunch of messages have come in for me already. I'm kind of blown away. Some are from book publishers—HarperCollins, Simon & Schuster, and a few others whose names are familiar. And there are a couple of "call me" messages from literary agents. The part about my duffel bag full of writing must have gotten their attention.

When Betty reads me the names of the agents, one of them seems familiar: Dean King. I realize that's the name I got from Jeremy, the old writer who came up to our five-minute poetry table, back when we were first getting going. It's an encouraging coincidence.

My first call is to Jackson Publishing, to somebody called Jennifer Simkus. It turns out she is an editor, and we chat for a bit. She really dug the *60 Minutes* piece and wants to know if we would please come up to their offices on 53rd Street to talk to them about some book ideas. I say I think we can squeeze her into our schedule, and we both laugh. She is very enthusiastic and says they want to meet with us ASAP, and we make an appointment for the following morning.

Next I call Dean King's number, and when the receptionist answers, I ask her where their offices are located. I remember that Jeremy told me King was not far from the park. It turns out his literary agency is just a few blocks east, on Horatio Street, so I decide Sarah and I should just drop by, and after sitting in the sunshine for a few minutes admiring our old stomping grounds we head over.

His office is in a skinny, old building, but when we step out of the slow elevator, there's an expansive lobby with shelf after shelf of beautiful new books. I introduce myself to the receptionist and tell her Mr. King had called me, and we take a seat, flipping through some of the books while she buzzes him.

King doesn't keep us waiting long, and he comes out beaming warmly and welcomes us. He's a tall, lanky, sharply dressed guy, way older than me but with a lot of energy in his step. He leads us back to his roomy office, and we have a long, relaxed conversation. He knows the basics of our story from the show, but he has a lot of questions, and we end up sharing all kinds of anecdotes about our time in Washington Square Park especially. He says that aspect of our story had particularly moved him. Back in his younger days, he'd spent a lot of time in the park, hanging out, listening to music, and reading, and the *60 Minutes* piece had made him realize how he had lost track of all that even though he was so close by.

"That's why I picked up the phone and called you," he said. "The park had something to do with me getting into publishing and working with writers in the first place. It's been a long run, and your story took me back to where I began."

I can tell King really likes us, and he takes the time to explain what an agent does, and what he thinks we should go for in terms of publishing. He says timing is important, and that being on the most popular feature news show there is gives us a great opportunity, and we should take advantage of that. And we need to be careful in making any deals. His role as a literary agent is to look out for the interests of his clients and be a kind of ally. He says he admires what we've done and wants to be our agent and represent us with publishers. He says books are only part of it. He thinks there might well be movie or TV interest in our story as well. And we should be thinking about other projects we might want to do later because we might be able to offer a publisher a multiple-book package.

Sarah is a little quiet at first, but she soon opens up to him and is her usual hilarious self, telling him about the nine dogs and the five-minute-poem thing and how exciting it was performing in Penn Station for the hordes. I tell him about meeting Jeremy months ago, and how he'd encouraged us and given me King's name but warned us not to mention him. King laughs good and loud at that and says he hasn't talked to Jeremy in years, but treasures the memory of "fighting the good fight" on his behalf back when he was just getting started in the agenting business. "He was a better writer than he thought," he says, shaking his head. "God bless him."

Sarah and I exchange a look, and I tell King that we want him to be our agent. He says he would be honored to work with us, and we all shake on it. Something in me relaxes. I feel like we're in good hands.

I tell King we are going to need his help in sorting out all the possibilities in front of us. I show him my list of messages from publishers and tell him we already have an appointment with HarperCollins the next day.

He mulls it over for a bit, then suggests that Sarah and I go ahead and take that meeting by ourselves, and not mention him, just see what the publisher proposes, then let him know.

"Don't sign anything without talking to me!" he chuckles.

Sarah and I head back over to the park and decide to drop in on the rev and update him on how well our day is going. He's glad to see us, and we all sit at the top of the steps as usual and talk about how crazy and great the night before had been. I tell him about our new ally and admit that I am scared about what's next.

"I am Poet, and I write poems," I tell him. "But I really don't know what I'm doing. I know Ginsberg and 'Howl,' and I've stood at the snowy fork in the road with Robert Frost a few times, but I am pretty naive about poetry, to be honest."

"That's not really honest, Poet," says the rev, shaking his head. "There's plenty you don't know, sure, but you want to learn, and you will. The most important thing is that you have an amazing delivery system. You can perform and touch people with your words. You can make a soul connection with an audience. That's the thing. You keep at this and keep going, and you'll figure out how to send higher and higher voltage through that wire. Yes, learn all you can from what other poets have done, of course, but keep on not being afraid to be whatever kind of poet you are."

There's a moment of silence as I take all that in.

Then Sarah says, "Amen!" and we all crack up.

As we're walking back to the shelter, Sarah says, "I'm worried about the meeting at HarperCollins, Poet. Shouldn't you be wearing a suit?"

"Yup. I'm going in my birthday suit. Harper published Allen Ginsberg. They should be able to deal with it."

"Jesus, Poet," she says. "You've only been a celebrity for twenty-four hours, and you're already obnoxious."

CHAPTER
SIXTY-FOUR

We splurge on a cab going up to the HarperCollins building on 53rd Street, and I get a receipt, figuring I will be able to expense the cost because I seem to have a shot at being taxed on a publishing income soon. The company offices look just like I'd hoped they would: an older building, the lobby busy with people coming and going, a big bank of elevators, with blowup posters of the covers of bestselling books and displays about the company's illustrious history.

Sarah and I go up to the front desk and tell the uniformed guy on duty that we have an appointment with Jennifer Simkus, and he tells us what floor to go to. When we get off, Jennifer is waiting for us and introduces herself enthusiastically. She's about Sarah's age, with curly hair and glasses. She isn't dressed formally, but with style, and I suddenly feel a rare bit of self-awareness about our funky street-worn attire. But she is warm and welcoming and immediately comments on Sarah's vintage Stones t-shirt.

As we walk down the hallway past a sea of cubicles and into her small book-lined office, Jennifer and Sarah are talking a mile a minute. In her office there's just enough room for two visitor chairs, and we settle in. I scan the spines of all the books on the shelves while Jennifer slips out and brings back tea for Sarah and two coffees. Hers is in a big mug with a Groucho Marx quote that cracks me up: "Outside of a dog, a book is man's best friend. Inside of a dog, it's too dark to read." Within minutes, we are all relaxed and talking away, and I can tell Sarah feels as comfortable with Jennifer as I do.

Jennifer says she wants to tell us about some publishing ideas she's had, based on the *60 Minutes* piece, and hear whatever feedback and other ideas we may have. In about an hour, the three of us are going to go to a bigger meeting, which will include people from publicity, sales and marketing, and subsidiary rights, which, she explains, is the department that sells excerpts to magazines, licenses books to book clubs, and offers film rights to movie makers. I immediately feel like we are edging into the big time. It's exciting.

We talk about writing for a bit, and then I pull my poems out of my duffle bag. I show her a few of my favorites, and then she roams through the stack for a while, reading. She asks us about our various performances and how that experience has been for us, and then she and Sarah get into a lot of detail about Sarah's life story, the highs and the lows.

Jennifer says she's been thinking that there are two books. One would be the story of our journey, the whole thing—each of us separately and then our life together. That, she feels, has great potential as an inspirational book. And she thinks there could easily be a movie version or a TV movie. Plus, she thinks our experience with performing, and our good-natured improvisational approach to it, will make us attractive for TV interviews and magazine articles. She thinks the two of us should write that book together. She'll help us, as our editor, and if we get to a point where we feel we need an outside person to help us with the writing, that's an option. But, she says, she thinks we can do it ourselves if we get off the streets and have an actual apartment to live and work in.

She also wants to publish a volume of my poetry, which is music to my ears, though also terrifying. But she wants me to take some time, again, get settled somewhere and write some more. She sees the poetry book and the "our story" book as two parts of a whole. She's already pitched this idea to her colleagues, and they all want to meet us, which is why we're going to the bigger meeting. She asks us if her two-book idea sounds good to us, and while I am kind of hemming and hawing toward an answer, Sarah says, "Fuck yes!"

I give Jennifer a thumbs-up, and she smiles.

On our way to the big meeting room, Jennifer takes us into another office and introduces us to a publicist named Karen, who is very high energy and has piles of paper all over her desk and an assistant who comes in and hands her notes three times in the five minutes we are in there. Sarah and I are a great team, Karen says, and she is very keen about working with us. The assistant comes in again and says, "Everybody's ready!" and we all troop off to the big meeting.

It goes really well. In fact, I am kind of floating above the table, though Sarah and I are holding hands under the table, which might be keeping me from going up and bouncing off the ceiling. Everyone goes around the table and introduces themselves, and all of them have seen the *60 Minutes* segment and have good things to say about it. One of the salespeople seems surprised when she suddenly chokes up while talking about it—about Sarah—and says, "See? It's a great and moving story! And we want to help you tell it more completely."

Jennifer gives everybody a kind of recap of what we've been talking about with her and goes over the two-book idea. When she's finished, she looks around the room and asks, "Anybody like to add anything?"

Sarah says, "Yes. If those two do well, you can publish my how-to book, *The Art of Being A Wiseass*."

Everybody cracks up, and the conversation rolls around the table freely as people offer all kinds of ideas about how to publish the books and work with us to promote them. They all think that my writing sessions with other homeless people and Sarah's helping other recovering heroin addicts are important parts of the story and need to be emphasized in our book. A lot of ideas get put on the table. It's pretty heady stuff, and I am trying to stay calm.

When it comes back to me, I tell them what we are looking for: a significant advance. We hope to get enough to get us off the streets and into an apartment with some stability for the future, which is essential not only for our health but also so that I can get custody of Josie—and so we can write. I tell them that I don't have any pretensions about my poetry, but that Sarah and I have been out there in public performing together long enough that we know for a fact that we can reach people and get them to respond, that we can touch people's hearts because we've suffered enough on our own. And I tell them that we would love to have our story help other people in whatever ways it might—as inspiration, entertainment, and information.

The guy Jennifer had introduced earlier as the publisher says that they all really admire us—and have enjoyed us, which is even more important. They all understand what we are looking for, and he thinks the commercial potential is considerable, especially given the TV and movie possibilities.

"Hear me now and remember it later!" Sarah suddenly pronounces, loudly, and there's a confused silence. "I will not be played by Julia Roberts. She's brilliant, but she's too old. Hell no. Not gonna happen."

There's a burst of relieved laughter. They're keeping up.

I ask them if Sarah and I can step outside for a moment to confer, and when we come back in, I tell them that we have been living on our guts and our instinct for a long time, which have served us well. A bunch of publishers have asked to meet with us, and they are the very first people we've talked to. But we feel very comfortable with them, and if they are willing, we would like to shake hands to pursue an agreement exclusively with them. In consideration for which, they will promise not to rip us off, and to be as generous as they can.

"We trust you," I say. "As we should. You not only published Allen Ginsberg, but also *The Runaway Bunny* for God's sake. And I'm *The Runaway Stockbroker*. It's a good match. And that might be our fourth book!"

Jennifer looks around the room and exchanges a glance with the publisher, then she turns to me and Sarah and says my proposal sounds good to them. But, she adds, they can't make a deal with first-time authors—especially a substantial deal like this one is going to be —without insisting that we obtain the services of a literary agent, to be sure our interests are protected. She says they can give us a list of half a dozen agents they've worked with before and who they recommend.

It feels really good to be able to tell her we already have an agent. We'll have Dean King call her in the morning, and they can begin negotiating toward a deal right away. Everybody gets up and shakes our hands warmly, and it's all good wishes and we'll talk more soon and great to meet you. We end up with just Jennifer again, and as she walks us back to the elevator, we all agree the day couldn't have gone any better.

"It's going to be fun working with you, editor!" I say as we shake hands, and Sarah and I step onto the elevator.

We wander around the busy East Side for a bit, our heads spinning. Then we step into a small park that has a waterfall and benches and sit down in the shade. I pull out my phone and call Dean and tell him what happened, and he seems as pleased with the outcome as we are.

"Making publishers compete with one another for a book is the way to get the most money," he says. "At least that's how it usually works. But your path has been weirdly unique all the way so far, so why change now? I'll give Jennifer a quick call to make contact. Then how about you and Sarah come down and see me tomorrow morning at 11, and we'll talk about what terms you want me to get for you, okay? Now please go treat yourselves to dinner. Or lunch. Celebrate! Things are going well."

I tell him we'll see him in the morning and hang up. Sarah and I sit listening to the splashing of the water for a while, and then agree that we aren't going to tell anybody about this news yet. It's a deal in progress, and we don't want to jinx it. That night, we sleep peacefully. Our bellies and our hearts are full.

CHAPTER
SIXTY-FIVE

By noon the next day, we've been wandering around for hours, talking about the book deal and what we should ask for. We end up in Union Square Park and plop down on one of the old wooden benches and go over the notes I've been taking on my yellow legal pad. It's a strange feeling to be at such a huge crossroads and have the chance to get some things we want. So, what the heck do we want? Well, to get a place, obviously. And to have the publisher spread the payments out, so we know we'll be okay for as long as possible and can build our new life.

But we'd also like to help the people who've helped us and share our good fortune somehow. So, we keep adding all kinds of ideas to our list, whatever we can think of. Sarah wants them to send copies of the books to homeless shelters all over and run ads in the free papers homeless folks hand out in the big cities.

"But obviously," I say to Sarah, "one of the most important things of all is a new T-shirt for you."

"Wait—you hate this shirt, don't you, Poet? And now it comes out, after all we've been through! The Stones are too much for you, aren't they. Holy Jesus, my coauthor is a pussy. Okay, fine, put me down for a Carly Simon sweatshirt. Extra large. Happy?"

"Deliriously. But I'm going to put in that you also get a dozen vintage Stones shirts—*Hot Rocks, Let It Bleed,* even *Exile on Main Street* for God's sake. And I want them in pristine condition."

By the time we've shared a bratwurst with sauerkraut and a cold can of Mountain Dew from one of the park's lunch carts and gone over our list and pruned it down to the things that we're serious about, it's time to head down for our meeting with Dean King. It's great strolling along through the busyness of Broadway, past the Strand Bookstore and all its sidewalk carts packed with used books, through a steady flow of people streaming past, all urgently headed to do urgent things —and today we too are on our way to an important business meeting. It all feels pretty hopeful, until, in the elevator, Sarah and I look at each other and realize that both of us are really nervous. After scrappling around for so long watching every nickel and dime, it's stressful to suddenly have so much at stake.

But once we are back in Dean's office, sipping the coffee he's brought us, joking with him, and having him tell some good stories about some of the interesting publishing deals he's been involved in over the years, we realize everything is fine. Not only does he think even our more wacky ideas are worth talking about, but he has his own list of ideas, and his are pretty good. So, we go through both lists and talk each item through, and we see how good he is at all this. And in the end, we agree about everything.

He says he's going to work up a deal memo and send it to our editor. I tell him if we get half of the things we're asking for, I'll be happy, and he laughs and says, "Poet, I think we'll do way better than that. These things you're asking for make sense. Relax, okay? I'm serious. I think the publishing gods are smiling on you two. On all of us."

He tells us he'll call us after he and Jennifer have had a chance to go over everything. He walks us out to the lobby, and as the elevator doors are closing, at the last second, he gives us a double thumbs-up.

We hang out in Washington Square Park for a while, sitting by the fountain and listening to a guitar player we haven't seen in months who goes by Ace Harvey. The most striking thing about him is that he plays and sings without taking the lit cigarette out of his mouth. While we sit there, I can't stop thinking about the deal, and the feeling that there's something else we missed, something we should have asked for. And then I suddenly tune in on Ace, who's singing a song I've never heard before, and hear the words, "Every passing stranger is a book you haven't read." Bingo. I realize what I had missed.

Just then Sarah pops up, "Come on, Poet, let's go see the rev. It's time to share the good news!"

And off we go.

As we walk into the church, the rev is walking right up the main aisle toward us and just keeps coming, throws his arms up wide, and enfolds us in a classic huge Rev hug. "You crazy kids," he's smiling. "What's the news? Did you survive being on the news?"

"More than survive, Rev. Everything is great. I mean it's going to be. I think..." I don't know where to start so I stop.

"Use your words, Poet. That's what you're good at."

I laugh, and he leads us outside. We all sit together on the top step, and we tell him about the deal we don't have yet—but seem likely to get.

"Holy shit," he says, shaking his head. "And I'm authorized to say that, by the way. I don't know if 'happy for you' even begins to describe what I'm feeling. But at the same time, I'm completely not surprised. The Force has always been strong with you two. I think we're in the episode called *The Homeless Strike Back*."

"Rev," beams Sarah, "we don't know exactly how it's going to turn out yet, but we're definitely going to end up with a roof over our heads. And a TV, so Poet can stop haranguing everybody on the street with his sweet words and just stay home and watch music videos on YouTube. And you can come over and join him. You know you are family, and you've been a holy fucking rock for us. And the church and everything you do is so important, so, however this turns out, we want you to know that we'll be able to pitch in financially, with the programs—counseling, health care, whatever you think will help people the most."

"Well that's well and good. Amazing really, seriously. Verklempt..." His feelings well up for a second, joy and sadness together in his eyes. "But what I really want is for you two to keep showing up! More poems. More Poet and Sarah. You two are the real money."

"Okay," I announce. "That's it. I'm going to write a poem tonight, and I'll unveil it at artists night. It's about three goofballs who are on such a roll that they don't know what to do, and the first line is 'We had a freaking love fest on God's front porch.'" I reach over and offer him my hand. "You the rev. Are now and ever shall be."

It's time for us to head uptown to make it to the shelter on time. We promise the rev we'll let him know if our dream comes true, or if we wake up, whichever happens first.

CHAPTER
SIXTY-SIX

It's late morning, and we head back to Union Square and have just splurged on a couple of coffees when Dean calls. We take a bench, and I get out my tablet and take notes while he brings us up to speed. I have him on speaker phone so Sarah can be in on the conversation—even though I despise people who share their phone conversations. We're in a pretty remote section of the park, and I don't think anybody will hear us but pigeons. Let them hate me for a few minutes; I can take it.

Dean says the good news is that Harper is eager to accommodate our requests because we have given them exclusivity, and he and Jennifer have been able to work everything out pretty easily with just minor adjustments and clarifications. In fact, she really likes a lot of our more unusual ideas, talked them over with colleagues in various departments, and everybody else is on board too, enthusiastic even, and coming up with new angles and ideas.

"Wow," I say. "That's pretty good news."

"And there's some more," he chuckles. "The rest of the good news is that there isn't any bad news. Everything just kind of worked out."

Dean says Harper has agreed to a great advance—something unprecedented for him. He got exactly what he asked for—in technical terms, as Sarah put it, a shitload of dough. It's a two-book deal for the our-story book and the poetry book, but with an option clause. They get the chance to make an offer on anything else we write, before anybody else even sees it, though we aren't required to accept an offer from them. Nice.

There are all kinds of details about splitting up income that comes from movies, TV, magazine excerpts, book club editions, and foreign language editions—all of which Dean took care of. If any or all of that happens, we'll be golden. But even if the only money we get is the advance for the books, we'll be okay. And they were cool with the part we've been most concerned about: breaking the advance up in pieces so it keeps coming to us, bit by bit, over the next few years.

"Oh my God, we'll be able to make our rent, Dean," says Sarah. She is smiling hard, her eyes are squinted shut, and I know that deep inside she is beginning to let go of her long-borne fear.

As for the fun stuff, all the things we just made up on our own, Harper is not merely accommodating our ideas, but embracing them, and have come up with some of their own. We've agreed to do the kind of publicity most authors would want to do out there in public—readings and signings in bookstores and radio and TV interviews—and they've also agreed with our proposal to do readings and workshops at homeless shelters across the country. And they have agreed to work on ways to involve other organizations to distribute a lot of free copies of our books at those events. They even float the idea that maybe eventually, as I keep doing the writing workshops, we can someday publish an anthology of writing by the homeless writers I will work with.

They are equally keen to promote the book by working with Sarah in the same ways, linking up with local recovery organizations, holding workshops, doing readings, and giving away some copies of the book. We'll both do all the publicity together, whichever community we're working with. Clearly, the publisher has embraced the idea of figuring out as many ways as possible to help the our-story book do some good, and we've offered them two entire universes to work with.

But Harper agrees with us that aside from that, we'll also promote our story as a great, entertaining, inspiring tale about a couple of crazy kids who went sane. I can't wait to see Sarah mixing it up with

Stephen Colbert and getting crazy with Ellen. I'll just stay backstage and watch on a monitor.

By the time Dean goes over all the things the publisher is interested in doing, my head is spinning. We are looking at a win-win-freaking-win-win scenario. The stars have lined up for us, though behind my sense of joy and awe I also feel a bit of panic. I'm actually going to get to do what I've been saying I wanted to do all along. The only catch is: What if I can't do it? Do I have what it takes to pull all this off? Sarah does—no question. She's going all the way and bringing everybody with her. So, I guess all I have to do is hold on tight.

While I'm riding out that moment of panic, Sarah and Dean have been talking about the deal.

"And, Dean," she says as I tune back in, "I wasn't kidding about my book on kick-assery. Our book is going to kick ass. And then I'm doing a kids' book, and I'm going to use a lot of glitter pens on the illustrations, so look out."

He laughs and assures her that any book she comes up with will be covered under the option clause.

When we've covered everything else, I say, "Okay, Dean, there's something else, and I hope it doesn't screw everything up." And I tell him about my Ace Harvey epiphany, which Sarah and I had discussed and agreed on completely the night before at the shelter. "We have overlooked one key issue, Dean, and it's make or break for us."

In our strategy meeting, he had explained that most publishing contracts give the author a modest number of copies—a dozen or so. But we need to find a benefactor to buy 500 copies of the book, so we can inscribe them all and give one to everybody in our shelter, everybody in the church program, all our homeless pals around Washington Square Park, and our friends in Penn Station.

"Everything else has gone so well," I tell Dean. "And I know this is a lot to ask."

He laughs. "I'll ask Jennifer, but I am certain they'll be okay with that, Poet. Given the size of this advance, I'm absolutely sure it's not going to be an issue. Plus, it's a beautiful idea, and they will be glad you thought of it."

"Okay." I'm relieved. "So, we're down to the last, most important question," I say, pausing to drain the last gulp cup of the cup of coffee we could barely afford. "How soon can we get the first part of the advance? To be honest, we'd like to buy some clean clothes. I've started to care, now that I'm gonna be a published author."

Sarah laughs.

"Good idea!" he enthuses.

"And," I add, "as nice as our cots are, we want to try sleeping in a bed. We might like it. So, we want to upgrade from a shelter to a hotel as soon as we can afford to."

"Understood." He says he'll call Jennifer right away about the free books, then draw up fresh copies of the contract. He'll call us in the morning to confirm, and then we can come down to the office and sign them. It will take a few days to get the initial payment from Harper, but he's going to get a commission eventually when the advance comes in, and meanwhile he's happy to loan us a chunk up front, personally, to get us started.

I'm very moved. "Wow," I manage. "That feels like you're really going an extra mile for us. Thank you."

"Hey, Poet," he says. "My job got a lot more interesting a few days ago, and today I'm actually having fun. Thank *you*."

CHAPTER
SIXTY-SEVEN

I have no idea if I'm dreaming this, or if today is really happening. Dean is wildly energized when he greets us in the lobby of the office, and right away he takes us into a meeting room. "Okay, kids!" he enthuses, "you two sit down right here and just give me a sec!" and he zips out.

Three contracts are laid out in a row on the conference table, and before we can even look at them, he's back, settling a big mug of hot coffee in front of each of us and rushing back out to return with one for himself. "All right," he says, sitting down and shoving a contract over to each of us, "let's get caffeinated and go over these."

And for the next while, we all sip and read, and Dean answers our questions and explains various points, emphasizing that we basically got everything we asked for, right down to the 500 copies.

"You see there in the next paragraph after that one, that you do not get final control over the jacket art or the title, but you get consultation. I'm sure you and Jennifer are going to work together well."

"Damn!" says Sarah, cocking her head sideways and giving Dean a look. "She better like my title idea." He and I brace ourselves. "*Harry Potter and the Homeless People.*"

"Or maybe," chuckles Dean, "*Harry Potter and the Goblet of Poetry.* Or how about *The Girl with the Pilot G2 Tattoo.* Okay," he says, sliding us each a pen, "pick up your wands and let's make some magic happen."

Sarah and I each sign all three copies, and the agreement with his literary agency that Dean's already talked to us about, and then we all lean back in our big soft chairs.

"Done," says Dean. "Let the magic of writing begin. Well, not today of course. First, we have to get you out of the shelter."

"You did a great job, Dean," says Sarah, and I nod. "Poet and I really, really appreciate all your efforts, even though I know there's a hidden camera in this room, and a bunch of clowns are about to jump out blowing horns and laughing at us, cause this is an insane joke, right?"

"Wrong!" laughs Dean. "Don't you remember clause 47? We went over that. It says you two are going to be insanely happy. You deserve it."

Then he says he has figured out the next step. He is going to follow ancient publishing protocols that have not been evoked in years, and in honor of the hard path we've traveled, he has reserved two complimentary nights for us at the Washington Square Hotel, and they are expecting us. Sarah and I exchange a look. We know it well. It's just past the north end of the park, and we've passed it a million times and fantasized about how much fun it would be to stay there.

"Meals are included!" says Dean. "We've got to get you reacquainted with indoor living and privacy right away, and get you rested up. So, get on over there this afternoon and check in. And I made a dinner reservation for you, but not until 8, so you'll have time to relax." He pauses. "I even took the liberty of inviting Jennifer to meet you for breakfast in the hotel restaurant as well, so you can just, you know, start thinking about the project. But she won't get there until 10 am, so you can sleep in!"

Dean says he'll send the signed contracts up to Jennifer right away, so they can have them countersigned and get the initial payment headed our way. "Meanwhile…" he hands me an envelope. "This is $3,000. Don't blow it all at the track. Or if you do, put it all on 'Poet and Sarah.'"

Before you know it, we hug the poor guy half to death, head downstairs, and walk a block or two and right into a bank that's within shouting distance of the park. We set up two checking accounts with a thousand bucks in each. Because neither of us has been running up any debt or defaulting on anything, our credit ratings are in good shape, and we walk out with debit cards. I stuff the envelope with the rest of the money into my duffel bag. And there we are, back in the park, sitting by the fountain, dazed, holding hands, and smiling. I mean, really smiling, I'm emotional.

After a while just sitting there, it's like we wake up from the same dream and both have the same idea. We need to go back up to the shelter and tell Cindy what's going on, about the great madness.

We head uptown at a good clip. It's a pretty a good hike, but we are in an ecstatic state. We get up there, settle into Cindy's office, and give her the good but weird news that we are moving into a hotel for now. We also tell her that, as with the rev, we plan to help the shelter out and will, of course, keep on being part of the shelter family and doing our workshops.

"You've been our home away from the sidewalk, Cindy," I say.

"And," Sarah adds, "you have the best mac and cheese in town. No way we're walking away from that!"

We thank Cindy for every single thing she did for us, from our in-the-corner cozy cots right down to our cell phone.

"A signed copy of each book for you, Cindy. The very least we can do," and we head down the hall and out the front door.

We wander back to 6th Avenue, head downtown, and soon find ourselves descending into Penn Station on the escalator. We arrive in the quiet part of the afternoon; it hasn't started hopping yet, but it will soon. Back on very familiar ground, we go around to all our station friends and say hi and catch up. I buy a couple papers like I'm going to write my news, though I'm not, and Sarah gets a smoothie like she's going to drink it, and she does.

We end up in the waiting room where we used to do our shows, and sure enough, there's a milk crate sitting over against the wall. I hop up on it.

"Commuters, want to know what's going down in this crazy town?" I orate in echoing tones.

A woman who is walking by hears me and comes over to us, excited. A regular! She misses our show! Where have we been? Are we okay? We fill her in on the basics of our improbable good fortune and our book ambitions, and she asks if she can take our picture. Of course! Sarah and I step up on the milk crate and hug each other, balancing there together, smiling.

"This is the way it ends!" I shout, raising my arm and pointing to the ceiling. "Not with a bang, but with a book!"

"Two of them!" yells Sarah. The woman cracks up and wishes us well. It feels like a nice coda to an improbable day.

"You know," says Sarah. "I'm taking this milk crate with us. If we do our job right, it may end up in the fucking Smithsonian. But at least we can use it to hold some snacks in our hotel room tonight."

We head upstairs to the shops and load up on Chex Mix, Oreos, and Cheese Nips.

CHAPTER
SIXTY-EIGHT

"Do you think we'll ever have that much fun again, Poet," asks Sarah, smiling as she stares at the breakfast menu in the hotel restaurant. "Or have we already peaked too soon—dinner, room service, and then three movies. Maybe we overplayed our hand."

"But it was freaking wonderful."

"It was. And if it is downhill from here? Worth it. I especially liked the part with the bed, and the forty-five-minute shower this morning. And the coffee maker in our room."

"And when we were dancing at 2 am. That was all right," I chuckled.

"My favorite thing," smiles Sarah, "was when you opened the window to throw that dinner roll out naked seeing if you could hit the Hanging Tree in the park, which is like 500 yards away. You might have been slightly inebriated by that point, Poet. But you got a good arm and a great dick."

I crack up.

"It's basically insane that we're here, a block and a half away from where we met, and we're both wearing new clothes, and I'm about to order Eggs Benedict. It's freaking me out, in a good way."

"Me too, Poet. I'm having the egg scramble."

Half an hour later, our editor Jennifer has joined us, and we're into our third pot of coffee and talking a mile a minute. She's brought us a big canvas book bag that says READ in huge letters on the side, and it's full of recently published HarperCollins books she thought we'd enjoy. And she included half a dozen for Josie.

"You're a very good editor," I laugh. "I can tell already!"

We talk for quite a while about the our-story book. Jennifer is very encouraging and wants us to start thinking about it, even if we aren't ready to write. "In the background, all the time. And just take notes," she says. "Whenever you think of an idea, or something that you might want to put in the book, just write it down quickly."

The most urgent thing is for us to find a place to live. But she's right: We can get started, even if only in our minds, until things settle down.

I tell Jennifer that I think maybe Dean, our agent, sent us to this particular hotel for a reason, whether he knew it or not. Plaques and photographs are subtly displayed here and there, and as I take them in one by one it dawns on me that this is a kind of magic place, a way station visited by many creative people over many years. Hemingway stayed here en route to serve as an ambulance driver in WWI. Chuck Berry stayed here, and Bo Diddley, and the Stones. Bob Dylan and Joan Baez lived in room 305 for a while. Even fucking Dee Dee Ramone stayed here. And Albert King. All of which I take as a good sign. I feel like we are here to relax, exhale, calm our exhausted minds, take a deep breath, and begin to summon up our creative powers for the journey ahead.

Jennifer reiterates her offer to have someone transcribe my hand-written poems to get me started on the poetry book, but I wave her off. "I really think typing up everything I've written is something I need to do myself. It'll be good for me. Some of this stuff is ancient, and I might hate it, so reading it all in order will help me get going on fixing it up and on writing more. The worse the old stuff sucks, the more motivation I'll have to write better stuff."

The night before, during our delirious dinner of joy in this very dining room, Sarah and I had made some basic decisions, which we share with Jennifer. The advance is big enough that we are both going to get Macs and a printer. From here on out, we're going to be living with words, so we need dope computers for inspiration.

Jennifer seems pleased by our news, but with an odd smile, she bends down, reaches into her bag, and carefully lifts out something big. "You're right," she said. "Good call. But until the money comes through, maybe this will get you underway." She unzips a slim cloth case and slides out a computer. "This is for you. One of our editors recently upgraded, and we had our tech crew clean up his old machine and empty it out, for whoever comes on board next in the editorial department. But we decided you should have it instead. So, you can start writing as soon as you want."

"Take it, please," she says, handing it to Sarah. "And if you do get new computers for yourselves, then Josie can use this one when she's with you. Sound like a plan?"

Sarah opens it up, stares at it, smiling big time.

"The charger's in the pocket on the side," says Jennifer. "You folks are cleared for takeoff."

"Wow. I'm seeing the future," says Sarah. "And it's silver."

"Thank you, Jennifer," I add. "As unlikely as it sounds, I'm almost speechless. I shouldn't be surprised editors are light years beyond pencils and green eyeshades by now, but youre really kicking our asses up there into the tech stratosphere." I turn to Sarah. "I think my trusty old Pilot G2 might have some serious competition."

CHAPTER
SIXTY-NINE

Hotel life is good. By the next night, we've watched two more movies, and Sarah is reading her second novel, working her way through the bagful Jennifer brought. And I've typed eighty of my oldest poems. Some of them have some juice, some power, and one of them made me cry to see how lost and angry I'd been. A few are awful, and some of the others could use some work. But a lot of them are okay, and they all definitely look better typed up. My handwriting is sometimes a little funky.

Sarah and I talk about Josie a lot, about how to get her into our life. And Jennifer comes by again, brings us a bottle of wine, and talks with Sarah and me about memoirs and various ways to write them. She's not pushing us, but she's helping us, getting us thinking about how to tell our story.

We have one more day in the hotel when Dean calls us and says the publisher fast-tracked the initial payment and wired the money over. "It's in my account," Dean says. "I think it's time for you to see your friendly neighborhood real estate agent."

An hour later, we've looked up a couple of places on our computer and are on our way up 6th Avenue, feeling pretty giddy. Suddenly Sarah jumps on me, and I carry her piggyback, and I'm singing loudly, making up new lyrics to the theme song from *The Jeffersons*.

Sarah immediately takes on the chorus parts: "Well, we're moving on in (movin' on in), to the West Vill, (movin' on in) to a beautiful brownstone in the sky, We're moving on in (movin' on in), to the West Vill (movin' on in). We finally got a piece of the pie."

I stumble and go down on my knees, and Sarah falls off, and we crack up big time. We just lie there on the sidewalk laughing, as a cute little white dog on a leash leans in and sniffs Sarah's face, making her laugh even harder.

We go into the real estate office, which is just off 6th Avenue on a side street. It's a really nice place, with contemporary sofas, and everything is white, including the reception desk. I tell the gal sitting there my name, and she says an agent will be out shortly.

While we're waiting, Sarah leans over like she's confiding in me. "Poet," she says softly. "There's one thing. One request."

"What's that?"

"I don't want a building that has a laundry room in it. There used to be one in my building, but I always had my clothes done at the dry cleaners, and every time I went by and saw other tenants doing laundry, I felt guilty. So, I'm a diva. I don't do laundry. Or feel guilty. No laundry room."

"But I do laundry!" I said.

"Bullshit!" she snaps. "You had somebody else do it. I bet you had a laundress."

"Well, I do it now. And when we get a place, I'll do yours too. It will be my pleasure."

"And you'll never make me feel guilty about it?"

"Never."

Sarah holds out her hand and we shake. "Deal!" she says. "Just don't machine dry my delicates."

I crack up.

The agent has walked up, and we both pop up and introduce ourselves. His name is Casey, and he leads us down the hall into his office.

"So, what can I help you folks with today?"

We explain that we are looking for a furnished apartment, as close to Washington Square Park as we can get without spending an insane amount of money. And we need to move in right away.

"What's the rush," he asks. "Where do you live now?"

"We're homeless."

He laughs. But then he can see from our faces that we aren't kidding. "Seriously?" Suddenly his face lights up. "Wait a minute, you're the Penn Station performers! I saw you on YouTube and on TV! How cool." He reaches over and shakes our hands again. "But how are you going to pay for an apartment? Is panhandling that lucrative?" He grins, hoping he's made a joke.

"We got really lucky," I say and explain the whole situation, about our book deal and how we've been in a hotel for a few days.

"What a great story," he says. "I hope I have exactly what you need. How big a place are you looking for?"

"Two-bedrooms, furnished, and not fancy. Ideally with a laundry room in the building." I smile at Sarah.

"And I'd like a headboard on the bed," adds Sarah. "I like to read."

"She's voracious!" I add.

"That's it? Two bedrooms, laundry, and a headboard?"

"The second bedroom has to be sweet and cozy," I say, "with a window that's not on an air shaft. It's for my daughter. I want her to love it."

"Aside from that, we're not picky," adds Sarah. "We've been living in a park, a church basement, and a shelter. So, anything you've got will probably be fine."

Casey turns his big computer screen at an angle so we can see too and starts showing us places. The first few are insanely fancy, but eventually he comes to one that looks like home—clean, nice simple furnishings, a huge table, and little desk over in the corner. It's one floor up from the street, it's not too far from the park, and it has some windows in front and one in the bedroom on the side.

"That's where we live, Poet," says Sarah.

And I know she's right.

Sarah doesn't even want to go look at it. "I know that's the place," she insists.

And in less than an hour, we've worked everything out. Deposits and rent are paid, everything is signed and sealed. We have keys and Casey's phone number for any questions that come up. We are beyond happy.

"Before you go," says Casey, "can I please get a picture of the three of us, with me holding up a sign that says, 'I rented Poet and Sarah an apartment!' for my Facebook page. I would really love it."

"Of course!"

Casey gets out a big marker and some paper and does a nice lettering job, and he takes the selfie, with the sign held up in front of his chest. Sarah can't resist giving him rabbit ears, of course.

"I love it," he beams and walks us out and shakes our hands again.

Suddenly, we are back out on the street, but no longer homeless.

Casey insists on giving our new apartment a freshening up that afternoon, so we aren't taking possession until the next morning, which is fine with us because we plan to enjoy our last night of hotel living.

"I'm going to miss this big-ass TV, Poet," laments Sarah as we lie sprawled out on the big-ass bed, eating chips and cruising channels.

"Don't worry. I'll get you one for the new place. At least a middle-ass TV, and maybe even a big-ass one. Or maybe we'll get a huge-ass TV. Apparently, beggars *can* be choosers."

CHAPTER
SEVENTY

A week later, we are so settled into the new place that everything that came before seems dreamlike. We have breakfast together and marvel that there's a wall and windows between us and the outside world, and that we can sit around in our new pajamas for hours if we want and nobody sees or cares.

Some mornings, I go out and get us a newspaper, and sometimes I bring back gigantic coffees, though we've also got a coffee maker in the kitchen and are putting it to good use. We each picked out our own mugs and got two extras for when we have visitors. We have saucepans. We make soup; we make oatmeal. It's like we're kids at a party, all the time, playing house.

We've both got Macs, and each of us has settled into a workspace: Sarah at the big table, me at the little desk in the corner by the living room window. But sometimes she goes into the bedroom and leans up against the headboard, and I can hear her clickity-clacking keyboard. I can get by as a typist; she's incredibly fast.

We go to Best Buy and settle on a middle-ass TV, and we have already spent some quality time watching trashy reality shows. With Sarah, it's a participatory sport. "You jealous bitch!" she'll yell at the screen, when one tipsy housewife turns on another.

It's hilarious. I've always hated reality TV, but not when I'm watching it with Sarah. She makes anything fun.

She has even made the thing I hate most in the world fun: shopping for clothes. We've gone on clothes-hunting expeditions several times together, and I loved it. She tends toward vintage, and I'm in a lifelong rut of averageness. But one time we agreed that we could each pick an entire outfit for the other. I got her a bright summer floral print dress, with flip-flops and a big straw hat. And she made me look like the guy I've always wanted to be: casually hip, cool, fun. And I'm sporting a brand spanking new pair of my trademark white Nike Air Maxes.

Sarah has never looked more beautiful. No matter what she wears, to me she's always had a "I'm not trying to look hot, but I am smoking hot" look. With new clothes, a home, eating well, sleeping well, drug-free, secure, I didn't think she could possibly get more beautiful, but she did. She looks happy.

I stroll through the park in the afternoon and over to the church to see the rev, but he isn't there. I write a note for him and leave it, "Please come bless our new home. The Yankees are playing the Orioles tonight." And I give him our address.

I go back out into the park and sit and write for a while—old school, G2 Pilot pen and yellow legal pad—and take in the scene. It's been a while since I sat on this familiar bench. I say hi to a few old homeless friends I haven't run into in a while. It feels weird to be all cleaned up. I tell them about our adventures performing in Penn Station and how we're writing a book together now. They're happy for us, and I buy everybody hot dogs and drinks and we sit and visit, and I slip a few people a few bucks. It's good to see everyone, and we part with hugs, and I head, strange as it seems, for home.

When I come into the apartment, Sarah is eating mint chocolate chip ice cream straight out of the carton and watching *The Ellen Show*.

"You know, Poet," she says. "Ellen's a dancer. And I'm a dancer. Do you have what it takes today?" She jumps up onto the couch and starts bouncing up and down. "You gonna dance with me, Poet?"

Now she's gyrating like she's in a club at 2 am. Now she's leaning over and gripping the edge of the table. She's twerking.

"You can't handle this, Poet."

I just stare.

"C'mon, chicken shit, get on up here and dance with me. Ellen wants you to. Ellen commands it!"

I keep gawking, watching her enjoy her own insanity.

"Come up here, Poet. Get some of this."

"Some ice cream? Thanks! That would be great." I pick up the carton and scoop out a mouthful, then slam the carton down, leap up onto the couch, put my hands on her hips, and boogie.

"That's it, Poet! Turn off the writing mind, loosen up. We're dancing a poem called 'Leaves of Booty.'"

Considering there's no music on we get a pretty good groove going, and before you know it Sarah is leading me into the bedroom.

"The rev is coming over to watch the game tonight," I mention.

"Plenty of time," smiles Sarah. "Dancing is romantic, Poet. And don't you forget it."

It turns out to be a beautiful afternoon.

CHAPTER
SEVENTY-ONE

When the rev is visiting us, Sarah starts lamenting about how she misses their tuna sandwich lunches at the top of the stairs outside the church.

"You know, Sarah," says the rev, with a sheepish grin, "I don't actually like tuna fish. I ate it with you every day because I knew you liked it."

"You fake-liked tuna?" shouts Sarah. "Reverend, that's a sin!"

"I was trying to get through to you and gain your trust."

"It worked. But…with tuna?"

"I would've eaten anything."

Sarah points to the door. "Reverend, you have to leave. You can't be a guest in my home. I don't respect a man who lies about fish."

"But I'd eat tuna any day to get to visit with you, Sarah. How about you stop by for a tuna sandwich tomorrow, for old time's sake, at noon?"

And they both crack up.

"Okay," she says. "But you're eating the whole sandwich. Even the crust."

"It's a date."

While they are having their tuna feast, I head out into the park and find a quiet spot. It's time to make the important phone call I've been dreading, but also looking forward to.

Lauren picks up. "Hello?"

I flounder for a second, then say her name. She doesn't recognize my voice and sternly asks, "Who is this?"

"It's Evan."

"Evan, like, the poet Evan? My homeless husband who performs in Penn Station and makes ten cents an hour?"

"Well, more like $12, but yes. And one time it was eighty bucks."

"Well, that Evan doesn't live here anymore." Her condescension is clear.

"Thank God he doesn't. I'm sure we're both happier for that. How is Josie?"

"Josie who used to have a father? Who has been gone for the past year? That guy? Where has he been?"

"Building a better life for her."

"Right."

"And making himself a better father. Listen, Lauren, I need to tell you some things, so please just relax and let me talk a bit, okay? Please."

The silence encourages me.

"I need to tell you what happened. I think you'll be glad to hear it."

I wade in and tell her about how unhappy I'd been, and how unhappy I know she was too. How that night of the party something had snapped in me, and I'd had to leave, in order to figure out what was wrong and how to go on living. I apologize for not being able to tell her at the time, for letting our marriage get so broken that we couldn't even talk to each other anymore.

"I don't blame you, Lauren. We were both miserable and unable to see what was happening, or make it better."

I tell her that launching into the unknown and living on the street had let me see everything clearly for the first time. How writing for people had made me happy. How I realized I had been living the wrong life, and we had both suffered for it. How grateful I was that somehow I had found my way to a better life, doing what I was meant to do. But that leaving Josie was the worst thing I'd ever done.

"We clearly aren't a couple, and maybe we should never have been. And I'm sorry life together was so hard. I know you are happier without me, and I'm happier too. But I thank God every day we were married, because our marriage brought Josie into the world, and the joy of her existence makes everything we endured worthwhile. We did something good for the world, Lauren."

I tell her that we should divorce, but that it doesn't need to be hard to do that and that I want her to be completely taken care of financially. And I want to be Josie's full-time all-the-time dad.

"But you're homeless, Evan."

I explain that I no longer am and give her the basic outline of my new life: I have work, an income, and a place to live. And a partner.

"I figured. I saw her on TV. I'm seeing someone too."

"I'm glad! You deserve to be with the right person."

I tell her I know she loves Josie but doesn't love being a mom. And if she will grant me full custody, with visitation rights for herself, I will give her everything she needs. I have a plan that's pretty simple, one that will work for all of us.

"I'm listening."

I tell Lauren I want her to liquidate half our assets and put them into a trust fund for Josie, who'll get partial access at twenty-one and the rest when she's older. Lauren can have both houses, including the one in the Hamptons, and the cars, and 45 percent of everything else. The last 5 percent will go into a retirement fund for me—"in case I'm not as good a writer as I think I am."

"This is real? You're not drunk?"

"Of course not. I'm completely serious. I want us both to live the lives we want."

Lauren stumbles a bit, says a few things, and I can see she is confused, but maybe has softened a bit from the surprise of what I'm saying, and is maybe open to it.

"Don't say anything more right now. Just think about it, okay?" I tell her that right now the most important thing for me is to see Josie. "It was terrible that I felt I had to leave her, and I need to apologize and reconnect."

I want Josie to come visit me, see my new place, meet Sarah, and let me tell her what happened. Lauren agrees to have a car bring Josie into the city on Saturday at 9 am. I thank her and hang up. My head is spinning. But after a few minutes sitting there, I can breathe again. There's hope.

CHAPTER
SEVENTY-TWO

Saturday morning, I wake up at 6, and I am so nervous I can't stand it. I start the coffee machine, while Sarah comes out of the bedroom dragging the blanket behind her, curls up on the couch, and watches me fidget and pace. I don't need the coffee. I am already hyper, my mind racing. My hand is shaking as I fill my mug.

"Evan, you're going to make yourself sick. It's going to be okay. Bring your coffee over here and talk to me."

I take a sip and sit down beside her.

"Listen and listen closely," she says in a soothing voice, putting her hand on my arm. "Kids don't forget. She is still your daughter, and she loves you. She'll be excited to see you. She doesn't see this through your eyes. What she remembers is how she loves being with you, and she'll be glad to be back with you."

"She's not going to understand why I went away. How do I explain that?"

"Just tell her the truth. You had some important things to take care of, you missed her like crazy, and now you're back in her life, and you won't ever let it happen again."

"Should I tell her about my writing?"

"Of course. Tell her what you are doing. Writing is a big part of who you are, and she'll love that. Let her into your world, Evan. You want her there, and that's where she belongs. Poet is who you are and have really always been. She'll see that you're happy, and she'll be happy too."

I like what she is saying, but I am shaking my head with doubt.

"The only thing that matters is that she knows you love her. Take a deep breath. I know you feel awful about what happened, but over time everything will work out. You know it will."

I put the coffee down and snuggle in next to Sarah, and suddenly she's nudging me awake, and it's almost 9.

I give Sarah a kiss and rush down and wait on the stoop. It's a beautiful May morning, a perfect day for the park, and I feel much more relaxed. Josie and I will go out to breakfast, then hang out in the park for a while, and later I'll bring her to the apartment and she'll meet Sarah. A big black town car rounds the corner and is coming down the street, and I leap to my feet.

And there's Josie, climbing out and looking over and seeing me. My heart is enflamed. My vision clears. My lungs filled with joy. In ten months, she got so big! And her hair is longer. She's the most beautiful thing I've ever seen.

I drop to my knees and open my arms, and she rushes into them and gives me a wonderful crushing hug. When she says in my ear, "It's alright, Daddy. It's alright," I realize tears are running down my cheeks.

"Oh. I love you so much, sweetheart! I'm so sorry I've been gone! I love you so much!" And we both are laughing.

"Daddy, we need to waddle," she says. And we do. Penguin voice. Big "aargh aargh" sound.

I talk to the driver briefly, and then Josie and I are off. She's perched up on my shoulders, and we bounce along all the way to the diner. As usual, Josie puts her hands over my eyes for a few seconds then takes them off, shouting, "Don't trip, Daddy!" and I pretend to stumble.

We slide into a booth in the diner and agree that we are both on the all-you-can-eat pancake diet, and we order them up, along with hot chocolate. It's a long, wonderful meal, and I never want it to end. Josie fills my ears with delightful stories of all that she's been up to. She is shocked I haven't seen *Frozen* nor *Despicable Me*. She says she read the final Harry Potter book on her own, with no help. Me reading the first one to her out loud seems like a lifetime ago. I can see that even in ten months she's grown up a lot, and I've lost time with her that I'll never get back.

I tell her the basic outline of what happened, how I hated my job and had been unhappy, and Mommy was unhappy, and we had not been getting along. That it wasn't Josie's fault—we both love her. But I needed to leave, though I hated to leave her, and that I had come to Washington Square Park to learn how to write and had lived there for months. I tell her that I'd first visited it when I was sixteen and loved it even then. And now I know it's a magical place, and I have been looking forward to showing it to her, and that I think she'll love it too.

From there the day opens up like a good dream. We wander through the park, sit here, talk there, swing on the swings together, and watch the amazing dogs in their dog zone. I show her my favorite trees and the fountain, and we stop to listen to various musicians. As the morning hours pass, she tells me more of what I've missed, and I tell her more of what I've done. She mentions that Lauren told her that Lauren and I were mad at each other. She asks if I have any friends or if I've been alone all this time.

I tell her that I have a couple of new friends, and my best friend is a wonderful woman named Sarah, and I show her where we set up our poetry table and how I wrote poems for people and Sarah wrote them out and decorated them. I show where we used to "camp."

She giggles. "Really, Daddy? You slept here? Weren't you afraid?"

"A little maybe, but it was an adventure. And Sarah was with me, so that made me braver."

We stop by where the chess guys are all playing their games, with watchers watching the slow-but-interesting action.

"Hey, Poet!" one yells, and a bunch of them look up and give me shout-outs.

"Damn, Poet. You clean up good!" says a big guy named Franko, with a grizzly grey beard.

"Hey, guys! I'd like you all to meet my daughter, Josie!"

Josie waves and smiles and they all melt. We chat and hang around a while, and I tell her stories about them, and Josie laughs.

When we are walking away, she asks me why Franko called me Poet.

"Because I've been writing poetry, Josie. All the time! And I love it so much. Poet is my nickname now, and a lot of people call me that. In fact, a lot of them think that's my real name."

"I'm still going to call you Daddy."

"Of course! You're the only person in the world who can call me that. I love being Daddy, and I always will."

We're sitting by the fountain eating salted pretzels, with some jazz guys playing a little ways away from us. Suddenly Josie says, "My friend Kara's parents got divorced. And so did Andrew's parents." I keep chewing. "Are you and Mommy going to get divorced?"

I sigh. I somehow didn't anticipate we would get so far into things so fast. My daughter is smarter than I am.

"I think we are, sweetheart. I didn't expect that, but I think that's what we need to do. But she's always going to be your mommy and I'm always going to be your daddy. Things are going to be different, but okay. You and I are still going to waddle and do everything we like to do together. We just have to work things out a bit."

"Okay." She's quiet for a while. "Where is Sarah? Where does she live?"

"Well, she's my roommate, Josie! She lives with me in our apartment, and we'll go meet her later. I talk to her about you all the time, and she's really looking forward to meeting you. And she's my writing partner. We're writing a book together."

"Are you in love with her? Is she your girlfriend?" She smiles at me.

"Yes, she is my girlfriend, and I love her very much. And I know you're going to like her."

"Am I going to I live with you and Sarah, Daddy, or with Mommy?"

"Mommy and I are working on that now, Josie. I want you to spend as much time with me and Sarah as possible. When we rented our apartment, we got you your own room, and it's waiting for you. Should we head over there now so you can check it out? And meet Sarah?"

She jumps off the bench and takes my hand. "C'mon, Daddy, let's go!"

CHAPTER
SEVENTY-THREE

I open the apartment door slowly so as not to surprise Sarah. I realize she's in our bedroom with the door closed, so I can show Josie the apartment. I bring her into the living room. "What do you think?"

"I like it. The color on the wall is nice, and the sofa looks comfy. Can I sit on it?"

"You can jump on it. Do whatever you want. This is your home too."

"Really? I can jump on it?"

"Yeah, if you want to, go ahead. Sarah eats ice cream while jumping on it all the time. She's quite a couch-jumper."

Josie giggles and goes on into the kitchen, looks out the windows, and looks at my desk.

"This is where I've been writing poems," I tell her, flipping through some of the loose sheets of paper.

"Can I see my room?"

"Of course! Right this way."

We go in, and she checks it out slowly and approvingly.

"I figured you'd want to put up your own decorations. I was going to get you a Harry Potter poster, but I didn't know which one you'd want. Sarah is a big Hermione fan, and she hates Draco."

"Daddy," she says in a what-a-moron voice, "everybody hates Draco. I like my room. Where's Sarah?"

I am sure Sarah has been listening at the bedroom door, hearing every word. "Is there anyone here named 'Sarah'?" I ask in a booming voice. "If there is a Sarah here, please report to Josie's bedroom immediately."

I hear the door open, and Sarah comes in with a big grin on her face. She drops to her knees so she is at face level with Josie and sticks out her hand, and they shake. "Hi, Josie, I'm Sarah."

"So, you hate Draco, huh."

"He's the worst."

"There are at least two kinds of boys, Josie. You've got your Harrys, and you've got your Dracos."

"Well, what's my daddy?"

"Oh, he's definitely a Hagrid. Big and goofy."

And we all crack up.

We all sit on the floor, and Sarah and Josie are off, talking about all kinds of things. Sarah says she already knows a lot about Josie, that she's a Taylor Swift fan, likes pancakes, can beat me at tetherball, and loves animated movies.

"What's your favorite movie, Sarah?"

"*Shrek.*"

"I love *Shrek* too. Do you know when my birthday is?"

"I do. It's March 27th."

"Wow, you do know a lot about me."

"Your Daddy loves you a lot, and he can't stop talking about you. I know he's missed you. And he's missed waddling with you."

Josie smiles.

We all have sandwiches and sit and talk at the big dining room table, and stories and jokes are flying. I realize how natural it feels for the three of us to be together.

It's getting late, and I know the car will be coming to pick Josie up soon, and I tell her that today has been one of my favorite days ever.

"Today was the best, Daddy," she says.

"I knew you and Sarah would like each other," I say.

"Sarah is like a big kid!" laughs Josie. "But a really big kid."

"We'll get you back here soon, Josie," I say, nodding to myself.

"Sarah, next time I come over, can we please watch *Harry Potter and the Deathly Hallows*?"

"Absolutely. Let's take a weekend and watch all the Harry Potter movies in a row. That would be fantastic. And we'll eat ice cream and Doritos!"

"Cool!" says Josie.

I see the car pull up to the curb, and we take Josie downstairs. While Josie and Sarah share a huge hug, I go around and talk to the driver and give him an envelope. I come back around and swing Josie up and around and around in a big Daddy hug. "I love you so much, sweetheart. I'll talk to Mommy, and we'll get you back here as soon as possible! I love being with you."

As the car pulls away, Josie keeps waving from the window until it turns the corner and she is out of sight, and we keep waving too.

Sarah turns to me. "What was the envelope?"

"A note for Lauren. It just said, 'I meant everything I said to you on the phone. Let's talk.'"

CHAPTER
SEVENTY-FOUR

Two months, later we're living in a wonderful new world. The papers have all been signed, the legal details attended to, and Josie is living with us for good. She'll spend a week with her mother in the Hamptons in August, but I doubt Lauren will exercise her visitation rights much more than that. School is out, and Josie is full-bore into summer, already becoming familiar with every corner of the park and making friends there at the playground. The walls of her bedroom are already covered with drawings and posters.

Sarah and I are writing nonstop, working on our book all day, and I'm writing poems at night in the park. Jennifer comes by once a week to pick up new material and hash out editing questions with us. Our delivery deadline is almost upon us. The covers have already been designed. The sales force is excited. The pressure is on, and we are loving it. Sometimes when we are both typing away, me at the desk and Sarah at the table, I'll stop and yell to her, "Hey, Sarah, look at us! We're writers!" And she always answers with a whoop, and on we go.

Now that things are settled, we've been reconnecting with our friends again. Sarah and I have each done a few workshops back up at the shelter, and I've read at two poetry nights at the church. It feels a little odd at first, but as soon as I get going, reciting one of my new poems, the energy comes to me, and I am back in the groove. But both the rev and Cindy know that we have to get the books done. Once they are turned in, we plan to focus on teaching and reaching out to other folks, helping others the way we have been fortunate enough to be helped. We just have to get this huge task complete, and then our energy can flow into that.

Sarah and Josie have become close. They've watched *Frozen* so many times I've lost count. After the third time, I leave it to them. But I am beyond happy to be actively Daddying again. My life feels complete, almost.

One afternoon, Josie and I are in the park and she asks me, "Daddy, are you and Sarah going to get married?"

I stop, look at her, and point to a bench, and we sit down.

"I'm glad you asked me that. I've wanted to talk to you about it. Josie, I love her so much, and I do want to marry her. Would that be okay with you?"

"Of course, Daddy. I love Sarah, and I know she loves you."

I tell Josie that I have been working on a secret plan, and now that I know for sure that she is okay with Sarah and me getting married, that she has to keep it secret and not tell Sarah that I am going to ask her.

"That's a good secret, Daddy. I won't say a peep."

A week later, I tell the gals I have some errands to do and not to expect me home until afternoon. I head over to the rev's church, so I can recruit him into my scheme. I tell him the plan, and he's on board. Over the next few hours, I hike and subway all over town to various stores, seeking out particular items as if I were on a treasure hunt. By late afternoon I've completed my mission and am back at the church, handing the rev a black duffle bag that looks exactly like the one I lived out of for so long. I emphasize to the rev that it's essential that he leave that bag in the place where I tell him, at exactly 2:55 the next afternoon. The deal is sealed, and as the rev and I head out the door of the church, he sees a young scruffy-looking guy sitting on the steps to the side and the rev indicates he and I should go over to him.

"Hey, Trevor!" he says. The guy stands up. "This is my friend, Poet. You guys need to meet."

I stick out my hand. "Hey, Trevor, how you doing?"

He can't be more than nineteen, and he's not only disheveled, but a little shaky. He's clearly having a hard time.

"Hey, Poet, good to meet you," he says, barely looking up at me.

"Where you from, Trevor? The city?"

"No, I moved here from Portland a year ago. I don't have any family left out there, and I thought maybe coming to the Big Apple would change everything."

"What is it you want to do?"

"I don't know. I just don't want to be living on the streets, worrying for my life."

"Let me tell you something, Trevor, and the reverend can back me up. A few months ago, I was in pretty much the same situation. I was homeless. I had no money. No place to go. I felt alone, and you know who helped me? This man right here, the rev. Listen to what he says, hear the advice he gives you, and he'll help you see the way forward. I love this man, and he loves everyone."

"You were homeless?"

"You bet I was. And I'm not ashamed to tell people, and you shouldn't be either. Some people just fall on hard times, or get their ass kicked by life. It doesn't mean you're a bad person."

"Amen," said the rev.

"Hey, Trevor," I say. "I don't know if he's told you, but the rev has all kinds of events here. You should hang around and be part of it. I come to the open mic nights and read poems. Maybe I'll see you at the next one, okay?"

"Okay. Maybe I'll see you there."

As the rev walks me down the stairs, he puts his arm around my shoulders, "Who told you that you could take over my job, kid?"

"Sorry, Rev, I'm just feeling the love is all. You're *still* the rev. Tomorrow at 2:55!"

"Absolutely."

As the other part of the plan, I tell Sarah and Josie that I have a surprise for them the next day, on Saturday. I am going to take them on an expedition to show Josie parts of the city that we haven't explored yet. I make it sound just a little mysterious, and they like the idea. To prepare the final part, I stay up until 3 am.

CHAPTER
SEVENTY-FIVE

My backpack is stuffed full of food and drinks, and off we go. It's a beautiful day, warm but not hot. I take them up to the High Line, the abandoned freeway that has been turned into a magical park in the air, the best walk in town.

We make our way clear to the north end, then come down, and walk over to the West Side and stroll south, as close to the Hudson River as we can get. I point out all the sights—Hoboken, Jersey City—and we admire all the barges, ships, and Circle Line tour boats moving up and down the river. It's a perfect day to be out and about—lots of bike riders, dogs happily walking, people sitting, sunbathing, talking. It's pretty crowded, and we end up ready for a break on a small makeshift boardwalk along the water, where people stroll past and there's a bit of green turf we can plop down on and eat.

I unload the treats, and we hungrily savor every bite as we stare out over the river.

As I'm steering us back into the Village, wanting us to end up at the park, I try to time it just right. I'm telling Josie stories about various old buildings we pass and the famous people who used to live in them, or still live in them. As we come across Bleecker Street and turn left, it seems like we're going to arrive right on time.

"I'm pooped, Poet!" says Sarah suddenly. "Do you think we can call it a day go home and watch a movie?"

"Almost. One more thing," I say, white-lying a bit. "Jamie said she has a new song and wants us to hear it. She said we should be at the fountain by 3, and we're almost there. Let's go."

A minute later, I suggest we cut through the alley, and Sarah's eyes light up.

"Yes! Take us there, Poet. It's where it all began."

"Right this way, Ms. Jones," I say and lead the way across the street and into the alley. Up ahead, lying on the ground in the spot where we used to sleep, is a duffel bag.

As we get nearer Sarah asks, "Poet, what the hell is that? It looks like your duffel bag."

I take her hand and say, "Sit down here please, and Josie, you too." I smile and nod toward the ground next to the row of bushes. Sarah looks at me strangely, and then sits down cross-legged, and Josie does the same.

"What's going on here? You have a sneaky look, Poet. I don't like it."

"You will," I say.

"Josie," I say, "this spot is where Sarah and I shared our first kiss. This is where we fell in love, and spent a lot of time, right in this spot. It's a very special place for us."

"Wow," said Josie. "This alley?"

Sarah looks confused but doesn't say anything. I sit down next to the bag and begin to take items out. The first one is a Clash T-shirt. "This is what you were wearing when I met you."

I pull out a bag of markers and glitter pens. "And these are what you used to turn my poems into beautiful pieces of art."

I pull an entire plastic milk crate out. "And this is the stage you gave me the courage to get up on."

A toy plastic microphone: "And this represents the voice you gave me the courage to find."

A puffy warm knee-length parka: "This is the winter coat I wish I could have given you, back when we were always cold."

An electric heating pad: "This is the warmth you gave me, body and heart, that kept me going."

A Pretty Lights CD: "This is for the concert—or as you called it, the sweat fest—that we went to at the Fillmore."

A bag of bubble gum: "Because it lasts forever."

The final thing I take out is a bundle of papers: "And this is the poem I wrote the night I began the journey that brought me here to the park. And brought me to you. It's in this bag, underneath everything else, to remind me how lucky I am that my life brought me to this moment."

I take a ring out of my pocket and get down on one knee. "Sarah Jessica Jones, I want to be your husband, and Josie," I look her way, and Josie is beaming at Sarah, "would like to be your step-daughter." I turn back to Sarah, beaming, and I ask, "Will you please marry me and make all three of us very happy?"

Sarah drops her head down for a few seconds and doesn't move, and I don't either. Then she looks up, cocks her head to the side looking into my eyes, takes the ring, looks at it closely, and looks back at me. And as she slides it onto her finger, she laughs out loud and whispers, "Yes."

We're all laughing and crying. Considering we are in an alley, it's a pretty good moment. And then we all waddle together out into the park.

CHAPTER
SEVENTY-SIX

The honeymoon starts as soon as we are engaged. It feels like everything is falling into place. Life is good, and Josie is happy, making friends in the neighborhood and loving the park. She really wants us to get a dog, but I point out that she already has at least ten—all the dog friends she's been making by hanging out at the dog run. Of course, Sarah's former beau, Bruno, was Josie's first dog-crush.

Sarah and I are locked into a wonderful, productive work rhythm, writing for hours every day with discipline, which is in large part because we have a looming, unbreakable deadline. The publisher insists that they need to put the books out in the fall. They call it a crash schedule, which sounds ominous, and it will only work if we turn the manuscripts in at the start of summer.

Our editor, Jennifer, comes by every few days, and we work on the new pages together. She weighs in, sometimes urging us to go further in a certain area, or gently waving us off from something that she doesn't think belongs in the book. The three of us make a great team, and after just a few weeks Jennifer tells us she sees no need to hire an outside writer. She likes what we are doing and says each of us has a strong voice. I take it as a good sign that she chuckles so often when reading through a new section.

After the big "yes" moment in the alley, Sarah and I realize we don't want to rush to make the wedding happen. For one thing, it will be a lot of work to figure out what the heck kind of event it is going to be. And we want to settle into our life with Josie first and let that become normal for all of us. Plus, of course, writing the books is swallowing up all our time and attention, not to mention stressing us out. So, we figure we should get the books finished up and turned in first, and then we'll have the summer to plan, and we can get married in the fall.

For me, the torture part of work is the poetry collection. I spend weeks just typing everything up, and I do it in backward order, typing up my most recent writing first, then painfully working my way back. Some of it seems so pathetic that I feel sick. Fortunately, this is going to be a *selected* book of poems, so I cull like crazy and focus on the ones I like. By the time I've made it all the way through the entire pile of yellow paper that I hauled all over New York City for ten months and have typed up everything back to my earliest work, I still have a big pile of unrejected candidates to choose from.

Meanwhile I've started reading a lot, and there are piles of library books all over the apartment. But I find myself drawn to kid's books, so I can read to Josie, and to novels. I can't read too much poetry or I get self-conscious and hate myself. And I don't want to be influenced to write like anybody else. I just want to write like me—like a better-writer version of me.

I've read several books about writing and about writing poetry, and the main thing I've picked up is that rewriting is as important as writing, and I now I find myself rewriting like crazy. Sometimes I start playing around with a really old poem, and I get lost in doing it, and by the time I come out of it and realize that the poem is done, there are three times as many lines as there were at first, but maybe only a couple were there in the original version. Every day I marvel that the publisher agreed to doing this book and has given me this incredible chance to write and learn.

Over at her work station, Sarah rolls right along with it and takes delight in what she's writing. Sometimes she'll read me a hilarious line as soon as she's written it and crack herself up. Other times, after we knock off for the evening, we'll settle in on the sofa and read each other our favorite passages from the day's work. As I get nearer to the end of my poetry manuscript, I decide to finish it with "The Ring," a poem I wrote for the day I asked Sarah to marry me.

One evening, we're having a glass of wine and taking turns reading things to each other out loud, and I read this poem to her.

"I know I'm far from perfect," it begins. "I know life can be unfair. But every day I thank God you're in it, and I bow my head and say a prayer."

It ends with an emotional crescendo, me pledging myself to her and explaining that the ring symbolizes my devotion and commitment. At one point, I'd asked our friend Jamie to write music for it so I could sing it to Sarah before I went down on my knee, but it seemed a bit much. I changed my mind, and I'd gone with the duffel bag instead.

When I finish reading the poem, I look up. Sarah is staring at me. She slowly gets up, comes over to me, embraces me softly, and whispers in my ear. "Two words," she says. "Greeting cards."

Then she hugs me wildly, shaking me side to side and muffling her laughter, but when she pulls away, I see that her eyes are teared up.

"I'm not completely joking, Poet. It is also a beautiful poem, and I love it. I'm so lucky. Thank you."

Josie has been making friends up and down the block, and I've never seen her happier. The rev and his family take her out for dinner one night a week, usually at one of the many excellent pizza parlors in our neighborhood. For Josie, the Emersons are the grandparents she never had, so much so that she calls the rev "Grandpa Rev," which I think is hilarious. And whenever Josie calls him that, his smile glows as cheerful and bright as the golden arches of a McDonald's.

Josie and Sarah are pretty much inseparable. They are magic together. Josie follows Sarah everywhere, even into the bathroom, and Sarah does the same. They talk and talk and talk and make up crazy, fun things. One day, I realize that maybe I am now my daughter's #2. In fact, it's no contest.

At the same time, Josie and I are closer than ever. For bedtime reading, we go on binges, like a big run on Shel Silverstein. I've gotten her four of his main books, and every night we each pick one up, and we read his weird and funny poems back and forth to each other.

One night, she says, "Here's the last one for the night, Daddy. It's about you!" And she reads me the final poem in *Falling Up*, which begins:

> *Underneath the Poet Tree*
> *Come and rest awhile with me…*

After I tuck her in, I go outside, sit on the stoop, look out over the park, and count my blessings. One. Two.

I'm also grateful that things are going so well with Lauren. As soon as we finished all the vast amount of paperwork involved in our divorce and Josie moved in with me and Sarah full time, Lauren sold our house and moved in with her divorce attorney, an older guy who I have a feeling is loaded. Like Lauren. Now she seems happy, and we are in a good place. She no longer resents me, and I have accepted her for who she is. She has visitation rights to see Josie twice a month, but sometimes she gets so wrapped up in bouncing back and forth between Aspen and the Hamptons that she has trouble working Josie in. But Lauren and I are comfortable communicating and making arrangements for Josie going back and forth. It's a huge relief that we navigated our way past all that anger.

The publisher has been doing its publisher work, showing us various stages of editing, rough pages, cover ideas, and publicity plans. It all happens fast in a matter of months. They clearly know what they are doing, and we move rapidly toward the books' publication dates.

Some mornings, Sarah and I wake up and one or the other of us will ask, "Is this really happening?" The books are scheduled for release on September 25th—which happens to be Shel Silverstein's birthday, which I of course take as a blessing of sorts. We allow a month from that date for us to work with the publishers on whatever brouhaha the book is going to cause and decide our wedding will be on October 17th. That's the day the Beatles recorded "I Want to Hold Your Hand"at EMI Studios in London, which I figure will put an appropriate love resonance blessing under the proceedings.

From time to time, we have the rev over and talk about the

wedding. When he agreed to plant my duffel bag in the alley, he did so with one caveat: that he would get to officiate. As if we were going to ask someone else. But we do need to plan the ceremony, and at first, we aren't seeing it eye to eye.

Sarah definitely wants a *wedding* wedding, and the rev insists it has to be at the top of the steps in front of the church, looking out over the park. He's very excited about the party afterward and seems to picture it as a movie extravaganza. "We'll shut the whole park down, Poet! It'll be nuts! We'll get huge speakers and blast the music out, and we'll have the whole park filled with dancing! Thousands of people!"

We all laugh, and before you know it everybody is throwing out over-the-top ideas. Josie says she thinks we should arrive in a horse and carriage. I propose that all the guests bring sleeping bags, and we spend our wedding night sleeping in a pile in the middle of the park. Sarah says we should get married on the Imagine Circle in Strawberry Fields in Central Park and have the party at the bandshell.

"And everybody wear roller skates!" adds the rev.

"And let's invite the Rockettes!" adds Sarah.

I calm everybody down and come back to the idea of getting married in Washington Square Park, which is after all the first home we shared. But maybe the party after the ceremony can be small, not so epic?

"Come on, Poet. This is your wedding day," the rev says. "Go big or stay single. How about we get four high school marching bands, and each one marches into the park from a different corner, all playing the same song?"

"Boys!" shouts Sarah, commanding silence. "I'd like to remind you that I would like everyone to look at me, not at a flock of freaking tuba players. I'm going to be wearing my most formal T-shirt, so I want some respect."

"Or," I pause. "we *could* just go over to city hall and…"

"BOOOOOOO!" Everyone drowns out my facetious suggestion.

The banter goes on for weeks, every time we are together. But in our calmer moments, we do manage to piece together a realistic plan. It's going to be sweet. But first there's this book thing.

CHAPTER
SEVENTY-SEVEN

The night before our publication day, I wake up every hour. I cannot sleep. I go into the living room and try watching TV, then go back to bed. Then I'm on the sofa watching TV again, and then I'm back in bed. Four times. I feel like I'm going to explode with nervous energy. Some of it is great: People are going to read our book! But some of it makes me feel sick: People are going to read my poems!

I'm completely agitated while we all get dressed and eat and we walk Josie to school. We wave hi to her teacher, hug Josie, and leave.

When we are back out on the sidewalk, Sarah turns on me. "Enough with this bullshit!" But she's smiling. "This is one of the most exciting days of your life, and of mine. So, you can't be miserable. Fuck that! As of today, we're writers, and you're a poet."

"You're right," I admit. "This is supposed to be fun, right?"

"Poet, if you can't enjoy today, then go back to Wall Street. You're a professional writer now, and this is your first day. We're going to walk over to Barnes & Noble right now, and you are going to clock in to your new job, and we are going to buy copies of our own fucking books, sit down in the café, read them, and freak out. Okay? Are you with me?"

"Jeez," I fake moan. "Can't you ever let a guy be miserable?"

"If that's what you want, you are marrying the wrong girl, you misanthrope. You'd better go find some cranky bitch. It ain't me, babe."

"Okay, okay. Let's go see what we look like on the cover of a book."

She jumps on my back, and I carry her down the block.

Weeks before, for some reason Sarah and I both came up with the same idea. We asked Jennifer not to send us early finished copies, which she'd offered to do a couple of weeks earlier when the first sample books came to her directly from the printer. We wanted to see them for the first time in a bookstore, the way readers would. And as we walk the dozen blocks north toward the big Barnes & Noble store on Union Square, it feels like we are heading to the hospital to have a baby—or babies, actually, fraternal twins. We've seen all the stages leading toward the finished books, but we want to be surprised by the actual, finished, printed-on-paper-with-a-beautiful-cover books themselves.

I take Sarah's hand and hook it through my raised elbow, and we formally promenade through the front doors and into the colossal store as if we are walking down the aisle of a church. In fact, it feels a bit like a temple of books. How many books are in here? A bazillion? And somewhere amongst the throng are our two. It is humbling and exhilarating at the same time. We are being initiated into an ancient, vast brother and sisterhood of writing.

We walk past a few big stacks of hot bestsellers and a big wall of shelves filled with coffee mugs, reading lights, and chocolate, and then we come around the corner and see two big sections featuring the newest books—fiction and nonfiction. We stop in front of the huge nonfiction section and are holding hands, both of us scanning and scanning and scanning over all the book covers and then suddenly: There it is. *Poet and Sarah: A True Tale of Homeless Love.* On the front cover is a drawing of us lying in the alley on my duffel bag, on our backs, looking up at the sky. They got all the details right: Sarah's black nail polish, her hair up and frizzy, Clash T-shirt, short jean shorts, black boots. My frayed grey T-shirt, beat-up jeans, and Nikes. I have a shaggy beard, and I am wearing my Yankees cap. We each take a copy down and start thumbing through. It's beautiful.

On the back are some advance quotes about the book and a recent photograph of us, "cleaned up nice," as they say. The flap copy tells our story. It's a lot to take in. I flip to the acknowledgments page and make sure they got in the part where I thank the Pilot G2 pen. When I chuckle, Sarah looks over at it, then says, "Hey, Poet, give me your Pilot G2 for a sec."

I pull it out, and she opens up her copy of the book to the title page and turns it toward me. "Excuse me, Mr. Bloom, would you please sign your book for me? My name is Sarah."

"Well, that's a lovely name." I sign, "To Sarah. I love you. Poet."

I look up at her and gasp. "Oh my God, are you Sarah *Jones*? That really hot former model? Is that you?"

"You mean really hot formerly homeless model."

"Yes! Excuse me. Would you please sign your book for me? My name is Evan."

"Where are you from, Evan?"

"Great Neck, Long Island."

"Oh, the place rich people jerk each other off?"

"That's the place!"

She signs, "Evan, keep writing. Love, Sarah."

We turn back to the big shelf and realize that my book of poems is right below our book. It's smaller and thinner and green, with a beautiful painting on the cover, showing Washington Square Park and a man sitting with his legs crossed on a bench, writing on a yellow legal pad. The book is called *The Arch of Heaven*, and as I hold it and slowly turn through the pages, I feel like heaven is pretty much where I am now. All those years alone writing in my office, locking my poems away, then all those months writing outdoors in the park, and now here I am, reading my own words in Barnes & Noble. And I have discovered who I am—just a normal guy with an odd gift of some kind who wants to help people feel something. To feel the love I feel. Finally.

We take our copies over to the café and drink as much coffee as we can over the next three hours, reading our books and watching our shelf. In that time, customers buy fourteen books. What does that mean? Is that pretty good? Does that suck? What if we keep selling at that pace? We'd sell fifty books a day! And there are what, 300 Barnes

& Noble stores? Are we going to sell 15,000 books in one day? Wait, that's insane. We don't know what we are talking about. We end up laughing, giddy with the weirdness that we are sitting there with our books thinking this way.

"Oh shit, Poet! What about Kindles?"

And we crack up all over again.

Yet, three weeks later, our book makes it onto the *New York Times* bestseller list. And if that isn't wild enough, it moves up to number three, and for one brief shining week, my poetry book even makes it onto the bottom rung of the list. We see people reading our book on the subway, in the park, and in coffee shops. We get recognized now and again, and people are warm and enthusiastic, telling us how our story has encouraged them, cheered them up.

We do all kinds of interviews, including one on NPR with an amazing interviewer named Terri Gross. We do book signings in two big New York City bookstores, and we get interviewed onstage at the 92nd Street Y. It just keeps coming, and we enjoy every part of all of it.

One of the weirder sweet moments is when Josie and I are walking through the park one afternoon, and I see someone sitting and reading our book in the exact spot I was in when I met Sarah.

At our readings, we tell a bit about our lives before we were homeless and talk about our lives on the street and in the shelter, and Sarah talks about her recovery. I usually read a couple of my poems, and then we take questions. I like the Q&A best because it's when Sarah really shines. At any event, she'll bring down the house more than once and usually with something that's not just funny but also insightful.

Everyone knows that homelessness is as big a problem as ever, and in some areas is getting worse. And people seem anxious to hear about it and ask how they can help, which gives us the opening to talk about our workshops. Now that we've gotten such strong encouragement from readers, I find I am more confident in the writing workshops I've been doing. And I get ideas from the questions people ask at the events.

Sarah, of course, has never had any hesitation in her group work, but even she seems maybe a little bit bolder because of all the public speaking we find ourselves doing. She's still doing the news group at the shelter and has even added a couple more shelters. And she's helping other people step up and start groups in their shelters as well. And the idea of doing writing workshops with homeless people is spreading. I go to lots of shelters and encourage people by talking about what's happened in the groups I've led, and how writing has helped people figure out the way ahead for them. Like I did. Not bad for a couple of former hermits.

As soon as we got the book deal, we knew we'd use some of our advance to help the rev with his projects. Once the initial wave of publicity is over, and once it's clear we're going to get even more money because our advance from the publisher has already been earned back, we start talking to him about the best way to do that, and over the next couple months we come up with several plans.

The most important thing we can do is fund the rev's shelter and clinic, so he knows his bottom line will be covered for the foreseeable future. And I've started helping him counsel homeless young people, and that's very rewarding. I love watching how he finds ways to get through and connect. We see transformations. And I'm his backup man. And I'm Exhibit A: proof that it's never too late to change your life.

CHAPTER
SEVENTY-EIGHT

On the night before our wedding, Sarah and Josie stay with the rev's family. I'm not supposed to see my bride until we meet at the altar. For my bachelor party of one, I sit at my desk mostly and work on my vows. I keep trying to make them perfect, even though I realize my words will never be adequate.

The ceremony is going to take place at noon, in front of the church, at the top of the steps as the rev originally insisted. We've spread the word, basically inviting everyone we know. Plus, anybody who happens to be in the park is utterly welcome to join in, and we're hoping people will. The rev has rustled up a lot of chairs, so we're ready. We've invited Cindy and everyone else from the shelter, all our friends from the church and the park, the folks up at Penn Station, Petra, Josie's school friends, all the neighbors, our editor Jennifer and all the folks at Harper, our agent Dean King—we even track down his author Jeremy. As I walk toward the church, I see Dean and Jeremy on a bench together laughing. I catch glimpses of so many familiar faces and look forward to the celebration after the ceremony.

But right now, all I can think about is my vows, and I can't wait to see Sarah and Josie in their finery. They have been shopping and whispering and planning for weeks. Last night, as they were leaving for the rev's, I told Sarah I couldn't wait to hear her vows. She smiled and said she had a surprise for me.

"Is it a poem?" I asked. She just smiled.

Now it's 11:30, and I take the long route to the church, to keep moving and not get nervous. I think I'm looking pretty good. I assume that Sarah is going to wear something eccentric, so I've bought a funky tuxedo—hunter green with black lapels, and I have a green flower boutonniere. I kind of feel like a pool table. And I've actually paid someone to give me a haircut. And I'm sporting brand new Nike Air Max sneakers—black to go with the tux.

As I come up on the chess corner of the park, Bobby yells, "Hey, Poet, all chess games will be suspended for your wedding. We're all gonna be there, man, to watch you get hitched."

"No comment on your duds, brother," says Ricardo. "A for effort though. But I'll tell you one thing that's guaranteed: Sarah and Josie are going to glow. You're a lucky man."

I laugh and keep walking. "Wrap up your games, guys. One day I'm gonna learn how to play and kick all your asses."

"I got you, Poet!" yells Reggie. "Come back and see me when you're a married man, and I'll show you everything you need to know. Checkmate!"

As I get near the church, I see that everything is arranged perfectly. The rev has gone all out. There's a white carpet leading up the church steps, at the top a makeshift altar, and a podium with a microphone. There are big containers of flowers all over the area, on every flat surface, and card tables and chairs over on the sides and at the back. All the park vendors have moved their carts and wagons in around the edges. People have already filled a lot of the seats, and more are streaming in. A jazz quartet is playing a beautiful Bill Evans tune, and there are kids scampering around. It feels like the wedding area is a village itself, a village within the Village. There's an energized buzz of conversation in the air. People sound happy.

Inside the church, the rev greets me with a hug that's even a little bigger than usual. "Are you ready?" he asks. "Did you perfect your vows last night?"

"I wrote something. I hope it's okay. But as long as I can at least make *you* cry, I'll be satisfied."

"Well, your odds are good. This might turn out to be one of the best days of my life. So far, so good! God bless you."

The rev sends me out of the chapel and tells me to go sit by the fountain and wait for my cue. I circle around and arrive there and sit for a while on the fountain rim. Not surprisingly, the ceremony seems to be running late, and I don't mind. I've spent plenty of time sitting in this spot, and now as I look over toward the church at everyone gathered for our wedding, I'm at peace.

In my mind, the whole journey flashes past in an instant—from me getting out of the limo and surrendering my fate to the world, to this moment, about to commit my life to Sarah. And in that moment, I realize that she and I have already been married for a long time.

I hear Jamie's guitar, and that's my cue. I walk through the park I love and think of as home, and through the seated, smiling crowd and nod and smile at friend after friend. I slowly climb the steps, savoring each second, and when I arrive at the top, the rev gives me a big smile, as do Donna and Holly, who are to his left. We all stand there while Jamie finishes the song, and then there's a moment of silence before the reverend asks everyone to rise. Jamie starts playing "Here Comes the Bride," and everyone turns.

Josie is walking down the aisle first, sprinkling flower petals from a basket. Her dress is beautiful, cornflower blue with a big yellow ribbon at the waist. Behind her comes Sarah, who is so beautiful I actually gasp. At the bottom of the stairs, Josie takes Sarah's hand, and they walk up together.

Then suddenly Sarah is there beside me, and I can't speak.

"Nice jacket," she whispers. "Did you borrow it from 'Clyde' Frazier?"

"You look incredible," I say quietly. "I thought you were going to find some funky vintage dress. That looks like it cost $10,000. I feel like an asshole."

"You are an asshole, but you're the love of my life. So, let's get married."

She squeezes my hand and gives me the deepest, most radiant

smile I have ever seen, and all is well. To be honest, I don't know exactly what happened next, or what was said, except I know the rev talked about love, how it can change you, listening to your heart and trusting your intuition, and being ready to recognize it when someone special comes into your life. I remember smiling at Josie, and I remember at one point when the rev was getting emotional Sarah making a funny face at me, and I remember feeling like my spine was on fire.

Sarah said beautiful things, and I read a poem about her and quoted the moment when I introduced myself to her saying my name was Poet, and she responded, "What's your last name—Tree?" That got a good laugh, but it was an easy crowd. I remember our vows only vaguely. The next thing I remember clearly is the rev pronouncing us husband and wife, and Sarah, Josie, and I standing together at the top of the stairs and everybody cheering, and us walking carefully down the white-carpeted steps while Jamie played "When the Stars Go Blue."

The next thing I know, Sarah and I are standing in the middle of the fountain, sharing a long kiss. And then there are hours and hours of fun and food, and relaxed conversations go meandering past, and everyone is aglow and at a rare level of peacefulness. Josie and I go over to the dog run and play with all the frisky friendly dogs for a while. Even they seem unusually happy.

Sarah and I stand in our five-minute-poem spot while our friend Henry takes our picture so he can later do a painting of us as a wedding present. There are hundreds of moments of joy and friend-ship. Our wedding is everything we could have imagined wanting it to be.

We've made plans to slip away at some point and spend our wedding night alone. I've told Sarah I've made some special arrange-ments, and Josie will be staying with the rev and his family.

The party is still going strong, but as the evening deepens, I look at Sarah, and we both know that it's time. We quietly tell Josie goodbye and all share another family hug.

As we move across the park, hand in hand, I say, "Let's go sleep in the alley."

Sarah laughs. "We'd need your duffel bag for a pillow."

"It's already there."

"Wonderful, Poet. You are such a good planner. And so thoughtful. Really. Shall we just sleep in our wedding clothes?"

"That's what I had in mind. There are some blankets in the duffel bag."

"I am so relieved. I was afraid you were planning some fancy hotel for us. I've always thought the alley should be our honeymoon suite. But don't try anything, Poet. You know I don't put out in the alley."

"Can I at least massage your stomach?"

"You'd better. How else will I fall asleep?"

Before long, we're in the alley, all settled in, arms around each other, in full wedding attire and blanketed up, watching the night sky and listening to the life all around us.

"You know, Sarah. This is truly the most comfortable bed I've ever slept in. Or on."

She kisses me gently. "We deserve a good night's sleep."

"We do."

After five minutes of silence, Sarah says, "Remember that surprise I have for you?"

"Oh! I forgot all about that. Excellent. What is it? After today, nothing could surprise me."

"Are you sure?"

"Absolutely."

It's silent again, and I turn, and Sarah is looking at me calmly, suppressing a smile.

"What?"

"I'm pregnant."

"What?" I whisper hoarsely. "What? You are? For real?"

"For very real, Poet. Get out your notebook and your Pilot G2 pen. We've got to start working on names."

Sarah falls asleep with her head on my chest, and I kiss her forehead. As I hold her, I realize that I have found heaven. Heaven is not in the sky: It is in your heart. All I am is filled with love, now grateful for every moment of my life. I have made peace with the past—the seclusion, isolation, Wall Street, Lauren, my parents, everything. I realize they were just a steppingstone to this moment. Everything in life is a learning experience. Every experience shapes who you were, who you are, and who you will become.

Listen to the voice—the narrator in your mind who tells you who you truly are. I am a thirty-five-year-old man lying in an alley—a poet, writer, public speaker, advocate for the homeless, husband, and a soon-to-be father of two surrounded by love. That's all I ever wanted to be...

ACKNOWLEDGMENTS

To the greatest father in the History of the World, Michael Gendal—my best friend and roommate. Dad, you are the funniest man alive. We've been laughing for 42 years, and our laughs are eternal. No father and son have ever spent more time together, and I've loved every second of it. Thank you for taking care of me and always being there. Your dedication to my health and well-being brings tears to my eyes. I love you, Dad. St. John's will win a National Championship before you're gone. I promise.

To my sister, Marisa "The Beef" Gendal. My greatest joy in life has been being your big brother. You will always be my favorite person on the planet. My #1. There is no one I'd rather spend my time with. Double Trouble will ride again. Ohana…

To Dr. Jay "The Jackson" Gendal. We are The Bipolar Boys! You are my second father. This novel is not possible without you. You have helped me every which way my entire life. Where would I be without you? Love you, Man!

To Josh Gendal, lead guitar player in the world-famous songwriting team of Gendal & Gendal. You are the little brother I never had. Educating you on music and writing songs with you has been incredible. Love you, Dude!

Uncle Mark, Stephanie, Jeff, and Stacey, the Gendals are royalty. Is there anyone better than us? I feel blessed to have such an incredible family. Love you all!

My best friends and brothers, Drew Eisenberg and Michael Gorman, the three of us have done everything together. I can't imagine my life without you. Every day I thank God for you both and feel blessed to have had you by my side my whole entire life. School, camp, sports, girls, family, The City, West 10th, partying—we've done it all together, from the cradle to the grave and beyond. I love you both.

To my friend, John Donato, one of my greatest gifts was you coming back into my life and resuming our friendship. The Who will always be better than Zeppelin!

For Jeremy "The Bone, Jabrone" Lieberman. Shimidimiyayha! No one makes me laugh harder. Doing our podcast was a highlight in my life. I will always be grateful for how your parents took care of me after my mother passed away.

Special shoutout to Dylan and Hayley Gorman, Uncle Scotty loves you, Mandels, I didn't forget you. I love you too.

Jennifer Bright, you have been sent from above. All your last-minute editing and organization was a Godsend. Thank you!

For music, the symphony of my soul, I want to name anyone who's ever picked up an instrument, but I have to give special recognition to Phish, the Grateful Dead, and Taylor Swift. Phish and The Grateful Dead's music has served as my religion and shaped my life in every way imaginable. I want to thank Taylor Swift for renewing my faith in songwriting and for being the most incredible artist and the best role model for young girls.

To every artist in every genre ever, to anyone who has ever been touched by the power of music, to anyone who has ever sat down to write a song or poem, I hope somehow this novel resonated with you.

Pilot G2 Pens, yellow legal pads, and my black duffel bag—my soulmates. I've spent so much time with all of you. I love you!

ABOUT THE AUTHOR

Scott Gendal has written more than 2,000 songs and poems with a Pilot G2 pen on yellow legal pads.

Scott wrote both the book and lyrics to the rock musical "Your Biggest Fan," which is currently in preproduction.

A standup comedian, Scott performed and worked at Carolines Comedy Club in New York City.

In the summer of 2017, Scott wrote 5-minute poetry for passers-by in New York City's Washington Square Park.

Scott is originally from Dix Hills, Long Island and is a graduate of Hofstra University. He currently resides in New York City and Delray Beach, Florida.

That's All I Ever Wanted To Be is Scott's first novel.